Tourist Trap

Tourist Trap

A novel of the Jarnian Confederation
Sue Ann Bowling

iUniverse, Inc.
Bloomington

Tourist Trap

iUniverse books may be ordered through booksellers or by contacting:

iUniverse
1663 Liberty Drive
Bloomington, IN 47403
www.iuniverse.com
1-800-Authors (1-800-288-4677)

ISBN: 978-1-4620-2958-7 (sc)
ISBN: 978-1-4620-2960-0 (dj)
ISBN: 978-1-4620-2959-4 (ebk)

Printed in the United States of America

iUniverse rev. date: 07/01/2011

Other books by Sue Ann Bowling

Homecoming

Critical Acclaim for Homecoming:

Well-written science fiction expands the imagination. It is a book genre that explores the outer limits of reality, based on the reasoning and endless possibilities of science. Unfortunately, there is too much science fiction on the market today that has left this creative path of exploration, and instead offers readers a constantly rehashed mix of starship battle scenes and evil alien races bent on taking over the universe. Fortunately, in *Homecoming*, Sue Ann Bowling takes the reader back to the foundations of sci-fi, offering a completely original story, with both fresh ideas and sound science .... *Homecoming* is a truly compelling book. The author has done a superb job of creating characters that are well rounded and emotionally real. The plot is original and thoughtfully crafted, and the supporting science is fresh and exciting .... the reader will turn the last page hoping that a sequel is on the way.
ForeWord Clarion review by Catherine Thureson

While "Homecoming" has an ending that confidently wraps up all the loose ends in this part of Roi's life, I'm left with the hope that Ms Bowling might one day let us see how Roi is doing as an adult. If you're looking for a science fiction adventure that has some thought behind it, I highly recommend this story.
Reader Views review by Marty Shaw

CONTENTS

Characters

Amber: Technically Roi's Human slave, but in fact a companion of Roi's who will be freed as soon as she completes her education. Born free, and planning to study medicine.

Davy: Roi's Human attendant and physical therapist at school, now freed.

Derik Tarlian: Lai's High R'il'noid half brother, Lai's heir until Zhaim's birth. Roi's former owner.

Elyra Faranian: R'il'noid chief geneticist of the Genetics Board. She has a child Wif's age by Lai, but is currently in a relationship with Derik.

Feline: Wif's Human mother, now free and a member of Roi's household.

Flame: Technically Roi's Human slave, but in fact a companion of Roi's who will be freed as soon as she completes her education. Born a slave and not all that interested in freedom, but very attached to Roi.

Kyrie Talganian: High R'il'nian Confederation adjudicator, assigned to Falaron.

Lai: the last surviving R'il'nian until he discovered Marna, with whom he is now in a close relationship. He is the effective ruler of the Confederation.

Marna: The last survivor of the R'il'nai of Riya, a distant planet colonized long ago by the R'il'nai. Healer. Foster mother to Roi, and in some ways more his parent than Lai.

Penny Ansdor: Falaron tour guide, Human.

Roi Laian: High R'il'noid son of Lai and his lost Human love, Cloudy. Born a slave; now 18 and just graduated from Tyndall, an exclusive boarding school.

Timi: Technically Roi's Human slave, but in fact a companion of Roi's who will be freed as soon as he completes his education. Born free, in a culture based on starship trading.

Wif k'Roi Laian: Roi's High R'il'noid son, 3 1/2 years old.

Xazhar k'Zhaim Laian: Zhaim's High R'il'noid son, formerly Roi's schoolmate and rival at Tyndall.

Zhaim Laian: Lai's older son and formerly his heir, now displaced from the heirship by Roi.

A complete list of the characters in both Tourist Trap and Homecoming can be found at http://www.sueannbowling.com/ . The glossary is at http://sueannbowling.com/glossary_297.html .

Background

Go back, over a hundred thousand years, to the time of the last interglacial. Imagine an alien starship designer, a R'il'nian named Jarn, stranded on Earth when his latest design proves to have some unexpected flaws. He befriends a group of primates, strikingly similar in appearance to himself, and eventually becomes part of their tribe, mating with their women and, totally to his surprise, having a few children. Some of those offspring even inherit his lack of aging and his esper abilities.

Over the next few thousand years his genes spread, and he guides the Humans that result into a short-lived civilization capable of building starships to his plans. He himself and some of his descendants return to the stars; others choose to stay on Earth, where their force-grown civilization is soon forgotten as they spread from Africa over the planet.

Those who followed Jarn to the stars create their own civilizations, with some help and protection from Jarn's R'il'nian relatives and led by those of Jarn's descendants expressing most strongly his abilities of conditional precognition and telepathy.

The telepathy is important in protecting the Human planets from the Maungs, whose life cycle is totally incompatible with that of Humans. (Although adult, healthy Maungs are no threat to Humans—and prefer different planets—their reproduction can result in Humans parasitized by what should be a Maung nervous system. R'il'nians are not affected, and consider the Maungs as valuable trading partners.)

Now fast-forward to the time when Humans on Earth are rediscovering agriculture. A new disease has arisen among the star-faring Humans. Kharfun syndrome is not serious for them—similar to a mild case of flu. But it is deadly to those leaders with a high fraction of R'il'nian genes, and lethal to the pure R'il'nai. Finally Humans and R'il'nai working together find a cure and a method of immunization, but only a small fraction of the R'il'nai, and almost none of the crossbred R'il'noids, survive. The Human planets are threatened both by the Maungs and by their tendency to war on each other. The surviving R'il'nai are in decline, their already low fertility driven even lower by the aftereffects of the disease and by the immunization, which also affects fertility. Eventually a few of the Human leaders petition the R'il'nai to try hybridizing again with the Humans, in hope of producing individuals capable of detecting Maung infestations and stopping wars—duties the R'il'nai have become too few in numbers to continue.

Thus the Confederation is born. The pure R'il'nai continue to decline, but their place as peacekeepers and guardians against the Maungs is taken by the new hybrids, the R'il'noids.

The natural increase of the R'il'noids is insufficient to keep up with the growing number of Human-occupied planets in the Confederation. Shortly after the Saxons invade Britain on Earth, a R'il'noid, Çeren, develops a laboratory method of increasing the number of hybrids produced. He also develops a measurement, the Çeren index, which is used to rank R'il'noids according to the fraction of active R'il'nian genes their chromosomes contain. Those with a Çeren index of 72 or more (half their active genes are R'il'nian) are defined as R'il'noids, subject only to Confederation law.

Fast-forward yet again, to about the time of George Washington's birth on Earth, and we come to the start of *Homecoming*. Only a single R'il'nian, Lai, is left alive in the Confederation, and he is mourning his lost Human love, Cloudy. Humans are now running the last R'il'nian planet, Central, which has become both the de facto capital of the Confederation and the hub of the slave trade in the Confederation. Then Lai discovers that Cloudy left him when she learned she was pregnant—against the orders of the Genetics Board. Their slave-reared son, whom Lai names Roi, is alive, paralyzed by Kharfun, owned by Lai's half-brother Derik, and refusing to believe anything he is being told.

Beyond the borders of the Confederation is Riya, settled long ago by the R'il'nai. Here Marna is the sole survivor of a planet-wide epidemic, kept alive only by her determination to warn off any other R'il'nai who may find the doomed planet. She was on an isolation satellite studying a different disease when the epidemic started, but now the life-support system of the satellite has broken down. Can she avoid being infected, two centuries after everyone she has ever known has died? Does she even want to?

When Lai finds evidence of Riya's existence, he journeys to seek it out. On the journey, Lai is forced to recognize that his heir by Çeren index, Zhaim, is not fit to take over his job as coordinator of the Confederation. But he has little choice in the matter, as selection by the Çeren index has been cast in stone by the Human inhabitants of the Confederation. Lai finds Marna and manages to save her from Kharfun syndrome, and she becomes a mother, mentor and Healer to Roi, who shares her rare talent of Healing. Roi, although demonstrating increasing intelligence and mastery of R'il'nian talents as he progresses through the Tyndall school, cannot at first be Çeren indexed because of the Kharfun. Eventually, at sixteen and a half, he is found to have a higher Çeren index then Zhaim. Meanwhile Derik has given him his three closest slave friends, the people who had become his surrogate family during his slave years: Flame, Amber and Timi.

Now a year and a half has passed, and Zhaim, still resenting the fact that Roi has replaced him as Lai's heir and the future leader of the Confederation, is attending the graduation ceremonies at Tyndall.

Preface

Central: Zhaim
Northday, '38

Zhaim looked at Tyndall's graduating class on the platform, and struggled to keep his features neutral. All of the graduates were crossbred, and most were R'il'noids. Many, like Zhaim, showed that heritage in their similarity to Zhaim's father, Lai—delicate features and eyes that clearly showed the metallic tracery common among R'il'noids, even at this distance. Zhaim himself, he was proudly aware, could have been his father's twin, black haired and bronze skinned, differing only in that Zhaim's eyes were ice and silver while Lai's were gold-veined green.

He had no problem with the class second, his own son Xazhar, beyond the fact that Xazhar should have been class first. But the—thing—that was class first .... Empaths were necessary, he supposed, but they were *not* suited to rule. And his father's preference for his bastard, slave-reared son over legitimate and properly socialized R'il'noids was going to destroy the Confederation if something wasn't done.

The brat didn't even look R'il'noid—more like its Human dam. It had yellow eyes that showed their gold flecking only if the light was just right, and white hair that marked it as carrying the gene that had prevented Lai's lover from ever being approved for the crossbreeding project. It should have been aborted, or killed at birth, but its dam had bolted before that could happen. And not only had Lai accepted it, it had actually proved to have a Çeren index higher than Zhaim's, thus replacing Zhaim as Lai's heir.

Zhaim glanced sideways at the only two R'il'nians in the school auditorium—the only two survivors of their species. Lai and Marna. Weak survivors. Far too easily swayed by sentiment, too sensitive to the emotions of others. Marna especially, and her red-gold hair and dark ivory skin didn't even look like the R'il'nai he was used to, though her silver-veined dark blue eyes were typical enough.

Someone was going to have to do something, Zhaim thought, or the whole Jarnian Confederation was going to collapse around their heads. Over a hundred thousand years of R'il'nian rule, with the assistance of the part-human R'il'noids like himself, and all about to be torn down because his father refused to face reality. When—not if—Zhaim, as the ranking R'il'nian-Human crossbred, replaced his father, the Jarnian Confederation would be ruled properly, not allowed to drift as his father had let it. His eyes went back to young Roi, standing as class first at the far left of the platform. Somehow, he had to get rid of the bastard empath that had usurped his position as Lai's heir. The Confederation needed a strong leader, not a jumped-up slave.

Lai wouldn't agree with that, of course. In fact, Zhaim thought, he'd have to make damn sure his father never even suspected anything. But if they really let the bastard go off-planet on that idiotic vacation trip it wanted .... Zhaim never was sure, afterward, just when he had crossed the line between wishful thinking and planning.

Chapter 1

Central: Roi
4/1/38

"But he's not even eighteen yet," Marna said. "A manhood Challenge?"

Roi winced inwardly. Most of the time he enjoyed the way Marna had all but adopted him since his own mother had never been found, but there were times when her concern was downright smothering. After all, he'd taken care of himself for most of his life, and that life, as a slave, had been a lot harder than any of the adults around him realized. He glanced pleadingly toward his father, Lai, and Lai's half brother, Derik.

"Marna," Lai said quietly, "he's R'il'noid, not R'il'nian. Half Human. And Humans mature a lot faster than the R'il'nai."

"Zhaim hasn't," Marna snapped back, and Roi was hard put not to cringe. That was his own worst nightmare, that he might become like Zhaim, treating others as things rather than people. Some of his former owners, like Derik, had become good friends since he had been recognized as his father's son, but he still had no reason at all to trust Zhaim, and very little inclination to let his older half-brother near him.

"At the moment," his father replied, "I'd say Roi is considerably more mature than Zhaim in his attitude toward other people, even if he is several centuries younger in chronological age. And it shouldn't be too difficult a Challenge. He'll have his slave friends with him, and an experienced guide." His soon-to-be ex-slave friends, Roi hoped. Derik had given him his three closest companions two years ago. He wasn't comfortable about owning slaves, having been a slave for so much of his own life, but right now they were not ready to make their own way through the world.

"Matter of fact," Derik said, "they'll have the same guide Coryn did two years ago. You commented yourself on how much good the trip did Cory. As for the challenge aspect, over half of the planets in the Confederation

1

have some kind of test or challenge before granting adult status. Thanks be they now recognize each other's tests! My first adjudication was on a planet with a manhood test based on surviving an encounter with a particularly nasty specimen of the local wildlife. They wouldn't even listen to me 'til I passed the challenge, and they weren't really happy about the way I did it."

Roi fought back a grin. He hadn't heard of that particular incident before; a lot had happened in Derik's fifteen centuries, and he hardly expected to know all of it. But he knew his uncle well enough to guess that Derik, by far the best xenotelepath among the R'il'noids, had handled the challenge by using his talent to make friends with the critter—whatever it was.

Elyra, who'd moved in with Derik a year ago, winked a chocolate eye at Roi. Like Derik, she gave the impression of being monotone, with skin, hair and eyes the same color. But where Derik was all golden brown, she was the color of milk chocolate, and small enough to fit under Derik's arm. Not that there was anything small about her personality!

"Marna," Lai said, "are you picking up any precognitive warnings of trouble for Roi?"

Marna shook her copper-gold head. "No," she said, almost reluctantly. "And I've certainly tried hard enough. Maybe you're right, and I'm just being overprotective. If Roi really wants the Challenge, I'll withdraw my objections. But Roi, promise you'll keep in mind-touch with us, and don't push this Challenge to the point that you're in serious danger."

"That's the advantage of a Challenge journey on Falaron," Derik put in. "If the guide or the Company decides they are at real risk—say due to an unusual incident like an earthquake—they'll give them extra help. The Challenge is more sheer endurance in relatively primitive conditions than anything else."

So they would let him take the Challenge, after all. Lai had given him the trip as a graduation present yesterday, but he and Marna had both balked initially when Roi had said he wanted to take the full Challenge journey. Derik had backed Roi from the start. He'd been rather careful not to comment on how the Challenge aspect of the trip would help Roi's reluctance to make decisions that affected others, for which the young R'il'noid was grateful. He disagreed with Derik on that. If his decisions affected others, those others had a right to influence those decisions.

He'd miss his son Wif, now three and a half. But the kind of traveling they'd be doing was no place for a child Wif's age, even if Wif's mother Feline had wanted to go with them—which she emphatically did not. Leaving Wif with the child's overly possessive mother did bother Roi, but his own parents—he thought of Marna as a second mother now—would keep her from doing too much damage. His own mother .... Lai hadn't been able to find what had become of her, though he said he'd tried, and Roi had no reason not to believe him. She'd been sold, he said, not long after Roi had been sold away from her, and while he had tracked her through several owners, he had eventually lost the trail.

Four days to pack and be ready to go. And now Marna had finally given her permission, they could really start packing. Roi had been wanting this trip ever since Cory had taken a similar trip, though without the Challenge aspect, and he'd already set up the parameters. They would be dog sledding, hang gliding, riding horses, whitewater rafting, and rock climbing. Sailing, too, but that was really because Timi had insisted on it. They were all good at riding and hang gliding, and since the Challenge did not absolutely forbid the use of esper talents, Roi had little doubt of his ability to control the dog teams. The rafting would be the only thing really new, and he looked forward to that.

Timi
4/4/38

"Got your packing finished?" Roi asked, on the eve of their departure.

Timi flinched a little as he turned to answer. "Except for a few things I can't put in 'til the last minute," he replied. "I just want to take a walk around the corridor system before we leave. Alone. Do you mind?" He knew his tone was sarcastic, but these meetings, exhilarating as they were, frightened him, as well. The one thing he could not be was relaxed and casual, but he could hardly explain that to Roi.

His owner looked at him, a slight frown wrinkling his forehead. "I wish we could just be friends, like we used to be," Roi said.

"We were slaves together, then, instead of slave and owner," Timi replied. "Maybe when I'm free ...."

Roi nodded. "Have a good walk, Timi," he said as he turned back to his own packing.

Timi almost ran into Amber as he turned toward the corridor. She jumped back, laughing, and repeated Roi's question. "Got your packing done?"

"All but the last-minute stuff."

She tipped her blond head and looked hard at him. "You don't look very excited. I mean, how many slaves get to go on a trip like this? Even Derik said he wished he had the time for that kind of thing."

"A month on horseback? I can think of things I'd rather be doing."

She wrinkled her nose at him. "Well, the rest of us like riding. And we'll be sailing, too. You're good at that. I hope Flame and I don't get seasick."

Timi forced a laugh and headed on down the corridor. They weren't really corridors, of course, but small rooms with jump-gates at each end. He had started early, afraid of interference, and he deliberately chose a long route to his destination, walking by windows that opened on late-evening scenes varying from seacoast to mountains. Most were too dark to see anything without pressing his face against the windows, and he strolled unseeing, trying to understand his own attraction to the R'il'noid he was going to see.

Zhaim was dangerous. He understood that, from what Roi had told him. Zhaim was Roi's half brother, but the two had as little as possible to do with each other. And Timi remembered all too clearly the time when Zhaim had tried to force Roi to sell him. Could he really believe Zhaim's more recent assurances that he had simply felt Timi was being wasted in Roi's hands? Zhaim *had* gotten Timi that desperately wanted conditional acceptance to the Space Academy, when Roi hadn't managed—or perhaps hadn't wanted—to do anything. Oh, Roi's tutoring had helped, but that same tutoring somehow left Timi feeling hopelessly stupid at times. Everything came so easily to Roi! And Roi was so complaisant. Even if Roi found out about this evening, Timi thought, the worst he would do was look hurt. If Zhaim cared about anyone, he would care enough to kill.

Timi turned into a side corridor that led directly to the guest garage, pushed open the door, and looked for Zhaim's silver and gray skimmer. There was supposed to have been an Inner Council meeting tonight, though Roi had been let off his usual observer status, and Zhaim, who was blocked against teleporting into the Enclave complex, should have come by jump flyer. Sure enough, the skimmer was in its usual place, with Zhaim swearing into an open access hatch.

Timi hesitated a moment, and Zhaim looked up. "Timi!" he said. "You know something about these things. Why won't it start?"

Timi relaxed in a glow of pleasure as he walked over to peer into the opening. "It was all right on the way in?" he asked.

"Fine, but now it acts like someone else is trying to start it up."

Timi moved around to where he could see the status panel of the little craft. "Try it again," he suggested.

The status panel confirmed that the finger panel was recognizing Zhaim, but the start command was getting only about halfway through the system. Timi thought for a moment, mentally going over the starter circuit. There were a couple of places where something could have been jarred loose.

"Hey," Zhaim said, "what's this I hear about your getting a vacation?"

Timi grimaced. "We're all going to Falaron for a couple of months. We'll be traveling from the Spine Range down to Safeport along the Surprise River. Roi wants to make it a Challenge journey, so it's not exactly going to be a vacation." He opened a side access panel, finding and tightening a loose plug. "There's the problem, I think. Try it now."

The machine purred into life, and Zhaim swiveled sideways in the driver's seat. "Good job, Timi. You've got a real talent with electronics." His expression turned serious.

"You said a Challenge? That sounds a bit on the dangerous side." Zhaim's voice was concerned. "Timi, I worry about you. Roi's just too reckless where his friends are concerned. I know it sounds silly, but will you accept a small gift from me? A luck piece? And keep it hidden. Roi's still pretty prejudiced toward me." He grimaced.

Timi hesitated. He knew perfectly well that Roi would not approve, but he was sick of looking for Roi's approval. Zhaim might frighten him, but there was a thrill in defying that fear that Timi found increasingly difficult to resist. Then Zhaim reached into a pocket and pulled out a pendant carved of some translucent flame-orange material. A cat-like creature, with slanted slits of eyes and one paw lifted in warning. Not an expensive piece, he thought, but one that appealed greatly to him. Timi's hand went out, almost of its own accord, and Zhaim smiled as he dropped the braided leather cord over Timi's head.

"Matches your eyes," the R'il'noid said with a smile as he turned in his seat. "Have a good trip, Timi."

Zhaim

Not until he was back in his own home did Zhaim allow himself to gloat over his success. He now knew roughly where on Falaron Roi and his friends would be for the next couple of months—a piece of information he had been quite unable to worm out of his father or anyone else who knew. He had planted a locator beacon and control circuit in the party. That was certainly worth pulling a plug loose to put the brat in the right frame of mind to accept his "gift."

And he hadn't expected a Challenge journey. He had assumed that Roi would be closely guarded during his vacation, but on a Challenge journey the group would be very much on their own. This could be an opportunity he would be a fool to miss. Zhaim owned a hunting lodge on Falaron, more as a matter of prestige than anything else. Officially, the place was closed for the season, but that would be easy enough to get around. And from the lodge, it shouldn't be too difficult to eavesdrop on the Company communications. Maybe he could even get a tap on the finders the party would be carrying, as a backup for the beacon on the slave.

Zhaim was not particularly good at long-range precognition. But over the last two years he had discovered that he could use his considerable short-range talent to affect the precognitive warnings of others. He had used this ability for over six months now to hide any precognitive warnings of danger to Roi. Evidently he had been doing a good enough job that Lai had been willing to accept the Challenge journey.

He still did not dare attack Roi directly while Lai or Marna were anywhere near. But if they were both called out of the Central system .... Could he arrange that, somehow, without attracting any suspicion to himself?

There was the situation in the Kablukolelli Cluster. He had been amusing himself for some time now by egging on the most extreme religious leaders of the four stellar systems that made up the cluster. It wouldn't take much to start a holy war by now, and since the four systems had entered the Confederation separately, any such war would require the immediate attention of a Confederation mediator. If he manipulated his puppets right, Zhaim thought, the situation could rapidly become so explosive that Lai would have to handle it personally.

Had he himself left any tracks? No, he had been very subtle in his manipulations. And he would continue to be just as careful that nothing pointed to any outside agitator.

Marna. He didn't understand Marna as well as he did his father, but he knew better than even to consider attacking Roi the way he wanted to if Marna were anywhere close enough that a mental scream from Roi could reach her. But how could he lure her far enough away that Roi could not reach her without the boosting he'd be unable to find on Falaron? The bastard had barely learned the basics of using his esper talents to protect himself, but Marna was so attuned to her apprentice's mind that Roi could probably reach her on Central from Falaron. The wilderness planet was only about ten light years away, after all.

He walked down the corridor to his bioengineering laboratory as he thought, planning to check his latest experiments with the virus he had been engineering. If he could manage the side effects, he thought, this would be his greatest triumph yet. A planet where no food animals could survive, and he had not only worked out the cause, he had found a solution. Of course the side effects of immediate application would result in killing most of the planet's population, but he was sure he could find a way of preventing that. And then—he half closed his eyes, seeing himself watched anxiously as he released the virus, and then the adulation, the population of the planet shouting his praise, even the Inner Council once again giving him his proper admiration!

The latest experiment only confirmed the others. If he released the virus now, the result might as well be a plague.

A plague.

Marna was a Healer. A planetary plague was one kind of bait Zhaim doubted she could resist.

Was it worth giving up his triumph for a chance to destroy his rival?

And if his father ever suspected ....

He shuddered a little, remembering a lecture delivered several centuries before, the first time he had tried to justify doing what he wanted by the fact that planetary laws did not apply to High R'il'noids. Zhaim considered that a minor recompense for his labors for the Confederation. His father ....

"They don't apply because there have been cases where we couldn't do our jobs without running afoul of some ridiculous local regulation," Lai had exploded. "It's been justified because we save millions of lives, and we can't do that if we're dead. I don't ever again want to hear of your perverting that to suggest that you have a right to kill people at your pleasure because you've saved other lives!"

Plenty of others thought that way, Zhaim thought resentfully. After the lecture he'd kept his hobby well hidden from his father until the bastard's explorations had brought it to the old R'il'nian's attention. And if the old fool could get as upset as he had about the deaths of a few slaves, how would he react to the death of half the population of a planet?

They couldn't trace it to him, he thought. He hadn't even mentioned this particular research project to anyone, because if he failed, he didn't want it known. He'd leave it to Marna to handle the side effects. Once Roi was dead, he might even help handle the crisis. He'd be a hero—not as much of a hero as if he'd taken care of the side effects before he'd released the virus, but certainly not a plague spreader. He looked at the culture vat, considering the best way of getting the virus to its intended host.

And if it didn't work right away, a Challenge journey had all kinds of possibilities for accidents. Playing with the weather would be safest, he thought, if not nearly as much fun as actually getting his hands on the party. He looked at the culture tanks, seeing clouds swirling on a planet ten light years away, and smiled.

Roi

An interwoven knot of arms and legs, with the heads evenly spaced around it. Yes, that was what he would make of the three, with enough motility left that they could writhe a little. He'd have to nick the vocal chords, of course, to tone down any screaming, but he'd long since solved the problems involved in grafting the blood supplies together .... *What am I thinking? I'm not Zhaim!*

"Of course you're not," Flame's voice came from beside him, and Roi turned his head to find her across from him in the levitation bed. Nightmares again, strong enough that he must have cried out aloud in his sleep. He didn't usually have nightmares with Flame beside him, though.

"I must have rolled away from you," she said.

He went back over what he remembered of the dream. Timi's departure must have triggered it, he thought. His friend hadn't told him where he was going, but he was well aware of Timi's increasing fascination with the R'il'noid who'd once tried to kill him.

No, he wasn't Zhaim. But they were both R'il'noids. He could kill with his mind alone—he knew that, from early experience as a slave. He'd feel his victims' emotions—but one of the things he'd had to learn in studying Healing was how to control that. If he used that knowledge .... Just how much like Zhaim was he?

Chapter 2

Penny sat primly on her seat in the departure lounge for the shuttle, wishing she dared to tuck her feet under her. She hadn't met this particular client, though, and she wanted his first impression of her to be one of competence and authority. She glanced quickly at the doorway, and then back to the information on her lap pad as she registered the entrance of a middle-aged couple. Her client should be an adolescent, several years younger than Penny herself, with three slaves of about the same age.

She shook her head at the images she called up. Slavery was not legal on Falaron, and the three slaves could claim their freedom the instant they set foot on the planet, four days from now. Her client, Roi Laian, had been told as much, but had refused to change his mind about taking his slaves along. Penny sniffed as she studied his image. Altogether too pretty for a male, she thought. Deep bronze skin and golden eyes contrasted sharply with pure white hair. All of her clients were spoiled rich boys, but this one's looks probably had every girl he met swooning over him. Well, she wasn't going to.

She had first become a guide for the glamour and the excitement, but she'd recognized almost from the start that Falaron company clients were mostly the type she could barely stand in a professional relationship, and wanted no part of personally. Then she'd broken up with Nevin, who resented her exposure to off-planet men. Her off-planet clients, mostly boys younger than she was, were even worse, though there had been a few decent ones, like Coryn.

Coryn and his father Derik had both spoken to her about her current client, the son of the last R'il'nian, Lai. "You'll like him," Coryn had said. "He's nice—a little too nice, maybe. I sure wouldn't put up with some of what he takes! Mom says it's because he can't hurt someone else without feeling their pain. Father says it's partly because he was raised a slave. When I met him at school, he still didn't believe he was really free. He's better now, but still a little too goody-goody to be true. He's smart and a terrific esper—one of very few who can beat my father at pattern chess. But you're safe—he won't use his talents to manipulate people."

Derik had supplied more factual information, things that were beyond her access in the planetary computer. "He's Lai's son, and High R'il'noid," he had said. "His mother was not approved for the cross-breeding program. She and Lai were lovers, and when she realized she was pregnant, she bolted and hid. She was enslaved illegally, and Roi was thought to be a slave until three and a half years ago, when he came down with Kharfun syndrome. That told us what he was—Humans simply don't show those symptoms from Kharfun—but it left him completely paralyzed for close to a year, and still only partly in control of his body when Lai brought Marna back to Central, two years ago. She's pretty well adopted him and managed to treat the paralysis, but it's been a long recovery. There's no way he could have handled the physical challenges of this trip even six months ago, but I don't think he'll have any problem with it now. We still haven't been able to trace what happened to his own mother." He'd sighed and looked away before he went on.

"I'd bought him, with three other dancers, nine months before he got sick, so I'm partly responsible for his lack of self-confidence. The three slaves he's taking with him are his old friends, and that's how he thinks of them. They'll be free soon, and I think he's being responsible in insisting that they get some education first. Penny, I liked what I saw when Coryn came back. Roi needs even more encouragement to make his own decisions. Give it to him, will you?"

Too good to be true, she reminded herself, and paged on to review the other three images. The younger slave girl, she thought, could disappear on Falaron with no trouble at all. Amber's tanned skin, golden hair and blue eyes mirrored Penny's own coloring, and even the general cast of their features was similar. The older girl, Flame, had milky skin, copper hair, and green eyes, with features closer to classical beauty. Penny had made a point of including extra sunscreen in the trip supplies for her. The slave boy, Timi—well, he'd stick out like a high-intensity light on Falaron. Skin and loosely curled hair were jet black, and gave the impression of being polished until they gleamed. He'd been smiling in the tri-dee, and his blackness was relieved only by the whiteness of teeth and the whites of his eyes, and the flame-orange of the irises. Penny frowned down at the tri-dee. She was sure she had seen coloring like that before, but she couldn't think quite where. Not on Falaron, certainly.

She glanced up again at the sound of chattering in the entryway, then closed her lap pad and rose to her feet. In person, the distinction between her client and his slaves almost disappeared—she could be looking at a very expensive quartet of pleasure slaves. If she hadn't known the white-haired boy owned the other three, she would never have deduced it from their behavior. In another way they reminded her irresistibly of Coryn's group: Coryn, his friend Ander, and both of their girl friends. The natural leader in that group had been Tina, Ander's sister and Coryn's lover. In this group Roi should be the leader—but body language said that Timi was in charge. She thought of what Derik had said, and nodded to herself. Part of her job, then, would be to facilitate the transfer of leadership from Timi to Roi—without alienating Timi.

"It's two days out to the jump-point, and another two days from the jump-point in the Falaron system to orbit," she told them after they had exchanged introductions. "There'll be a short tour once the inter-system ship gets going, just to be sure you can find the facilities, and a longer one tomorrow on the operation of the ship. We should all take the short one—you need to be able to find the dining area and emergency stations and get back to our quarters if nothing else. Take the longer one only if you're really interested in space flight. Come on, let's find our seats and get webbed in for takeoff."

Flame
4/6/38

So far, Flame thought, the trip seemed likely to be boring. Not that she really objected to boring—it was certainly better than what she'd experienced as a slave since birth! But with her perfect memory—eidetic, Roi called it—she hadn't needed more than one quick tour of the ship and a brief study of the maps in the handout to know her way around. Timi planned to go back to space, Amber was studying space medicine, and Roi was interested in everything, but the only thing Flame had seen worth a return visit was the ship's store. They'd had some tunics in luscious colors, and furs she longed to run her hands through.

"Do I need to go with you?" she finally asked. The others were deep in a discussion of how jump-ships worked as they waited to start on the in-depth tour. "I'd a lot rather see what they have in the ship's store. And they said the best view screens were the ones right here in the passenger lounge."

Timi rolled his eyes and Amber looked torn, but Roi just smiled at her. "Fine with me," he said, "but .... Penny, will she be safe alone? Maybe you'd better take off the slave chain, Flame."

Flame hesitated, her hand protectively over the small emerald hanging at her throat.

"I'll go with her," Penny volunteered. "I've taken the ship tour lots of times."

Roi looked relieved. "Fine. Flame, just remember we're going to be in the wilderness for the next couple of months. Don't get anything that can't be stored until we go back."

Flame laughed aloud. "Oh, I don't have to *buy* anything to shop. And I'll keep my eyes open for the kind of things you like, too, Amber. Maybe they'll have some new perfumes. Or something really good to eat." She jumped to her feet and looked over at Penny, who was also rising. "Lets go." Eager as she was, she reached out for Roi mentally, feeling his mind touch hers in the light contact that would allow her to call on him quickly if anything went wrong.

"Don't expect bargains," Penny's voice came from behind her as they walked toward the shop entrance. "This is basically a tourist ship, you know."

"I know. But don't they run a loop? I want to see what they have from other planets on the loop."

"Qaba silk from Katun, and some lovely furs—not that I can afford them—from Frosthome. But you could probably get them cheaper on Central."

"Oh, I'll just be looking, unless I see something I'd like to have on the trip." By now they were across the passenger lounge, and Flame pushed her way into the store.

It smelled of leather, flowers, chocolate and incense. Jewels sparkled from a case on the back wall, and clothing racks spilled a waterfall of brilliant color. Roi's tineral dance, Flame thought at once, and reached for his attention. *Wouldn't those do for costumes?* she thought.

They certainly mimic the colors of the jewels, he thought back, and she caught his image of Marna's pet, Ruby—a feathered, winged monkey in shape, with a voice like a viola. *See if we'd be able to move in them.*

She moved to the rack of tunics, finding the styles flowing and the fabric almost weightless. *There's a talent show the last day of the trip*, she thought hopefully. *You brought the chip with the tinerals singing, didn't you?*

Timi'd have fits, he sighed mentally. *Dancing for a professional like Loki he'll go along with, but not performing for strangers. It's too tied up with slavery, for him. But maybe we can perform it for a select group, some day, and you're right. Those are exactly what we need for costumes. What are those odors? Amber's interested. Wants to know if there's anything she could use in her perfume making.*

Essential oils and resins. I'll wait until she can come back with me. Right now I want a closer look at those furs.

She felt his chuckle. *And check out the chocolate? Better remind Penny to be sure some's packed.* Flame grinned. The others might prefer coffee, but it set her nerves to jangling unpleasantly. Chocolate woke her up without making her high.

The furs were wonderfully soft when she picked them up and rubbed them against her cheek, but they were not suitable for a wilderness trek. She was turning to leave when a flash of copper and green caught her eye. A moment later she was lifting a green velvet hood, lined and framed with a red-gold fur so soft she could barely feel it. She found a mirror and tried it on, smiling in delight at her reflection. "Is it terribly overpriced?" she asked Penny. "Could I wear it on the trek?"

The guide placed the hood in the reader and pursed her lips. "It's expensive, but for that quality of fur—no, it's a reasonable price. And yala fur's durable as well as warm. I'd have to modify the helmet you'd wear for the hang gliding so you'd have ear buds—you wouldn't be able to hear the regular helmet speakers through the fur lining. But I can have that done before we leave. And it'd certainly be practical enough for the first stage, dogsledding on snow."

"Then I'll take it. Roi said we could use his account." She felt Roi smile at the back of her mind, but also felt that most of his attention was elsewhere, with Timi. *Thank you, Roi*, she thought as she started toward the sweets counter.

It was too bad, she thought privately as she walked, that Timi let Zhaim influence him so much.

Timi
4/7/38

Timi wasn't thinking about Zhaim at all, or even remembering to be angry with Roi. He was looking in shocked surprise at the young jump captain, who was looking back at him in just as much surprise and more than a hint of outrage.

Slaves—and other inhabitants of Central—came in every possible color combination. Except Timi's. He knew he'd been captured and sold by pirates as a child, knew he'd been raised in space before that, even remembered, dimly, his murdered parents' faces, as black-skinned and amber-eyed as his own. Almost-black skins were common enough, usually with black hair and dark, dark eyes. But he hadn't seen anyone else with his own true black skin and light eyes since he'd been enslaved.

Until now.

The jump captain's eyes weren't quite the rich copper-red of Timi's, more of a smoky topaz color. But his skin, and hair, and the cast of his features left no doubt that he came from the same stock as did Timi. As he himself obviously believed.

"You are of the Clan," he said as he surged to his feet, his voice almost accusing. "Who dared to enslave you? Who claims to own you? You?" The rest of the tour had melted back from the three, and the jump captain turned on Roi, as the one of the little group not wearing anything around his throat. "Name his price, and I buy his freedom. We do not leave our own in bondage."

"He's not for sale," Roi stated quietly, and the jump captain's fists clenched.

"Not for sale? You would keep him from his family, then? You monsters of Central are not unknown to us, but the Clan has its ways. Better you sell him to me now, and live!"

"My family's dead," Timi tried to say, increasingly certain he did not want to be rescued by this man, but the jump captain seemed not even to hear him as he continued to berate Roi.

"Oh, SHUT UP," Amber exclaimed with unexpected force. "Men," she added under her breath as all three turned to face her. "Roi couldn't sell either of us if he wanted to," she told the stranger. "We've both got conditional manumissions on file. Now why don't we go somewhere private and get this sorted out?"

"Use the officers' lounge," the system captain ordered, glaring at all four. As they left, led by the jump captain, the guide cleared his throat and resumed his explanation of bridge procedure.

"I apologize for losing my temper," the jump captain said stiffly as they entered a dimly lit room with several small tables surrounded by comfortable chairs. "I am Filomako of the Clan—and Clan simply are not left in slavery. You are?" he looked questioningly at Timi as they sat down at one of the tables.

"I'm Timi," the young man answered, "and this is Roi Laian, and Amber. We were all three slaves together, along with Flame. She's exploring the ship's store. Then his father found Roi, and freed him—well, I guess they just said he'd never legally been a slave, since he's R'il'noid—and later our old owner gave us to him. Roi's father says that Amber and I probably aren't legally slaves, either, but we have to know our home planets to prove it. Amber's found hers, but she doesn't want to go back, and anyway the conditional manumission's likely to be faster than proving she isn't legally a slave. We haven't even been able to figure out what planet I come from."

Roi nodded. "Far as I'm concerned, the slavery's never been more than a legal fiction that lets me take care of them until they're able to take care of themselves."

Filomako frowned down at the table. "You are a son of the Clan, and we do not claim a planet. If your parents are not present to guide you, such is the duty of every Clan member. How did it happen that you fell into slavery? No, wait. The telling of tales is dry work. Will you all drink with me?"

"Just fruit juice, please," Roi said quickly, and Timi shot him a resentful look.

Filomako nodded approvingly, and tapped out a pattern on the tabletop. "Goldenfruit juice, then," he said, and almost at once a tray floated to the table, loaded with a pitcher of golden liquid and four mugs. They all helped themselves, and Filomako turned again to Timi. "Proceed," he said.

Timi frowned at the tabletop, trying to remember a past he had long put behind him. "I grew up on a ship, I think," he said slowly. "Anyway, I remember I just about panicked the first time I saw open sky and felt gravity that was everywhere, and they beat me for it."

He paused, and Roi said quietly, "His record chip shows he was first sold when he was about eight years old, and he still remembered a lot about the ship when we first met, a couple of years after that. Including how to read and write and use a computer and basic math. He taught me, when we were both slaves."

Timi looked at Roi in surprise. "That's right; I'd almost forgotten. I learned not to remember, later, because it hurt too much, and the memories would get me doing things that got me into trouble."

Roi was chewing on his lower lip and looking guilty. "I think that's one of the things I may have helped you forget, a little," he said. "You aren't still mad about it, are you? I didn't know how to do it properly, then, and you were about to get yourself killed, and I was worried ...." His voice trailed off.

Timi fought back a flare of anger. It wasn't as if Roi hadn't confessed to what he'd done shortly after Derik had turned them all over to Roi, and Timi had never really doubted Roi's statement that he'd intruded in Timi's mind only because he'd feared for Timi's life. It still rankled, but this was neither the time nor the place to start a fight about something that he had accepted two years ago. "Understood," he said, and looked back toward Filomako. "I'm pretty sure pirates got the ship."

"You were very graphic about it, a time or two," Roi said dryly. "I think I could get the memories back to the surface, but you'd have to deal with them all over if I did. And I'd rather not try to help until Marna's around."

"If you don't feel confident about trying, I sure don't," Timi replied. "So—I think my parents looked pretty much like I do, except my father had a white streak in his hair. And the gravity varied a lot. I remember that. Free fall one day, twice normal the next. Even from place to place at the same time. I think my mother used to be mad at that, and my father would just laugh and say it made for variety." He scowled in concentration. "There were some other people like us, I think, but all grownups. And sometimes the ship would feel—dead—and then once I saw what I thought was a demon, with pale skin, and my mother said it was a customer." He shook his head in frustration. "That's about all I can remember."

"A Clan ship, then," Filomako said thoughtfully. "Probably a small one, if the artificial gravity was indeed erratic and you were the only child. Most likely a cargo ship, or you would have seen more paleskins. Still, we would have records." He looked over at Roi. "Now, what is this conditional manumission?"

"Timi's been pre-accepted to the space command academy on Central," Roi replied. "He needs another year of basic schooling before he enters, and we'd planned to continue as we've been doing, with lessons from the Enclave computer and me tutoring him. The manumission takes effect as soon as he graduates from the academy. That way if he needs help while he's still in school, I can be sure he gets it. Amber's is the same way, except she's going in for space medicine. And I'm pretty sure Timi told me once his father was the astrogator and his mother an engineer. Maybe she was mad about the gravity fluctuations because it was her responsibility."

For the first time since they had seen him, Filomako smiled. "Yes," he agreed. "And her mate would belittle a problem that might be taken as her responsibility." He looked directly at Timi, eyes grave. "And it is good that you are coming back to us, back to space. We of the Clan will have to investigate this situation—never have we left the rearing of one of our own to others! Still, the teachings of the Academies are not to be belittled, and that you should have both heritages may be some compensation for your years of slavery." He fell silent, brooding over the mug he held in both hands.

"Captain Filomako," Roi said, "we've told you about Timi—what we can tell you without messing with his mind. But none of us knows much about the Clan. I've seen mention on the Big'Un—uh, the main Confederation database—of people who live entirely on starships, and have an economy based on trade and building starships in debris belts. But are you all related? Of the same physical type? I've been trying to find a planet Timi might have come from, both to clarify his legal status and in case he might have relatives alive, but we simply couldn't find one with his physical type. Is the coloring typical, for instance?"

Filomako smiled again, more broadly this time. "Oh, yes. We are not a large group, so there has been much marriage between relatives over the years. The heavy skin and hair pigment are adaptive, and so are the light eyes—the iris isn't translucent, like most light human eyes; it has a strongly reflecting layer below the pigment. Like a cat's retina, but the iris instead. We all have black skin and hair, and eye color varies from green through various shades of yellow and orange to almost red. And we are very close knit."

Never have thought that from the way he reacted to you, Roi's mind whispered into Timi's.

Timi grinned mentally. *He does act downright possessive of me, doesn't he? But I kind of like the idea of having relatives again.*

"Most of us," Filomako continued, "live and work on our own ships, or in the shipyards. Many of the young singles, like me, take positions on other ships as part of our training, but I shall go back to one of our own ships, some day. Timi, you may have grown too far away from us to want to do that, but you should still plan to get part of your training after you graduate on a Clan ship. We have techniques you will not learn in a school—as witness my position on this ship, at my age. And I think your—friend—is right that we should try to find any close relatives. It would help if you could remember the name of your ship."

"I think I could probably bring that up without triggering the piracy memories," Roi said thoughtfully. "Just never occurred to me that it would be that important. Want to try, Timi? It might have been part of the computer logon sequence."

Timi nodded. "Sure, we could try for that," he said. He tightened the grip of his hand around Roi's, looking into the R'il'noid's eyes. He was aware of Roi's mind-touch, gentle and supporting as always, and then he was logging onto the ship's computer, chafing at having to do his assigned lessons when he'd much rather play in the cargo hold. The acknowledgment screen came up, and he looked at what had become a pattern to be ignored.

"The *Stellar Breeze*," he told Filomako.

"Last heard from ten years ago," the man confirmed. "Oh, we memorize the names and last reported contact of missing ships. If there is a Clan ship on Falaron, they can contact the Mothership. It might take as much as months, but we shall find out who your parents were, and if they left any relatives. Where will you be?"

"Out in the wilderness on Falaron, for the next couple of months," Timi replied. "Then back at the Enclave on Central. Uh, captain? You said I might find a position on a Clan ship after I graduate. Would Amber be welcome, too?"

"Like that, is it?" the man replied. "It would depend on the ship, I think. *Some* of the Clan get very upset at what they call miscegenation. Those of us who have spent time on out-Clan ships are generally more tolerant. But even I would have problems with a half-Clan child aboard a Clan ship." He smiled ruefully at Amber.

"You said there was a lot of close breeding in the Clan," Roi said. "Any medical problems from that?"

The jump captain nodded. "Alcohol intolerance, for one," he said. "Do not ever have anything to do with a drunk Clan member. I do not say that new blood would not be a good idea, objectively. Only that the reaction would not be objective. Well, that lies in the future." He finished his juice and stood, waiting for the other three to follow. "My deepest apologies that I lost my temper; I really did not understand the situation."

Timi smiled as he stood. "It's all right," he said. "Nice to know I may have relatives somewhere."

Central: Zhaim

An opportunity wasted, Zhaim thought disgustedly. The control circuit he had planted on the black slave allowed him to sample the creature's thoughts and memories at will, but he hadn't bothered until several hours after the meeting with Filomako. If he'd been in contact during the meeting, he would have made sure Timi had said some things that would have put a few more cracks in the bastard's already fragile self-esteem. He paced across the room, hardly noticing the mountains beyond the window, or the softness of the furred floor under his feet. There wasn't much he could do to his rival physically until the group was on the surface of Falaron, and not much then until he could get Lai and Marna out of the way. Psychologically, though .... He'd keep closer track of the black's experiences from now on, he decided.

Chapter 3

"Growler, walk on." Penny glanced back over her shoulder, saw that the blue and yellow teams were following at the intervals to which they'd been trained, and moved her red-harnessed team into a trot with a quiet "hup-hup." The color coding, she thought amusedly, was breaking down already. Her own violet parka, the color of the Company logo, clashed with the red of her dogs' harnesses and her own sled. Timi in gold and Amber in blue did not look out of place with blue sled and harnesses, but Roi's red, Flame's emerald green, and the yellow of their harness and sled made a combination that was almost painful to look at. Whoever back at headquarters had come up with the color-coding scheme should try to live with it.

Neither of the girls was having any difficulty with her team. She hadn't expected them to, after the check drive back at the Company headquarters this morning. If they were going to have trouble, it would have been while they were taking the dogs from the airvan cages and harnessing them. But when she'd asked them if they remembered how to harness the dogs, Flame had responded promptly: "The color of the main part of the collar identifies the team. And team harnesses are all the same color as the sled and tugline—that's the line down the middle of the team. The inner stripe on the collar matches the loop at the back of the harness. Each collar has a number—1 is the leader, and they follow in order, with the even numbers to the left of the tugline. We fasten the sled to something solid, fasten the loop at the back of the leader's harness to the front of the tugline, and he holds it straight while we fasten the other dogs' harnesses and collars."

Roi's body language and voice tone had told the dogs quite clearly that he was in charge, and they had accepted his dominance without question.

Now if he'd just do the same in his dealings with other people .... The three teams trotted northward in file, the Spine Range towering to their left. Snow squeaked under the runners, and the dogs' breath puffed out in brief clouds. Falaron's sun, already declining toward the mountains, shone warm on Penny's left cheek, while the right side of her face burned cold with the wind of their travel.

They reached a point where the dogs had to move to the steeper slope near the mountain front to get around a ravine head. "Everybody stop and passengers out," she called back cheerfully. "We take this stretch one at a time. Roi, Timi, activate your forcewebs and walk until we're back on the level, and then we'll switch places and you can drive for a while."

She led them carefully around the ravine head, then stopped her team and watched as they followed her, one at a time. Amber had resumed her parka as the wind began to bite through her sweater, and its teal blue harmonized with the slightly darker blue of the sled and towline as she voice-guided Snowflake around the arc of trail. Snowflake looked pleased that her driver's commands agreed with the route that the old leader would have taken anyway. Timi followed. He'd set his forcewebs for a long, narrow base of support with slip forward only, and skied confidently along the uphill part of the trail. When he turned back downhill to the plateau, it became obvious that he had set the webs to have almost no friction against sliding forward, and came down so fast he had difficulty staying upright. Amber smothered her laughter quickly, but it was apparent that Timi's feelings were hurt. Oh, blast, Penny thought. Now he'll be trying to prove himself for the rest of the afternoon.

Flame had left her copper hair loose under the fur hood, and her emerald jacket was bright against the snow. Her black leader, Nip, threatened to get away from her near the high point of the trail, then suddenly steadied. Roi's mind touch, Penny thought. Well, it wasn't as if he didn't use it responsibly.

Last Roi himself skied over the trail. He seemed at first to have more control than Timi, but two-thirds of the way down the near side of the trail he managed to lose his balance completely and sat down, hard. Managed, Penny thought admiringly, was the operative word. The others laughed heartily when the scarlet-clad figure elected to slide down the rest of the slope sitting, and Timi's good humor was totally restored. Yes, Penny thought, in some ways he really was the leader. But he shouldn't have to make a fool of himself to keep the others happy.

The next section of trail, after the boys had taken over the driving, was level and well enough packed to make excellent footing for the dogs. Once satisfied that the two boys were controlling their teams well at a trot, Penny decided to let the dogs, still fresh, have the run they so obviously wanted. "Growler, Hike!" she commanded, and her team broke into a lope. She heard Timi and then Roi repeat the command to their teams, and the girls' squeals as the dogs' flying feet kicked snow into their faces.

She looked back a time or two, and when she saw the smiles began to fade a bit, and felt her own face stiffen with the wind of their speed, she called, "Growler, ease back, boy, steady," and touched the brake. When they came out of the mountains' shadow to a sunny spot, she stopped her team and downed them. The dogs gulped snow, heated by their run, as she turned to check the other two sleds. "Ready to change places again?" she called. "Our night camp's almost in sight from here."

They all pulled scarves over their faces before continuing, and the scarves were soon icy with their frozen breath. The shadow of the range stretched farther and farther away to their right, and the dogs' breath and their own trailed after them in clouds. A gibbous moon, faint in the daylight sky, rose slowly above the still sunlit eastern horizon. "Hey, it's big," Roi said.

"We've got a big moon," Penny agreed, "and close. That's why we have such strong tides." They headed down into a broad valley, the dogs loping downhill and dropping back to a trot as they climbed the rise on the far side. A hint of violet appeared low in the eastern sky, and sunlight no longer touched the horizon. The ground leveled out again ahead of them, and a new and distant horizon appeared suddenly beyond the near one they'd been struggling toward. A little farther, and a dark square appeared in the blue shadows and grew until it was a small log building, incongruous in this treeless wilderness of snow, with firewood stacked as high as the roof, a cluster of well-spaced doghouses to one side, and several hitching posts in front.

"Luxury accommodations," Penny laughed as she guided her team toward a hitching post, set the brake, and snapped the short line at the back of the sled to the ring on the post. "Timi, Roi, can you take in an armload of wood apiece and get a fire started in the stove? There should be kindling inside. The rest of us'll get the dogs tied."

By the time all the dogs were chained and investigating their night's accommodations, there was smoke coming from the cabin's chimney. It was still cold when they went in the door; it would take time for the metal of the stove to heat enough to warm the well-insulated cabin. But the fire was properly started, and would soon be demanding more fuel.

"We'll need snow to melt for water, and more wood for the fire," Penny said. "Somebody get these big pots filled with snow, so I can start fixing the dogs' supper, and we'll have to keep dumping snow in as it melts. The reservoir on the back of the stove needs filling, too, and we'll want wood enough to completely fill the wood rack, there."

Roi grabbed one of the pots while she was still speaking, and had it back, heaped with packed snow, a couple of minutes later. Amber had located the pile of clean buckets by the door and grabbed Timi, and the two were ferrying snow to the reservoir.

Roi studied the reservoir and the size of the buckets. "I could teleport snow into the reservoir," he offered. "It'd be a lot faster."

"I'm sure you could," Penny agreed as she located the dog food mix in the cabin's supplies. "We could also look at the scenery out of closed snowskimmers instead of freezing our faces on dogsleds, and build luxury hostels with hot and cold running water and resident chefs. But this is a Challenge journey. I know, the teleporting *would* be work, for you. But it wouldn't seem that way to the others, and you'd be cheating them by taking more than your share of the work."

Roi's face was serious as he thought that out, then he grinned at her. "All right, ma'am," he said cheerfully, saluting her with an empty bucket. "OK if I use TK to get *lots* of snow in each bucket?"

Penny laughed and shooed him out, then divided the dogs' meal into the pots and began stirring. She had her clients dump several more buckets of snow into the pots before they resumed filling the reservoir, and then had Roi fill a smaller pot for their own supper. By the time the reservoir was full of half-melted snow, the aroma of the stew was beginning to compete with that of the dog food, and the dogs outside were yodeling frantically at the odors seeping from the cabin.

The boys went back to hauling in wood while Penny and Amber fed the dogs and Flame watched their dinner, and the wood stand was close to full when they reentered the cabin. Penny had lit a couple of oil lanterns earlier, and their light was warm and welcoming after the cold moonlight outside. The smell of the stew had all of their mouths watering, and the little building had warmed enough that both parkas and vests were heaped on the bunks. Roi had found the dishes and piled them on the rough wood table. "Go ahead and dish it up, Flame," Penny said as she added a few more sticks of wood to the stove.

They discussed sleeping arrangements as they ate, the girls laying claim to the upper bunks. "Too bad the beds aren't wider," Flame said wistfully. Penny, reminded of the morning she had awakened to find Flame in Roi's bed on the ship, thought that this was one aspect of having slaves along she found hard to accept. Then she thought of Coryn's group, with Coryn and Tina always in the same sleeping bag, and decided she was being unfair.

She sent the four out to get more snow for the reservoir while she used the dog pot as a dishpan. Later they would take turns with cooking and washing up, but this first night she wanted to get a feel for how they handled the simpler chores. When she had finished the dishes and rinsed out the pot, and no snow had appeared, she pulled on her parka and stepped outdoors to look for the group.

The cold burned her face and took her breath away, and the contrast between moonlight and shadow made it hard to see anything at first. Breathless laughter greeted her ears, and she finally located the group. All three slaves were on top of Roi, vigorously washing his face and hair with snow. He seemed to be laughing as hard as his slaves were, so she left them to their play, shaking her head.

They came indoors a few minutes later, buckets heaped with snow and faces suspiciously demure. Both Roi and Timi had snow in their hair and eyebrows, and commenced digging it out of their sweater necks as soon as they shed their parkas. "We still need more snow for water, if we're to wash at all," she pointed out, and then had to stop Roi, who'd promptly grabbed two buckets, from heading out the door. Enough snow had melted while he'd been trying to dig it out of his clothes that his white hair was plastered across his forehead and water ran in rivulets down his face. When she put her hand on his shoulder, she found his sweater was sodden.

"You can't go out wet like that," she scolded. "Or Timi, either. Aren't you all a little old for that kind of nonsense?"

The laughter went out of Roi's eyes, and he ducked his head. Flame glared at her in his defense. "We never had a chance to play when we were young, Penny," she said. "This is the first time ...." Flame gulped and fell silent, and Penny had a sudden, bleak glimpse of just how unlike her usual spoiled clients these four were.

She sighed. "Well, we'll just have to ration water. You girls can't bring in all we should have by yourselves. Or are you wet too?" Not as wet as the boys, but wet enough, she decided.

Central: Zhaim

Ten light years away, Roi's school rival Xazhar stared out over a seemingly endless vista of ice cliffs, snow and clouds. "I'm bored," he said. "Bored, bored, bored."

So, Zhaim thought sourly, am I. Not least with you.

He had begun the habit of bringing Xazhar home each firstday as much to hurt Roi, then being ignored by his father, as because he wanted Xazhar's company. Later, Xazhar had proved a useful source of information as to what was going on at Tyndall. But Zhaim had made sure he was never in a position to invite his son home for school holidays, and even a few days of actually living with the boy had set his teeth on edge.

Part of his frustration and boredom had nothing to do with Xazhar, of course. For several centuries his chief artistic pursuit and avocation had been the creation of sculptures of living flesh, mostly Human, though he had begun to experiment with blending species, and even a few combinations of plant and animal. He knew his father disapproved, but he had been unable to resist embellishing his old home at the Enclave with some of his less obvious creations. And the brat had invaded that sacred ground, even before its Çeren index was known, and tattled to their father. Zhaim should have crushed it then. He had tried to discipline it instead, avoiding what would then have been no more than unpleasantness from his father, only to find once it was Çeren indexed that harming it would bring the death penalty on his own head.

And his isolated eyrie, chosen to avoid his father's notice that he was continuing his hobby, had become a boring prison. Even Xazhar noticed that.

He maintained his own computer, and so far he did not believe that his father knew what information he accessed. Weather reports on a dozen planets would in any case look routine. So far, he saw no instabilities on Falaron he could exploit. So far.

Falaron: Penny
4/10/38

Penny's bed faced a high window opening toward the west, so when an anguished cry awoke her the first thing she saw was the gibbous moon, almost hidden behind the flank of a mountain. After midnight, she thought muzzily as she groped for the portable light on the floor by her bed. Her hand struck the textured plastic, and she flipped on the light and played it around the room, looking for the source of the moaning.

Roi. His face was twisted in such misery as Penny had never seen on a human face, his head whipping back and forth in helpless despair. White legs came into view above and beyond that head, as Flame scrambled hastily down the ladder from the upper bunk and dropped to her knees by Roi's head, her hands cupped around his face. "Roi," she called gently, "Roi! Wake up, love. It's just one of your nightmares. Ah, that's better," she added as the golden eyes opened, pale in the bronze face.

"Flame?" he whispered raggedly, and his arms wrapped around her, pulling her body toward his. Flame darted an apologetic glance toward Penny as she slid into the narrow bed beside him, and Penny flicked off the light and made herself go back to sleep.

***

"It's not his fault," Flame said the next morning. She and Penny were packing a lunch while Amber and the boys reloaded the sleds and hitched up the dogs.

"Why should a nightmare be anyone's fault?" Penny replied, but Flame hurried on.

"He'd been having them three or four times a night for a year and a half when Derik gave us to him. Oh, we all have nightmares, but Roi's were almost continuous. We found that sleeping with him stopped them. Slaves never sleep alone; if you're not in bed with the Master you're in reach of other slaves, or piled up to keep warm, and that's all Roi ever knew unless he was being punished for something. Then after his father rescued him of course he had a bed to himself, but it just reminded him of pain.

"At least one of us always sleeps with him at home, and then he's all right. The bunks on the ship were close enough I could stretch my hand up to his over our heads, though he still got restless a time or two. Here, though ...."

"Once we're down on the plains we'll be camping out and using sleeping bags," Penny told her, "and they'll seal together to make double bags. Can you stand these narrow bunks for another fiveday or so?"

Flame's face relaxed in relief. "Oh, of course," she said. "You should have seen us all piled into that invalid bed they had him in when we were first with him! But the look you gave us on the ship, when he was extra restless and I crawled in with him to quiet him—well, I didn't think you approved."

Penny felt the heat in her face. "I like him—and you—too much not to be disappointed when it looked like he was being just another master using a slave," she forced herself to admit.

Flame looked at her thoughtfully. "I know what it's like to be used that way," she said, "and so does Roi. What we have together—all of us, even Timi, though he doesn't want to admit it any more—has nothing at all to do with that. We *care* about each other. And we didn't do anything but hold each other last night, or on the ship, but once we've got a little room it probably won't stay that way. By *my* choice, not his."

Penny smiled. "You couldn't possibly be as bad as Coryn and Tina, and I didn't mind them. I was just misinterpreting what was going on. And I'd like to apologize for that."

Flame tucked a last piece of dried fruit into the lunch pouch, and smiled at the guide. "People misunderstand us pretty often," she said. "They don't often apologize."

Roi

The pace was faster on the following days, with longer intervals between driver changes. They continued to run north, above tree line, detouring down into a ravine or sometimes even a patch of scrubby trees for a windbreak at their lunch stops. Roi hardly thought about his nightmare. It had just been one of his usual ones, where he found himself acting as Zhaim did, and Flame's touch had been enough to reassure him that he was still himself.

The moon rose later and fatter each day, and then began to collapse until it was close to a half circle barely above the eastern horizon before they slept. Roi, unused to a moon of any sort, found its changes fascinating.

I could keep track of the days by that, he thought, even without a calendar.

By the sixth day on the trail, they were well ahead of schedule, and Penny let them all stretch out and relax in the increasing warmth of the noon sun while they ate. As the afternoon of that day wore on, the sun seemed if anything to grow hotter, and the sky lightened in color. The snow began to drag at the dogs' feet, and held back the runners of the sleds. Penny led them higher, more into the shadow of the mountains, but this took them across an area that the wind had swept almost bare of snow.

Roi was driving, and keeping a sharp eye on his team, when he saw the right wheel dog flinch. "Hold," he snapped, setting the brake. "Penny!"

The guide turned and looked back, and then halted her own team. Flame jumped out of the basket of Roi's sled to take his place at the handlebars, and Roi ran forward, his attention all for the possibly injured dog once he saw that Penny was aware of the situation.

The right wheeler, Rust, was trembling a little, blood staining the sparse snow under her left front paw. Roi threw aside his mittens and reached for her emotions, steadying her as he lifted her foot. Blood trickled over his bare hand. When he turned the foot he saw that the cut was shallow, though bleeding freely.

"What happened?" Penny asked as she fell to her knees beside him.

"A rock flake, I think," he replied. "I stopped the team the instant I felt her flinch. It's not too deep, but it hit a blood vessel." He thought for a moment. His Healing ability was not widely known, and he wasn't sure about revealing it to Penny, but he couldn't help feeling the dog's pain. "Emergency enough to use my talents?"

"What can you do for her?"

"Heal her." He wiggled uncomfortably. "I know you don't want me using esper, but I don't see why she should have to suffer."

"Get her down on her left side, so I can get a good look," Penny said.

Roi moved his free hand to Rust's head, urging her mentally to lie down. It took some careful doing to get her down without tangling the harness, but once she was flat he twisted the foot so Penny could see it.

The guide groaned. "Wheelers are almost as important as leaders, and she'll have to be carried for at least a couple of days. Could you really speed the healing? How long would it take?"

"Five, ten minutes," he replied. "The new skin will be a little fragile, but it won't hurt her any more, and she'll be able to work on it with no further damage if we pad it a bit. Dogs are easier to Heal than people. They don't know it can't happen."

Flame had been digging in the sled bag while they talked, and she straightened up as Penny nodded agreement to the Healing. "Here, Roi," she said as she tossed him a bag of candied fruit. "Get that into you first. He needs extra energy to Heal," she added to Penny.

Penny looked dubious, but she nodded approval.

Roi repositioned Rust as he chewed and swallowed a handful of fruit, moving into the dog as he rolled her until she was on her back, leaning slightly against his legs. The red of Rust's coat, almost the color of Flame's hair, shaded to a warm cream on her underbody, making her look like a patch of dusty snow among the rocks and sand. He closed his eyes, feeling through Rust's mind into the damaged foot and accelerating the healing of the cut. Vaguely he was aware of Penny telling Flame to find the dog booties and the two girls putting them on the rest of the team, but most of his attention stayed with Rust until the Healing was complete.

"We shouldn't have tried to take them across this without booting them up," Penny said as Roi felt her kneel at his side again.

"All right?" he asked as he again twisted the paw for her inspection. "I didn't want her getting back up on the foot until you'd checked it and gotten some protection on it. She needs some kind of skin lubricant or salve and then padding and maybe one of those boots like you put on the rest of the team."

Penny spread the toes where the cut had been, but aside from the new pink skin the cut was gone. "Looks great," she said as she pulled out a tube of salve and began smearing it over the scar and pads. A bit of soft fluff went next, and then she slid on one of the fuzzy yellow boots to hold everything in place. One of Rust's hind feet seemed to bother her as well, and she put a dab of salve on it before pulling on the rest of the booties.

Roi gave Rust's belly a last scratch before he guided her to her feet. Tarball, the other wheeler, backed her ears and looked imploring. "You'd better pet the rest of them a bit before we move on," Penny said. "Otherwise they'll be picking on Rust out of jealousy."

She returned to the other teams, and began showing the others how to apply the boots. Roi took to the driver's position and moved his sled up with the others'.

Penny met his eyes just before they pulled back out. "Healing," she said. "Nobody's able to Heal any more, except maybe the Lady Marna. No crossbred's ever been able to Heal. What are you? Inner Council level?"

"Marna's training me," he replied. "For the rest, you don't know anything. You never even asked the question." Had he gotten his message across to her?

The rest of the afternoon was uneventful. The haziness of the sky and the warmth of the air continued, as did the drag of the snow on the runners. But the dogs seemed much better able to handle the sticky snow once it no longer balled up between their toes.

When they reached the seventh night's shelter, the first short beginnings of icicles were forming on the northeast corner of the roof, and Roi saw Penny frown uneasily. "Problem?" he asked.

"The route I'd planned for tomorrow's mostly on frozen watercourses, and we'll lose quite a lot of altitude. With it this warm, there could be water over some of the ice. We may have to use an alternate route. Get the wood in and start the dog food, will you?"

Well, if he was busy with the wood and packing the dog food pot with snow to melt, Penny couldn't have him help cook the food they would eat themselves. He took in enough firewood to get the stove well started, and then packed the big dog food pots with snow. Penny added the dog meal to the pots and stirred it in, and then directed Roi to carry the pots out to the sledge she had positioned outside the cabin door. "You can help me feed, tonight," she said.

He cheerfully hauled the sledge between the doghouses while Penny ladled the food out for the hungry animals. The dogs seemed to like it, and Roi took a cautious fingerful himself. "Roi! That's *dog* food!" Penny scolded.

Roi grinned and sucked his finger. "Tastes better than a lot of slave rations I've had," he commented. "Probably better nutrition, too."

Penny shook her head. "No wonder you haven't been complaining about the food. Or about helping with the work, for that matter. Come on. The girls ought to have supper ready by now."

Amber and Flame hadn't actually done any more cooking before the trip than Roi had, but they seemed to be learning this skill faster than he was. Even Timi had managed to make soup without burning it, and Flame's biscuits actually impressed Penny. Roi washed the dishes while Penny got out her map and began to study it. "It's still warm out," he said as he finished his task. "Look at the way the eaves are dripping. Let's play a while before we go up to that hot spring Penny told us about."

Penny grinned. "Go ahead. I need to study the map and pick an alternate trail for tomorrow." The four made a rush for the door and through it.

"Look," Flame said before they could even put on the forcewebs. "The snow doesn't fall apart." Before Roi could react, she had flung the loose ball at his head.

His parka hood was down, and he yelped as it caught him in the ear, then grabbed a handful of snow himself and sent it flying toward Flame's hood. She laughed and threw herself flat in the snow, and the white ball flattened itself against the back of Timi's head.

Amber, already packing a loose ball, giggled at the sight even as she sent a return shot toward Roi, who was laughing as he ducked Flame's next snowball only to collide with Amber's.

Timi was also grabbing for snow, making a pile of snowballs rather than throwing them at once. Roi was too busy ducking the girls' shots and lobbing snowballs back at them to pay much attention to Timi, and he was caught totally by surprise as Timi's missiles began to slam into all three of them. One caught him in the face hard enough to hurt, and another actually knocked him down.

He felt his cheek, and then lowered his mittened hand to see blood-streaked snow in the palm. What was Timi up to, anyway? A snowball shouldn't have cut his face! He sent his perceptive sense into the snowball, and felt not only ice, but rocks. Anger grew, and he slammed Timi down into the snow with his mind.

"Dammit, that hurt, Timi. I wasn't even aiming to hit you."

"And you don't make snowballs out of sopping wet snow under the eaves, or put rocks in them!" Penny must have been watching, as she stormed out of the door.

Timi pushed himself to a sitting position in the snow, the rest of the snowballs piled at his side and his face puzzled. "I, I'm sorry, Roi. Don't know what got into me. I didn't hurt you too badly, did I?"

Roi wasn't hurt, but what had he himself done? He'd decided long since never to use his abilities on others without their consent, and now he'd used them to attack Timi over a stupid snowball. That was the kind of thing he'd sworn *never* to do! He closed his eyes and reached into his own mind and body, calming himself.

"Nothing I can't Heal," Roi replied as he sat up in the snow. "Sorry I lost my temper. You said there was a hot spring, Penny? I'll take care of it there."

The heat of the spring soothed tired muscles and left them almost too relaxed to resume their snow-damp clothes and walk back to the cabin. "Penny," Roi asked as he dumped a final bucket of snow into the reservoir, "are we going to be able to use the dogsleds tomorrow? It feels like it's still getting warmer, instead of cooling off. The dogs were already having problems this afternoon. What do we do if the snow really starts melting?"

"Help the dogs pull, if we have to," Penny said. "If it's this warm tomorrow we'll have to change course a little, that's all. Nothing major." But her eyes went to the growing icicles hanging from the cabin roof, and her face was worried.

You mean you hope it's nothing serious, Roi thought. I can't seem to get anything solid, but it doesn't feel right to me.

***

"So what do you have for me?" He kept his voice bored, but his eyes were running hungrily over the slave dealer's merchandise. Any could be his; he owned most of the company. But he was looking for more than a useful body. Terror. Defiance. Something he could get his teeth into.

"In the back room, My Lord." No slurred honorifics here; the man was even more frightened than the slaves he sold. "A bit too much for the average buyer, but not for you. And healthy—they'll last a long time. If you would follow me, My Lord?"

There were four in the room, three sluts and a brat. All were chained, and the brat, at least, would have been at his throat otherwise. Not that the sluts—a redhead and two blonds—looked much tamer! Plenty of spirit for him to break. And strong. Vital. Would the brat's blackness spread to the lighter skins of the others, when he grafted them together? He smiled, letting them see the cruelty in his eyes.

Not me! Not me! Roi's mind was screaming. Was this another nightmare? He struggled to wake.

"Roi!" Flame's whispered voice came through. When he managed to open his eyes, her head was upside down as she leaned over the edge of the upper bunk. "Good thing we'll be using the sleeping bags soon! Come on, love. Wake up. You're safe."

It wasn't his own safety that bothered him, though. His reaction to Timi's attack might have triggered the dream, but why had Penny been a part of the group? Was he turning into another Zhaim, as he had feared when he first found out he was Zhaim's brother? But he couldn't tell Flame about the dream and her part in it. And this bunk, unlike those in most of the cabins so far, was too narrow for her to join him.

He glanced around the room, barely visible in the starlight that filtered through the windows. The others were all asleep, resting for what promised to be a hard day tomorrow. As should he be, and Flame. "I'll be all right, now," he told her.

She looked doubtful, but her head vanished. Roi lay still, trying again to bring tomorrow into focus. Still blurred. Maybe if they took along extra food and supplies from the cabin .... The waning moon was high enough to shine in the south window before he managed to get back to sleep.

Chapter 4

The first thing Penny heard when she woke up the next morning was the dripping of water. Roi was already up and dressed, looking out the window into the pre-dawn darkness. He turned toward Penny, a worried frown on his face. "Isn't it awfully warm?" he asked.

"Too warm to sled on the streams," she agreed. "We'll have to take the alternate route, and it'll be a long day. Better get the others up; I want to get on the trail as early as possible, while it's still cold. We may have to picket the dogs, and if we do, we'll fasten individual short drop lines to a long line we can stretch from tree to tree. And yes, we should be in the trees by evening. But for right now, it's your turn to make breakfast."

"Oatmeal's on the stove," he replied, but it was clear that his mind was even less on cooking than usual. Well, there wasn't too much he could do wrong, with oatmeal. Was there?

There was. Roi's friends, who'd normally eat anything, had peculiar looks on their faces, and when Penny tried a spoonful, well creamed and sugared, she almost choked. Burned, to start with, and overloaded with salt. She forced herself to eat half the bowl, but she doubted Roi would have noticed if she'd thrown the whole thing out. He himself went through an entire bowlful, apparently never tasting what he was eating, and kept looking worriedly at the window.

Roi remained tense and on edge as they loaded the sleds, and disappeared into the cabin about halfway through the job. When he reappeared, he was dragging a weather sheet with a cooking pot, most of the stored food, dog food, weather sheets and blankets from the cabin piled on it, and had a number of extra drop lines and a coil of rope over his shoulders.

"Roi," Penny told him, annoyed, "we won't need that. We won't even have space on the sleds for it."

"We will if we use the forcewebs instead of riding," Roi replied. "Penny, I get hunches sometimes. It's a form of conditional precognition. With the training I've had the last few years, I should be able to do better than just knowing this is important, but somehow I can't get beyond the hunch this time. I *know* we'll need this stuff, but I don't know why or where."

Timi groaned theatrically. "We'll all be ready to drop by noon," he complained. "Roi, are you still mad at me from last night? I *told* you I didn't mean it."

"No," Roi said shortly. "But we're going to need these. Trust me, Timi. Please?"

He's not going to back down, Penny thought as she looked up from putting booties on one of the dogs to study her client. She glanced beyond Roi to the pale blue sky and sagging snow. She needed to reinforce his initiative, she remembered, and with weather this unusual, perhaps she should listen to the boy. If the snow kept thawing, they might have to stop and camp, waiting for the snow to melt or harden. "All right," she capitulated. "Just remember when your legs get tired from skiing whose idea this was."

The skiers quickly shed not only parkas and vests, but sweaters as well. A warm wind followed them from the south, and the soggy snow dragged at sled runners and forcewebs alike. Penny had decided to stay at high elevation as long as possible, and kept the line moving north along the mountain front long past the point she had planned to drop down onto a minor tributary of the Surprise River. Shortly before the time she planned to stop for lunch she led them east, following the crest of a broad ridge between the forested valleys of the North Fork and South Fork of the Surprise.

They didn't stop for lunch until well after noon. By then dogs and handlers alike were dragging, except for Roi. The young R'il'noid was strung tight, unable even to sit down with the others and eat. Instead he prowled restlessly as he chewed, rearranging the contents of the sled bags, checking the tightness of dog boots, and turning repeatedly to check the northwest sky. Penny glanced that way herself, but could see nothing beyond the general haziness of the atmosphere. Even the mountain front they had just left had a glassy, unreal look.

The guide had planned to take a long lunch break to rest the dogs, who were sprawled out panting in the unnatural warmth. Somehow Roi had his team on their feet and pulling out, with Amber driving the blue team behind him, almost as soon as they had finished eating. Penny had little choice but to follow, fuming with anger. Screaming at Roi when he moved the pace up to a lope had no effect, nor did attempting to stop her own team. Growler slowed only briefly at her "whoa," then glanced ahead and resumed his lope. How dare her client take over the mind of her lead dog!

When Roi abruptly turned right off the trail, heading down toward the South Fork, Penny lost her temper completely. "Growler, *hike*," she shouted. "Catch up with that idiot, drat you!" To her surprise, the dog obeyed, sprinting to catch up with Roi's team, and Roi stopped his team to wait for her. Timi and Flame, breathless from the near-racing pace Roi had set, joined them.

"What do you think you're doing?" Penny sputtered at the R'il'noid. "The dogs can't stand this pace in heat like this! And we've got to stay as high and cold as we can. Get back on the ridge trail!"

"They won't have to stand the heat much longer," Roi replied. "Look." He pointed behind and to the right of his southward course.

Penny glanced northwest, and froze. Thick clouds were boiling down from the north, already hiding the northernmost of the peaks that had been visible an hour earlier. "Equinox blizzard," she gulped through lips gone suddenly stiff. The warm wind still puffed lightly into her face when she turned back to the south, but only lightly. Warm and wet, and when the cold air coming down from the north met that moisture .... Hastily she thought back to the area maps she had studied so carefully. Roi had turned at the right point, she realized. The slope from the ridge was relatively gradual here, and there would be game trails into and through the woods. Penny opened the red sled bag and pulled out her portable map, wishing she had the chip to provide a detailed map of the valley. Roi, looking over her shoulder now, put his finger on an area the low-resolution map showed as spruce forest. "There," he said. "Can you lead us from here? I'm just going on instinct."

Penny shook her head. "I don't have a detailed map, so your instinct is probably as good as anything I can do, beyond getting us into the trees and spotting game trails. I'll lead to start, because the other teams are used to following mine. When that storm hits us, the temperature is going to drop, fast. Get your sweaters on now, and make sure your vests and parkas are where you can reach them in a hurry. And stay close together. The storm front should blot out the sun a few minutes before it actually reaches us. When that happens, stop, group up, and get your vests and parkas on. Roi, you take the lead at that point, if we haven't found shelter yet."

Roi nodded and reached into his sled bag, pulling out the rope he'd loaded that morning. "How about roping together then?" he asked.

"Cut a couple of pieces and tie them to the sleds for the skiers to hold on to," Penny replied. "The dogs will follow the lead team by scent. Just keep the pace slow once the storm hits. We won't be able to see the trees until we run into them, if it's as bad as it looks." She glanced around the group before moving ahead, driving her panting team toward the trees at a fast lope. The south breeze had died entirely, and the mere cessation of air motion was allowing the remaining snow to cool the air noticeably.

Growler reached the edge of the trees, swinging without guidance into a well-marked game trail, and Penny had to concentrate on keeping the sled upright. "Steady, Growler," she called, and glanced back to check on the others.

"Let him have his head," Roi called from the last sled in line. "I'm guiding him."

Penny nodded and shifted her concentration back to the sled. It was light but bulky, higher than wide, and it was a constant struggle to keep it from tipping over or hanging up on a tree. They could use the three sleds as three sides of a waist-high shelter, she thought as she dodged tree limbs. Set up the picket lines for the dogs radiating from the shelter, with guide lines from the shelter for the handlers. The dogs could eat emergency bars or even the dry meal mixed with snow if they had to, though she hated to reward them so poorly for their efforts. Not that they'd have much better themselves. If this was the kind of storm she suspected, they wouldn't be able to keep a fire going. She wished that she could call in an airvan before the storm hit, but as this was a Challenge journey, she had only an emergency caller, not a com, and there was no way she could transmit the nature of her problem.

The trail wound briefly toward the northwest, and Penny gasped in dismay as she got a glimpse of the sky. The boiling clouds that filled almost half the sky looked darker now, with a white curtain sweeping across the high ridge they had just left. The trail ran into a small clearing just as the clouds raced across the face of the sun, and Growler stopped as the other two sleds pulled up beside hers.

"I've got a mind-link set up among the four of us, for communication and location," Roi told her as he struggled into his parka. "Want me to bring you in, too? I'll set it so I won't pick up anything you don't deliberately aim my way."

Penny hesitated, hunting through the handlebar bag for her heavy mittens. The mere idea of the violation of her mental privacy left her nauseated. Once the storm reached them, however, the communication such a mind link could provide could literally be the difference between life and death.

"He's not talking about invading your mind, Penny," Flame said quietly, pulling the fur ruff of her hood forward to protect her face. "And he's very good at ignoring everything except what you're trying to communicate."

There was a kind of sighing roar as the first gust from the north struck the spruce trees over their heads, and the temperature seemed to drop as they stood. They'd never be able to hear each other once the storm really hit. "All right," Penny said through clenched teeth, and braced herself for the invasion.

"Good," Roi said as his team trotted out of the clearing. "Bring up the rear, will you? I don't think it's more than a few more minutes." He sounded intensely relieved, she thought, and wished he'd go ahead with whatever he was going to do to her mind.

"Well, do it," she finally shouted at him as she swung her team in after the other two. The wind was roaring overhead now, sending occasional icy fingers down to slap at their backs as they raced for shelter.

You don't think you're hearing *me in this, do you?* Roi said, his voice as clear as if he were sitting next to her in a quiet room. *For right now, just talk aloud if you want me to hear you. I'll show you how to reach me without actually opening your mouth after we get into shelter.*

Startled, Penny tried to examine her own mind. There was no feeling of all of anything out of the ordinary except, perhaps, a very slight increase in awareness of her surroundings. None of the symptoms she'd been taught to associate with an attempt at mind control were present, and that in itself frightened her.

Penny, I'm not reading your mind, but I'm a high-level empath, and I can't help feeling your emotions. What's frightening you? The tone was concerned.

"I've been taught to recognize mental invasion," she said anxiously, "and I can't feel anything like that. What are you doing?"

Well, I'm not invading your mind, he replied, and she felt his amusement. *I'm just holding a very light communications link. Add to that the fact that I have a very soft mind touch, what Marna calls the Healer's touch, and you shouldn't feel anything.* A snow flurry drove into the side of her face, and for a moment the world seemed to vanish around her in a white blur. A branch exploded out of the whiteness, coming toward her face, and she barely had time to duck as the team took her past it. *I'm going to intensify the link so you can share my perception of what's around us,* Roi's mental voice continued.

The first flurry dissipated, allowing her to see Growler, Timi skiing behind Amber, and a small sphere of forest around them. Amber's team faded into the whiteness of the sphere's boundary, and Roi's was completely lost in the thickening snow. The feeling she'd been taught to associate with telepathy came, very slightly, and abruptly she knew when Snowflake started into a bend in the trail, and felt Flame's and Roi's positions ahead of the old leader. When the next flurry wiped out vision, she retained awareness of the whereabouts of trees and the others in the party, and it even seemed that trees and branches threatening the sled or her face were abnormally intense in their blackness. When she closed her eyes as a spit of snow blew into her face, the awareness intensified. After a few minutes, she began to trust Roi's guidance enough to keep her eyes closed.

We're here, Roi's voice came into Penny's mind, and she opened her eyes on blinding snow. In the few minutes since the first flurry the temperature had dropped so far she was wishing her parka were heavier. She groped for Roi's awareness of their surroundings, trying to visualize where to set up the picket lines. They stood in a very small, brushy clearing, small enough that the dense wall of spruce surrounding them kept out most of the wind. *Sleds in there?* Roi asked, and her feeling of their surroundings concentrated on a hollow where the brush had been flattened. In her mind the hollow was suddenly surrounded on three sides by the sleds, with waterproof weather sheets below them and stretched above the sled tops as a roof. Sleeping bags and blankets made a nest inside the shelter.

"Cut a dozen or so of the young spruce, put the branches under the bottom sheet, and lay the poles across the top of the sleds so the snow won't collapse the sheet on top of us," Penny said. "And in this storm, we'll need a sheltered latrine area with a snow floor. Can you pick up a picture from my mind?" Without waiting for an answer, she visualized an addition to the shelter, with weather sheets forming a tiny bump-out on one of the front corners. Then she added the dog pickets in three loops, running through heavy brush that would give the animals some shelter from the wind until the snow provided the insulation they would need.

Higher, came Roi's mind-voice, and her visualized picket line attachments moved upward on the trees she had picked, the individual drop lines doubled in length as the extras Roi had brought were snapped into the ones already present.

"So they can work their way up if the snow really drifts into the brush, without getting tangled in the main picket line," Penny agreed as she set the snow brake and fumbled in the sled bag for the picket line Roi had restowed at the top of the load. He had already snapped the extra lines on, at lunch, she thought, and she hastily fastened the near end around the tree she had picked. Flame loomed up suddenly at her side, bending to unfasten the tugline and hook it to the picket line. The dogs seemed to understand the situation and approve the campsite, and several were already trying to burrow into the brush.

Timi appeared out of the driving snow on the other side of the sled to assist Flame as they maneuvered it toward the hollow. "Put the left side inside the shelter," Penny said. "There's a side opening there we can use to reach the supplies. Timi, there's a force blade in the handlebar bag. Better get those spruce boughs in for insulation before you start moving the other sleds. You're going to need the sleds' weight to hold down the ground sheet. Put about half the poles on top of the roof sheet. It's just about impossible to tear, but it could sure blow away." She grabbed the collar of her left wheel dog, Stockings, worked his harness off, and led him to the farthest of the droplines.

By the time she and Amber finally got the rest of the dogs out of harness and snapped to the droplines, Timi and Flame were maneuvering the last sled into position over the edges of the sheet-covered mattress of spruce boughs. "Where's Roi?" Penny asked.

Timi snorted and nodded toward a sleeping bag wrapped in a weather sheet in the lee of a pile of spruce poles. "He didn't feel like helping out with the camp chores tonight," he said.

"He collapsed from exhaustion, that's what happened," Flame blazed back. "It takes energy—a lot of energy—to do what he did to get us here, especially bringing you into the link. He needs food and warmth, or he's really going to be in trouble."

"We all need food and warmth," Timi snapped. "At least the rest of us are doing something about it!"

"You think we'd even have made it here without the energy Roi spent?" Amber replied. "Timi, what's gotten into you lately? Roi's doing what he can for us; he can't do that and make camp too."

Penny knelt by the sleeping bag, turning back a fold of the weather sheet to look at Roi's face, and pressed the backs of her fingers against the angle of his jaw to check his pulse. His color was definitely greenish, and his heartbeat, like his breathing, was fast and shallow. "Better let him rest," she agreed with Flame. "Let's get a roof on this."

The four worked together to lash half the poles across the top, lay a second waterproof sheet over them, and lash most of the remaining poles over the sheet to hold it down. They dragged Roi in his sleeping bag into the shelter as soon as they had the roof on. The snow was piling up on the crude roof by the time they had finished it, and the dogs were almost buried.

Penny grabbed an overlooked spruce branch and crawled into the shelter, brushing out the snow that had blown in before the roof had been put on into the latrine area. The extra blankets and food Roi had insisted on loading into the passenger space of the sleds were piled with the sleeping bags in the back of the crude hut, where the snow accumulation was least. The dogs had to be fed, but the dog meal Roi had taken from the cabin would blow away if they tried to feed it in a wind like this. And there wasn't really enough of it, or of the extra human rations, either, if they were stuck here for more than a day or two.

"We'll have to feed emergency bars," she muttered to herself as she rolled onto her back to survey the ceiling. The others were piling spruce boughs on top of the sheet, she saw with approval, and putting more poles over them. The roof was already almost opaque with snow that had blown into the boughs and stuck.

"Bars?" Roi inquired, and she turned to see him with his eyes open and his face turned toward her.

"Emergency rations for the dogs," she replied as she dug out an emergency pack and unsealed the plastic bag surrounding it. The dog bars were on top, but there were emergency bars underneath meant for human use, and she decided that would have to be their supper tonight. It was quiet enough in the shelter they could talk aloud, though the roaring of the wind outside was still audible.

"You three start making a nest with the blankets and sleeping bags," Penny told the three slaves, "and I'll get the dogs fed. We won't be able to do anything with the dog food from the cabin until the wind dies down. It needs cooking, and we can't keep a fire going in this. We'll use the emergency bars for now." Bracing herself against the increasingly cold wind, she wiggled backward out of the shelter

Timi had used poles and spruce boughs to block most of the space between the ends of the two sleds forming the side walls of their shelter, Penny saw with approval, leaving only a narrow opening over which he was hanging a translucent weather sheet. One of the spruce poles stuck out of the other side of the opening, and the upper end was tied loosely to one of the tall spruce. They could keep an air hole open by wiggling it.

She pulled two bars from the pack as she reached Growler, and poked them into the snow near the dropline. An eager nose brushed her mittened hand as she withdrew it, and then she worked her way down the picket line to the next dropline.

The pale gray of the driving snow was darkening by the time she followed the last picket line back to the shelter. "Water?" Roi asked as Penny started to crawl in.

Penny handed the human food bars to Amber and opened the bag that had been wrapped around them. She had to scoop snow into the bag by touch.

"Get your boots and parka off and slip them under the open end of the sleeping bags," Flame's voice came out of the darkness when she returned, "and then crawl in between me and Amber. We made one big bag, almost double thick, so we can share each other's warmth." The light came on again, aimed at the ceiling. Three of the roomy bags had been sealed together to make one that filled the width of the shelter, with the other two wrapped over the top and sides and finished off with blankets. The rest of the blankets were lying between the oversized bag and the floor sheet, with parkas and boots stuffed between the blanket layers and doubling as pillows. Timi's black face and amber eyes looked out at Penny from the near end of the sleeping bag, with Amber's blond head snuggled under his chin. Roi was at the other end of the bag, with Flame's arms wrapped around him, and the space between Flame and Amber was obviously waiting for Penny.

She didn't really like the idea of sharing the sleeping bag with the group, but right now, she decided, survival came first. Sighing, she pulled the rest of her body into the shelter and began working off her boots, dismayed to find how much snow had sifted into them.

"I made Roi eat some dried fruit, when he first started staggering," Flame's voice said. "But now I'm hungry. I know it's probably too early for supper, but it seems a long time since lunch. Do we have anything we can use for supper here?"

"Emergency bars," Penny replied. "Amber has them. But they'll make you awfully thirsty if we don't wait for the snow in the bag to melt."

"I'm recovered enough to do that," Roi said. "Hand me the bag, would you, Penny."

***

None of them slept immediately after eating. Penny lay between the two other girls, going over their supplies in her head. Her sled carried two days' worth of emergency supplies for dogs and people alike, though after tonight she wasn't sure their jaws would survive eating the rock-hard bars for two days. Roi's plundering of the cabin supplies had added several packets of freeze-dried stew—enough for a day for all of them, she thought—and two days' worth of dog food, though the cabin supplies would be useless until the wind died down enough that they could build a fire. She could use the emergency caller, but there was no way the Company could get a flyer to them through weather like this. Should they ration food? she wondered . Roi was clearly going to need extra food if he was going to continue using his odd talents to help them. Timi's sarcastic comments while they were eating had made that clear. But giving him the extra rations he needed would only escalate the growing friction between Roi and Timi.

At least she knew now that Roi could and would take charge in what he considered an emergency. Derik's comments had apparently referred more to his willingness to take responsibility than to his ability. She wiggled onto her side, her back against Flame's, so that she was looking at the back of Timi's head.

Timi

Timi lay facing the far sled, his body stiff with resentment. Dammit, Roi was supposed to be able to see that kind of thing coming. The R'il'noid had failed to do his job, and then had slacked off on the camp chores as well. And Amber .... He thought of Amber as *his* girl, but you'd never know it from the way she'd jumped all over him when he'd started to say what he'd thought of Roi's behavior. He refused even to listen to the part of his mind that insisted that Roi was probably doing the best he could.

Someday he'd be free, and he wouldn't have to be bound by Roi's decisions. That freedom depended on Roi—one more cause to resent the friend who had now become his owner. He refused to admit that his resentment of Roi was largely because he hated feeling he owed the other boy anything.

Amber

Amber lay with her back against Timi's, feeling his tension against her own spine. She loved him, but she loved Roi, too, and the fighting between the two was tearing her apart. She was going to grow old some day. Timi would age with her, and Roi would not, and because of that she had decided long since that she should not plan on staying with Roi. She sighed and shifted position a little, and felt Timi jerk into renewed stiffness behind her.

She didn't have to stay with him, she reminded herself again. She had already started her medical training, and once that was finished she could go pretty well anywhere she pleased. She'd chosen space medicine with the idea of staying with Timi, but any of the colony planets would welcome a doctor.

Maybe she ought to forget about Timi, she thought miserably, and just try to make her own way through the Confederation. But the thought of losing all of her oldest friends was hard to face. Why did Timi have to be so difficult?

Flame

Flame lay on her side, Roi's back snuggled into her stomach and her arms around his body. Timi was being an ass again, she thought sleepily, but there was nothing unusual about that. She hoped for Amber's sake that he'd get himself straightened out soon, but as long as she had some part of Roi's heart, she was content. A blast of wind reached through the trees to shake the roof of their fragile shelter, and she listened for a while to the storm outside. Nothing to worry about; not as long as Roi was with her. She nestled closer, and felt him snuggle against her body.

She smiled and nuzzled the nape of his neck. Timi and Amber might be eager for freedom, but she honestly didn't care. The worst of slavery, for her, had been the lack of choice—and she'd never have to worry about that with Roi. More than that, he needed her. He might even need more than her, if Timi and Amber left. She wished they wouldn't, but she knew better than to think Roi would stop them if they really wanted to leave.

Roi

Roi lay quiet and wakeful for a long time after the other four had dropped off to sleep. How had he ever managed to miss a major storm like this? It was clear enough now, almost stationary over their heads, and when he settled himself to look ahead, he knew it would snow all day tomorrow, and most of the next day as well. So why hadn't he been able to feel anything but a generalized warning earlier today?

Weather forecasting was one of the easiest uses of his talent. Conditional precognition was largely a matter of being able to sense the probabilities of various things happening. If the future could be affected by his own actions, or by those of another person, he could concentrate on a particular course of action and read what the probabilities would be if that course of action were followed. Since the future weather was generally determined by the present state of the atmosphere, and not by willful human choices, forecasting the weather didn't usually require much in the way of following alternate futures. Oh, there were times when a particular state of the atmosphere could evolve into two or more totally different states, and those were the times when it was sometimes possible to influence which of those cases would occur—by dumping in a few extra ice nuclei, or adding a little extra heat or moisture. So far, Roi's training in actually changing the weather had extended only far enough to recognize those states, but he hadn't picked up even a possibility of a storm this morning. Of course he hadn't really been looking for one, either.

He wiggled onto his back, trying not to disturb the others, and listened to the wind howling outside their flimsy shelter. The weak, chilly draft from the opening had almost ceased. The snow must have drifted completely over the door, he thought, and went back to worrying at his problem. Something was significant about what he'd just been thinking, he suspected, but he couldn't quite follow what it was.

He thought back farther, increasingly dissatisfied with himself. First he hadn't been able to talk Timi into the dance the others wanted, then he'd failed one of the easiest precognitive tasks, and finally he'd had to push himself almost to the point of collapse to save the group from his failure. What kind of a R'il'noid was he, anyway? Not a very competent one, certainly.

Finally he rolled over again, fitting himself against Flame's stomach. Her breathing and the damp silk of her hair against his face gradually calmed him into sleep.

Central: Xazhar

Xazhar fought back a yawn as he looked out the window, and then hastily turned his head away from his father as his jaws opened in spite of his effort to keep his face still. He was more bored than ever, but he doubted that his father wanted to hear that.

"You *could* study," Zhaim suggested. "You did not learn everything you could have at Tyndal, you know."

"I probably learned a lot more than if I hadn't been competing with Roi," Xazhar replied. Why couldn't his father accept Roi's brilliance? It wasn't fair. If Roi hadn't showed up, Xazhar would have been class first, and with a lot less effort than it had taken to earn his place as class second. And he couldn't really blame Roi. In some ways he rather liked Roi, but he was also bitterly jealous of Lai's son.

"Roi and his slaves got a vacation trip for graduation," he added aloud.

Zhaim's eyebrows rose as he turned to look at his son. "You want a vacation in a wilderness?" he asked, looking amused. "With slaves for company and no modern conveniences?"

"It's not all wilderness," Xazhar replied. "The Confederation plasmaball finals start the 18th in Wilderness City, and the eating establishments alone are worth visiting Falaron, from what I've heard. Even you've hunted there. Don't you keep a hunting lodge, even?"

"Wrong season," Zhaim replied with a yawn. "And the lodge is shut down. Still, get through that science module on the computer, and I'll think about it."

Chapter 5

Falaron: Penny
4/17/38

Amber was no longer at Penny's back when the activity in the cramped shelter woke the guide. Faint light filtered through the weather sheet across the entrance, and a brighter but still grayish cone surrounded the spruce pole at the air hole. Amber and Flame were checking the parkas and boots for moisture, while Timi and Roi were maneuvering the next row of emergency supplies out of the sled. "We need to get the dogs checked and fed," Penny said abruptly, pulling herself out of the sleeping bag.

Roi nodded. "How many packs do we need for their breakfast?" he asked. "Forget your boots, I'm 'porting it out, unless you object enough to want to feed them yourself. How much per dog?"

Penny considered their situation, and decided Roi's use of esper talents was justified. "Two-thirds of a bar per dog. We'll feed three times today, to help keep them from thinking they're hungry. Do you know," she continued, "I had the most incredible dream last night. I thought the trekmaster formally approved your feeding the dogs that way."

Roi grinned at her. "And she's sending out the map chips for this area, and spare power packs for the lamp, by teleport express? No dream, Penny. Your trekmaster told my father about the storm and he got worried and woke me up telepathically. He'll probably be back to me within an hour or two to set up the teleport. Soon as Kyrie's up, in Wilderness City. She's adjudicating here for the next decade or so, and since I've met her, Father thought she'd be the best person to handle the teleport. Why don't you pass around breakfast while I'm feeding the dogs?" He set the dog food pack down beside the sled and began unwrapping it and breaking a third off of each bar.

"I can do the dividing," Amber told him. "Penny, hand me one of those people bars for him, will you? He needs the energy to teleport the dog food. Matter of fact he should probably have double rations, if he's going to be involved in a long-distance link later on."

"We may not have enough food for that," Penny replied soberly.

Timi wiggled over to where Roi had left the water bag the night before, and picked it up. "Almost empty," he said. "Anybody want a drink before I get more snow?"

"You'll have to wait for this one to melt without help," Roi warned, his voice indistinct around a mouthful of emergency bar. "I've got to conserve energy for feeding the dogs and linking with Kyrie. At least I hope it's Kyrie, and not some stranger." He picked up one of the shortened bars and closed his eyes briefly. The bar vanished, and he reopened his eyes. "Growler's got a good appetite," he told Penny with a grin.

"You're not putting it into their stomachs, then?" Penny asked.

Roi looked indignant. "Course not. Have you any idea how hard that is? Anyway, they *like* gnawing the bars, and it gives them something to do. And if they didn't break it up with their teeth it'd be in too big a lump for them to digest properly." The bars were vanishing from his hands as fast as Amber broke them up and handed them to him. *Penny?* his mind touched hers. *Snowflake's on some kind of medication for arthritis, isn't she? If you've got it with you, I will put that right in her stomach.*

Penny's stomach lurched. Snowflake was one of the best client team leaders in the Company string. When she had begun favoring a shoulder last season, several of the guides had clubbed together, without the knowledge of the Company vet, to buy anti-inflammatory drugs to hide her lameness. "Don't tell the trekmaster, Roi, please," she said as she hunted through her sled bag for the drugs they were currently using to keep the old dog going.

You mean a vet hasn't seen her? Penny, wouldn't it be kinder to retire her? Sleeping in the snow is not what that shoulder needs. He paused for a moment. *What does the Company do with dogs too old to work?*

"They keep a list of people who'd like a retired trek dog. But there's never enough homes, and they try to place the sound dogs first, the ones that don't have the stamina left for cross-country work but could still work on a recreational team. I doubt they'd even try, with Snowy. They'd just kill her."

She handed Roi the pill, and saw him frown as he studied it. *You'll kill her with this stuff, if you keep it up,* he told her. His face blanked out with the look that meant his mind was elsewhere, but the pill stayed in his

49

hand. Finally he turned his head back toward Penny. "It's getting colder out," he said. "If we brought the leaders in here, they'd help keep the place warm." Penny nodded, puzzled. Bringing the dogs in would help keep the cold from Snowflake's shoulder, but she'd still go lame without the medication. *Trust me,* Roi's mind whispered in hers.

"I'll go get them, if everybody's willing," she offered, but Roi shook his head.

"I'll undo the snaps and tell them to come in," he said. "That's hardly any work at all, compared with 'porting the food out. You make sure anything they might eat is in the sleds. I can get across the idea that anything in the sleds is impossible for them to reach, but getting them to ignore food lying around loose is a bit much to ask them." A moment later the weather sheet over the door brightened as some of the snow against it was knocked away, and a furry white head thrust through the opening.

"Snowflake," Penny said as she grabbed the blue collar and pulled, "get on in here and quit holding the door open. Come on, Growler, Nip. Just lie down and keep our feet warm."

Growler and Nip cocked their heads, looked at Roi, and lay down next to the weather sheet. Snowflake made a beeline for Roi's place in the bag and waited while he wiggled back in and sat with his back braced against the sled. Then she sat next to him, carefully, with the lame shoulder against his side.

"Snowflake!" Penny scolded. "Roi, push her away. She's got better manners than to get in someone's face like that."

"I told her to," Roi said absently. "I want to check out that shoulder. Mmm ...." Snowflake leaned against Roi's shoulder and relaxed as Roi's eyes closed.

Roi and the white dog sat unmoving while the others finished their morning chores. Finally Roi opened his eyes, and Snowflake got to her feet and padded over to join the other two leaders. As far as Penny could tell in the confined space, she displayed no trace of the slight limp she had shown when first brought in. Roi yawned and stretched, then rummaged in the yellow bag for more of the candied fruit. "Better ask Kyrie to send more sweets, if I'm going to keep this up," he mumbled. "Father did say something about sending us more food."

"Roi, what did you do?" she asked as she sat beside him and tucked her legs into the sleeping bag.

"Same thing your pill would have done, but only in the shoulder where she needed it," he replied between bites. "That stuff you've been giving her affects the whole body." He finished three more mouthfuls of the fruit, licked his fingers and checked the area around him for crumbs, and wiggled deeper into the sleeping bags. "Penny, if someone offered a retirement home to a specific dog, would your dog retirement board or whatever go along even if the dog was a bit gimpy?"

"The head vet's in charge," she told him. "He'd probably try to talk your someone into a sound dog. Roi, are you offering Snowflake a home? How would you get her back to Central?"

"Teleport her. It's the kind of stuff I'm supposed to be learning now, so I can probably get Derry to help me pattern it. Actually, I can give a good objective reason for wanting her. She's really sensitive to human thoughts, like my dog Smoky. I want to know if that ability can be bred for. Besides, Marna's training me as a Healer, and we're just getting into degenerative diseases. We're both learning—pure R'il'nians don't get them, and of course there weren't any Humans on her planet, Riya—and we're working with animals to start. I know enough now to manage the symptoms, but we're working on a real cure. At worst Snowflake would have a good home, feeling at least as well as she would with your pills. At best, she could be completely herself again. And maybe help us learn to help people who are crippled with similar problems."

"The company doesn't normally release retired animals for research, so I don't think I'd mention that," Penny said. "But with your father's position, if he requested her for you, I bet the head vet would jump at the chance of a good home."

"I'll ask him this morning," Roi said. "That way my asking for her will be on file before they pick up our teams when we switch to the hang gliders." He wiggled the rest of the way back into the sleeping bags and closed his eyes.

Kyrie

Kyrie?

Kyrie Talganian opened one eye, observed that the still sunless sky outside her east window was barely shaded pink along the horizon, and buried her head under the pillow.

Kyrie, wake up. It's Lai. I need your help.

It hadn't been a dream. Lai was really trying to contact her. *Lai?* she thought blearily, without removing the pillow. *Help? At this time of the morning?*

It's almost midnight here. Remember my son, Roi?

Sighing, Kyrie removed the pillow and rolled over in bed. It was at least an hour until her normal waking time, but then it was probably an hour after Lai would normally have been asleep. *Yes, of course.*

Roi and his friends are on a Challenge journey in mid-continent, east of the Spine Range from you. They're weathered in and got out of their map range running for cover. I need somebody on Falaron to teleport a map chip and if possible a couple of small power packs to them, and you're the only teleport on planet that he knows. Maybe a little extra food; they're going to be tight, and Roi's going to need it if he's doing a lot of esper work.

All right. She was sitting up and swinging her legs over the side of the bed, now. Still blinking the sleep out of her eyes, she walked into the small sanitary cubicle. *The storm was the main topic on all the newscasts yesterday evening. They're saying there's been nothing like it for over a century, and even the forecasters missed it until late yesterday morning. Where's the stuff?*

The Falaron Trek Company will get it to you midmorning. Right now I just want to make sure you and Roi can handle the link without difficulty.

Give me five minutes to wake myself up the rest of the way. She felt Lai's mind weaken its contact with hers and reach out, far to the east. Bringing Roi into the link, she thought as she cleaned her teeth. She had four adjudications scheduled for the morning, with only one break. Activating the computer's scheduling program, she ordered it to deliver a message to the Company that they must get the chip to her by the beginning of her break, or she could not promise delivery until a good deal later in the day.

Ready? Lai asked, and she felt Roi's mind alongside his father's.

Hello, Roi, she said. He felt a little peaked, she thought critically.

Not enough rest after 'porting food out to the dogs and doing some unplanned Healing, he told her, *and we're running out of candy.*

Hmm. Do you like that ground almond-wild orange confection they make here?

Sure.

I can take it or leave it myself, but the Falaron trade representative has been inundating me with the stuff. I don't know if he's trying to court me and doesn't have the nerve to say so, or if he wants me to send the stuff to all my friends and hopes they like it enough to order more. If I eat it myself I know exactly where it will go, and my hips are quite broad enough already. Why don't I teleport you a box, for practice?

Roi turned to his friends, and Kyrie felt their enthusiastic response. *We'll all be delighted to help you save your figure, Kyrie,* he told her, and Kyrie felt Lai's amusement in the background.

She found the largest of the boxes, the one containing several different varieties of the stuff, and lined up her teleport. There were no landslide areas set aside on Falaron, so she balanced potential energy and momentum by moving water from the snow pack near Roi down to the Wilderness River. She felt Lai's approval of the smoothness of the teleport, and resisted the impulse to preen a bit.

Looks like everything's under control, if the Company lives up to their end of the deal, Lai said. *Kyrie, could you contact Roi about once a day with a weather report until they're back on their planned route?*

Of course. Early evening all right with you, Roi? She had to smile at his enthusiastic sampling of a piece of the candy dipped in chocolate. In the front of the shelter, a white dog whined and licked her lips. *Extra warmth,* Roi told them mentally, at the same time he admonished the dog that candy—especially chocolate—would make her sick.

Father, he added mentally, *could you ask the trekmaster if I could have Snowflake when she retires? I want it on record before they pick her up. She's a little gimpy and they might kill her if she doesn't have a home waiting.*

Kyrie felt Lai's wry amusement. *You're going to overflow that east wing just with rescued animals,* he said. *I suppose you're planning to Heal that gimpiness? All right, I'll see what I can do. Enjoy your vacation.*

Lai's mind slipped out of the link, leaving Kyrie and Roi. *Go back to sleep, Kyrie,* the boy advised her. *He woke me up a couple of hours after midnight. I was so sleepy I thought at first he was dragging me back to Central for another stupid Council meeting, but he'd just heard about the storm and got worried.*

I'd barely get to sleep before the wakeup call, she said ruefully. *Might as well stay up and watch the sunrise. Roi, you're Inner Council level, aren't you? You can tell me it's none of my business, but don't give me that line about Kharfun interfering with Çeren indexing after more than three years. I know better.*

She felt his mental grimace. *We're trying to keep it quiet so I can grow up a little bit normal*, he said, *but I'm starting to wonder if that's even possible. I tested 139. And don't you dare tell anybody!*

And Zhaim knows you outrank him.

The whole Inner Council knows, and the Genetics Board, and Flame, and now you. Timi and Amber know I'm Inner Council, but not that I test higher than Zhaim. Far as anybody else knows, I haven't been Çeren indexed yet. Zhaim was there when they first tested me, two years after they found me. Talk about mad!

After that business with Timi, then. I think he suspected before that, Roi. Be very careful.

Kyrie, isn't there any way of using that legal order you made to stop him from—well—seducing Timi? I mean, your order keeps him from approaching Timi, but it doesn't do a thing to stop Timi from approaching him.

Oh, dear. She paused and thought as she watched Falaron's sun appear, a thin, red line defining a misty horizon. *I'll think about it, Roi,* she said finally, *but if you can't stop it, I doubt the law can.* Her waker buzzed softly, and she reached over to shut it off. *I'll contact you again about noon your time.*

She felt his mind drop away, and considered what he had just told her. A Çeren index higher than Zhaim's? That meant that Roi was now Lai's heir. No wonder Lai had been worried enough to assure himself his son was safe when he heard about the storm. She was surprised that the R'il'nian had let Roi out of his sight, especially considering Zhaim's attitude. And Zhaim trying to make friends with Timi? She didn't like the sound of that at all.

She was one of an increasing number of R'il'noids horrified by the thought of Zhaim taking his father's place some day. The realization that Lai's successor would instead be the almost compulsively responsible and caring Roi left her light-headed with relief as the knowledge began to sink in. Instead of the rather austere clothing she usually wore when she adjudicated, she picked a knee-length tunic in sky blue. It did nothing to disguise the fullness of her hips and breasts, but it suited her mood.

The news screen was melting through a series of targeted advertisements even as the voice-over reported the latest doings of the planetary government. Kyrie glanced at herself in the mirror and grimaced at a tri-dee of a sumptuous meal accompanying today's menu at one of her favorite restaurants. Not 'til you get some fat off, my girl, she told herself.

Why anyone would actually pay for the privilege of being dragged across country and eating poorly cooked camp food when the planet had such superb cuisine was beyond her understanding. Not that Roi had seemed to mind, and she'd caught a glimpse of the concentrated food sticks they'd had for breakfast when she'd teleported the candy to the group. She shuddered. Then she paused as the food sticks and the gourmet meal juxtaposed themselves in her brain, and a slow smile spread across her face.

"Gralen's," she told the communicator, and a moment later the manager's face was on the com screen.

"I want a meal for five delivered, in full stasis containers and including table service," she told him. "At the Confederation Justice building, before midmorning. Enough that they can nibble all day. Set up the menu so they can sample a wide variety of your specialties. It's for a group of snowbound adolescents with excellent appetites, and at least one of them knows something about fine food."

"Wines?" the manager asked.

"Of course. I'll leave the selection to you, but I should warn you that Lord Derik Tarlian will be sharing the bill with me—and he will certainly check your selections."

The man bowed his head politely. "At the Justice Building, by midmorning, Lady Kyrie," he said. "It will be my pleasure to supervise the order personally."

Roi

"All that, for a chip and a couple of power packs?" Penny asked.

Roi shook his head, feeling as puzzled as Penny looked at the size and mass of the box he'd just helped Kyrie teleport into the shelter. "Even with heavy packing, it shouldn't be any bigger than one of your mittens. This is more the size of one of the dogs; there's hardly room for it in here. And it feels like there's stasis containers in it." Carefully, he located the seal tape and pulled it, then folded the box lid back.

There was a package the size he'd described on top, marked with the Company logo. He handed that to Penny, who promptly opened it, pulled out the chip, and began opening the back of her map to insert it. "What else?" she asked without raising her head.

"Bunch of stasis containers, labeled 'Gralen's'," he replied, "and a pile of single-use plates and bowls and stuff."

Penny jerked her head up. "Did you say Gralen's?" she exclaimed. "That's the best restaurant in Wilderness City! I've never been there, but they say people come from all over the planet and even beyond to eat there."

"Y'know, I think I've heard Derik mention Gralen's," Roi said thoughtfully as he lifted out one of the containers and cracked the stasis seal.

"Your Adjudicator friend's making sure you don't starve," Penny said wistfully.

"We," Roi corrected her. "There's a menu card. 'Wilderness Luncheon for Five', see? And the numbers by the items are keyed to the stasis containers. So help me, they've even sent a table of sorts. Five little short-legged trays. I'd better send the dogs outside while we eat. I hope most of it's hot; my stomach's already tired of coping with stuff that's half frozen. Read the menu and see if things are supposed to be eaten in numerical order, will you, Penny?"

The dogs padded to the entrance and out as Penny scanned the card, Snowflake looking wistfully over her shoulder as she departed. A gust of frigid air burst in as the door flap was pushed aside and the snow knocked off, and Timi hastily grabbed the weather sheet and slid the box over the free corner to hold it down.

"Broiled aurochs tenderloin, pit-roasted baby peccary with tropical fruit sauce, salmon *a la Gralen* …. Roi, there's way too much here for one meal."

"And wines chosen to complement them," Roi added as he picked up a second card. He saw Timi's face light up, and determined to ignore his own unease. "I think it's meant to be a kind of sampler, with just a few bites of each all around. Ought to keep us busy most of the rest of the day, deciding what we like best. He grinned. "Bless Kyrie. She positively flinched away when I thought of the food bars this morning. Guess she thought we needed something to keep us from getting bored."

"There's a note on the back of the menu," Penny said as she turned the card over. "It says 'I trust Derry has trained you well enough to appreciate these.' What's she talking about?"

"Gourmet snobbery," Roi said indistinctly, nibbling carefully at a crisp yellow-orange strip. "Mmm. Try this, Penny. Container 1. What is it?"

Central: Zhaim

"You're sure Roi's safe?" Derik asked.

"Oh, yes," Lai replied. "Kyrie's keeping tabs on them until the storm blows over. Sent them out a meal from Gralen's. She said she'd send half the bill to you."

Derik laughed. "Tell her I'll take her and the kids out to dinner there when they're back."

"Problems with Roi's party?" Kaia asked.

"They got caught in a once-in-a-century blizzard," Lai replied, "but they're waiting it out quite comfortably."

"*Very* comfortably, with catering from Gralen's," Derry chuckled, and then closed his mouth as Zhaim entered the room.

If he hadn't already known from the black slave's mind about the way the party had escaped his storm, what Zhaim had overheard from outside the door would not have meant much. As it was, he had obtained one very useful piece of information: not one of the other Inner Council members seemed to have any suspicion that the storm was anything but natural. He smiled pleasantly and forced his reactions behind tight shields. Not until he had returned home, to the building perched high in the vee between the Cancairn and Snowfire Ranges, did he allow his anger to surface.

He'd *worked* for that storm. Found and twisted the trigger points that would turn a minor seasonal storm into a major blizzard, allowing frigid air from the poles to sweep down on the unsuspecting party, carefully blunting any precognitive awareness in others, even in his father and his consort. Roi should have died in that storm. He wasn't experienced enough to teleport the others to safety, and with his silly sense of responsibility, together with Zhaim's careful blocking of the boy's precognitive sense, he should have been too hypothermic to get away by the time he realized he was in any real danger. Zhaim wanted to get his hands on his half brother's body, or better yet, get his hands on the whole group. He knew Roi well enough by now to know he could hurt the boy far more through his friends than through any physical injury. For a few moments he let his imagination soar, planning the sculpture he could make of the four, blending them into a single intertwined being.

No, that was too dangerous to risk. He could blur his father's precognitive sense up to a point, but if Roi were missing, and any trace of him or his party was found in Zhaim's hands—the risk was too great. If his father and the Lady Marna were called well away from Central, of course—say a few hundred light years—well, he was working on that. He still wouldn't be able to risk keeping them for the time needed to build the sculpture he envisioned. In fact, they would have to die and their bodies be destroyed—or at least the causes of death well disguised—fairly quickly. Old-fashioned torture would have to do, much as it pained his artistic soul. There would still be danger to Zhaim himself, but that lesser danger he might risk. At this point, he'd have to be careful even with the notoriously unpredictable weather on Falaron.

Or was there another way he could reach out to hurt Roi through his friends? Zhaim paused, running back over the memories he had used his "good luck piece" to strip from Timi's mind. That gourmet meal from Gralen's had included an assortment of fine wines, and remembering how Timi had reacted to the discovery of those wines .... Zhaim grinned broadly. He'd hardly have to nudge his pawn on this one.

Falaron: Roi

"Roi," Amber's voice penetrated Roi's sleep. "Roi! Wake up!"

"Mmph?" Roi mumbled sleepily, and then jerked into wakefulness as his automatic mental nose-count came up one short. "Where's Timi?"

"He, he said he needed another drink," Amber said. "You know how mad he was when you teleported the rest of the wines out into the snow."

"He was so drunk he was incoherent," Roi said, shuddering inwardly at the memory of Timi's tirade when Roi had tried to control the other boy's wine consumption. "Amber, you didn't believe that nonsense about my trying to keep the wine all to myself, did you?" He stopped short, suddenly realizing the implications of what Amber had said. "Do you mean he went into the storm to try to find the wines? They're back where we had lunch just before the storm! How long has he been gone?"

"I don't know," she said miserably. "I was more asleep than awake. But his place in the bag isn't warm anymore."

"Damn him!" Roi snarled as he struggled to free his parka and boots from the bedding. "Did he at least take his winter gear? I'll have to go after him, dammit. He'll have been lost in ten steps, in this."

"Wait just a minute, here," Penny's voice broke in. "You're not going out in this by yourself. I don't need *two* of you lost; one's bad enough."

Roi glared at the voice in the dark. "If you want to help, find the emergency light. I won't get lost, and I'm the only one of us who won't.

Perceiving what's out there for the rest of you takes a lot more energy than just doing it for myself."

"Can't you just guide him back mentally?" Flame asked.

"Already tried. He's shielding from me." That had been one of the first things he'd taught his friends once they had been reunited, and he was close to regretting it now. "I'll have to locate him by density and body heat. I think I can feel him off to the south, but I'll have to get closer to be sure." He finished shrugging into the heavy parka, and twisted around on the blankets to where he could pull his boots onto his feet, blinking in the sudden glare from the emergency light. The door opening was at Timi's end of the shelter, at the far end from the ventilation pole, and the snow there was disturbed. The three lead dogs showed no interest at all in going out into the storm. He wrapped the scarf completely over his face, knowing he wouldn't be able to see enough through the snow for his eyes to be much help anyway, and pulled the hood of his parka over it.

Penny handed him the light as he wiggled through the opening, but between the scarf and the violence of the snow, it wasn't much help. He turned it off, saving the power for Timi's eyes. The snow in the lee of the shelter was almost hip deep, and when he reached out to find one of the picket lines, he found snow drifted above it in places. He could feel Timi's track, the snow denser than its surroundings beneath the fresh snow filling the slot left by the other boy's passage. Downwind, he thought, at least to the extent that the wind had a direction.

His legs were chilled and aching within moments as he forced them through the snow, and his breath turned the scarf into a mask of ice. He reached the end of the picket line and paused, feeling ahead of himself with his mind. Undisturbed snow, mostly, and trees, with an open swath beyond the trees where the snow was wind-packed. Beyond that was softer snow and more trees, and the half-filled slot of Timi's trail. He should have put on the forcewebs, but he didn't want to take the time to go back for them now. He felt along the trail, able now to ignore the denser and warmer regions behind him that marked the dogs' positions, and found a body under the snow, still warm. Alive? He thought he could detect some movement. Breathing, perhaps, or the circulation of blood.

Roi wasn't comfortable with teleporting to a place he'd never been before without another mind there to home in on. Right now, though, he didn't want to take the time to fight his way through the crusted snow in the exposed swath. He reached toward Timi mentally, hoping he could reach Timi's mind from here, but felt only angry repulsion and a raging thirst. Bracing himself, he centered his mind on the soft snow just beyond his friend's body and thought himself there. The effort tired him more than he had expected, and he staggered and went down on his knees beside Timi. Should have levitated, he thought.

He turned the light back on, setting it down where it would shine in Timi's face.

"Come on, get up," he said, shaking Timi's shoulder.

"Lemmie lone," Timi groaned, turning away from the light. His eyelashes glittered with ice. "Thirshty. Whersha resa wine?" Abruptly he rolled over, vomiting into the snow.

Roi's lip curled in disgust. "Didn't you *listen* to what Filomako said about your people and alcohol? Come on, let's get back to the shelter before you freeze to death." He struggled to his own feet with some difficulty, and pulled at Timi's shoulder.

"Too tired," Timi mumbled. "Gotta rest first."

"You rest and you're never going to wake up, Timi," Roi snapped. He couldn't reach Timi's mind to motivate him, at least not without doing permanent damage. Bracing himself, he grabbed Timi's arm and pulled, adding telekinesis to help lift the staggering boy to his feet. He reached out into the wind to find the shelter, a tiny hollow around the warmth and density of the three girls. It was hard to keep struggling into the wind, harder still to force Timi on. He was getting tired himself, and colder by the step, but he gritted his teeth and struggled on.

The trees had broken the force of the wind up to now, but once he entered the open swath the wind almost knocked him off his feet. The snow was crusted here, not quite enough to hold his weight, but enough that his thighs were bruised repeatedly by the chunks of wind-slabbed snow he was dragging Timi through. He paused twice to increase the circulation to his feet. Were they cold, hurting like hell, or just numb? he wondered absently, and then realized that Timi's shields had dropped to the point that he was feeling Timi's body as well as his own. The wind cut through the frozen scarf and the cold glued his eyelashes shut, and with a start of horror he realized that he had drifted away from the line back to the shelter. He could teleport himself back, maybe—but he wasn't sure he had the energy left to do even that, and there was no way he could take Timi with him.

He struggled on: lift a leg and break the crust with his knee, then drag the leg through the slightly softer snow underneath until he could balance on that leg to break out the next step with the other leg. Timi staggered behind him, almost falling several times, and his mind ached from the effort of keeping the other boy upright. Snow had sifted into his clothing, somehow, and he knew he was cold but no longer felt it.

With an abruptness that caught him by surprise, the wind died down, and he went to his knees as he tried to break through a crust that was no longer there. Back in the trees, he finally realized, and reached out for the faint impression of the shelter. It had drifted off to the side again, and dimmed to the point that he could barely feel it. He struggled on, no longer even sure he was moving in the right direction, until his foot caught on something under the snow and he fell full length, Timi almost on top of him. No wind here. He needed to rest just a minute, to recover a little strength.

Whatever he'd tripped over wouldn't let him. He was pulled about, grabbed with teeth and shaken, and all but deafened by a sudden cacophony of barking. Something dragged the scarf away, and warm breath puffed into his face. He pulled the light from the snow, and recognized Rust wiggling out from under him, while Snowflake licked his face. "Roi?" Flame's voice shouted in his ear, and then he was being dragged through the snow. That was the last he knew until morning.

Chapter 6

The noon light finally woke Timi, dim as it was in the shelter. "Well, it's about time," came Penny's voice, and she sounded anything but happy.

Timi winced at the sound. His head was pounding, his stomach was protesting, and his mouth felt as if it was stuffed with dry, musty rags. "Need a drink," he tried to say, but his mouth was so dry he wasn't sure he had actually made a sound.

Penny sniffed audibly. "You can have a drink of water," she said coldly. "No more alcohol on this trip! Of all the idiotic things to do! Even I've heard that Clan members don't have a head for drink, and the jump captain told you that clearly enough. You could have frozen to death out there! Would have, if Roi hadn't been crazy enough to go after you, and if it hadn't been for the dogs you'd *both* be dead.

"Well, there'll be no more of that. Now let me check your hands and feet again. I still can't believe you didn't both get frostbite!"

She didn't even pretend to be gentle with the checking. Timi looked hopefully at Amber once Penny had finished her examination, but she merely handed him the water bag. "Better clean yourself up," she said.

Roi was no better. "I got my lecture earlier," he responded to Timi's complaints about the guide's scolding.

Penny

The storm finally blew itself out late that afternoon. It was still bitterly cold, but the snow had stopped and the wind, never as fierce in the trees as it had been overhead, had died down to a mere whisper. After two days tucked into the combined sleeping bags, unable to stand upright in the low-ceilinged shelter, the group found the temptation to get out of their refuge and feed the dogs themselves overwhelming.

Roi sent the lead dogs out first, urging them to trample down the snow in front of their shelter. Even at that, the travelers crawled out to find themselves surrounded waist deep by the fluffy stuff. The picket lines were invisible under the snow, and there was no sign of the picketed team dogs. Snow lay on the lower branches of the spruce surrounding the little clearing, but had been blown away from the tops. Sunlight touched those tops, and they turned to find bits of blue sky visible between the trees to the west, with the low sun glinting in bright beads through the branches.

"A full bar apiece tonight," Penny said, "they'll be working again tomorrow."

"Why not cook them up some hot food?" Roi asked.

"We ought to be able to manage a fire now that the wind's died down," Timi agreed, "and not just for the dogs. I'd like a hot meal, too. And a fire to sit around, for that matter."

At least he sounded like he was finally over his hangover, Penny thought. And she'd checked both boys' feet and hands again before they'd come outside—no sign of frostbite, though she'd been worried about Timi. She looked around the clearing again, this time checking for possible fuel. Several dead spruce had been blown down, and even the healthy older trees had a good many dead lower branches. They'd have to cook the dog food in shifts, she thought, since the cooking pot Roi had brought was so small. But cooked food would get liquids into the dogs as well as saving the last of the concentrated food. She had been worrying about whether the dogs were eating enough snow, and concerned about dehydration when they had to start working again.

"Good idea," she told her clients. "Over here, Amber, where there's not so much brush. Help me trample down the snow. Flame, you break dead branches off and bring them over for kindling, and Timi and Roi can get one of those dead spruce over there."

She activated her forcewebs, using a snowshoe setting, and walked over to the tree where she remembered tying her picket line, Growler lunging and swimming through the deep snow behind her. Dogs fairly erupted out of the snow all around the tiny clearing as she tied Growler.

***

"So what's the plan for tomorrow?" Roi asked after the increasing cold had driven them from the cooking fire back to their shelter. "Can we sled in this stuff?"

Penny pulled out her map. "We'll take the South Fork route," she said. "With normal conditions, it'd be less than half a day from here to the cabin. Like I said, the river itself will probably be passable, though there may be drifts in a few places. Getting to the river through this deep snow will be the hard part." She ran her finger from their camping place, visible as a pinpoint of light on the map, to the riverbank. They had come a good third of the way from the tree line to the river during their race for cover. The remaining two-thirds was a tiny fraction of the distance to the cabin, but after their experience of feeding the dogs, that tiny distance seemed almost insurmountable.

"Now," Penny said, "the key is to get the snow packed as much as we can before the dogs have to try to get through it. Roi, you and Timi are the heaviest, so you two lead. Adjust your forcewebs as snowshoes so you're sinking as far as possible while keeping a slow walking pace. Ideally, about knee deep. I'll follow you to start, with the forceweb booties on my team, and my team and sled will pack the snow even more. We'll try driving the other two teams after mine, and hope we've packed the snow enough so they can get through. Otherwise, we'll take my team forward until the other two are almost out of sight. That won't be far, here in the woods, and then you boys will have to walk back to the girls with the webs for the next team. Do all of your walking in the same trail. Flame, Amber, we don't normally do this, but I want you to walk ahead of your teams, for a final trampling. Roi, I'm counting on you to stop any attempted runaways."

Roi nodded. "I don't think I'll have to," he said. "Where would they go?"

Penny had to smile at that. "If we can't run normally down river, we may have to plan on sleeping out again tonight," she warned. "But I hope the worst will be over by the time we're on the ice."

Central: Zhaim

There were other kinds of accidents than weather, Zhaim thought as he flew back to his aerie from the latest Inner Council meeting. Too bad his ploy with the black slave hadn't worked better. As it was, Roi had been firmly reminded that he couldn't use his esper abilities unless his body was functioning properly. The bastard wouldn't take a chance on getting badly chilled again. At least there was still no indication of suspicion on his father's part, nor had he heard anything that made him think the bastard had told anyone about Timi's escapade.

Zhaim glanced around the living areas, wondering where Xazhar had put himself, then shrugged and headed for his laboratory. He had some work to do—in strict privacy—over the next day or two.

Xazhar was not only in the laboratory, he was working in the electronics section. Zhaim scowled. He had not planned to involve Xazhar in Roi's downfall. He didn't care for the way his son's personality was developing, for one thing—he wasn't sure he could trust the boy. Especially if Lai started questioning him.

"Any interesting results?" he drawled cheerfully.

"I'm trying to build an improved plasmaball controller," Xazhar replied, "since you won't let me go to the tournament."

Zhaim raised his eyebrows in affected surprise. "You really are serious about wanting to go?"

Xazhar programmed a pause into the computerized assembler and turned to face his father. "Of course I want to go," he replied. "I've been captain of the Tyndall team for the last two years, in case you've forgotten. And we won the Schools Trophy this year, even though I had to put most of my energy into studying. I'm not interested in playing professionally, but I'd sure like to see the top teams in the Confederation. Who knows when the tournament'll be this close again?"

Zhaim paused as if he were considering the matter, though in fact he was hugging himself inside at the thought of getting Xazhar out of his way. Electronics were not his own strongest point, and he was afraid Xazhar would be able to follow what he planned to do if the boy were anywhere around the laboratory. For that matter, it would be better if Xazhar never even knew his father had been working in that section. "Sorry," he said finally, "somehow the tournament didn't click with me when you first mentioned Falaron. You wouldn't miss more than the first day or two if you took tomorrow's flight, would you?"

Xazhar's face lit up. "First few days are mostly to eliminate the weakest teams," he replied eagerly. "I can really go?"

Zhaim nodded. "Hell, I was in a bad mood the other day. You deserve a break from studying just as much as that little prig Roi does. Can you be ready for the morning flight tomorrow? It'll mean getting up hours before daylight, here, but if you can catch it, you'll only miss the first day. I'm pretty sure I've got pull enough to get you tickets for the games." Get the boy engrossed in the tournament, Zhaim thought, and he might as well be at the farthest frontier of the Confederation.

Xazhar was hastily shutting down his experiment, putting everything in stasis until he got back. "I'll be ready, all right," he said. "Father, this is wonderful of you. You really think you can get me tickets, even? Maybe in the real game arena, instead of a virtual arena?"

"I'll get your flight and accommodation reservations, and see what I can do about arena tickets," Zhaim assured the boy. They'd be saving a small block of seats for Confederation officials and guests, he thought, and Kyrie Talganian owed him for her judgment against him a couple of years ago. If she would agree to let Xazhar attend as her representative, Zhaim could really be sure that his son would be kept out of the way.

Falaron: Roi

The travelers began dismantling their shelter and repacking the sleds by the light of the stars and a thin sliver of crescent moon the next morning. The air was still and bitterly cold, and their breath left trails behind them. Scarves clogged with ice, and eyelashes froze together. When they started hitching dogs, the clearing turned into a shallow bowl of fog, silver under the stars.

"It should stay clear and warm up quite a lot today," Roi commented as he checked Rust's feet. "That's what Kyrie said last night, anyway. And did I tell you the Company's approved letting me have Snowflake? They looked at her age and said she was overdue for retirement, and Kyrie volunteered to take her until we get back. So she'll be going straight from where we drop the dogs to the adjudicator's villa in Wilderness City."

Penny was checking the harness on the blue team when Roi said that, and she flung her arms around the white leader's neck. "You've got a home, Snowflake," she said. "Oh, Roi, I'm so glad to know she'll have a chance. Did the adjudicator know how she led us to you two?"

Roi refused to meet her eyes. "I didn't tell her about that," he said. "I did tell her no more alcohol, though."

Penny grinned at him. "If you left that first lot out in the snow, it'll be snow brandy by now," she said.

Timi licked his lips and looked wistfully at Roi. "It's not fair. You drink it."

Roi sighed in exasperation. "Good wine, because I like the taste. And I've got the enzymes to break it down so fast it's ATP and sugar before it even gets into my blood stream. I couldn't get drunk if I tried, Timi. The girls could; they've got normal Human enzyme systems. From what Filomako said, I suspect you don't even have those. I may have a glass of wine now and then, but I don't go fooling with Vroom or stuff like that that could mess up my mind like alcohol does yours."

"Enough," Penny said firmly. "Let's get the rest of the dogs hooked up."

The sky had brightened to blue and the first rays of the sun were just touching the treetops when they started working their way toward the river. Timi and Roi walked ahead, taking turns leading. When Roi looked over his shoulder Penny, forcewebbing behind the sled runners, was keeping Growler about a team-length behind them. Flame was following, stepping high on her forcewebs and stamping them down, and Nip, the first creature to try the trail on his own feet, was following close behind. The yellow team dogs were lunging and struggling in the deep snow, Roi thought as he looked back, but they weren't actually swimming in it. Amber behind them was skiing as much as walking, and Snowflake was leading the blue team at a steady, purposeful walk.

The two boys entered a clearing and started across it. Something odd about the way the snow seemed to bounce under their forcwebs, Roi thought, and then Timi, leading at that point, dropped out of sight. A moment later Roi felt himelf falling. "Growler, whoa!" he heard Penny shout behind him. Roi could just see her over the snow when he glanced back.

What had happened? He ducked, and saw a tangle of branches with Timi trapped within them. Snow was roofing the bent-over trees, but it wasn't solid enough to support dogs or people, with or without forcewebs.

He stood, turned and looked back. "Penny," he called, "set your brake solid and send Growler hard left until he pulls your sled around at right angles."

"Are you all right? What is it?" Penny called as she shifted her team.

Roi frowned in concentration. "Feels like a lot of trees bent over or lying down. Birch and willow in a bit of a ravine, I think. The snow's bridged them over, but there's just air underneath. Whole clearing's the same way. We'll have to go around. Timi, are you all right?"

"Yes," the other boy replied, "but I'm stuck. Got my foot caught between a couple of branches, I guess. It hurts."

"Go ahead and use your talents, Roi," Penny called out. "Including finding safe trails to the river."

Roi nodded and reached for the snow. Might as well lift all the snow from their path, he thought. When the air cleared, the snow had vanished from a broad strip running back to the sled. At least three of Penny's dogs had been on the snow bridging the downed trees when she had stopped them.

Roi ducked his head and began working his way under, over and through the interlaced branches to where Timi stood. Once there, he knelt "Put your weight on the free foot, Timi," he said, "and I'll see if I can pull the branches apart." He managed to free Timi's foot without further use of his talents, but there was no way he was going to bother with finding a way through the tangled brush back to Penny. For that matter, he doubted that Timi could manage the distance—he'd felt the sprain while disentangling the foot.

"I'm going to levitate us out," he called to Penny. "Flame, dig out some candy, will you? I'll need something before I try to Heal Timi's ankle." Penny's face whitened she watched the two boys rise slowly out of the tangled branches and move through the air toward her, dropping lightly to the ground by her sled. Timi's lips were compressed, and he caught at the red sled to keep his balance. Almost all of his weight was on his left foot.

"How bad is it?" Flame asked as she handed Roi a couple of the remaining pieces of Kyrie's candy.

"Nasty sprain," Roi replied. "He can't keep on breaking trail with it that way."

Penny had already unsealed her sled bag and pulled out a couple of rolled-up sleeping bags. "Sit on this," she told Timi as she stacked them beside the sled. When he obeyed, she deactivated his forcewebs and began unfastening his right boot.

Roi gulped down the rest of his candy and knelt beside her, gently sliding his hands under hers. "I can Heal it with the boot on," he assured her. "Ready, Timi?" When the injured boy nodded, Roi settled back on his heels and closed his eyes, his hands cradling the injured ankle. Thank goodness Timi had learned to trust his Healing, at least! The bones were intact—he'd been pretty sure of that from his quick examination back in the brush. He had to Heal the ligaments for immediate strength, though, and that took work. When he opened his eyes, Timi pulled himself to his feet, carefully testing the right ankle, then grinned. Roi remained kneeling until Flame put another piece of candy in his mouth and ordered him to chew.

The sun had moved noticeably higher in the sky by the time they resumed their journey, and they were beginning to feel its warmth on their faces. Roi and Timi still led, but this time Roi, his parka pockets stuffed with the few remaining pieces of Kyrie's candy, was casting ahead of them with his perception, carefully selecting the paths where the snow would pack to give good footing. Rabbit and bird tracks began to appear in the fresh snow in and alongside of the winding animal trails they followed, and at one point Roi stopped short, looking to his right. "Look," he said softly, and the others looked the same way to see a lynx, its head turned to watch them. After a moment it decided they were no threat and lowered its head to pick up a fat ptarmigan before it turned and loped away between the trees, its large, furry feet allowing it to travel without sinking into the snow. "Got its own forcewebs," Roi chuckled.

"The forcewebs copy its feet, you mean," Penny replied.

It was almost noon before they reached the South Fork. Roi had finished Kyrie's candy and was staggering a little as they walked out onto the wind-packed snow topping the river ice. "Lunch stop," Penny called out as she set her brake just inside the trees. The air had warmed a good deal more than the sun by itself could account for, and while it was nothing like as hot as the day before the storm, the dogs were panting and more than willing to lie down and rest.

Roi needed Timi's support as they came back to the sleds. "Penny, are there any more of those emergency bars left?" Timi asked. "He's about done in. We shouldn't have eaten so much of that candy in the shelter."

"And we're out of sweets," Flame said anxiously.

Penny pulled the sleeping bags out of her sled again, rolling them out on a weather sheet to give Roi a dry place to sit down. Thanks to Kyrie's bounty they still had a full pack of the emergency rations left. "Let's save those for Roi," Flame suggested. "Don't we still have a packet of dried stuff from the cabin? We could have that for lunch."

"And Roi rides in one of the sleds this afternoon," Amber said firmly. "Don't argue, Roi. You've done more work during the storm and again this morning than the rest of us have done on the whole trek so far."

"In the sled, yes," Penny agreed as she lit a small fire of dead branches culled from the spruce around them. "With the emergency food supplies just about finished, we can transfer enough of the cabin stuff out of the yellow sled that you can ride. And Amber's right. You've done more than your share today. But if you have the energy to do it, after lunch and an hour's rest, I'd really appreciate it if you could keep on feeling out the trail ahead of us."

Roi swallowed the bite he'd been chewing and turned toward her. "Feeling for what?" he asked.

Penny pulled the last package of dried stew from the cabin supplies they still carried on the yellow sled, and dug deeper into her own sled, coming up with the pot Roi had brought from the cabin. "Thin ice, deep drifts, overflows hidden by snow, or air pockets, to start with," she told him as she began packing snow into the pot, and then added the stew mix. She covered the pot and placed it carefully on three flat rocks she'd arranged in the center of the fire. "Overflows that aren't hidden, for that matter," she added. "Flame can continue to drive the yellow sled, with you riding, but we'll put you two in the lead. I'll give you the rest of the emergency bars to carry with you. They won't give you energy quite as fast as the sweeter stuff, but if you nibble on them regularly you should be able to make it to the cabin all right. And once we get there, I want you to stretch out and relax while the rest of us do the evening chores. For that matter, you rest right now. Flame, keep an eye on him and the fire, will you? I want to get the forcewebs off my team, and give all of the dogs a snack."

"Lie down," Flame ordered. She tucked another sleeping bag around him. He closed his eyes for a moment, and the next thing he knew Penny was offering him his share of the stew and the sun had moved noticeably in the sky. Two hours, he estimated.

The afternoon was as smooth as the morning had been exhausting. The first time Roi felt an overflow and had Flame lead them back into the deep snow among the trees Penny, evidently having some doubts about Roi's leadership, stopped to investigate the river ice from the bank, using a long branch. The branch penetrated perhaps a hand's width of dry snow. It took her no more than a minute to brush away the dry snow and confirm that saturated slush lay knee-deep over the sound ice beneath. After that, she followed the yellow sled without question.

The sun was still well up in the southwestern sky when the river they followed joined another one, and within half an hour of that they reached the cabin. There were marks in the snow where a van had set down since the storm, and footprints going to and from the door.

"Nobody here now," Roi said as Penny pulled her sled up beside Flame's.

"Why don't you get on into the cabin and see if they left anything?" Penny suggested. "Timi, take an armload of firewood in with you and get a fire started, and see that Roi rests."

The Company had indeed left a considerable amount. The stove had a banked fire burning, and the reservoir was full of hot water, as were the two covered pots sitting on the back of the stove. The firewood rack was loaded. Emergency rations to replace the ones they had used were piled on the table, along with three more boxes of Kyrie's surplus candy, a document from the Company confirming Snowflake's transfer to Roi, fresh clothing, a stasis container with steaks and fresh vegetables, and a portable weather receiver with a folded note addressed to Penny. When the guide came into the cabin, she grinned as she read the note.

"They've decided that weather receivers are to be standard equipment in the high country from now on," she told them. "They did get a warning out to the cabins, but we left early, because of the heat. And I'm to use the cabin com to let them know we made it this far. Roi, there's no hot spring here, but there is a tub of sorts, and plenty of hot water in the reservoir. Why don't you clean up while I com the Company, and then lie down? I'll build up the fire and get the dog food and supper going, and Timi and Flame can finish unharnessing. Amber, you bring in snow to replace the water Roi uses."

Roi glanced at the bunks, and noticed with relief that they were wide enough that Flame could sleep beside him. He hadn't had nightmares in the emergency shelter; maybe he could avoid them tonight.

***

The next day's run was almost routine. They had lost more elevation than they had realized the day before, and lost even more during the morning, swinging away from the river repeatedly to get around half-frozen waterfalls and steep rapids. Both sun and air warmed rapidly, and during their lunch stop the wind rose again, blowing strongly from the mountains behind them. By the middle of the afternoon their parkas were again piled on the sleds. The spruce and birch were now intermixed with alder, aspen, fir and a few pines, and the clumps of snow on the south branches of the evergreens had transparent laceworks of ice around their edges.

"Snow-eater wind," Penny told them. "The snow's melting, but the air's so dry it's evaporating most of the water before it can run off. We may have to wait a day or two before we glide off the ridge—we can't do it with a tailwind like this—but we'll have the cabin for a base, and there are some pretty hikes in the area, and one or two nice ski runs."

The river began to show streaks of open water as the afternoon wore on. The trail was now entirely along the north bank, and a faint roaring sound reached their ears whenever the wind dropped slightly. The valley walls, although still low, were steepening, and Penny led them entirely away from the river at a point where a path split off to the north before it curved back to the east to cross a rough bridge over a broad, mostly frozen tributary.

The trail wound through pine and aspen forest, the pines singing in the wind while the roaring to their right grew steadily louder. Blue sky became increasingly visible through the trees ahead of them, and they finally came out of the trees entirely, into a clearing with a gentle, snow-covered slope rising before them and only the sky behind it. "We'll leave the teams here," Penny called back. "See the hitching posts? Fasten the sleds just like you do at the cabins, and down your teams."

The remaining snow was no more than calf deep, and they walked up the slope five abreast, Penny was watching them as if waiting to see their reactions, Roi thought. What was ahead?

The slope ended in a level area, perhaps four arm spans across, surrounded on three sides by a low stone wall. Beyond the wall, the ground they stood on vanished in a sheer drop. From the base of the drop gently rolling plains, green and tan patched with the remains of snowdrifts, stretched away into blueness, the horizon a faint, almost invisible smudge of pale indigo. Broad loops of water reflected the sky, barely visible in the distance but becoming more distinct closer up until a raging torrent appeared far below their feet. He walked to the right end of the wall and looked over.

The river disappeared briefly beneath their perch, but as he followed its invisible course backward with his eyes it reappeared far below them, boiling through a narrow gorge whose opposite wall was as sheer as that beyond their own vantage point. The head of the gorge was half hidden behind the spray of an enormous waterfall, its center flow dropping unbroken from almost the height of their vantage point to the gorge far below, flanked by regions on either side where multiple shorter drops took the water from step to curving step until it disappeared in the spray. Ice covered the rocks bordering the upper part of the falls, and hung from the surrounding trees.

"We were sledding on that?" Roi asked.

Penny laughed. "It's the same river, yes," she said. "But it's been joined by two large tributaries since the cabin, along with a fair amount of snowmelt. The snow hasn't *all* evaporated, even with the snow eater. And you may recall we didn't actually stay on the ice all that much today."

"That's right, we didn't," Flame chimed in. "It's absolutely beautiful. What does it look like from below?"

"Nobody knows, really," Penny replied. "See the way the gorge curves, so the side we're on is almost in front of the falls, and then it bends around the other way, in a kind of s-curve? Well, you can't see the falls from the plains, at all. The neck of high land we're standing on is in the way. The only way you could see the falls from below would be to run a boat up the gorge. One of the early explorers did, supposedly. That's how they say Surprise Falls got their name, and the river was named after the falls. But nobody's done that since I've been working for the Company, at least, and I don't think anyone's done it and survived since before I was born. People try, of course. But it's a rather expensive way of committing suicide."

Roi was measuring the width of the gorge with his eyes. "Wonder how hard it'd be to get in there with a glider," he remarked.

Penny caught her breath in horror. "Don't you even *think* about it, Roi Laian," she gasped. "The winds in that gorge are totally unpredictable."

Roi grinned at her. "I can levitate, remember? And perceive the winds. Oh, calm down, Penny. I wasn't thinking about trying it this trip. And I'd want to study it quite a while under different wind conditions. Might be fun to come back with Uncle Derry and try it someday, though."

"Where do we jump off?" Timi asked. "I don't like those parapets, even on the side away from the falls."

"Oh, not from here," Penny said. "To tell the truth, this area's got a force screen a little beyond the parapet—just in case someone gets dizzy looking over into the gorge. See where tonight's cabin is?" She led them back to the left side of the viewpoint, and pointed to a small brown rectangle, perhaps twenty minutes' walk along the edge of the cliff, topped with a smudge of lighter tan. "Well, that stretch beyond it is our takeoff point. The basalt flows give a nice, nearly vertical cliff for about half the height, but the shale and sandstone below the basalt weather to a reasonably smooth slope. Then there's enough shale and sediments up on top to give a rounded lip. With a light east wind, it's streamlined enough there's hardly even a rotor. Where we are it's volcanic all the way down, and it tends to be very rough. Ready to head on to the cabin? We'll be here another day at least before the wind changes enough that we can take off, and you can hike back over here tomorrow if you want."

Timi looked relieved. "Good," he said. "My tri-dee recorder's in the bottom of the sled, and I want to get that waterfall on chip."

Penny

Roi didn't need a tri-dee recorder. Penny had seen him working with a pad of textured plastic sheets and a carbon marker on other occasions, but that evening was the first time she had time to watch what he was doing. A sketch of the waterfall was growing under his hand, and she stopped short behind him to admire it. His hand slowed, and he turned to look up at her, his face embarrassed.

"I'm sorry," Penny said, backing away. "I didn't mean to pry. But that's the most beautiful picture of Surprise Falls I've ever seen."

He looked back at the picture. "Do you really think so?" he said doubtfully. "I mean, there's no depth, and I don't have any colors with me, and I couldn't get all the details ...."

"You can get that in a tri-dee," Penny told him, "and I've seen hundreds of them. You've got the heart of the Falls, somehow. Is that what you've been doing, evenings after we've settled down? Sketching what we've seen that day?"

Roi nodded. "Yes. Uh—would you like to see some of the others?" He looked hesitant, as if he couldn't believe she would really want to see them.

"I'd love to," she told him, and spent the rest of the evening looking in wonder at dozens of sketches—mountain vistas, the saiga and musk oxen they'd seen the second day, a pika harvesting overlooked seeds in the same area where Rust had cut her foot, moonlight on the snow, the dog teams striking out along the mountain front. The dogs themselves, with their personalities shining through the sketches, and finally a page with half a dozen sketches of Penny herself—harnessing dogs, scolding with part of a snowball in her hair, laughing as she touched noses with Growler.

"You should see what he can do when he's got proper materials," Amber said proudly.

"I'm impressed enough by this," Penny assured her. "Roi, you don't want to carry those down in a glider. Pack the finished sketches with a note to hold them 'til we get back. The Company will pick them up along with the rest of the gear we won't need any more after we take off. And if there's anything any of you will want on the rest of the trip but don't want to carry down with you, pack it up with a note to get it to the plains base camp. I'll trigger the pickup call when we leave for the drop-off, and they'll move it down while we're flying."

Flame thrust her jaw out. "We'll be wearing our cold-weather gear, won't we? Well, I'm wearing my hood. They can pick it up with the parkas."

Penny sighed. Had she remembered to modify Flame's helmet? Well if she hadn't, this cabin had a com. She could contact the techs and get it modified tomorrow, while they were exploring the area.

Chapter 7

Falaron: Roi
4/21/38

Roi sat on the parapet, leaning far out to study the cliff face beyond the cabin. They wouldn't be flying today; the wind was still steady over his shoulder. But he'd made half a dozen sketches while Timi was recording the falls, the forest and the rest of the party, and he wanted to get a good look at where they'd be flying. Probably tomorrow, if he could trust his weather sense at all. Since the blizzard, he wasn't sure he could.

It had been his turn to make breakfast, and he was relieved that his cooking stint was over for the day. He could do most things well, but not cook. Flame was with Penny back at the cabin fixing lunch, and Amber was helping Timi.

He leaned over a little farther, levitating slightly to steady himself. "Roi!" Penny said sharply, from behind him. "Get off that wall. That's a long drop!"

Roi turned his head, annoyed. "I'm not going to fall. There's a force field beyond the wall—not only did you tell us about it, I can feel it. Besides, a clear fall's not something I have to worry about." He jumped to his feet on the top of the wall and stepped off—out and up, climbing invisible stairs until he was twice his height above the wall and a similar distance out from the cliff face, and pivoted to face Penny. "I can levitate, remember?"

"Show-off," Timi muttered under his breath. Roi refused to acknowledge the comment, though to himself he admitted that either Derik or his father would have been a good deal harsher.

Penny gritted her teeth and glared at him. "If you are quite through trying to give me heart failure, lunch is ready," she said, and turned to stalk off.

"I don't think she was amused," Timi snickered as he and Amber joined Roi and the three of them followed Penny back to the cabin.

Roi still felt justified in using levitation to lean out and get a good look at the cliff face. Going through the motions of walking on air—well, maybe he had gone a little too far there. But he wasn't about to say that to Timi.

Lunch was somewhat strained until Roi, feeling increasingly sheepish but not willing to admit it aloud, asked if there were anywhere they could try out their gliders with the wind blowing from the mountains. "That cliff's an awfully big step for the first time in a new glider," he said.

"They're pretty standard," the guide replied. "Hangin' Free's, full compensation, full support slings. But yes, there is an area where you could try them out, about an hour's hike west. Remember the Little Surprise, the last big tributary we crossed yesterday? From the bridge the trees would have hidden it, but there's a bedrock island farther north that's high enough to serve as a takeoff point for short flights. The wind's lightened up enough it should be fairly safe."

Full compensation? "Penny," Roi said, "I've never flown full compensation. It's going to feel like flying a log."

"Never?" Penny asked, raising an eyebrow. "And how long have you been flying?"

"A year and a half, since Derry started teaching me formally. More like four years, since the first time Derry took me up, back when I was his slave. He let me take the control bar pretty often then, too. He never flies at more than half compensation, more often a quarter. And he never let me, either, when I was learning. I had to fly close to an hour with no compensation before he'd let me fly without his supervision."

"An hour? With *no* compensation?" Penny sounded skeptical.

"Yes! Oh, all right, Penny. I was showing off this morning. I shouldn't have been using levitation the way I was. But I really am used to half or quarter compensation, and at full compensation a glider's going to feel so unresponsive I'll have a hard time flying it. At least let me check it out."

"Anyone else want to check their glider out?" Penny asked. "We could all hike over to the hill this afternoon and do some test flying. But Roi, you'd better really be good if I'm going even to consider letting you weaken the compensation on yours."

At least she was considering the possibility.

The gliders were stored in a shed a little distance beyond the cabin, along the edge of the cliff. The snow, soggy and melting though it was, was painfully bright in the noon sun. The trail from the shed led into birch and aspen forest, with patches of pine. The gliders themselves were little more than wings with supporting slings, guided as much by weight shifts as by the control bar, and breaking down to light but long fabric bundles easily pulled on a long sled. "Color coded again," Roi commented as he heaved his scarlet wing onto the sled.

"I need to keep track of who's who when we're flying," Penny pointed out. "And if I'm above you, which I intend to be as much as possible, what I'll see is mostly the wings. For communication I have a helmet for each of you, with a radio—we'll practice using those today, too. Flame, we'll see how yours works with the hood, since you insist on wearing it. We three girls will start out in the lead, to pack the trail a little, and the boys can bring the sled. We'll switch off halfway there."

The woods here were filled with birds. Most were familiar to Roi—chickadees quarrelling merrily over birch seeds, cardinals, early thrushes looking affronted at the snow, and others, familiar and unfamiliar, whose names he did not know. It wasn't a day for conflict, and even Timi's good-natured grumbling over having to pull the sled was belied by his rivalry with Roi over who could pull harder. They almost ran the girls down more than once, and Penny looked relieved when she was able to send them ahead while she and the two girls took over pulling the sled.

"Race you to the edge of the woods," Timi challenged as soon as they were well in the lead. "No fair using esper, either."

"Ski or snowshoe adjustment?"

"Skis," Timi replied, pausing to adjust the settings on his forcewebs.

It was an even race, over the distance. Timi had the advantage of sheer strength and power, but Roi was more agile and his endurance, always better than Timi's before his paralysis, had finally returned. The trail had been engineered for the sleds and curves were gentle, which favored Timi, but by the time they burst out of the trees Roi was closing the gap between them. "I won," Timi gasped, collapsing onto a downed tree."

"Another twenty strides and I'd have had you," Roi replied. He, too, was breathing hard, but he stayed on his feet, flipping off his forcewebs and walking in circles on the gravel bar where they had stopped. He could barely see flashes of color among the trees that must be the three girls. "Good thing we both left our jackets and vests on the sled. We're going to want them when the girls catch up, though. That must be the hill Penny was talking about. She said it was an island. Let's scout for running water."

By the time the rest of the party rejoined them the boys, aided by Roi's ability to perceive unsound ice, had scouted a safe trail. "Most of the current's on the other side here," Penny commented as they maneuvered the sled along the trail spiraling up the hill. "Do remember that you want to land on the east side of the river or on the island itself. Otherwise there's been enough thawing you might have a hard time crossing."

Roi could feel the air rising as it struck the upwind side of the island, and even a few thermals over the darker spruce forest on the riverbanks. Plenty of lift for a short flight, he thought as he triggered the setup button, stiffening the struts and expanding the scarlet fabric bundle into broad wings above the cradle in which he would lie. When he reached for the control bar to adjust the compensation, however, Penny shook her head. "Not until I've seen you fly with full compensation," she said.

"Penny, I'll be clumsy. These things are unstable by design. I know how the compensation acts. There's a small computer that changes the curvature of the struts, the length of the cables—even the camber of the wing fabric—to keep the glider in straight and level flight. Fine if you want to fly straight and level, but you have to fight it to do anything else. It's the instability that lets you maneuver. I can fly with no compensation at all, but I prefer about quarter compensation for long flights."

"He means it," Timi unexpectedly supported him. "We all watched when Derik was testing him on uncompensated flight. Three quarters of an hour with Derik watching and calling maneuvers. Then they started playing tag." He grinned at the memory. "Lai was speechless. Marna said it looked like fun and from then on she and Lai just glared at each other. Derik never did get him to make a serious mistake, and he admitted later he was trying."

"Lord Derik?" Penny frowned. "He seemed—well—a little too staid for that when I met him."

Timi howled with laughter. Roi felt his jaw drop open. "Uncle Derry? Staid?"

Flame just stared, but Amber said, "Hedonist, libertine and an absolutely terrible practical joker—but I don't think anybody's ever called him staid before. Wonder what he'll say when I tell him." Even Roi couldn't keep a straight face at that.

"Nevertheless," Penny said, "you demonstrate to me that you can handle a fully compensated glider before I let you decrease the compensation. Take off from the top of the hill, stay in the updraft on the windward side until you've climbed high enough to maneuver, do a nice open figure eight, and then land back on top of the hill."

It was a good thing Penny had specified a nice open figure eight, Roi decided as he struggled to keep the glider in the curtain of rising air over the windward slope of the hill. He had to fight the compensation even for the zigzag he needed to climb, and while he could perceive the thermals easily enough, there was no way he could turn sharply enough to keep the glider in one. Still, if he were going to do nothing but glide off the cliff down to the plains, he could see the point of the compensation. About the only possible mistake a flyer could make with full compensation was to fly into the ground instead of landing on his feet, and the support slings were even designed to allow that. He might as well be just a passenger, Roi thought as be brought the glider in to the hilltop, rotating his body as he stalled the glider to land on his feet.

Penny nodded grudging acceptance as he landed. "All right," she said. "You can try it with half compensation."

"Quarter?" Roi pleaded. "And there's a thermal over there. Too small to stay in with full compensation, but with quarter compensation I can. I'd like to get enough height to really look the terrain over."

Penny sighed and moved to where she could watch over his shoulder. "I want to see you reset it."

Normally Roi would have reset the compensation mentally, but if Penny insisted on watching, that was out. Carefully he teased open the access portal in the left uptube of the control triangle and extracted the tiny pick he needed to reset the compensation chip. The spring-loaded access portal kept trying to close until Timi reached over to hold it open. "Thanks," Roi said absently as he carefully adjusted the tiny switches, checking his work mentally when he was done.

"Same pattern," Penny told him, "except you can fly free for about half an hour after the figure eight unless I call you in. Remember to stay between the river and the cliff—there's going to be a downdraft to the lee of the cliff today, and I don't want you to risk getting caught in it. Timi, you're next. Get your glider set up."

This time Roi's glider responded properly, turning easily to stay in the updraft until he was high enough that Timi's wing was a toy taking off from a tiny island in the braided river. He could see the spray rising from the falls, and the endless blue plains beyond. Closer at hand, he was aware of the rising curtain of air he rode, and the thermals rising from the dark trees. He broadened the loops of the flat figure eight he had been flying and heard Penny's "all right; go have fun," in his earphones. He couldn't see her face from this height, but her voice was smiling.

The thermals weren't very tall, and so narrow he had to circle tightly to stay in them. But they gave him enough height that he could see the Surprise, and follow with his eyes the route they had taken the day before. He watched Amber's blue wing take off, and then Flame's green one. One at a time they followed the same drill he had: climb the updraft over the windward slope of the island, a broad figure eight to demonstrate control, and then a few minutes of flying free, getting the feel of their gliders.

All too soon Penny began calling them in, starting with Timi, by now the lowest. Roi straightened his glider reluctantly, leaving the thermal behind as he began to lose altitude. One at a time the others landed, and finally it was his turn to fly into the hill from downwind. He wisely decided that Penny would be more impressed by a precise, safe landing than a flashy one, and landed smoothly just before the top of the hill.

"No levitation?" Penny asked.

"None. I did perceive the lee downdraft and compensated for it, but I couldn't help that."

Penny nodded reluctantly. "All right. You can fly quarter compensation tomorrow. Get your gliders broken down and on the sled. Timi, you're doing supper tonight. We've already discussed the menu, so you'd better head back to the cabin as soon as your glider's packed up. I want to talk with Roi, so he and I will haul the sled back."

Penny

"Uh, Penny?"

Penny glanced over at Roi, pulling at the other towrope. They were alone, as the two girls had taken her words as a tacit order to leave, and gone ahead with Timi. Roi looked worried. "Not your flying," she hastened to reassure him. "That's much better than I expected. It's just that—well, while you were aloft Timi said some things about you and Derik ...."

"That he had ulterior motives in teaching me to fly, back when I was a slave?" he replied, looking more amused than angry. "He probably did. But Penny, I was born a slave. From the time I was a baby I was taught that my owner had the power of life or death over me, just on a whim. My first priority was staying alive. Then keeping my friends alive, if I could. Freedom was a distant third—I never really thought it was possible.

"Derik was the first owner I'd ever had who was kind to me. I was scared to death he'd sell me—he did sell slaves then, though he doesn't since he bothered to find out what happened to those he sold—and I knew he'd taken slaves as lovers in the past, and kept them for all their lives. He was interested in me, yes—and I'd happily have seduced him. Not because I wanted the physical side of things, but because it looked like the best chance I'd ever have to stay alive and keep my friends with me.

"Timi doesn't think that way—he was a captive, and for him freedom came even before survival. What Derik wanted from me—for him it really was a fate worse than death. We've all been raped—that's part of being a pleasure slave. For me, it was what I'd been raised to expect. For Timi—he used to get downright suicidal, and I think he assumes I ought to feel the same way. I don't. I never really hated Derry, or feared him, and we've gotten to be good friends since he understood how I really felt. Timi's never quite been able to accept that."

"I'm not sure I can."

"Who said you have to? Look, Penny, your culture's monogamous, mildly patriarchal, kids are raised by their genetic parents, and sex is assumed in public not to exist. Especially between two individuals of the same gender. Central's totally different. I'd like to get rid of slavery, but the rules for free Humans are centered on making sure every child is wanted and cared for. Infertile sex is mostly ignored; fertile sex takes a lot more hoops than your marriage does. Mostly aimed at making sure the child's interests are protected, though genetics comes into it sometimes—like I can't ever have children, because my kids could be espers with Coven syndrome—insane—and that's a combination nobody wants to risk. That's why I was born a slave—my mother had the same combination I have, and she was afraid I'd be killed if anyone found out she was pregnant. I've got Wif, and maybe grandchildren through him, some day, but that's it." His expression was wistful.

"Couldn't a Healer take care of that?"

Roi shook his head. "Not a genetic problem that affects every cell of the body, and keeps the nervous system from developing properly. Wif'll be the only child I ever have."

Penny looked down. They were crossing a little meadow, and the declining sun behind them cast long, blue shadows from their feet. Roi's distinction between fertile and infertile sex shocked her, but in spite of herself she thought about her younger sister. Bonet was a third child, and as such she would have to leave Falaron by her twenty-first birthday. Falaron's wilderness character was the basis of its economy, and to keep that wilderness character they had to control population. Infertile sex wasn't unknown on Falaron, but it certainly was not discussed openly. She couldn't wish her little sister unborn, but what would become of her? Bonet's attempts to find jobs on other planets had been fruitless, and within a couple of years she would probably be forced to sign up with one of the big colonizing companies. With no premium, she'd have no choice at all of where she'd be sent.

And how many families did she know where more than half of the children would have to leave Falaron? Some of the younger children weren't even decently educated, as parents were expected to pay for most of the education of children beyond the second. Funny—she'd never thought before about that being a logical consequence of the morality she'd been taught. "So how do you think it should be?" she asked, half defiant.

"Penny! I'm just a student, not a social engineer. I did have to study quite a few societies last term, and I've talked a bit with Father. But there's no one right answer. It all has to fit together, I know that much. The religion and morality, the economics, the ecology. If one changes the others have to as well. I do know that all working societies have to balance the tension between individuals and society, and they all have some way of assuring that children are protected and socialized into the society at the rate they're needed for replacements. And imposing change from outside usually doesn't work. Especially where religion's involved."

"So what should I do?"

Roi stopped short, turning to face her. "About what? Penny, I'm not reading your mind. Even during the storm, I wasn't trying to pick up anything you didn't push my way. I hate invading another mind. It makes me feel filthy. And I probably couldn't tell you what you should do anyway, even if I knew why you think you should do something."

"Oh," Penny said as she also stopped. She could feel her face warming. "It's the third children and beyond. They have to leave the planet. And I worry about my little sister."

Roi frowned down at the snow. "From what I know you have a right to worry. Planets that accept immigrants without premiums or special abilities are generally those with such high death rates that immigration's the only way they can keep population stable—and some of the companies aren't much better than slavers. You winced when I mentioned infertile sex. Is that part of the moral code here?"

Penny felt herself blushing again. "Yes, at least for our own people. We accept that visitors may not go by the same rules."

Roi grinned. "Good thing, since we're all sterilized. It's reversible on the other three. But it's planetary affairs, then, and the Confederation can't do a thing. And religious, which means an externally imposed change wouldn't work anyway. If you want a suggestion, I'd say find out exactly what happens to some of those emigrants and publicize it. But it's going to be slow. Probably several generations." He bent to pick up the towrope he'd dropped. "Shall we go on?"

Penny leaned into her own towrope, and they walked together into the denser belt of trees that fringed the edge of the bluff. Neither spoke again until they were unloading and stowing the gliders, and then they avoided any serious discussion. *What's happening to me?* Penny wondered as they skied back toward the cabin, watching the sunset light fade over the plains below. *I've had lots of other clients who didn't share my beliefs, but they've never had me questioning what I believe before. And Roi wasn't even arguing with me, or trying to make me change my mind. Something he said made me take a fresh look at the consequences of what I believe, and I didn't like what I saw. And I still don't know what to do about it.*

They deactivated their forcewebs at the cabin entrance, sniffing hungrily at the odors escaping as they opened the door. "Smells a lot better than my cooking," Roi told Timi with a grin.

Anything would, Penny thought, her mood lightening as she reminded herself that Roi, too, had his weak points.

Chapter 8

They all slept well that night—too well, Roi thought later. He woke to find the sun slipping over the edge of the world and the others just beginning to stir. "How's the wind?" was Amber's first question, and Penny yawned and picked up the weather receiver from the floor by her bunk.

"The satellite map looks good," she reported after a moment.

Roi threw back the covers and padded across to the north window, shivering as the chill air washed over his bare skin. "Pine needles are blowing the right way," he reported as he detoured by the stove to build up the fire. "Whose turn is it to cook breakfast?"

"Mine, I think," Amber replied, "since Timi did dinner last night. Toss me my clothes, will you? I'm getting dressed before I get out from under the blankets."

Roi found his own clothing as well as Amber's and Flame's, and stayed in front of the stove to dress. Timi and Penny had left their clothing in reach from their bunks.

"We're getting special treatment since we were snowbound, I think," Amber commented as she dumped fresh milk and eggs into a bowl of flatcake mix. "Fresh food in stasis three days running." She opened another container and stirred the fresh blueberries it held into the batter.

"Enjoy it while you can," Penny told her. "This cabin and the last one are easy to get supplies to. Once we're down on the plains we'll be picking out tent sites instead of heading for cabins, and if we want anything but dehydrated stuff we'll have to catch it."

"Like what?" Roi asked dubiously. He wasn't sure he wanted to eat food he'd just met alive.

"Fish, for starters," Penny said. "Birds—grouse, turkey, ducks. Hares. It's early for berries, but there are lots of edible buds and shoots and tubers—though most of the tubers have probably sprouted by now. Who's going to bring in a little more firewood? The rack's almost empty."

Roi finished pulling on his parka and mittens. "I'm just going for it," he said as he let himself out into the chill morning.

The sun, still too low in the sky to compensate for the bite of the east wind, blazed into his face. Far below, a gray-white blanket rolled like an ocean around islands of higher ground. Roi activated his forcewebs and snowshoed around the cabin to the woodpile. When he pulled a few of the upper logs into his arms there was a sudden flurry of motion as a tiny, reddish animal with a stubby tail bolted for cover deeper in the pile. Smiling, he closed his eyes, feeling for the mote of life and surprised to find the woodpile alive with the little creatures.

"But why do we need more wood?" Timi was asking as Roi came back into the cabin. "We'll be leaving right after breakfast, won't we?" He set the last plate on the table and went back to the cupboard for eating tongs and mugs.

"Not if we want to find any thermals," Roi said. "It's pretty well fogged in below right now. And we don't really want the sun right in our faces anyway, do we? Let's wait 'til it's higher. Maybe even after lunch, unless the wind's likely to change. Penny," he added, "what's little and rust-colored and mousy-looking and lives in woodpiles?"

"Red-backed voles, most likely," Penny replied. "And if they're in the woodpile they're probably in here. They're as bad as mice about moving indoors if they get a chance. Why they included them when they seeded Falaron is beyond me."

"I could feel around for a stray cat in Safeport," Roi offered, but Penny shook her head.

"We're not supposed to disrupt the local ecology," she said regretfully as she started out the door.

"Feeding the critters isn't?" Roi grinned after her as he shed his parka. "Amber, that smells wonderful. We're all going to know how to cook by the time we get home."

Amber made a face at him as she set a plateful of flatcakes on the table. "Some of us will," she said. "But if you think I'm going to waste my time cooking once we get home, you can just think again. Where'd Penny go?"

"She went out for more wood, I think," Flame replied.

"And to check on the fog," Penny said as she came back in the door. "Roi's right; we'll have to wait 'til it burns off."

"It's clear enough up here," Roi said. "You know, there's been a downdraft over the falls the last couple of days. There ought to be an updraft today, and I bet it looks a lot different. Why don't we hike over there this morning, and then fly this afternoon?"

***

Different, they all decided when they stood looking at the falls, wasn't a strong enough word. The gorge was half full of fog. Spray and fog were so intermingled at the falls themselves that the falling water seemed to blend into the mist almost as soon as it plunged over the cliff. Roi had brought a marker and pad, but made only a few very rough sketches—to jog his memory when he could get hold of a spray brush, he said. Surprise Falls did not lend themselves to firm lines this morning.

***

The fog had burned off by late morning, and they ate lunch before heading for the glider shed only because Roi insisted. "If I should have to grab somebody who's going into a tumble," he said, "I want some food in me." Penny backed him up, and they found cheese to go with flatcakes made from the morning's leftover batter.

The plains below were a soft mosaic of pale tan, green and brown, with occasional sweeps of black volcanic rock. "Good thermals there," Roi said as he pointed to one of the black areas, "and over the dark hill, there. I don't see any snow left. That orange rectangle to the northeast is the cabin roof for tonight, isn't it, Penny? Pity they had to make it so bright."

"They made it as visible as possible," Penny replied. "Remember that's where we want to land. You can't see it from here, but there's a wind flag in the flat area south of the building. It's a good landing area—sandy, and no rocks. We'll use radios again—yes, Roi, I know you could keep us in touch, but we're back to using esper only in an emergency, okay? If you don't think you'll make the right area, tell me where you think you're headed. And for goodness' sake try to land on this side of the Surprise, at least. The nearest ford is two days' ride downstream." She paused to unlock the door to the glider storage shed.

"Normally I'd be the last off, so I could watch the rest of you for any problems," she added, "but Roi's talked me into letting him take that post."

"If somebody has a problem," Roi pointed out, "I'm the only one that can do anything about it beyond yelling at them to use their emergency chute. So it makes sense to have me go last, and you lead since you know exactly where we're going."

"Right," Penny said as she led the way into the shed. "Amber, Flame, Timi, go ahead and get your gliders set up north of the shed, well apart. Roi, set yours up at this end, and I'll take the far end. We'll take off from north to south, one at a time. Soon as you're far enough out—over the middle of the toe slope should be about right—turn north and ride the updraft for height. Crab to stay as nearly over the vertical part of the cliff as you can, and watch me for when to turn back south."

They set their gliders up with the ease of long practice, breaking into two groups for setup and again for preflight checks, each inspecting another's wing before checking his or her own. "Call off your names in order if you hear me," Penny's voice came over the helmet earphone, "and tell me if you've completed your preflight." Roi heard Timi, Amber and Flame respond before he added his own name.

"All right," Penny said in their ears, "Give the person ahead of you time to turn and start climbing before you take off, but don't wait much beyond that. Call your name as you take off; I won't be able to see you. Let's go." She lifted her wing to neutral position and began her run over the lip of the drop. The wind caught her as she nosed down into it, and the violet glider lifted like a bird, turning and soaring northward along the drop-off.

Timi had found a part of the cliff where snow lingered and adjusted his forcewebs to skis. His amber wing took off even more smoothly than Penny's, with Amber's sapphire one close behind.

Flame had readied her emerald glider while Amber was taking off. "Flame," she shouted joyously as she ran over the edge. Her copper hair floated behind her as the wing lifted her, held back from her face by the fur hood she had insisted on wearing under her helmet.

Roi settled himself in the support sling as Flame turned northward, and looked beyond her to the line of jewel-colored wings soaring above the cliffs. He felt a brief sense of unquiet as he started his run, but not enough to really bother him. "Roi," he called out breathlessly as the scarlet wing lifted him off his feet.

The cliff was beautifully streamlined, and the air beneath him flowed as smoothly as honey. The cliff rim was dropping behind him, and the plains spread to the end of the world ahead, dotted with the warm columns of rising thermals. He could fly beyond the horizon on a day like this, he thought exultantly, fly to the lake that lay somewhere at the end of the lazy curves traced by the Surprise far below. He pulled in slightly on the control bar, accelerating to turn northward after the others.

The wing nosed over, diving so abruptly toward the toe of the slope that Roi was caught by surprise. Startled, he pushed out hard, using his whole body to throw his weight as far back as he could. Slowly, reluctantly, the wing leveled out into steady flight. Then, as swiftly as it had dived, it tried to leap upward into a stall. By the time Roi managed to get it settled into level flight, he found himself headed southwest, straight for the curtain wall before the waterfall and far below the level of the cliff top.

Cautiously he prepared for another turn, pulling in, sliding his weight to the left, and pushing out, keeping his movements feather light and mentally thanking Derik for insisting that he learn the nearly impossible feat of flying his glider totally uncompensated. The scarlet wing sideslipped violently and made a determined effort to perform a cartwheel, then changed its mind and tried for a back flip instead. Roi fought back with weight and muscle, his body drenched with sweat inside the heavy parka. This time he managed to keep track of his orientation, and when the wing surrendered into level flight, he was heading north within the updraft along the cliff front. Far above and ahead of him a violet speck swung out from the cliff and turned back southward, and Penny's voice came abruptly into his helmet. "Roi, what do you think you're doing? Are you all right?"

He swallowed hard and took a couple of deep breaths. "I'm having control problems," he said. "Stay clear." His mind was working frantically, trying to make sense of what he thought he'd seen when he started the turn.

Designing a glider was a battle between maneuverability and stability. Performance gliders like their Hangin' Frees were so unstable in basic design as to be almost unflyable. Micro circuitry controlling cable lengths and fabric curvature made them manageable. If a glider nosed forward too steeply, for instance, the compensation circuit would lengthen the nose cables and warp upward the trailing edges of tail and sail, thus lifting the nose away from the dive. A sideslip would be compensated for by lengthening the flight cable to the inside wing, changing both weight distribution and dihedral. There were other, more subtle changes in wing shape and angles, but the direction of change in cable length was fundamental to compensation.

When his glider had started to sideslip, the left wing cable had been in Roi's field of view, and he was sure he had seen it shorten.

Very carefully, he pulled back on the control bar, bringing the glider's nose down and increasing speed. He was watching for the nose cable to lengthen, and when he saw it shorten instead he immediately pushed out, bringing the glider back to level flight.

The glider's flight had been normal yesterday, but today the compensation circuit was somehow working backward, destabilizing the already inherently unstable wing instead of stabilizing it. He couldn't imagine how that could happen, other than deliberate sabotage, and in that case the sooner he bailed out the better. He moved a hand to the emergency chute on his chest, and felt a sudden unease. What if the chute had been sabotaged too? He reached into the package with his mind, and spat out a couple of curses from his years as a slave. The chute felt as if someone had tied it in loose knots and then stuffed it into the holding bag. He'd really be in trouble with that deployed.

Better try to use his perceptive and telekinetic abilities to get the compensation circuit straightened out, he decided, and reached mentally for the chip in the left upright of the control triangle. His mind touched something that should not have been there at all, and he cried out aloud and doubled up under the mental impact of a high-powered screamer.

Roi had felt screamers before, and managed to work through them after a fashion. This one, however, was far stronger than anything in his previous experience. Even a tight mental shield couldn't stop the pain in his head entirely, and levitation and teleportation were no longer even remotely possible. Whoever was responsible for the sabotage had intended for the glider to kill him. Any normal telepath, raised to depend on esper talents, would probably have panicked.

Roi, however, had been conditioned from birth to find ways of dealing with impossible situations without betraying his esper abilities.

His involuntary start had thrown the glider into another tumble, and his helmet speaker was raucous with cries of alarm from the others. "Shut up and keep clear," he snarled in response as he struggled to get the scarlet wing flying again. Somehow he leveled off heading more or less toward the orange roof, though he was too low now to make the distance without a thermal, and too wary of the blood-colored wing to trust his ability to circle in an updraft for height. The ground below was studded with boulders and cut by gullies, and looked almost as hostile as the suddenly unfriendly sky.

Both the screamer and the compensation circuits needed power, he thought. He had felt no difference in weight distribution when he'd lifted the glider for takeoff, so there was at least a chance that the small power pack in the right upright was feeding both. Carefully, almost holding his breath, he began working his hands toward each other on the control bar. When they touched, he maneuvered the left hand under the right. His right hand came up, working at the catch of the power pack compartment.

The catch had never been designed for mittens.

His breath sobbing with frustration, he brought his right hand back to his mouth and used his teeth to pull the scarlet mitten off and let it drop. It fell away to the rugged ground below him, turning over and over until it was so small he could no longer see it. Again he reached for the catch.

He had to adjust constantly for the changing wind resistance of his asymmetrical body position, and when the cover popped off of the power pack compartment, changing the shape of the streamlined upright, the wing tried again to escape his one-handed control. He thrust his fingers desperately into the power pack cavity, jerking the pack clear of the wiring.

The sudden silence in his head was deafening. Carefully he opened his mental shields, feeling for the nearest thermal. There, ahead and to his left, a small one, but rising faster than the glider's sink rate. He nosed down, shifted his weight left, and pulled up, feeling and seeing the glider turn into the thermal and begin to rise. He didn't think he could climb enough on this little sprat of a thermal to make the cabin, but with luck he could make it out of the broken land.

He looked down at the ground to his left, searching for his own shadow to help him estimate distance. *Two* shadows?

He turned his head and saw a large power flier pacing his glider, above and behind him, where most of the craft was hidden by the wing above him. Rage flooded through his body, and he gathered and channeled it toward the enemy craft, banking his own wing enough to see the markings on the craft that must have been responsible for his plight. He reached toward the flyer, with every intention of blasting it out of the sky, and abruptly saw the mammoth device, and picked up a hint of concern over his own plight from the vessel that had become his target. Horrified, he wrenched at the building rage, somehow transmuting it and changing direction toward where Central and his father should be, ten light years away.

Get this goddam baby-sitter off my back! he snarled into his father's mind, and felt Lai's shocked response.

Roi? He felt the surprise in Lai's mind-voice, and a distinct feeling of—respect?—that he had initiated contact at such a distance.

For once in my life can't you let me do something I want to do, on my own? Or am I as much your slave as I was Derry's?

He felt his father flinch at the accusation. *What happened, Roi?*

We're gliding down to the plains, I had a minor problem with the wing, and there's a Company flier pacing me. Get him off me now, or I'll arrange that we lose the finders. I mean it, Father. This trip may not seem like much to you, but it's important to me. He wasn't even sure why it had become so important, except that he'd never in his life had the opportunity to do something he wanted on his own.

A long moment of silence, as his shadow shrank on the ground below. *If I ask the Company not to shadow you, will you promise to contact me or Kyrie the way you did just now if anything happens that you need help? We can't afford to lose you, son.*

There was a sense of surprise from the craft shadowing his, and it suddenly accelerated and turned away. *Thanks,* he thought as he broke the connection.

The glider was responsive now, if cranky, and he thought back to Derry's lessons on his own uncompensated wing. He had sworn the task was impossible when he had first tried uncompensated flight. After the negative compensation he had just experienced, the natural instability of the little craft was a joy to work with. He didn't even want to think about what the glider would have been like if he'd been using full compensation, rather than a quarter.

An acrid smell brought his attention back from the world circling below him, and he groaned as he saw smoke pouring out of the empty power pack compartment. Cautious exploration with his bare right hand confirmed the heat in the left uptube, in the region of the compensation chip. Whoever had sabotaged his wing had made sure that the evidence would be destroyed, and the glider's misbehavior probably attributed to a short circuit. Come to think about it, he wasn't sure how much heat the synthetic that made up the control bar would stand without weakening or even igniting. As the orange roof came around in front of him again, he straightened the glider and headed northeast and down, dropping the nose for maximum speed.

"Roi?" Penny's voice was anxious. "Are you going to make the cabin?"

"No," he replied, "though I won't be far from it. I think I've got an electrical fire in the control circuit, and I'm in a bit of a hurry to get on the ground." Had he really been wise to get rid of the escort craft?

He heard Penny's sudden intake of breath before she continued. "I sent Flame and Amber straight to the cabin and told them to get the horses saddled and out here. I'll try to circle over you as long as I can to guide them, and Timi will follow you down."

The ground was closer now, and the air was so warm his parka felt stifling in spite of the wind of his motion. He felt ahead for thermals, and altered course slightly. He had no intention of flying any farther than he had to before setting down, so he didn't want to get into an updraft himself. But if he set down close to a rising column of air, Penny could use it to stay aloft.

"Penny?" he said. "There's a patch of grass ahead, fairly smooth, where I'm putting down. And another broken area, looks like an old black lava flow, north of it. The dark area's putting up a good thermal, if you want to use it to keep soaring near my landing spot." The violet and amber gliders were coming down from the northwest to meet him, and he saw them split apart, the violet wing swinging into the rising column of air while the amber one continued on, passing him on the left and disappearing behind the scarlet wing overhead.

The west edge of the grassy area was ahead, and he turned the wing into the wind for his final approach. He could see and hear the wind rattling last season's dead grass, now, and smell the new green blades, less than a finger's length long, poking up through the snow-wet soil. He pulled his feet free of the streamlined harness and pushed out just a little, killing speed and slowing his drop rate as he allowed his body to rotate to a vertical position. Then the grass was almost touching his boots and he pushed out hard, stalling the wing and slamming his feet into the ground.

Somehow he managed to crawl out of his support sling before his legs gave way and he sat down on the wonderful, wet, solid ground. There were still patches of snow, too small to have been seen from the cliff, hiding in the shade of the thicker tufts of dead grass, and he packed several handfuls around the hot end of the upright. Shutting off the air supply should help, too, he thought, and he replaced the cover on the power pack compartment. He must have dropped the power pack.

He couldn't think of anyone except possibly Zhaim who might have wanted him dead. And whoever had sabotaged the glider would have touched it, left traces of his personality behind. Reading objects wasn't one of his strongest talents, but Derry had told him often enough that his weakness in that aspect of esper work was simple lack of application. "You don't like eavesdropping," his uncle had told him, "and there's a lot of eavesdropping in reading an object's history. But that doesn't mean it's a useless skill." In this case, Roi decided, it might be a very useful skill indeed.

The cooling from the snow he had continued to pile on the upright, together with the reduction of the air supply, had pretty well stopped the fire. Closing his eyes and opening his mind to any lingering impressions, Roi reached out to put his hands on the control triangle. Himself, of course. Traces of Flame, who had helped him set up and inspect the glider just before the flight, and of Penny, who'd helped the day before. Neither, however, had touched the control triangle except at the top, where both had checked its attachment to the wing. The only fresh trace beside his own anywhere near the electronics was—Timi? From yesterday, when he'd held the compartment door open? But this felt more recent.

Roi felt a sick coldness growing in his middle as he probed deeper. Timi, and nobody else, had handled the access hatch since Roi himself had reset the compensation level the day before. Could Zhaim actually have succeeded in influencing Timi to the extent that the Clan boy would try to kill him? Roi could not believe that. Sure, they had disagreements, mostly about Timi's growing tendency to push what Roi saw as a dangerous flirtation with Zhaim. Roi could even imagine Timi attacking him in a fit of temper, as he had during the snowball fight. But a calculated murder attempt like this?

He pulled his hands back, wiping them on his parka as if he could wipe away the impression his mind had taken from the control bar. The wing hid his view of the sky, and he wiggled backward until he could see the violet glider soaring in wide circles almost over his head, and the amber one over his right shoulder, losing altitude in great side—slipping curves. He had no doubt of Penny's motives in choosing Timi to land and assist him. Timi was the strongest of the party physically, and they were all well versed in first aid. And—dammit, no matter what his reading of the control bar told him, he simply did not believe that Timi would knowingly have sabotaged the glider. Besides, his friend was good at electronics, sure, but esperelectronics was something else entirely. Timi couldn't have managed the screamer circuit. Not without someone guiding his every move.

The amber glider was low and almost behind him now, banking into its final upwind landing leg. Roi forced himself to open fully to Timi's emotions as the other boy flared and dropped to the ground a wing length away, yanking the emergency release on his support sling and starting toward Roi at a run almost before his feet were firmly planted. Love, concern, some anger, but directed at what he perceived as Roi's reckless flying. No trace of guilt, or even of suspicion that the glider might have been tampered with.

"What the *hell* did you think you were doing," Timi gasped as he dropped to his knees at Roi's side. "No, don't try to get up, dammit. Have you eaten anything? Can you keep anything down, after that? What *happened?*" He was checking Roi's pulse and breathing as he spoke, his mittens thrown to the ground beside them and his bare hands against Roi's skin.

Roi had always hated the thought of invading another mind unasked, even in emergency Healing. Derik had insisted he learn the technique of such invasion, assuring him repeatedly that there would be times when it would be necessary for his own safety to know exactly what was in another's thoughts. This, he thought glumly, looked like being one of those times. Hating himself even as he used Timi's hands against his face as a focus, he slid into his friend's mind.

Nothing. Timi had prepared dinner the night before, felt tired and gone to bed early with the rest of the group, and slept soundly all night. The group had been together all this morning. The only thing Roi could find that seemed even remotely suspicious was what seemed a brief hiatus of memory while Timi had been seasoning the thick soup he had made from the first night's leftovers. There was nothing really unusual in that; people did wander off mentally while their bodies continued to work. But they had all slept very soundly last night. Could something or someone else have drugged them, working through Timi's body?

The one thing he was sure of, Roi decided as he withdrew from Timi's mind, was that while Timi's body might have been used, Timi himself had no part in the murder attempt. If he reported that he thought the glider had been sabotaged, his father would certainly order a detailed reading of the equipment. Any competent esper would pick up what he had, that Timi had handled the glider. And Timi would be in a very large amount of undeserved trouble.

"Well, you look all right," Timi said grudgingly. "How 'bout monitoring yourself?"

Roi shrugged and winced at the pain in his shoulders. "Pulled muscles and a couple of bruises from when I slammed into the wing a time or two," he said. "It wasn't intentional, Timi. There must have been a short circuit somewhere, maybe something that jogged loose while we were sledding the wings back to the shed yesterday, and the compensation was totally screwed up."

"And of course you were too bloody stubborn to teleport, or levitate, or even use your chute," Timi came back. "Roi, I know you don't like it, but you're too important to take risks with yourself like that." He flopped back on his heels and began pulling off his parka.

For an instant Roi was tempted to tell Timi what had really happened. But Timi's ignorance of the sabotage and the screamer circuit was the best defense the young slave had. And if there was a legitimate reason for Timi to have handled the glider after as well as before Roi had test-flown it yesterday, maybe he could keep Timi out of any eventual investigation altogether. "All right," he said tiredly, "I was too shook up to think straight. Timi, would you mind packing up my glider? I don't think I can stand up right now."

In reply Timi jumped to his feet and started toward the red wing. "Better eat some of Kyrie's candy," he advised as he began the breakdown procedure. "Roi, are you feeling all right? Not right now, but since the trip started? I mean, your precog doesn't seem normal to me. I'd have thought you'd have caught that storm a long time before the local forecasters. And didn't you feel anything wrong with that glider before you took off?"

Roi frowned, thinking back to the top of the cliff. "It did feel a little odd," he said. "But the feeling was so weak it just didn't register. Same with the storm. The warm weather the day before bothered me, but it didn't feel like a real warning. Even less than the hunches I used to get before I knew what I was doing. It happens sometimes, and Derik warned me talents might fade in and out a bit at my age. It'll come back."

Timi paused to look directly at Roi, chin jutting. "Maybe you'd better start paying more attention to things feeling even a little odd," he said, and went back to folding up the glider. "Like you did before the storm. And eat something, for Clan's sake."

Roi tugged at the seal of his parka and shrugged out of the garment, wincing again at the pain in his shoulders. He'd have to Heal that, he thought as he searched through the parka pockets for the smallest box of Kyrie's confections. He thought for a moment the box might have fallen out during his wild maneuvers, then remembered he'd put it in his vest pocket instead and pulled it out. The sweet citrus and almond flavors blended as he chewed, and he felt the energy of the sugar surge through his body. "You were right about eating, Timi," he told his friend. "I feel better already."

"Good," Penny's voice said in his ear, and he jumped in response. He'd forgotten he still wore the helmet with its radio pickup and receiver. "The girls are almost to you; they should see you in a minute or two. Roi, if you're sure you're up to sitting on a horse, head back to the cabin with Flame. Timi, you and Amber finish packing up those two gliders—they're bringing the second set of storage bags and some weather sheets on one of the spare horses. Tie the two bags together so the gliders reinforce each other and wrap the weather sheets around them. As many thicknesses as you can. I'll head for the cabin and ride back to meet you, and once I'm sure Roi's not hurt I'll ride out here to help you skid the gliders back to the cabin. All right?"

Timi stood on the crest of the gentle rise, looking northwest, and began waving wildly. Roi felt the vibration of hoof beats through the ground, and struggled to his own feet. "All right, Penny," he confirmed grumpily. "But I'm not really hurt. There's no reason to stick the others with all the work."

"I think you'll find it's you against the other four of us on that," Penny told him. Flame's head, hair flying free, came over the rise to his north, quickly followed by Amber's and those of several horses.

Roi blinked hard when he saw the horses, thinking for a moment he must have hit his head on something, after all. They were polka dotted. Flame's mount was white sprinkled with round copper spots. Amber's, a little bay roan with curious dark lines on its nose, looked less exotic until it turned as she halted it. Then it became apparent that it had a large white area, punctuated by dark bay spots, over its hips. One of the two led horses had a black-spotted white body, but its neck, legs and chest were a dark mouse gray, set off by a black head and mane and a black and white tail. The other had markings resembling those of Flame's mount, but its spots were a lighter, sandy color, with a good deal of black mixed with the white of its mane and tail. Then Flame and Amber jumped down from their horses and slammed into Roi, and he had to concentrate on keeping upright.

"Somebody better grab the horses," he pointed out.

"Preferably before they trample my glider," Timi agreed, catching the reins of the horses the girls had ridden in. "Here, Amber, hold these, will you? I'll get my wing broken down." He hadn't taken time to do more than get his glider's nose down when he landed, and the wind had flipped it onto its back and skidded it almost to the edge of the grassy area.

Flame pulled back a little to look up at Roi's face. "The one with the buckskin spots is for you right now," she told him. "He's the quietest, Penny said."

"My shoulders are too sore to ride," Roi said. "Why don't I Heal myself while you three get the gliders ready, and then we can all go back together?" The request was too reasonable to ignore. Flame laid out one of the weather sheets for him to lie down on, and Roi stretched out, reaching into his body to Heal it at the same time he fretted over how much to tell Penny.

Penny

The radios were line of sight, and Penny lost contact with the rest of the group as she landed. The green and blue gliders had simply been left, flat on the ground. Normally that would have upset her, but this time she was relieved they hadn't taken the extra time they'd have needed to secure the gliders properly, and left her own the same way.

Her bay leopard gelding had been caught and left tied to the corral fence, and she saddled up quickly. Even if Roi returned at once with Flame, she could get to him faster by riding out to meet the others. And in spite of his assurances, she wasn't certain he'd be able to ride. She detoured into the cabin to get the large aid kit, discovering that the girls had left their parkas and helmets—and Flame's hood—tossed down anywhere. Had the girl been fixated on the hood, or on the fact that Roi had effectively bought it for her?

Of course none of them had thought to don the light riding helmets. She put hers on and grabbed the other four, tying them and the aid kit to her saddle. Then she mounted and headed south at a fast lope, following the trail of bent grass left by the other horses.

She kept reliving the moment she had turned and seen Roi's glider, almost halfway down to the plains and clearly out of control. What could have happened? She'd never heard of an electrical fire in a glider before. If the compensation circuits started firing at random, though .... She shuddered. She'd had to fly a glider with as little as quarter compensation as part of her training, and the very thought of malfunctioning compensation made her feel weak.

Her horse slowed briefly to a walk, lifted his head, and whinnied. A moment later he was answered, and she met the other four just on the far side of the next rise.

Roi, looking tired but otherwise fit, was on the gentle buckskin leopard that had been chosen as Timi's mount, leaving Timi to cope—barely—with the spirited body-blanketed grulla selected for Roi. They had roped the two gliders tightly together, wrapped the resulting bundle in layers of weather sheets, and attached the middle of the remaining rope to one end of the bundle, spreading out the ends in a Y with one end going to Flame's saddle and the other to Roi's. Timi's lathered mount was snorting and shying at the bundle, and sweat was dripping down the boy's black face. Amber's hip-blanketed bay varnish roan was watching the gliders warily, and even Flame's chestnut leopard had an ear cocked back toward the bundle she dragged.

"Roi, I thought you were coming straight back with Flame and leaving the gliders to the others," Penny said.

He looked at her with an expression of hurt innocence. "I pulled some muscles in my shoulders," he said gravely. "I lay down and Healed them while the others were packing up the gliders. Then the horse you said I was to ride turned out to be the only one beside Flame's that'd pull the gliders without a fight."

Penny sighed. She'd had clients enough who'd disobeyed orders before, but rarely one who came up with such consistently good reasons for doing so as did Roi. And he certainly didn't seem to be under any stress at the moment. "All right," she said reluctantly. "Roi, what happened? I looked back and you were way down and flying like you were drunk. Then you started tumbling. Why didn't you bail out, or levitate, or something?"

"Some kind of electronics problem, I think," Roi replied. "Some of the compensations were going the wrong way. Good thing I set them to only quarter strength yesterday. I know how to fly uncompensated, so I yanked the power pack. That's when smoke started pouring out and I realized there must have been a short circuit somewhere. But it was flyable enough without the compensation messing me up that I was pretty sure I could land it all right. Good thing that cliff's so high; I had time enough to get things under control." He glanced over toward the cliff, which had almost swallowed the afternoon sun. It seemed incredible that they had all been up there only an hour or two ago.

"You still should have bailed out or levitated," Penny told him. "And I'm going to tag that kite of yours to be gone over to the molecular level by our techs."

Flame's horse took a nervous step, shifting the bundle in the grass, and Timi's grulla, who'd just gotten up the courage to stretch out her neck and investigate, shied with a violence that almost unseated Timi. Penny's own mount danced backward a step or two. "Oh, get these helmets on and let's get on back to the cabin," the guide said, making a mental note to have a word with the horse trainers. Horses on this leg of the Surprise River route should be trained to drag gliders.

Falaron: Xazhar
4/23/38

The disembarkation area at Wilderness City seethed with people. Xazhar paused at the top of the ramp, looking for the MultiStellar Travel offices. They were supposed to have his accommodations and arena tickets, but from the number of team logos and banners in the crowd, he wondered if even his father had been able to get tickets to the arena itself. He finally spotted a sign, "Travel agencies," with an arrow pointing to the right, and joined the tide of passengers flowing in that direction.

MultiStelllar was supposed to be an exclusive agency, but just now people were ten deep in front of the counter. Xazhar paused, trying to catch an agent's eye. He was, he told himself, High R'il'noid, one of the elite of the Confederation, and should not have to wait on the convenience of mere Humans. When no one waved him forward, he walked up to the counter, pushing those unfortunate enough to be in his way aside telekinetically. Angry words erupted in his wake, but he ignored them.

"Xazhar K'Zhaim," he told the young woman on the other side of the counter. "You should be holding reservations and tickets for me."

"You'll have to wait your turn, sir," the agent started to say, then gripped the counter with both hands and closed her eyes as Xazhar's mental flick exploded in her head. The angry thoughts around Xazhar were suddenly replaced by recognition of his father's name, and people who had been pressing in began shifting toward the other end of the counter.

"I would suggest that you find my reservations now," the R'il'noid said smoothly. The supervisor at the other end of the counter muttered something into her throat mike, and the agent nodded and began keying her computer. "You're in an executive suite at the Mad Mammoth," she told him after a moment, "with full virtual hookups to the Arena."

Damn! Hadn't they been able to get tickets to the Arena? Xazhar scowled, noting with some satisfaction the fear on the woman's face. Virtual reality simply was *not* the same as being present at a sporting event, no matter what the promoters said. At least not for him. He remembered what Roi had once suggested, that he was not totally lacking in empathy, but responded so weakly that he actually sought out sources of strong emotion. He hadn't believed the suggestion, but could something of the sort account for his dislike of virtual hookups?

"My father requested Arena passes," he said sharply.

"Milord, Arena passes have been sold out for over a year. The Agency has made every possible effort, but we cannot force those people who have passes to give them up." She paused and swallowed. "If I might venture a suggestion, Milord?"

Xazhar nodded, scowling. "If it's a useful one."

"Your father is high in the Confederation government, Milord, and there will have been tickets reserved for Confederation representatives. You might check with the Adjudicator's office. At the moment, the Lady Kyrie is the highest Confederation official on planet, and while she attended the opening ceremonies, I have not heard that she is a great fan of plasmaball."

Neither, Xazhar, thought, was she any fan at all of his father. In fact, she was one of the very few people who had crossed his father and gotten away with it. But if she had any sense of what his father's continued enmity could be like, she might be willing to be a little helpful to Zhaim's son. "I'll consider that option," he told the woman as he took the Mad Mammoth chip.

***

He had been thoroughly wrong about Kyrie Talganian, Xazhar thought as he rode in the official surface van to the Arena the next morning. He had dropped his luggage at the Mad Mammoth and headed straight for the adjudicator's villa, thinking how he could best suggest the possible benefits to Kyrie of supplying him with tickets, without actually laying himself open to charges of extortion or bribery. Instead, he had found himself telling her how he had led the Tyndall team to victory in the last game of the Schools tournament. The adjudicator had listened with interest, and asked him a few questions about what he considered to be acceptable behavior at a major tournament.

As a player himself, he had no use for unruly fans and said so.

"So do you think you could represent the Confederation for me and act as host for the dignitaries I have to invite to see the tournament?" Kyrie had asked unexpectedly. "I detest the game myself, and I really can't take the time to escort the Confederation's guests. You understand plasmaball, and you are one of the very few High R'il'noids to have played it, even on the school level. That makes you just enough of a celebrity that I can pass off giving you the escort duty as a compliment to the fans you'll be joining in the Confederation box. Well?"

Xazhar leaned back in his seat in the van and grinned. Two ambassadors, a trade representative and a planetary administrator's spoiled son shared the van with him. At the moment, all four were craning their necks to look at the arena.

"Why's it such an odd shape?" young Cliffal asked as the van pulled up to an inconspicuous door.

Xazhar looked up at the building himself. "It is rather unusual, isn't it?" he replied. "You know that the playing volume itself is a prolate ellipsoid—well, a symmetrical egg lying on its side. The vertical walls and the generally elliptical floor plan of the building just make the whole thing stable, and provide for the amenities like food service, and rest areas, and of course the artificial gravity generators."

"This isn't a standard shape, though," Ambassador Konkliz remarked. "Usually they're larger, and a good deal flatter on top."

A young woman in Arena uniform bowed as she opened the van door and stood aside to let them get out. "Welcome to the tournament, my lords," she said. "I see you've noticed that our building's not standard. If you'll follow me, I'll explain why as I escort you to your seats."

Xazhar waved the four Human dignitaries ahead of him after their guide, then tipped his head back to take a better look at the building himself. In most plasmaball arenas, the ellipsoidal null-gravity playing volume was cupped in a more or less hyperboloid seating area that reached at least level with the top of the ellipsoid, and the gently arched roof started from the top of the seating area. This building looked more as if the roof followed the curve of the playing volume. He followed the others through the door and into a lift shaft.

"In most arenas," the guide was saying, "all but the most expensive seats are either far from the action, or require that the spectators lie on their backs to some extent, looking up at the playing volume. This building was designed primarily for virtual broadcasts, since we knew it would be impossible to accommodate everyone who wanted to see the playoffs. What seating there is was designed so everyone is within three to four rows of the playing volume."

That explained the shape of the building, Xazhar thought as he followed the group out of the lift shaft and along a short corridor carpeted in dark blue. The guide opened the panel at the far end, and stood aside to let them through. Xazhar paused and squinted through the playing volume before him, trying to see how the seats were arranged.

Their own seats, richly upholstered and equipped with full food and beverage delivery systems, were on the long side of the ellipsoid, midway between the two goals. Across the playing volume, Xazhar could see that seats at their level, though far more tightly packed and arranged several deep, extended around the circumference of the arena. Other tiers were stacked above and below their level, but Xazhar had to look almost directly at the top of the ellipsoid before he began to understand just how unusual the seating was. "You've got artificial gravity control on the seats as well as in the playing volume," he exclaimed. "As far as any spectator is concerned, they're sitting on a level surface and looking straight into the arena. But everybody else is tilted at least a little, even to the point of sitting upside down."

The guide nodded, her expression smug. "Perfect seats for everyone," she said. "The lifts to the upper levels are curved, to add to the illusion, and the artificial gravity is applied to the corridors."

Xazhar looked back at the seats overhead, and frowned. "Fail-safes?" he asked quietly.

"The seats are gimbaled to swing upright relative to whatever the local gravity happens to be," she assured him, "and we request that the spectators in the upper tiers web in. That's not necessary in this section, of course. The direction of the gravity field here is normal, though the intensity has been reduced slightly."

"Thought I'd lost a little weight," Xazhar said.

"They're changing gravity?" Cliffal asked.

"Have you seen a plasmaball game before?" Xazhar countered. He was sure from the conversation in the van that Ambassador Konkliz and the trade representative, Mizzar, were ardent fans of plasmaball, and he thought that the other ambassador, Rankin, that was it, had at least attended a few games. Fifteen-year-old Cliffal knew a lot of players' names, but had seemed confused several times over the way the game was played.

The boy shook his head reluctantly, not meeting Xazhar's eyes. "We're a low-tech planet," he replied unhappily. "I think plasmaball takes some technology we don't use. But I do follow the scores," he added hastily.

"That's hardly your fault," Xazhar replied. "Why don't you sit at the left end, there, and I'll sit next to you and explain the game rules and answer your questions?"

Cliffal's face lit up as he seated himself. "You've played yourself, haven't you, m'lord? So you'd really know the rules. Is it as dangerous as they say?"

"Not at School level," Xazhar replied as he sat next to the younger boy. "That's mostly because of details like requirements for protective gear and mandatory breaks if a player's hurt, though. At professional level, protective gear is optional, and a lot of players don't bother with much. And once a ten-minute set is started, they don't break for anything. Even a player's being killed. And that can happen if the ball hits an unshielded player. You know what a plasmaball is, don't you?"

"Ball lightning," Cliffal replied.

"Artificial ball lightning," Xazhar agreed, glancing out into the arena. The arena lights were coming up, and those in the spectator seats dimming. He could no longer see the other seats through the light in the arena. "That's one reason a low-tech planet can't support plasmaball. You need not only the technology to create self-sustaining plasmoids, but the right kind of controllers as well. Kind of electronic rackets to hit the ball with. Another is the fact that the game is played in free fall. They're shaping gravity in the seating areas here, and that's a bit unusual. But they always shape it to provide null gravity in the arena itself, so if your planet doesn't use artificial gravity, and doesn't have the personal motive systems to move around in free fall, you can't have plasmaball."

Cliffal grinned. "We've got artificial free fall," he said, "but only the police are allowed to use it. Crowd control. I hadn't heard of the motive systems, but I bet they're illegal."

"Crowd control," Xazhar chuckled. "I like that."

Chapter 9

It took several days before Roi recovered from his anger at his father—and his confusion and guilt over concealing Timi's possible role in the sabotage—enough to want to share his experiences with anyone back on Central. Even then he refused to answer Lai, but he was feeling increasingly guilty about shutting Marna out as well. Finally, he decided to respond when she attempted to contact him.

So you're enjoying the Falaron wildlife? she asked. *How does it compare with what you saw when you visited Earth?*

Pretty different. Well, Falaron was seeded when? A hundred thousand years ago, when Jarn's descendants were first spreading out to the stars? What I saw in Virginia was really different—no mammoths, or giant sloths, or sabertooths, and the horses were brought in by the settlers. But I saw some bones once, in a sinkhole. I'm glad they're still alive here. Marna, thank you so much for the color sticks. I wasn't expecting a birthday present on top of this trip.

The trip's a graduation present. You'll be getting a major birthday present from your father, but I thought you'd like the color sticks along on the trek.

I'll use them to make you a picture of the sabertooth attack, he promised.

Sabertooth attack? she asked, and he picked up a brief image of a large feline, patterned in dark and light green, charging directly at him.

Not on us, he assured her. *It went after a mammoth calf. Penny said the sabertooth must have been very young, or it would have known better than to try an attack with the mother mammoth that close. It must have flown twenty strides, and landed running for all it was worth. And it almost wasn't running fast enough at that—mamma mammoth was mad! Penny had us get back, even wearing the warnoffs—not from the sabertooth, from the mammoths.*

Roi felt Marna's laughter. *I'll look forward to your drawing,* she told him.

Central: Marna
5/5/38

The first rumors had reached Marna a few days before her mental conversation with Roi. Plague was for her the great enemy. She had watched, helpless, as her own planet and everyone she had ever known had died, two hundred years ago, and only the fact that Lai's ancestors, working with Humans, had found an answer to a similar plague had allowed him to save her. And now a planet far away, on the boundaries of the Confederation, was reported to have a plague of its own. The rumors grew, and finally, almost three fivedays later, the planet asked for help.

"So are you really needed?" Lai looked down at Marna, his hands gentle around her upper arms.

"Yes," she told him. "The pattern's wrong for an epidemic, Lai. It's some kind of environmental factor, and I can identify it and develop treatment faster than their doctors can. Enough faster that it might save several hundred thousand lives."

"That's not worth risking you."

"Oh, I'll stay in an isolation suit until I'm sure what's going on. I don't believe there's any risk to me, Lai. But I don't like leaving when Roi's off on that wilderness Challenge of his. Not when Zhaim feels the way he does about Roi. Not when so much has gone wrong already."

Lai's grip tightened. "You're sure you can't get anything more from the Riyan medical texts we transferred to the Big'Un? If we could somehow give Zhaim the conscience he seems to lack ...."

Marna shook her head. "Lots on identifying children who lacked empathy. Lots on the importance of early treatment. Some on the side effects. A little bit about how it was done—most of the training seemed to involve working with someone who already knew the technique. And nothing at all about treating adults, or why it was so important to catch children early. I think is had something to do with children not fighting the treatment, but I'm not sure. And so much has gone wrong already on Roi's trip."

"I don't like it either," Lai said quietly. "But they aren't all that isolated. The Company was pacing the flight, until Roi spotted them." He grimaced. "Roi was furious. I think it kind of broke the illusion they were really on their own. I'm afraid that's one of the things he's just going to have to get used to. But as far as safety goes, he's a lot better guarded than he was that first year at Tyndall. Know what Davy once told me was the primary thing to remember about Roi, Marna? He's a survivor. He'll be all right. And I think you worry too much about Zhaim."

"I'd still like to know what went wrong with that glider," Marna said grimly. "And I wish you hadn't given in to Roi about not keeping tabs on the group."

"They're all carrying tracers, and the Company tracks them," Lai replied. "Their report says a wire must have come loose from the chip and shorted another one. The whole compensation chip and its connections were so charred they couldn't be sure, and they're holding the glider for further investigation. Roi himself had reset the compensation level the day before, and he could have jarred something loose. I'll get over there and look at it myself, once the Kablukolelli situation is straightened out. Or send Kaia. Anyway, Roi handled the situation all right. Ah—Win hasn't said anything, has he?"

Marna chuckled, but there was something wistful in the sound. "Not since the day I met Roi. Over two years, now. I don't think he was ever real, Lai. Just my own subconscious, trying to keep me going when I had to absorb the full shock of thinking everyone else was dead. Maybe some precognition that you would find me. He did tell me to go with you, you know, that you'd have to give me the child he and I were planning. You will keep tabs on Roi, won't you?"

"At least Falaron's in easy teleport range, even unboosted. I wish you could just 'port out to Eversummer."

"So do I," Marna said, "if only so I could get there faster. It's thousands of lives for every day of travel, Lai. Maybe more."

"Three hundred and fifty lights is a long way," Lai said. "We don't have a good teleport who's been there to give you the coordinates, so the best we can do is boost you out to Songbird and put you on a fast courier for the last seventy lights. It's only two long jumps, and the courier will eat up the space between them. A couple of days, at most."

"Once I get going," Marna agreed reluctantly, and pulled back from his grasp to resume packing her medical kit.

She had spoken to Roi telepathically three hours earlier, right after the official plea for help had come in from Eversummer, and told him then about the problem. A syndrome that produced violent intestinal cramps, vomiting, diarrhea, dehydration and sloughing of the intestinal mucosa had shown up half a month earlier. Only when the deaths had reached thousands per day had the planetary authorities requested help. She had the statistics ready to share with Roi, and he observed almost as soon as she had that medical personnel brought from other areas to care for the victims were not affected. *And if you trace back where the isolated victims were about four days before they started showing symptoms, it was areas where a lot of the rest of the population got sick, too. Food, maybe, or water or air or even an insect vector. But there's no evidence it's passing from person to person directly, or even whether it's a pathogen or a toxin.*

Marna had agreed with his reasoning, and she had already advised the planetary authorities to screen food, air and water in affected regions. But she could do a lot more in person, especially in devising treatment for those already affected.

"Ready?" Lai asked. He had set the interface lounge out flat, with a single interface for the two of them. She gave her medical kit a final check before she latched it and keyed its levitation and follow-me units.

"Ready," she said, and walked over to stretch out beside him, reaching with him to draw energy from the fusion generator that powered the big computer. He turned to pull her close within the interface, cupping her cheek in his hand to turn her face to his, and she smiled at him. "At least Win's not jealous," she said lightly. When her surroundings became Songbird, the memory of his parting kiss was still on her lips.

Falaron: Roi

The trouble with this part of the trip, Roi thought as he angled his sketchpad to take advantage of the last light of the dying campfire, was that it got dark so early. The waning half moon would not rise until almost midnight. For now the stars were clear overhead, and the night air felt cool enough that Roi paused to seal the front of his scarlet jacket. This afternoon it had been so warm that he'd ridden bare to the waist for a while, though the others had retained their tunics. Flame had forgotten to reapply her sunscreen this morning, and her nose and forehead had been visibly red by the time they had stopped for lunch.

There was a soft snort out of the darkness to his left, and then a grunt and a thump as one of the horses lay down. Continuing sounds of tearing grass told Roi that most of the animals were still grazing. He opened his shields and listened briefly to the equine minds. Flame's mare, Token, was coming into season and cranky enough they might have to switch Flame to one of the pack geldings. A wolf howled from the other side of the river, and his own mare, Raindrop, jerked her head up and snorted apprehensively. Timi's buckskin leopard, dozing with his forelegs locked and one back hoof cocked, barely even flicked an ear at the sound.

The buckskin, Roi thought, would not have survived long on his own. He was safe enough here, though, with a warnoff and a creance both firmly attached to his neck rope.

Footsteps sounded behind Roi, and Penny dropped to her haunches beside him. "Ready to turn in for the night?" she asked him.

"About," he replied, turning the sketch so she could see it.

She chuckled. "Silly young sabertooth," she said. "I'm just as glad we didn't see him tossed from that angle, though. He looks like he's coming right out of the page. A warnoff's no protection against an animal that gets thrown or falls into it."

"It's still useful most of the time," Roi replied. "So are the creances, for that matter. Like invisible picket ropes. And the horses don't seem to mind at all."

"Why should they?" Penny yawned. "Most of them never go far enough from camp to find they're restrained."

"Well, I hated creances when I was a slave," Roi said.

"They use them on people?" Penny asked, shocked. "No wonder you looked upset the first time we put them on the horses. They really are great for letting the horses graze safely, though. I just hope we don't get a wild stud coming *into* camp, with Token in heat. The warnoffs aren't set for that." She stood. "Smother the fire when you're through, will you, Roi? I'm going to bed."

Roi studied the sketch again, and then decided there wasn't enough light to judge whether some of the lines needed darkening. He didn't usually make preliminary sketches, but he wanted his final drawing for Marna to be special, and he was finding it hard to decide exactly how he wanted to compose it. Flame's voice came out of the dark, silky and coaxing as she urged him to join her, and Roi grinned. He sometimes suspected that Flame was a weak latent telepath herself, and wondered if Token's condition was affecting her rider. Well, he decided, he had no particular objection if it was. He got up and stowed the sketchpad in the pack bag. Then he soaked the fire with the water they'd used to wash the cooking pans, and kicked sand over the soggy remains.

They hadn't bothered to set up the tents on such a warm, clear night, and as his eyes adjusted he could see the pale oval of Flame's face in the starlight. "What *would* we do if a wild stud came into camp," he mused aloud as he sat down by the double sleeping bag and began to pull off his boots.

Flame chuckled throatily. "I know what Token would do," she said softly. "Want me to show you?"

Roi grinned and stood to pull off the rest of his clothes. "Sure, show me," he said as he slid into the double bag with her.

***

The following day was even hotter. The girls applied sunscreen liberally to their upper bodies, and wore only breast bands above the waist. Neither Roi's bronze skin nor Timi's black one needed such protection, though Timi wore a loosely fitting, long-sleeved white tunic to reflect the heat of the sun. Roi himself rode bare to the waist. He considered riding barelegged as well, but remembered too well the chafe of the stirrup leathers when he'd tried that the second day.

They walked and trotted their horses through knee-high grass along the edge of the flood plain. The river swung in great lazy loops, now almost by the side of the trail, now out of sight, a quarter hour's ride to their right. Longhorn bison, their winter coats slipping away in patches to show the slick new hair beneath, grazed in small groups or lay down chewing their cud, and even the new calves seemed subdued by the unseasonable heat once the first freshness of the morning was gone. Twice they rode by the remains of calves whose mothers had been unable to protect them from predators. Lions were still feasting on one; dire wolves and a huge condor were quarreling over another.

By noon they were all the same shade of gray, their sweat-slicked skins powdered with the dust blowing off the river bars to the south, and their canteens were empty. The river was far out of sight to their right, and the sea of grass stretched endlessly in every direction they looked. The mountain front behind them had long since dropped completely below the horizon.

The horses, as sweaty and dust-caked as their riders, plodded up another rise, and Roi pulled Raindrop to a brief halt as they reached the top. "Stand," he told the grulla mare with voice and mind as he pulled his knees up onto the saddle and then stood erect on the black and white rump.

"See anything?" Penny asked, halting Freckles and pulling her map out of her saddlebag. The three pack horses, creanced to Penny's bay leopard, lowered their heads to graze as eagerly as if they hadn't been snatching mouthfuls of the fast-growing spring grass all morning, and Token squealed, switched her tail, and stamped a hind foot. Raindrop swiveled an ear as her rider shifted his weight, then lifted her head and nickered, her whole body vibrating under Roi's feet, as a gust of wind from the east ruffled the grass around her legs.

"Side stream ahead, I think," Roi said. "I can see treetops, anyway, and Raindrop thinks she smells water." He slid back into his saddle with an approving pat on the dark gray shoulder. "Good girl, Raindrop. You're starting to get some manners."

Timi laughed, white teeth flashing in his dust-covered face. "She sure needs some," he said. "I'd never have thought she'd stand like that after the ride she gave me."

Roi grinned. "Oh, I was cheating a bit on that one. Had a direct mind-link ready to clamp down on her if she tried anything. But I didn't need to, beyond making it clear to her what I wanted." He picked up the reins and shifted his weight forward, and his horse broke into an eager trot.

"That's probably the Bird River ahead," Penny called out as she trotted her horse alongside Roi's. "Map says there's a good gravel-bottomed swimming hole just upstream from the ford, and a safe drinking spring. Want to stop there and have a swim before lunch?"

A chorus of eager voices assured her that swimming, before and after lunch, would be more than welcome. Roi ran a light, assessing touch over all of the horses. A short run to the stream wouldn't overheat the well-conditioned animals enough to cause any problems, he decided. "Let's go," he called out as he let Raindrop break into a lope.

The trail led them gently downhill, the treetops seeming mere bushes ahead of them. Then the horses swung right and slowed to a walk, dropping single file into a narrow slot of a trail that led them down between waist-high dirt walls through foliage and among the cottonwood and willow trunks. The trees that had seemed only bushes from the plains above towered over their heads, and the bank behind them was almost invisible through their lower branches. The river was still Roi's height or more below the level of the trail.

The ground became first muddy, then increasingly gravelly as they approached the ford. "Don't let them drink more than a few swallows each right now," Penny cautioned as they rode into the wide, knee-deep crossing, "and keep them moving."

"How?" Flame called, and Roi looked back to see Token, ears flattened rebelliously, pawing at the water and totally ignoring her rider's heels and swats with the reins. Before Roi could reach out to the mare's mind, Token was going down in the water and preparing to roll. Flame kicked her boots out of the stirrups and landed on her feet, squealing at the chill of the water.

Roi was just in front of Token, so he turned back and used voice, mind and rein-ends to get the chestnut back to her feet, snubbing the mare close to Raindrop so Flame could remount. "You're not supposed to swim until we've unsaddled the horses, Flame," Timi laughed from behind them. His own buckskin lowered its head and started to paw at the water, and Timi hastily kicked his mount past Token and Raindrop.

Penny, looking back at them from the far bank, shook her head apologetically. "I've always liked the mares myself," she said unhappily, "but they've usually been given shots to keep them from coming in heat before the start of a trip. Token was supposed to be, but I guess it didn't take. Flame, you're good enough to handle Freckles. Want to trade mounts, at least until Token's herself again?"

"I'll think about it," Flame replied.

Penny

The swimming hole was another ten minutes' ride upstream. They stopped and unsaddled the horses in a grassy meadow just before they reached their goal, creancing them so they could graze and drink. The pool was a deep scour, warmed by the sun, with a steep bank on one side and a gravel bar almost cutting it off from the main current on the other. The only trees were head-high willows and one old cottonwood overhanging the steep bank. While they were undressing, Penny took one look at the sparkle of the sun on the water and reached for the sunscreen. "Get it all over you, Flame," she warned the pale-skinned redhead. "And Amber, you put on more than usual where you're not tanned."

"We'll take care of it," Roi assured her as he intercepted the tube Penny had tossed toward Flame. "Here, Amber," he added as he squirted generous amounts of the stuff on the girl's shoulders and hips, "let Timi rub that in for you. Turn around, Flame."

Penny had swum and bathed nude with other clients with only mild embarrassment. But for some reason she found the sight of the two boys massaging sunscreen into the girls' hips and thighs deeply disturbing. When Roi offered to help her apply a coat, she snapped at him, and then relented at once when she saw the hurt in his eyes. "I'll swim later," she told him. "Right now I want to get a couple of canteens filled and dig out lunch."

It was an excuse, she admitted to herself on the way to the spring, and the mere fact that Roi had not offered to help fill the canteens made her suspect that he had known she wanted to get away. She thrust the first canteen into the pocket pool where the spring bubbled up through the gravel, and considered the situation.

Part of her guide training had conditioned her to accept behavior from clients toward each other that was totally outside of her own behavioral rules. For some reason that conditioning was breaking down with Roi's group. Maybe, the thought welled up as she closed the second canteen, because she had come to think of them as friends, rather than just clients.

It didn't change the differences in perception that would make a bathing suit indecent in their eyes, she told herself firmly as she walked back to the swimming hole. Either you don't swim at all—and you'll have a hard time explaining that, in this heat!—or you swim nude like they do.

Roi

Roi wasn't even thinking of Penny. He was far too interested in Timi, or rather in what Timi had kept concealed under his clothing. Probably, Roi thought, since the start of the trip, since Timi hadn't worn an open-necked shirt since then.

It looked like a lump of carved amber, strung onto a braided leather cord to hang just below the hollow of Timi's throat. It was possible, of course, that it had something to do with Timi's new-found Clan identity. Certainly it set off Timi's Clan coloring. But Timi had been so ebullient about discovering a tie to his own identity that Roi couldn't see why he would have hidden a Clan emblem. Besides, Roi would have no reason to feel uneasy about a Clan symbol—and he did about this.

He could have probed it to make sure that it was in fact nothing more than a lump of amber. But after his experience with the screamer set to go off if he probed the glider's compensation circuit, he was reluctant even to try that. And if Timi had been hiding the pendant, in fact was still hiding it, under the water, he didn't want to antagonize the other boy by asking about it after the brief glance he'd had. Now if they were all out of the water, he couldn't help but notice such a striking ornament.

Thoughtfully he looked around the swimming hole where they were all resting briefly after an impromptu race. The water was cold—it was after all an unusually hot day for the middle of spring—and they would all feel like more activity soon. His eyes fell on the big cottonwood, not quite fully leafed out, with a broad branch overhanging the deepest part of the pool. "You know," he said thoughtfully, "we've got plenty of rope. Why don't we tie a rope to that big branch, so we can swing out over the pool?"

As he'd hoped, Timi was immediately caught by the idea. "Sure," he agreed as he rolled over and stroked to the lowest part of the bank. There was a grassy strip there that continued along the rising edge of the bank to the big cottonwood, but they had to cut through the willows to reach the packs. By the time they got back to the tree, they were watching where they placed every sore foot.

They tossed the silky synthetic rope over the branch and tied the ends firmly together in a huge, clumsy-looking knot big enough to sit on. By that time Roi felt it was natural enough that he should be interested in Timi's new ornament. "I like that," he commented, nodding toward the amber piece. "Matches your eyes. Where'd you get it?"

Timi stiffened briefly. "It was a gift, if you have to know," he replied.

"Oh? Anybody I know?" Roi kept his tone casual.

Timi hesitated and looked away. "Zhaim," he finally said. "A good luck piece." His expression as he looked back at Roi was openly defiant.

In all probability, Roi thought, he'd just found out how the glider had been sabotaged. If he was guessing right, that pretty piece of amber was an esper control circuit. In which case he *really* didn't want to probe it.

With that against Timi's skin, Zhaim could take over Timi's body pretty much at will. Timi wouldn't even be aware of the takeover. A moment's inattention on Timi's part, and Zhaim could have used the boy's body to drug the stew. He'd have chosen something that would affect Roi as well as the others, so none of them would have noticed if Timi had sleepwalked out to the glider shed. The fact that Timi had no memory of either event proved only that he had not been an active accomplice.

"I'd be happier if you threw it away, or cached it somewhere, or even stuck it in one of the packs," Roi said. "But I'm not going to make an issue of it." Mostly because he knew that if he made a fuss but failed to get Timi to remove the amulet, Zhaim would know about it almost at once. And if he did get it off by force, he suspected Zhaim would read that, too, and find another way of infiltrating the party. For now it was safer to let Timi wear the infernal thing and let Zhaim think Roi was too stupid to recognize a control circuit when he saw one. He did, however, give a cautious mental nudge to the thong. He could and would weaken that enough that he could get the thing off Timi fast if he had any reason to suspect that Zhaim was actually using it.

"Well, who goes first?"

The eventual reply was a chuckle from Penny, who came up behind them while they were politely deferring to each other. "Me," she said, grabbing the rope.

***

They ate a cold lunch in the shade of the cottonwood tree, letting the hot wind dry their wet skins. "We could just stay here for the night, if you like," Penny said. "We've made good time the last few days, and we're not on a fixed schedule, anyway."

Roi frowned as he looked around the little valley. It would be a pretty enough camping place, he thought, but there was something .... "Are you having one of your hunches?" Timi asked suddenly. "Because if you are, we'd better pay attention."

Roi looked at him in brief surprise, and then tried his old trick of thinking of alternatives while listening to the feeling in the back of his mind. "The valley's wrong, for tonight," he confirmed. "Dangerous—but I'm not sure how. Water ...." He scowled in frustration, thinking he could have done better than this when he was ten years old with no training at all.

Penny walked out from under the cottonwood and scanned the sky. "Just a few little puffballs of clouds off to the northwest," she said. "It doesn't *look* like flash flood weather."

Amber looked thoughtfully at Roi. "If you're not feeling the future weather properly," she suggested, "could you feel the weather right now and see if anything's building?"

Timi must have told her about his erratic precognition, Roi thought. But it was a good suggestion. He lay back on the grass and closed his eyes. The nearby air, while dry, was still so warm it had a fair absolute amount of water vapor. It got moister and cooler with increasing height above the ground, with the wind swinging slowly around from south to southwest, until a short distance above the tops of the few puffy cumulus. Above that the direction of the wind suddenly shifted around from southwest to northwest, and the air was dry and cooling off fast as he reached higher. He opened his eyes and took another look at the little clouds, trying to remember his thermodynamics. "I think we could get some thunderstorms building later this afternoon," he said. "Let's take one more short swim and then look for a site that's out of any possible flooding, but not where we'd attract a lightning bolt."

"Water's pretty cold to swim in with a full stomach," Penny said. "If we're going to stay in this general area, why don't we find a camping spot and move the horses and gear now to let lunch settle, and then we can swim for the rest of the afternoon."

"If the weather stays good," Flame said. "But I'd rather skip another swim than try to set up camp in a thunderstorm." She stood up and walked over to the willows where they had left their breeches and boots, and the others followed her.

There was a screen of willows between their swimming hole and the horses, and Flame led the way along the winding trail through it. "Where's Token?" she asked, even before Roi could see the clearing.

The little meadow was open and gently cupped, with no place in creance range where a horse could be hiding. Roi opened his mind to the horses' sensory impressions. Raindrop, Freckles, Dusty, Splash and the three pack horses, but no trace of Token. He called them all in with a suggestion of the grain in the packs, and reached farther for Token. He picked up the massed senses of a wild herd, perhaps an hour's ride to the west, and then, nearer, a flood of rampant equine sexuality. "Oh, hells," he groaned. "A wild stud *did* come in here, and he's driven her off. I can feel her, but I can't get through to her to bring her back. Flame, if I ever said you had a one-track mind, I apologize. That mare does, though. We'll have to go after her physically."

Raindrop nudged hopefully at his shoulder, and Roi reached into the small sack of grain they kept handy for catching the horses. He gave the grulla a handful before grabbing the horse's scanty mane and swinging onto the bare back. "I'll see if I can pick up which direction they went," he told the others. "You guys get the rest saddled and packed up. We'll probably have to split up; I don't want to leave the packhorses or our stuff down here on the flood plain." He leaned forward, sending Raindrop at a lope to the edge of the meadow. When the creance buzzed its warning, he leaned forward to turn it off, then turned Raindrop to circle the meadow just outside the range of the creances, his mind alert for any trace that a horse had crossed the line he rode.

He almost missed the escape route, dismissing it as their own trail into the meadow. But it didn't feel quite right, and he turned back. Yes, there were traces of a ninth horse on the trail, and of two horses moving in the opposite direction. He rode Raindrop on to the edge of a patch of damp soil and dismounted. Even he could see the prints of shod hooves traveling downstream toward the ford, and when Penny joined him, she pointed out the much smaller prints of an unshod horse overlaying their own upstream tracks. They followed the tracks far enough to confirm that the two horses had recrossed the river at the ford, and then rode back to rejoin the others.

The sun was even hotter than it had been earlier, and the sky overhead was blindingly blue. But two of the innocent-looking cloud puffs to the northwest were boiling up into great cauliflowers of cloud, with dark smudges at their bases, and Roi thought he could feel electricity building in the air. Amber had already organized the others into rigging the horses, and Timi was tightening the last of the pack saddles as Roi and Penny rode in.

"We'll have to split up," Roi confirmed to the others as he saddled Raindrop. "Timi, remember the knoll where I got on Raindrop's rump to look ahead? As I recall, it fell away pretty fast toward the Surprise, and then leveled out again. Sort of a notch in the hillside. It's well out of the flood plain, and under a bank like that it should be safe from lightning, too. Penny and I will go after Token, and the rest of you get everything up to the notch and set up camp. Figure it's going to rain and maybe even hail, and there'll be high winds. Amber, you ride double with Timi since you're lightest, and Flame can ride Splash and carry Token's saddle. Our fugitives followed our route in at least as far as the ford, so we might as well stick together until their trail splits off." He pulled on a shirt and tunic and checked the contents of his saddlebags, then pulled an extra package of candy, their sleeping bags and a couple of weather sheets from the load of one of the packhorses. "Did anybody refill the canteens after lunch?"

"I took Splash and got them all topped off while Timi and Flame were loading the packhorses," Amber answered. "Yours and Penny's are on your saddles."

They retraced their path at a steady jog trot until they reached the spot Roi had suggested as a campsite. Token's trail had actually branched to the right slightly before that, but Roi had already decided that they would try to cut between the eloping horses and the Surprise, rather than risk spooking the mare into a possibly flooding river. The wild herd was still where his first mental sweep had found it, on the flood plain of the Surprise where a meander took the big river well north, and Token was headed straight for the herd.

Penny

"I shouldn't let you get away with just taking over like that," Penny said as the two of them moved their horses into a lope.

"You disagree with what I did?"

"No, I don't," Penny admitted. "But I'm supposed to be in charge."

Roi grinned at her. "Penny, if you see me heading off in the wrong direction, say something. Argue with me. I've got some abilities you don't, but you've got a lot of knowledge I don't. Put 'em together, and we should do better than either alone. But be realistic. If you say 'go left,' and I say 'go right,' I know which way Flame and Amber are going to go, and I'm pretty sure about Timi. Even if I tell them to obey you." He straightened slightly, and Raindrop slowed to a jog trot. "We've got a ways to go, and we'll need to alternate gaits."

The northwestern sky was dark gray, now. Half a dozen growing clouds were leaning toward them, their tops spreading into fibrous anvils and darker veils hanging from their bases. Occasional streaks of lighting showed in those veils, and the white that always showed at the corners of the spotted horses' eyes had expanded to rings. "Their hearing's better than ours," Roi said. "They don't like the thunder."

The rolling land around them was a bright golden green in the heat of the sun, and a light south wind barely rippled the grass. When they came to a drop in the land level, Penny could see the cloud shadows, continuous far to the west and north, and several groups of animals near the sunlit river that looped ahead of them. "There's the wild herd," Roi said, indicating one of the groups. "Let's see if we can push them to higher ground, and hope Token and the wild stud catch their scent and stay on high ground, too." He leaned forward, settling his weight over Raindrop's withers, and urged the grulla down the steep bank.

Penny looked down, gritting her teeth. Roi and Raindrop seemed to be having no problems. She urged Freckles over the edge.

Both horses broke into a lope at the base of the slope, aiming a little to the left of the horse herd. Penny could see the horses as individuals now, striped duns the size of a child's pony, with dark manes and tails and pale bellies. Several had foals at their sides, but she didn't see a stallion. The part of the warnoff that tagged the two riders as not dangerous held until they were almost between the herd and the river, the horses milling nervously. It was the storm that bothered them, Penny realized, and it was in the direction of the storm they wanted to drive them.

A pale yellow mare with points and stripes that were more brown than black stepped out of the herd toward them, trailed by a reddish foal. Roi turned in the saddle, untying his rain poncho. Abruptly he straightened, flapping the crackling synthetic toward the curious mare's face. "Get out of here," he yelled sharply. "You want to get drowned, you idiots?"

Raindrop and Freckles were almost as startled as the wild mares, but by the time Roi and Penny got their mounts under control, the wild horses were well on their way to a relatively gentle portion of the bluffs bordering the flood plain. "That ought to move them far enough," Roi said, jogging Raindrop toward the climb to higher ground. "Let's get up there ourselves. That storm's coming on fast."

Thunder was audible to the riders as well as their mounts by the time they started up the slope, and the shadows of the clouds rushed toward and over them as they topped the rise. A wave of grass rippled out of the dimness toward them, and a chill gust from the northwest made Penny glad they had both put on tunics. Hastily she turned to untie her own poncho and put it on.

"There they are," Roi said, pointing east to where sunlight still gilded the prairie. Squinting, Penny was able to make out a tiny white figure topping one of the distant rises. Then the shadow of the clouds swallowed the rise, and she lost sight of Token. They pushed their nervous horses into a hand gallop, converging on the line between Token and the spot where the wild herd was milling nervously. "If we can get close enough," Roi panted beside her, "I can get enough of a mental grip to bring her to me."

Both horses were clearly visible by the time Roi unexpectedly pulled Raindrop to a halt, spitting out an expletive Penny failed even to recognize. "What's the matter?" she gasped.

"Prairie dog town," he replied, eyes closed and a look of intense concentration on his face. "They've got a couple of hundred paces of it to cross. If they're walking, they should make it all right, but I don't want to risk spooking them into a run."

Penny looked down. Her eyes hadn't quite adjusted to the sudden darkness of the oncoming storm, but the shallow mounds of dirt and mowed-looking grass surrounding them were unmistakable. A gust of unexpectedly cold wind hit her in the face, and she shivered under her poncho.

The little dun stallion seemed well aware of the danger, nose tucked and watching where he put every foot as he drove Token toward the rest of his harem. The tall white mare, her chestnut spots invisible in the gloom, was shaking her head fretfully, tired enough to walk but nervous of the thunder, not watching her footing at all. Still, she wasn't too likely to injure herself at a walk. Penny's hair seemed to be crackling under the poncho hood, and Roi led them down slope to where they could barely see Token's back.

Lightning was striking closer, now, and abruptly a bolt snaked down to the top of the knoll the runaway mare had just left, followed almost at once by a deafening crash. The fugitive horses screamed and bolted, the dun with his nose still tucked, weaving and jumping to avoid the deadly holes, and Token in a panicked flat-out run. Roi sent Raindrop to meet her at a gallop, reins flying loose, and yelled back at Penny to grab the pommel and let Freckles have his head. For a moment she tried to hold Freckles back, but then she saw that Raindrop was running like the wild stud, dodging and leaping to avoid the holes, and realized that Roi must be feeling out the holes and guiding the horse around them. When she dropped her mount's reins she found she needed the pommel hold to stay on as Freckles swerved and jumped.

Another flash of lightning blinded her as the first huge raindrops hit her face, and as the thunder accompanying it died she heard the shriek of a horse in mortal pain. When a more distant flash allowed her to see again, Token was down, screaming and flailing as she struggled to regain her feet. Penny couldn't tell how much of the water on her face was rain and how much was tears.

Roi was well ahead of her, and she saw him fairly throw himself from Raindrop's back to the frantic mare's head, pinning it to the ground with his weight. She couldn't hear anything through the now constant crash of thunder, but she didn't have to. Token's right foreleg was bent at an impossible angle, the end of the broken bone thrusting through the blood-soaked skin. Numbly she reached for her force blade as she dismounted. She'd never had to kill a hopelessly injured horse before, but she'd been told how to do it if necessary. One deep, hard slash just behind the jaw, the horse trainer had explained. Don't hesitate or make a shallow cut; it would only prolong the suffering.

Roi looked up, shouting at her, but she couldn't hear him over the sound of the storm, only see him shaking his head wildly at her. *Not yet,* his mind-voice came into her awareness. *Get me the aid kit, and then hold her head down for me. And forget about cutting her throat. I'll stop her heart if I have to, but only if I can't take care of the leg.*

Penny stared at him for a moment, remembering how he'd Healed Rust's foot. But that had been merely skin. To save Token, the bone would have to be Healed to the point that the mare could put her weight on it within hours. "Roi, there's nothing we can do for her," she told him. "Why make her suffer any longer than she has to?"

You may not be able to do anything for her, he told her, *but I can if we can keep her from going any deeper into shock. There's counterShock and Suppress in the aid kit. Get it to me!*

Raindrop came back and rubbed her head against Penny's shoulder, trembling and asking for human company in this cacophony of sound and light. Sighing, Penny pulled open Roi's saddlebag, lifting out a box of candy as well as the aid kit. "You'd better eat while you're getting her drugged up," she told him."

Roi nodded. "Stick a few pieces in my mouth while I treat her for shock," he shouted in her ear as he opened the aid kit, shielding it from the sporadic rain with his body. Hastily he pulled out an ampoule of counterShock, triggering it and pressing it against the angle of the trembling mare's jaw, then a second as soon as the first dropped away. By then Penny had the candy open and thrust two pieces into his mouth, and he chewed while dosing the mare with a third ampoule. "One's good for a large person," he muttered indistinctly as he scrabbled through the aid kit for the Suppress, "so five ought to be about right for a horse." Hastily he pulled the cap off a tube of Suppress and rolled back the mare's lip to smear the green gel onto the pale gums.

"I can get those into her," Penny offered, and Roi promptly handed her the painkiller.

"Give her four more," he instructed as he applied a fourth ampoule of counterShock, "and then we'll see how she's responding. It's pretty hard to overdose on either, but I'm not sure five's enough for a horse."

By the time the fifth ampoule dropped away from the mare's throat, a little color was coming back into her gums. "It's working," Penny said shakily. "Roi, why'd you risk putting counterShock that close to a vein?"

"Not close, in," he replied. "There's nothing wrong with injecting counterShock directly into the bloodstream. You don't normally want to take the time to find a vein, so the instructions say just put it in anywhere." He scowled uneasily at the sky, now almost black and spitting increasing amounts of rain, and stood up. "I'm going to get the saddle blankets and a weather sheet over her," he said, reaching for Raindrop's girth. Hastily he unsaddled both horses, and to Penny's surprise had them lie down between the two saddles and threw a second weather sheet over both of them, tucking the sheet under the saddles against the wildly gusting wind. "Keep your head down and get under the weather sheet against Token's chest," he warned her as he wiggled under the sheet next to the mare's back. "There's hail on its way. I can deflect the biggest stones, but the little ones will sting. The weather sheet will help."

Penny had thought the first scattering of huge drops was heavy, but what came next was like being under a waterfall. She threw a fold of the weather sheet over the mare's head, half afraid the animal would drown in the downpour, and looked wide-eyed out into the flickering of the lighting. White chunks, some the size of her fist, were bouncing off the soaked ground all around them, and when she looked upward through the translucent sheet she could see similar chunks heading straight for them and then swerving aside. She still had Roi's candy, and she reached across Token's neck to shove another piece into his mouth.

She found it hard to believe how still the horses were. Token's eyes were closed and her breathing deep and even, as if she had been sedated. The other two horses were making odd little noises, barely audible above the thunder and the splashing of the hail, almost as if they were whimpering. But they remained motionless, heads flattened to the ground and eyes completely surrounded by white rings. "I'm holding them," Roi said. "Any more candy?" She gave him another piece, and watched his face as he chewed. A little strained, she thought, but nothing like he'd been after Healing Timi's ankle.

"I've got emergency bars in my saddlebags," she told him, and then wondered how she could get to them.

"The hail's about over," he said. "I'll eat a couple of the emergency bars before I start working on the bone. We'll have to rig a shelter nearby for tonight, and try to build a fire. I'll have her on her feet by tomorrow if I can save her at all, but we won't be able to move her more than a couple of hundred paces tonight."

The downpour slacked off as quickly as it had started. Roi pulled back the weather sheet and struggled to his feet. His whole side and back were coated with mud, and looking down, Penny was suddenly aware that both she and the injured horse were lying in a shallow sheet flow of muddy water. So were Raindrop and Freckles, though in their case the weather sheet had been tucked under a saddle on the uphill side and had deflected some of the flow. Penny picked herself up and joined Roi in getting the two horses to their feet.

"Do we have a spare creance anchor?" he asked her. "They need to move around a little, but I don't want them wandering off in this prairie dog mausoleum." He picked up a bedraggled scrap of fur from the puddle uphill of the saddle, and shook his head sadly as he examined it. A prairie dog, Penny saw, drowned in its burrow and washed out onto the surface. Looking around in the growing yellow light, she saw similar limp bundles in all directions.

Hers was the uphill saddle, Penny thought. Luckily the saddlebags were waterproof, and she found the emergency rations and then the emergency creance anchor. "It's only good for about twenty strides' radius," she warned him as she set it up and Roi activated the units on the horses' neck ropes. "And I'd still like to know how Token got away wearing one."

"The stud bit it in two," Roi replied. "The electronics are in a cheap, weak, orange plastic box, and he chomped on it. Probably thought the warning buzz was some kind of insect. I hope it bit him hard enough to teach him that big orange bugs sting. I spotted some of the shards back where the trail crossed the creance boundary." He walked back to Token and knelt by her broken leg. "Let me get this tack-healed, and we'll see if we can find something dry enough to burn. We all need a fire."

"What can I do to help?" Penny asked.

Roi frowned at the twisted leg. "It's the leg on the side under her," he said, "so the ground will hold it fairly straight. See if you can scrape up enough mud to make a kind of raised platform, so it doesn't keep getting soaked. I'll clean out the mud that's already in it while I'm getting it lined up properly. I know, it looks awful. But I sterilized it and made sure the circulation was all right while I was getting the drugs into her, and it's a clean break. Should heal fine. I'll have a couple of the emergency bars while we're getting it propped up, and then you just keep poking candy into my mouth while I'm Healing."

There was a shovel—more of a trowel, really—in the emergency pack in Penny's saddlebag, and the rain that had fallen on high ground had run off so rapidly that the disturbed soil near the prairie dog holes was barely damp beneath the surface. Penny used her force blade to cut a square from one of the weather sheets and troweled a stack of the relatively dry dirt onto it. Roi nodded approval and had her wrap the weather sheet around the dirt into a kind of sausage that he then placed lengthwise under Token's leg, molding it to support the knee, cannon bone, and fetlock.

"Start poking in the candy," he said, and wrapped his hands carefully around the break. Gently he manipulated the fracture, straightening and aligning the bone until the leg lay fully supported and straight on the weather sheet, the bones back under the skin. Windows of blue sky began to appear in the west, and small islands of sunshine moved over the soaked landscape. As Roi finally sighed and dropped his hands away the sun found their knoll, lighting Roi's muddy white hair and the mare's muddy white coat with equal clarity.

Penny looked around, blinking in the sudden brilliance. "Did it work?" she asked Roi.

"It's tack-healed," he replied. "The blood vessels and nerves are completely healed. The bones and tendons and ligaments are sort of tacked into place. If she were a person, I'd put her arm in a sling and tell her to take it easy for a fiveday or two. Since she's a horse and she can't rest the leg for a fiveday, I'll give her a couple more sessions tonight and by morning the bone will be back to around three-quarter strength. She won't be rideable for a couple of days, but I doubt we'll get back across the Bird River that fast, anyway. She shouldn't stay flat too long, so I'll get her on her feet while I'm holding the injured tissues together in a couple of hours, and walk her out of the prairie dog town. Right now, let's find a camping place and see if we can get a fire started. I know I was broiling most of the day, but right now I can't even quite remember what it feels like to be too hot."

Their biggest problem turned out to be firewood. Trees grew only in stream bottoms, and the sheet wash that had piled mud over their own bodies was only a small sample of what had flowed into the streams. What had been a dry swale with a few trees that morning was a neck-deep torrent tonight. Even the Surprise had swollen enough to flood the groves along its banks.

"We'll have to try for a small tree that's uprooted and floating," Roi said as they walked back to the horses. The sun was glittering on the wet grass, but they hardly noticed that or the rainbow against the still-dark sky to the east. "What have we got with us, Penny?"

"Water, fire-starters, aid kits, a couple of emergency food bars, rain ponchos, sleeping bags and a couple more weather sheets wrapping them, air blankets, and rope," Penny replied. "And the clothes we're wearing. I wish we'd thought to grab our jackets."

"I wasn't thinking cold," Roi replied. "You start ferrying stuff to the campsite we picked, and I'll take Raindrop and try to rope us some firewood. Do we have enough food? I'm going to need quite a bit more to finish Healing Token."

"Half a box of candy and a couple of days' worth of emergency rations," she told him. "And all the roast prairie dog we can eat if you can manage a fire."

He grinned tiredly at her as he swung onto Raindrop's back. "I'll manage."

Chapter 10

Flame opened her eyes to grayness. The tent was still in place, she saw with some relief, and the saddles and packs were piled, wrapped in weather sheets, where they had left them. Timi's buckskin leopard was a misty silhouette grazing just in front of the tent, and the telltale on the creance anchor showed five active units in range, as it should. The way the fog thickened down slope, Flame thought, the other four horses could have been just beyond Dusty and she'd never have seen them.

The three slaves had shared a double sleeping bag the night before, huddling together for warmth and comfort after the fury of the storm. For Flame, there had been a huge, Roi-shaped hole in their togetherness. She wasn't even worried about Roi, really. They'd touched minds briefly around sunset, long enough to confirm that both groups had weathered the storm successfully, and for Roi to tell Flame that Token had been injured and he didn't want to move her that evening. She suspected that he'd left about as much out of his report as she had out of hers, but the texture of his mind had confirmed that he was unhurt. Still, she missed him more than she had thought possible.

She glanced over at Timi and Amber, sound asleep in each other's arms, then carefully wiggled out of the sleeping bag and into her clothes. The horses came at the sound of a moving human being, looking hopefully for their morning grain. They'd be working lightly if at all today, she thought, so she gave them only a handful apiece before pulling on her jacket and climbing to the top of the knoll.

The fog was pinkish gold to the east, and when she tipped her head back she saw blue sky showing overhead. Like the fog the morning before they had glided off the mountain front, she thought. Just a thin layer. It didn't feel as if it would be a hot day, but the fog would probably clear off. She wondered how long it would take Roi to get back, and resisted the impulse to attempt contact. He might easily have spent a good part of the night Healing an injured horse, and need every moment of sleep he could get. She hoped Penny had at least overcome her prudishness enough to hold him against his nightmares.

The grass was almost wetter than it had been after the storm, and she slipped a time or two as she worked her way back down the knoll. For a moment she thought she had lost herself in the fog—surely she had come downhill far enough to be level with their camping spot! Then she heard a horse stamp and whuffle off to her right, and when she followed the sound she discovered she had simply headed off the knoll in the wrong direction.

Timi and Amber were still asleep. Flame pulled back the weather sheet wrapped over the firewood Timi had insisted on collecting before the storm, and pulled out an armload of small branches. Timi might upset her at times, but she could do nothing but praise his behavior last night. Maybe the problem between the two boys was simply that Timi needed more responsibility, Flame thought as she built a small fire on the ashes of the one they'd managed to build after the storm.

She didn't want to lose herself again in the fog, so she used water from one of the canteens to fill the pot. Her own preference for a morning stimulant was chocolate rather than coffee, and she took advantage of being the first one up to please herself. If the other two wanted coffee, they could fix their own.

"Mmm," Amber's voice came from behind Flame. "Smells good. I take it the world's still here?"

"What little I can see of it," Flame replied. "I don't think the fog's very deep. Look, it's lighter to the east, even here."

"Did you contact Roi yet?"

Flame shook her head. "I didn't want to wake him up. He was awfully tired last night, Amber. I think he did a lot more Healing on Token than he admitted."

Amber chuckled. "Oh, we'll have some stories to tell on both sides when we get back together." She pulled her clothes into the sleeping bag and began to wiggle into them. "Ugh, these are still damp. But we got off easy, all things considered."

"And how," Timi yawned next to her. "Fogged in, huh? Flame, didn't you cook breakfast yesterday?"

"It's Roi's turn, but he's not here," Flame replied. "Anyway, you two were still asleep, and I was hungry."

"Missing Roi?" Timi asked, with surprising perception. "It's all right, Flame; I wasn't trying to scold you or anything. And that chocolate really does smell good. There's no need for you to pick up a double share of the work just because Roi's not here, though. Amber and I can help."

Flame turned her face away, blinking back tears. "Well, I do miss him," she said.

"Of course you do," Amber said. "We all do, but Timi and I have each other, so you feel it most. Here, I'll make some stick biscuits to toast over the coals."

"Any idea what it looks like higher up, Flame?" Timi asked as he pulled on his clothing.

"Blue overhead on top of the knoll," she replied, and felt herself blushing. "I almost got lost coming back down, though."

"Too many possible directions to go down," Timi grinned as he sealed his jacket. "I'll take a creance compass."

"I'd worry about coming straight over the bank," Amber said.

"Oh, I'll come back at an angle, and cut across when the beacon points cross slope," Timi assured them as he walked into the fog.

The two girls looked at each other, both suppressing giggles. "Nice job," Flame said. She was as aware as Amber that it would never have occurred to Timi that the direct line to the creance anchor would lead over the bank above the tent.

"He doesn't like being told things," Amber replied. "Some kind of male pride thing. Stupid. Let's finish making breakfast."

***

Flame?

Flame jerked her head up. The three had finished breakfast and tidied their camp, and Timi was considering what they should do next. "Roi's calling," she said aloud even as she gave the R'il'noid a warm mental hug.

How's the weather your way?

Fog. It's starting to break up, though.

Same here. I'd say another hour and it'll clear. Flame, any chance one of you could head up this way once it does? Don't take chances, but I'd like to know what kind of condition the creeks and swales are in. I'd just as soon give Token another day's rest if we can't get through all the way. And we could use our jackets, and some food. I ate a lot last night.

"He'd like a report on the creeks once the fog lifts," Flame said, "and some food if one of us can get through to him."

"You girls are the better riders," Timi said. "Flame, why don't you take Dusty and head west, and Amber can check the Bird River. Don't try to ford anything you're not sure of, Flame. Better yet, contact Roi every time you hit water you can't ride around, and have him guide you. Amber, you check the Bird and relay the conditions there to Roi, and then head back here. I'll see if I can find some more firewood, since it looks like we'll be here another night, at least."

Flame chuckled. "Roi says fine on the travel plans and he ought to leave you in charge more often. But don't count on finding any wood that's not underwater. They didn't have a chance to set up camp until after the storm, and he had to rope a dead tree that was floating down a tributary for firewood. All the spots with trees got flooded. The part of yesterday's trail that was near the river was completely under water last night."

An hour later, both girls headed out of camp under sunny skies. Flame was carrying jackets and extra food supplies for Roi and Penny, and if she could reach them, she would stay the night. Roi had insisted on constant light contact with both girls, and she could feel his mind in hers, comfortable and familiar, and a hint of Amber's beyond.

There was evidence of running water in several low spots on the trail. Grass was flattened toward the Surprise, and there were a couple of new gullies. A creek that had bubbled finger deep the day before was a muddy torrent. Amber's report on the Bird River came in while Flame was riding along the creek bank deciding where to cross, and Roi passed Amber's images on to Flame.

There must have been more than one storm on the Bird yesterday, Flame thought as she looked at the formerly small river through Amber's eyes. The muddy water was swirling through the treetops almost up to the level of the surrounding prairie. The meadow where they had left the horses, the swimming hole, the cottonwood they had swung from—even the spring must be under the racing water. *You'll have to filter the mud out of the water and then use purifier tablets,* Roi's mind-voice relayed Penny's instructions.

The creek water seemed to be moving at the same speed everywhere, Flame decided, so it should be shallowest where it was widest, and that was where the trail crossed, anyway. She relayed the thought to Roi, who seemed to have some reservations but agreed on her choice of crossing. Dusty was nervous but far more cooperative than Token, and they crossed without incident. *The water was above his knees, though, and really fast,* she told Roi.

Likely you'll hit worse, he warned her. *But we really need those supplies, if you can get through.*

She stayed on the trail they had followed the day before as long as she could, but when it dropped down a shallow incline to run near the Surprise she found herself heading down into the river. When she swung Dusty around and sent him back up the bank and then along the edge of the bluff rising over the trail, she saw that the Surprise, while not filling its flood plain, had spread out in broad silver runnels, filling old channels and making new ones. Those parts of the flood plain not under water were islands where herds of bison, camels and horses milled nervously. A group of mammoths were testing the water between their island and the bluff, and as she watched, they waded into the swirling current. Two calves were in the group, and the adults stayed carefully upstream from the youngsters. The water was not deep enough to force the adults off their feet, but only the uplifted trunks of the calves showed. Flame was relieved to see both calves scramble out of the water almost at the place where she herself had left the trail.

There must have been storms all over yesterday, Flame thought, to put that much water into the Surprise. Of course the river had been rising for several days. Penny had said that snow melt in the mountains to the west was producing normal spring floods. But Flame had never expected to find the main trail under water.

Dusty snorted and shook his head, and Flame sent him on, west and north. *Roi,* she thought at him, *should the Surprise be that high? I'm having to swing pretty far north.*

That's fine, his answer came. *You're heading pretty near straight toward us. We're camped just east of a tributary a little smaller than the Bird. There's one more good-sized creek between us, and you may have to cut away from the Surprise to cross it. But you don't have to worry about getting lost. You're only a little distance from where we dropped onto the flood plain to chase the wild herd up onto the bluffs.*

The rolling upland rotated slowly behind Flame as she rode on. The sun gleamed on the wet grass around her, and she noticed that here even the grass on gentle slopes had been washed flat by the pouring rain. Some of the vegetation looked bruised and cut, and once she saw a small drift of what looked like fast-melting chunks of ice. The soil, however, remained unexpectedly dry underfoot, with only a thin, treacherously slick coating of mud. *It came down so fast the surface mud sealed the ground and the rest couldn't sink in,* Roi's voice came into her mind. *And yes, that really is ice. We had quite a hailstorm here.*

We had a little, but only fingertip size, she told him. *We did have a tornado, though. I'll tell you about it when I get there.*

The ground was dropping ahead of her again, and water was rushing across the trail. This time she didn't even consider crossing where she was; the water looked more than swimming deep for Dusty and it gave the impression of moving faster than she thought the horse could gallop. Time to head upstream, she thought, and tried to reach out to Roi with a mental picture of her situation.

That's the one I was worried about, he confirmed. *Penny says it may be fordable half an hour's ride upstream, but contact me again before you try it.*

Flame turned north and trotted Dusty upstream, looking for a place where the water slowed or spread out. Her shadow fell almost directly ahead, and where the vegetation was beginning to recover from its beating, a halo showed around the shadow's head. The air had warmed to the point that Flame pulled off her jacket and tied the sleeves around her waist. She had so much tied to the saddle already that there was no place to fasten the jacket.

The ground leveled and then dipped a little, and the horse splashed across a small side stream, then another. After the third side stream, the main channel to her left seemed to open out, and Flame halted Dusty. *I think I might be at the crossing point,* she thought at Roi.

How many dips have you crossed? he whispered into her mind.

Three with side streams.

That should be it. Take a good look around for me, then back Dusty a couple of lengths so I've got a clear space to 'port to.

Flame obeyed, opening her mind completely to give Roi the coordinates he needed and pivoting Dusty all the way around, looking at the full circle of her surroundings so Roi could see them. Then she dismounted and led Dusty away. A moment later, Roi was suddenly there, dropping a finger's width to the ground where she had just been and turning to smile at her. His golden eyes had dark smudges under them, and there was a weariness in his stance that she hadn't felt in his mind touch.

Flame's eyes filled with tears as she ran to him and flung her arms around him. "You're all right? You're really all right? Oh, Roi, you look so tired. You didn't have nightmares on top of everything else, did you?" If he had, she'd have something to say to Penny, she thought grimly.

Roi hugged her back. "No, I didn't have nightmares. I was too tired to. Flame, we were both so wet and so cold last night that even Penny couldn't object to our sleeping together, and I don't want you teasing her about it. I'm tired because I've had to do a lot of Healing on Token. She broke her leg, and since she has to walk on it, I've had to Heal for full strength right away. And we're a little short on food for that much work. Roast prairie dog is good protein, and we're smoking some meat from a bison calf we found killed by one of the really big hailstones, and pit roasting the ribs for supper. But I need carbohydrates to Heal, and we're short on those."

Flame grinned. "Not now you're not," she said. "I've got biscuit makings, dried eggs, dry milk, and dried fruit as well as a couple of days' worth of freeze-dried stuff and a tent. And the rest of the candy." She paused to dig into her right saddlebag for the candy. "Here. Get this into you before you try to feel out that jumped-up brook."

Roi sighed with relief as he chewed on the candy. "Bet we're setting some kind of record for sugar consumption on a trek like this," he commented. "Penny says she's never had so many problems that justified esper work before." He reached out to scratch Dusty behind the ears. "Timi didn't mind your taking off with his horse?"

Flame snorted. "Gives him an excuse not to ride anywhere," she replied. "Roi, how long before you think we can get across the Bird River?"

Roi frowned and looked northwest, where puffy clouds were beginning to build up. Surely not another storm like yesterday's, Flame thought, and glanced anxiously over at Roi, who grinned back at her. "Not like yesterday," he agreed, "but I think we could get enough more rain today upstream to keep the larger streams pretty high. I doubt we'll get across the Bird tomorrow, anyway. And I don't really want to take Token across our little brook here today, for that matter. I think Dusty can do it all right, but—mmm. Be easier for him unloaded. I can 'port the saddle and load across. Want to try a teleport yourself, Flame? It'd save you a swim in that muddy water."

Flame looked at him in surprise. "Can you teleport me? I thought you said teleporting people was the hardest thing there was."

Roi grinned. "Not compared to Healing. It is hard for the same reason as Healing, though. Most people are convinced it can't happen, so they don't let it happen. You're very used to working with me mentally, and I think you trust me enough to accept what's reality for me. Want to try?"

"If you're sure it won't be too hard on you. You still look tired, Roi."

"Not as tired as I was before that candy," he replied as he unsaddled Dusty and tied one end of Flame's saddle rope to the horse's neck rope. "You did bring a load, didn't you? Let me get this across first, and then we'll try." He hefted the saddle and studied the far bank, and suddenly the saddle with everything Flame had tied to it was lying on the grass across the erstwhile brook.

"Easy as that?" she asked, and he grinned back.

"Easy as that. Just stand with your back to me, Flame, and lean against me. Look across the stream, just left of the saddle. Now close your eyes and go wide open, so you're seeing through my eyes. That's good. Try to relax your mind completely, and let mine be the only reality. Don't fight it when the scene changes; just imagine it's a scene cut in an entertainment chip. Want to be standing next to the saddle."

Flame looked at the saddle through Roi's eyes, trying to wish herself next to it, on the other side of the swirling water, with Dusty on the far bank. She could imagine how Dusty would look from the other side, lifting his head in sudden surprise to see them there .... "Attagirl," Roi chuckled behind her, giving her waist a sudden squeeze. Flame opened her eyes and gasped in shock. Dusty nickered plaintively from across the creek, and the saddle was almost brushing her left leg. "I didn't even have to work at it; you were right there helping out." He turned her around and kissed her, then continued to hold her against him as he looked over at the bewildered horse. "Come on, Dusty," he called as the end of the rope uncoiled itself and floated across the stream to him, "I'll steady you if you need it. It's just a little swim."

The horse switched his black-streaked white tail nervously and stepped toward them until his striped front hooves were planted just at the edge of the water. He lowered his head and snorted at the muddy water, shifting his front feet. Then, as Roi repeated his call and took up the slack in the rope, he plunged into the water. Within a few paces he was swimming strongly, only his head above the water. The swirling water carried him rapidly downstream, and for a moment Flame almost panicked. The bank steepened downstream of the former ford, and she was afraid the horse wouldn't be able to climb out. She glanced anxiously at Roi, who was frowning in concern, and then back at Dusty. The horse gave a sudden heave as his feet touched bottom, struggling upstream and toward the break in the bank.

"Good boy," Roi called gently, keeping the rope snug, "that's it. Come on, now, here to me. Flame, get him a little grain, would you? Come on, Dusty. Careful, that's a slick spot. That's it, almost here. Steady, steady, ah, that's a good boy." He took hold of the neck rope and led the horse the last few steps out of the creek. Flame was waiting with the grain, and Dusty chewed it eagerly while Roi and Flame pressed as much water as they could from his coat.

"There's some dead branches hung up just upstream," Flame pointed out. "Why don't we build a fire and have lunch and let him dry out in the sun?"

"Good idea. I'm still hungry. And I told Penny to saddle and bridle Raindrop and let her go if I called her. She should be here by the time Dusty's dried off a little."

"If he'd just stop rolling in the wet grass," Flame agreed.

Penny

Penny glanced around the crude camp. Raindrop's creance was attached to Token's neck rope, and for extra security Penny had tied the mare to their log with the saddle rope. The dead tree Roi had managed to drag out of the stream the night before was mostly broken up for firewood, though the thickest part of the trunk remained. Penny had spread the still-damp sleeping bags on it to dry, as well as using it as an anchor for Token. Supper was cooking in the pit they had dug with the trowel-like shovel, and there really seemed nothing left to do. Except, perhaps, a nap. Penny had not slept well the night before.

It wasn't that Roi had tried anything. He'd simply snuggled up against her and gone to sleep within minutes. She hadn't quite expected that, and the feel of his bare skin against hers had been disturbing. It had been well after midnight before she had finally dozed off, and she hadn't been able to sleep again once she felt him stir.

Penny glanced over at Token. The mare was grazing quietly, barely favoring the leg she'd broken. Penny still found it hard to believe that it was the same leg she'd seen with the bone sticking through the skin the night before. Roi had assured her that the wild herd, including the stallion, was trapped on the far side of Bison Creek to the west, so at least they didn't have to worry about a repeat of Token's abduction.

She walked over to check the green alder fire they had built to smoke thin strips of the bison meat. There had been plenty of uprooted trees floating down Bison Creek this morning, and Roi's ability to tie his saddle rope around a distant object telekinetically had brought them several freshly uprooted alders as well as enough additional dead wood to start a smoky fire. They had built a teepee covered with the dead calf's skin to keep the smoke in, and the meat would be cured enough to keep for a few days by morning.

What was really bothering her, she finally admitted to herself, was the scattering of the group for which she was responsible. It hadn't been so bad while Roi was with her and in contact with the other three. But since he had teleported off to help Flame, she had no contact at all with the other two groups. Raindrop's behavior in coming abruptly to her half an hour earlier and then trotting back and forth between her and the saddle had told her that Roi wanted the horse saddled and turned loose. They had agreed to that before he had left, vanishing with an abruptness that still sent chills down her back. But she felt more alone than ever, left with only Token and Freckles for company.

She made a last quick check of the camp and decided she might as well crawl into her sleeping bag and try to catch up on the sleep she had lost. Within minutes she was asleep.

She woke to the sound of suppressed voices, and blinked in surprise to find the sun low in the western sky. "Sorry," she heard Roi's voice as she pulled herself out of the sleeping bag, "we didn't mean to wake you up."

"It's about time somebody did," Penny replied. They had rebuilt the cooking fire, she saw, and it had burned down to a fine bed of coals. "How long have you two been back?"

"Couple of hours," Roi replied. "We stopped and had lunch after we crossed that so-called creek. What did you call it? Mosquito Creek? It was running a little fast for mosquitoes today. The water dropped some just during the hour or so we were there, though, so I'd guess it'll be passable even for Token by tomorrow afternoon. 'Specially if I get in a couple more Healing sessions."

"He did one more already," Flame said, "and I've got the dried vegetables soaking and the biscuits ready for the final mixing. Ready for supper?"

Penny's stomach growled, and the guide flushed with embarrassment. "I think I forgot lunch," she said sheepishly. "I crashed right after you left, Roi."

"Not used to sleeping with someone?" Flame grinned. Roi gave her a warning look, but she continued, "Actually, he takes quite a bit of seducing. At least the first time. He's perfectly safe, just to stay warm."

Penny's face was burning, and Roi's skin looked darker than usual. The worst part was Penny's own awareness that it was Roi's apparent indifference, as much as his physical closeness, that had bothered her. But she wasn't about to say that in his hearing.

"Let's get supper going," Roi said firmly, and Flame, catching his implied rebuke at last, dumped the waiting water into a plastic bag of biscuit makings and kneaded the bag to mix it. Roi got the trowel and began digging down to their improvised oven, and Penny put the foil package of vegetables on the fire to cook. By the time Roi had dug far enough to let out the mouth-watering smell of the roasting ribs, Flame had wrapped the biscuit dough in spirals around green alder branches and was toasting the stick biscuits over the coals.

***

"So how did you three weather the storm?" Penny asked after they had taken the edge off their hunger.

Flame grinned and licked roast bison juices off her fingers. "Well, we didn't have the hail you did," she replied. "But it was interesting, all the same. Roi, Timi did a marvelous job. I'd never have thought to get in firewood before the storm, but he and Amber went back to the Bird River on Dusty and Splash as soon as the tent was set up, and they dragged firewood and I stacked it almost until the rain hit us. Then he insisted we hobble the horses and creance them short. Amber and I really argued with him on that; we thought they should have a chance to graze. But Timi said if it got really bad he wanted to know exactly where they were.

"Then the clouds covered the sun and the sky got kind of a funny brassy color. Amber was up on the knoll, and she came sliding down looking really pale and saying a tornado was coming. I looked, and there was this long thing like a mammoth's trunk hanging down to the northwest, swaying around like the mammoth was hunting for a particularly nice bit of grass. We couldn't tell exactly which way it was moving, but it was coming more or less toward us. Timi said you'd picked the best place; that likely it'd come off the ground a bit if it went over the knoll, and we should hobble the horses and creance them tight right beside the tent and lie down ourselves.

"We could hear it roaring by then, and see lighting flashing inside the trunk. Then Timi made me lie down flat, but I lay on my back so I could see. Roi, it went right over us, but Timi was right. It came swooping over the knoll touching the ground—the grass on top was all swirled and torn up—but it didn't seem to be able to lengthen fast enough to come down right away when it went over that little bluff. It was like a big swirling tube over us, with lightning crackling all around the walls, and then about fifty paces beyond us it hit the ground again and dirt and grass just exploded up.

"The horses were screaming and fighting the creances and the hobbles, and a couple threw themselves trying to get away, but if they hadn't been tied close, it would have killed them. We all wished you were there to calm them down, though. That's one thing Timi was hopeless at, but at least he knows it and let Amber and me talk to them until they quieted down enough we could get the hobbles off without their striking out at us. The only really good one was Dusty. He rolled his eyes and shook so hard I thought he'd fall down, but he didn't fight the hobbles." She looked affectionately over at the horse, his tan body spots almost invisible in the gathering dusk beyond the fire. The sky lit up briefly to the northwest, where clouds had continued to gather through the afternoon, and Flame hugged herself briefly, glancing anxiously at Roi.

"Dusty," Penny said, "is about as close to fool-proof as they come. But standing still through a tornado is more than I'd have expected, even from him. Thank goodness we didn't have to go through *that* with Token."

"I probably could have held her down," Roi said, "but the hailstorm was bad enough. At least we got some fresh meat out of it." He reached over to cut himself another piece of the roast bison. "Any more biscuits, Flame?"

"Now how did I know you'd ask that?" the redhead grinned, and reached behind her for several additional dough-wrapped sticks. "Here, toast your own."

***

The next morning dawned clear and crisp, and Penny found herself missing the warmth of Roi's body against hers. Flame had brought one of the small tents with her as well as her own sleeping bag. Penny had chosen to sleep alone, but she had been sharply aware of the sounds coming from the double bag shared by the two on the other side of the tent.

No sense staying in bed, she decided, pulling on her jacket and walking over to the embers of last night's fire. By the time Roi and Flame woke, she had coffee brewing and biscuit dough, flavored with the chopped remains of last night's roast, cooking in the roasting pit. Token was staying close to the fire, her ears pricked and nostrils wide to the smell of baking bread, and Penny had chased her away twice by the time Roi crawled out of the tent.

"I'll give her another session while you're finishing up breakfast," he offered. "That'll keep her out of our food, at least. And I was so impressed by her being willing to pull the wings," he added disgustedly.

"She really is a good horse, usually," Penny said apologetically. "Of course the shots leave her physiologically in foal, so we don't have all this nonsense when they work."

"She's in foal now, I suspect," Roi said, his voice amused, "though I sure don't know what it'll turn out looking like. Probably the wild stud'll dominate."

Penny looked at him in astonishment. "You really think that little pipsqueak managed to breed her? Roi, they're not even the same species. And she was half again his height, at least."

"And cooperating to the hilt," Roi replied. "I don't know the details, Penny, but as a Healer I can tell you she's been bred. And unless I've really lost my touch, it took."

Penny groaned. "Oh, the Company's going to love this. At least we got her back. What really scares them is getting domestic blood into the wild herds. Roi, is there anything you could do to get her out of heat?"

Roi cocked his head and looked thoughtful. "Mmm—Marna hasn't taught me much about that, but I could try. It wouldn't hurt her, but it

139

might mess up the pregnancy. Her being in foal will do it soon enough, though."

"Great," Penny assured him. "As long as she can be ridden."

***

They spent the rest of the morning packing the smoked meat and breaking up camp. Roi had contacted Amber, who assured them that the Bird River, while still not fordable, had dropped to little more than half of its crest level. Token was walking and trotting completely sound, and by the end of the late morning Healing session, Roi could no longer detect any difference between the foreleg he had Healed and the uninjured one.

"You stay on Dusty 'til we get back, Flame, just to be sure," he told her as they prepared to saddle up shortly after their noon meal. "Token can carry the smoked meat and the food you brought, though."

"I hadn't noticed there was much left of the food I brought," Flame replied. "You were even hungrier than I thought."

They crossed Mosquito Creek at what they all now called Dusty's ford. The horses were belly-deep in a swifter than normal current, but the bottom was firm and the ford was uneventful. None of the smaller creeks and swales was still flooded, and they made good time back to the Bird River camp.

A month ago, Penny thought, she would have assumed that Roi's suggestion that Timi take more responsibility in setting up camps, and even his enthusiastic praise for the job Timi had done, was a bit of slave management to get out of work himself. After close to a month with the group, she recognized that what Roi was trying to do was help Timi along toward eventual freedom. One of the things she herself had been taught to do was a similar transfer of responsibility to her clients through the progress of a trek. Roi, she thought wryly, was going to be just as nervous at standing back and not interfering with Timi's decisions as she was when the time came to let her average client take a decision she herself would not have made. She was pleased to see Timi turn to Roi and say, "Look, you'll still warn me if one of your hunches is acting up, won't you?" and equally pleased to hear Roi say that of course he would, if Timi wanted him to.

The exchange took place as they were all riding over to have a look at the Bird River ford. The sun was low and red behind them, casting long

140

violet shadows that had Raindrop snorting and dancing at the movements of the strange purple creature on the grass. The other four had seen the area before, either through their own eyes or relayed by Roi's telepathy, but for Penny the flood wrack, caught high in the broken trees, was as much of a shock as the opaque churning of the water through a deep new channel where the ford had been. When they rode upstream along the high bank, they were able to look down at the beaver meadow, now just a wide portion of the river. Only the cottonwood, the limb they had swung from now a broken splinter, showed where the swimming hole had been, and there was no trace of the spring. If they had camped in the valley, they would never have survived.

Penny pulled her map from its case and keyed it for the Bird River. She knew it would no longer be accurate, but it was all the information they had. "There are a couple of possible fords upstream," she said, "but there's no telling how the flood altered them."

"So we go look tomorrow," Roi said cheerfully. "Would a current satellite image be within the Challenge parameters, Penny? And more candy? We're so low on candy I thought I might 'path Kyrie tonight and ask if she's still overloaded with the stuff. Be easy enough to ask for a satellite image. I doubt there'd be a new chip yet, but we could even try for that."

Penny relaxed and smiled. "It'd be downright wonderful, Roi. Ask her by all means."

Chapter 11

Falaron: Penny
5/15/38

The woodland-dotted prairie rolled to the edge of vision around the travelers, unchanging and unvarying in the broad distance, but constantly showing new aspects of itself at their feet. Tight whorls of leaves became buds that opened into flowers of every possible color, shade and shape. Birds that postured and displayed and sang, as they had near the mountain front, became less common, and hidden nests began to appear almost under their feet. Insects whirred and buzzed and clicked and fluttered around them, pursued by bank swallows and martins that in turn were alert to the hawks that rode the blue sky above them, a sky so huge and far away it made the five riders dizzy to look at it.

They had crossed the Bird six days earlier, after spending most of the day working their way upstream, crossing one swollen tributary after another. Finally they found a spot where Penny had felt it was safe to cross: a wide, shallow, slow-moving stretch.

Roi had been rightly uncertain about the safety of their crossing place, but had allowed himself to be overruled by the others. One of the packhorses and gone down in an unexpected hole. Before Roi could react, a floating tree had caved in the panicked animal's skull. Without the horse's mind to focus on, he had been unable even to salvage the animal's load, which had included most of their foodstuffs.

They were moving steadily east and down slope, journeying from spring into summer and from mountain-shadowed near-desert just east of the mountain front through shortgrass prairie with gallery forests along the rivers to tallgrass prairie with well-wooded river bottoms and increasingly frequent patches of trees even on higher ground. Antelope, camels and ground sloths were becoming rarer, replaced by deer. Mammoths, longhorn bison and the little striped horses remained common, grazing in ever more numerous herds, and the riders caught regular glimpses of the dire wolves, lions, short-faced bears and sabertooths that preyed on the larger herbivores, as well as seeing coyotes that were growing fat on young rabbits and ground-nesting birds.

By this time, the surviving packhorses were carrying little more than the tents and sleeping gear. Fishing was poor in the aftermath of the flood, and the Surprise still ran more than bank-full. Small stones were nonexistent in the deep soil of the prairie, so Penny had tried to bake a number of small clay weights in the previous night's campfire. She had fastened them together as bolas this morning, but the clay was of marginal quality and so far their efforts had brought only a rabbit and two grouse to hang at her saddlebow, and those at the cost of shattering almost a third of the crude weights.

Penny still found it hard to believe how completely Token had recovered. The red leopard mare was jogging shoulder to shoulder with Raindrop in the lead of the little party, both horses moving as soundly as the day they had left the cabin by the mountain front. As Penny watched, Flame suddenly rose in her stirrups, whirling the bola around her head twice before sending it into the tall grass to her left. She was off Token almost at once, running to the spot where she had aimed the weighted thongs. Roi had caught Token's reins, and Penny thought he looked a little green as Flame dropped to her knees to kill and clean her captive. But when the red-haired girl rose to her feet, holding the headless and gutted hare by its rear legs, he managed to smile and say, "Good throw, Flame."

Killing came hard to a Healer, Penny supposed. If it hadn't been for that thought, she would have had little patience with Roi, whose need for extra food to support his Healing had combined with the flood delay and the loss of the packhorse to leave them almost out of food. He had refused even to try the bolas, insisting he would never be able to kill a healthy animal and then eat it. In fairness, she had to admit that he had offered to teleport in food, and that she herself had vetoed the suggestion. A few missed meals were not an emergency, she had pointed out.

It was too bad that there were so few carbohydrate-rich plant foods available this time of year. Tubers had already given their stored food to new shoots, and it was too early for seeds or berries. Penny could only hope that the floods hadn't taken out the cache that should be within a day's travel, and that the Company had stocked it well enough that they could replenish their travel foods.

Roi was moving Raindrop away from Token, his head down and his attention obviously fixed. Probably some new kind of flower, Penny thought, exasperated. "Roi," she said sharply, "don't go wandering off like that." Freckles snorted and shook his head, sidling beneath her weight, and she brushed at an insect buzzing around his ears.

"Bees," Roi replied absently, and Penny took a closer look at the insects flying busily among the wild roses and clover around them. Fat, striped little insects, neatly patterned in gold and black, their wings buzzing as they darted from flower to flower. "Got a container, Penny? I think I can reach them mentally enough to keep them from stinging me, and they should have enough honey by now to spare a little."

The eggs they could gather and the animals they had managed to kill would provide protein and a little fat, but they needed carbohydrates, too, especially Roi. If Roi could find the bees' home base, the stored honey could provide what they needed. "Do they have enough minds for you to reach them, even to find their nest?" she asked doubtfully, pulling one of the packhorses up beside Freckles and digging a covered water bucket out of its load.

"They're heading that way," he replied, nodding toward a clump of trees to their left as he dismounted and hung his helmet on his saddle. "I'll leave Raindrop here with you and follow them on foot. If I should come back running, have her ready for me to mount fast." He slung the coils of his saddle rope around one shoulder, took the bucket from Penny and started toward the little copse, head up as he watched the returning bees.

Penny shifted uneasily in the saddle as she watched him walk away. She didn't think he was in any real danger. The warnoff he wore would protect him against most stings, and there had been nothing in his records to suggest any tendency toward allergic reactions. Still, it went against the grain to let one of her clients, even one as sensible as Roi, separate himself from the rest of the group.

He shrank as she watched, becoming little more than a smudge of bronze between the scarlet of his riding breeches and the white of his hair, grown out enough to flutter a little in the light breeze. Then he moved into the shade of the trees and was visible only when a stray shaft of sunlight touched his hair.

Roi

Roi wasn't as confident as Penny about the efficacy of the warnoff. He trusted the device to transmit its message that he was neither edible nor to be feared, but he also remembered Penny's comment about its uselessness against an animal thrown into the warnoff field. He suspected that intrusion into a bees' nest might override the "harmless" message of the warnoff.

He could feel the nest now, perceiving it as a swarm of brightness in an old tree fifty strides ahead. Several times his own height above the ground, at least, he thought. When he circled the tree, wincing as thorny underbrush clawed at his bare chest, he found that the bees were flying into an opening half an arm's length above the nest. He had been right about the honey, at least. He had learned enough about bees and honey that he knew bees stored honey in wax combs, but this was the first time he'd perceived raw honeycomb. It felt almost like something engineered, the wax matrix unnaturally perfect amid the sweet stickiness of the honey. Roi licked his lips in anticipation, studying the tree.

He could have teleported the honey he wanted into the covered pail, but since his experience with the glider he had decided that the trip was a good opportunity to practice doing things with minimal use of his esper talents. Not that he hadn't done so for most of his life, but that had hardly been conscious. This time, he intended to think ahead about how he could use his R'il'nian abilities, and then how he could manage the same task without his odd talents—or at least without more than peripheral use.

He would have to protect himself from the bees, and for that he thought that he would have to use esper. They didn't have enough minds as individuals for him to reach, but Roi sensed they were programmed to ignore intruders that smelled of the hive. Carefully he reached his mind into the brood chambers, then back into his own body, shifting his body chemistry until he himself produced the same odorous signature. Once satisfied, he tried inactivating the warnoff. Bees settled briefly on his body, seemed to verify that he belonged, and departed on their business. Their buzzing wings and probing feet tickled his face and chest, and he reminded himself not to react.

Moving slowly and carefully, he unwound the rope as he studied the branches of the tree. The opening had been enlarged at some time, perhaps by another honey seeker, and he thought he would be able to reach far enough into the cavity to get at the new combs. The branch just above and to the right of the opening was leafless and looked as if it was supported only by the hollow shell of the tree. Another branch, higher and to the left, looked healthier. He found a dead branch on the ground two trees over, and used his force blade to cut a piece as long as his arm.

Roi continued to study the green branch over his head as he tied one end of his rope securely around the stick. The rope was long enough, he decided, to reach from the branch to the ground, doubled. He clipped the bucket to one of the snaps on the elasticized waist of his breeches, and tied the free end of the rope to another of the snaps.

He needed three tries to throw the stick over the branch without using telekinesis to guide the toss, but when he bounced a few times on the doubled rope the branch felt as solid as the ground beneath his feet. Grinning, he braced his feet against the trunk of the tree and began to climb. His body answered his demands effortlessly. He remembered his struggles of two years ago, attempting to get from one side of a room to the other, unable to lift his body even a handwidth from the floor. His smile widened, and he took a deep breath that turned into a sputter as a bee nearly flew down his throat.

There were returning foragers swarming into the opening he had almost reached, and a constant cloud of bees brushing his body, verifying that he carried the safe hive-scent. He felt almost guilty about his deceit, but not guilty enough to change his mind about getting some of that honey. There was plenty of summer left for the hive to replenish its store.

His hand, reaching up along the doubled rope, touched the branch. He caught the rough bark, swung sideways to bring the other hand up beside it, and then increased the amplitude of his movement enough to swing himself up onto the branch, well above the hive opening. "Couldn't have done that a year ago," he said aloud, pleased at his own restored strength.

He pulled the rope up and knotted it into a seat, the way Derik once had shown him back in his slave days. He hadn't brought any tools to scoop out the honey, so he'd have to use his hands. They were filthy. He looked at his grimy knuckles and dirt-caked fingernails for a moment, and decided that it wouldn't really be cheating to teleport the dirt away.

He rechecked his scent as he lowered himself until he hung just beside the opening, with bees brushing his body as they went about their business. Much better than trusting the warnoff, he thought smugly. It never occurred to him that he had left the warnoff inactivated, or that animals other than the bees might be close by. His mind and eyes were so focused on the honeycomb he was detaching in fist-sized chunks that he didn't even notice the big, sand-colored cat several trees downwind.

Puma

The puma was puzzled. Its eyes and ears told it there was a prey-sized animal up in the bee tree, but its nose detected nothing but bees. It was hungry, and knew from experience that if it climbed onto any of several tree limbs, an unwary animal would sooner or later pass underneath. But feline curiosity was even stronger than hunger. Tipping its head from one side to the other, it watched as the strange creature climbed back to the tree limb and sat there for a few minutes.

Roi

Roi was blissfully unaware of the puma. He had fastened the lid on the top of the bucket and was chewing on a piece of honeycomb as he untied the knots in his rope and laid it back over the limb. The wax, he decided as he knotted the rope ends loosely together and dropped them to the ground, was rather pleasant to chew on, with a resilient texture and a faint taste of flowers and pollen. He clipped the pail of honey firmly to his waistband and began lowering himself to the ground.

He had clipped all kinds of things to his waistband before, but never anything quite as heavy as the full honey pail. By the time he was a third of the way down, he was all too keenly aware that he had lost weight on the trek, and as a result was well on the way to losing his breeches. He paused to consider the situation, and his breeches slid down another few finger widths. This left him hobbled mid-thigh, and uncomfortably exposed to the inquisitive bees. He strengthened the hive-smell and resumed working his way down the tree, having decided that TK'ing his breeches up and holding the hive-smell at the same time might be more than he was ready to manage yet. As for descending with one hand on the rope and the other holding up his pants—well, he didn't think he was quite up to the logistics of that, either. At least the others weren't there to see him!

Roi's boots were the only thing holding his breeches on by the time he reached the ground. He leaned against the tree and proceeded to get his pants back on, removing curious bees as he went. He stood erect only after he was quite sure there were no bees left between his breeches and his skin. The honey pail promptly started pulling his waistband down again, and he fastened it instead to the rope he wrapped diagonally around his chest.

Roi had followed the bees directly to their hive, scrambling through underbrush—most of which seemed to have thorns—and squishing through a few boggy spots. Now that he was no longer concentrating on the bees, he could see a winding game trail leading back toward the rest of the party. He swung into it, singing a song he had learned while studying Earth. It was meant to be a doleful song, with a rose and a briar—much like the undergrowth around him—growing from the graves of a young man who had died of love and the girl who scorned him. Roi thought the sentiment was ridiculous, but he liked the tune and sang it cheerfully as he strode along. He'd have to ask Penny if the story would make sense in her culture, he thought. There were few bees visible, any more, and he readjusted his scent back to normal. He didn't need to smell like a beehive when he rejoined the others.

Puma

The puma, paralleling the boy's course a few tens of strides downwind, tensed and blinked as the warm animal smell reached its nostrils. Meat. Something strange about it, yes, and it moved oddly and slowly, but there was no question in the cat's mind that this prey was well within its abilities. Lowering itself until its belly almost brushed the ground, the animal slid fluidly toward a tree near the edge of the little patch of woodland, a tree with a wide branch overhanging one of the few breaks in the brush surrounding the trees.

Roi

The edge of the wood was bright before Roi, and he could see the other four. They had all dismounted to let the horses graze. Timi and one of the blond girls—Amber, he thought since she was wearing blue, though it was hard to be sure at this distance since she had started copying Penny's pigtails—were talking off to one side, while Flame and the other blond checked the horses' feet. The midday sun was brilliant outside the shade of the trees, and he had to squint a little at the brightness. Roi shouted and waved, and saw their heads turn toward him.

He was never quite sure, afterward, whether he reacted to Penny's scream, his own late-waking precognition, or a hint of movement barely glimpsed from the corner of his eye. Whatever it was, he found himself diving toward and under a tawny mass hurtling toward him from above. Lions don't climb trees, he thought frantically even as he gasped at a sudden, searing jerk at his right shoulder. He kept rolling, broke loose, and found himself staring into eyes as golden as his own, but set in a snarling feline mask. Smaller than a lion, and more lightly built, but more than large enough to match an unarmed boy. He picked up hunger, along with the kind of confidence that let a house cat play with its quarry, and felt a cold knot form in his stomach.

The cat gathered itself for a second leap, and he tried desperately to counter its calm assumption that he was food. He thrust nausea toward the puma, trying to get across the notion that he was tainted meat, then decided that he didn't have time for that kind of finesse, and simply held the animal away telekinetically. He was shaking, painfully aware that he could have been killed if the cat had landed squarely on its first jump. The ground was trembling under his body, and he saw the tawny cat turn its head abruptly toward the sunlit plains. He glanced that way himself to see the other four galloping full tilt for the edge of the little woods, Raindrop and the packhorses running loose behind them.

He turned back to the tawny cat. The ears flattened and the animal shifted its feet uneasily, then turned and bounded back into the shadows of the trees. Roi sat up, wincing as the movement reminded him that the cat's claws had caught his shoulder in passing. He couldn't see the wound, but there was blood on the ground next to him, and from the look on Penny's face as she pulled Freckles to a sliding stop just outside the trees, she could certainly see the injury.

He had a good enough grip on himself by then to monitor his shoulder, and decided he had been lucky. The cat's strike had been aimed assuming its prey would jump away, and if Roi had done that, his own momentum would have helped set the curved claws deeper into his shoulder, probably ripping muscles in the process. His dive toward the puma had not only let him evade most of the force of the blow, it had actually slid him off the claws. He had three holes in the back of his shoulder—one that barely broke the skin, a deeper puncture, and one that was almost a tear, but only a finger width in length. They weren't clean and the tear was bleeding profusely, but removing foreign matter from his own cuts and punctures was something he'd taught himself as a child, and did now almost without thinking.

"Don't try to get up," Penny said as she rummaged in her saddlebag. "In fact, lie down. You've got to be in shock."

"Enough to need some more honey," Roi said, reaching for the still covered pail. "It didn't spill, anyway. Flame, could you get my medical kit? It's in my right saddlebag. I can Heal it, Penny. I'd just like a little of the herbal salve I carry."

Penny had found her own aid kit by then, and she and Flame came toward Roi side by side. "What I do not understand," she said fretfully, "is why the warnoff didn't work. That sort of thing just isn't supposed to happen." She knelt beside him, pouring sterile water from her kit onto a wad of fiber and dabbing carefully at the blood on his shoulder.

Roi froze, shocked more by his own stupidity than by the attack itself. "Uh—I inactivated it," he forced himself to say.

Penny

Penny stared at him in disbelief, her hands automatically continuing to clean the claw wounds. "You inactivated the warnoff?" she asked. "In the trees, in puma country? I thought you had some sense!"

"A puma? Is that what it was?" Roi asked.

"A puma," Penny agreed. "They like to drop down on their prey from above. Humans are easier prey than a deer, and a lot easier than an adult peccary. That's why we always, *always,* wear warnoffs. Whatever possessed you to inactivate it?"

Roi's face was pale under the bronze, and he refused to meet her eyes. "I was trying a different way of keeping the bees off," he said, almost in a whisper, "and I wanted to check if it would work without the warnoff. I was feeling so smug about how well it worked that I totally forgot about reactivating the warnoff. I'm *sorry,* Penny. Really. I can't believe I was that stupid."

"Neither can I," Penny said grimly. "Roi, I thought you had some sense. But this—you could have been killed! For no reason at all! Do I have to check your warnoff every day, like I would a five-year-old's? And fix the switch so you can't turn it off?" She was so angry it was hard to focus on his injured shoulder, but it didn't look nearly as bad as she had feared from the amount of blood. His head was still lowered and turned away, and his shoulders were hunched. "Look at me, damn you!"

He obeyed, looking up at her with an expression of abject misery, eyes close to tears. Penny felt Flame's hand close on her own shoulder. "Penny," Flame said quietly, "he's got the point. Back off."

For an instant the two girls locked eyes, and it was Penny who looked away. "He'd better have," she muttered angrily, and cleaned the last of the blood from Roi's shoulder with a fresh wad. She frowned at the shoulder. Hadn't there been three punctures? "Are you healing that?" she asked suspiciously.

"Yes," he said meekly. "Shouldn't I?"

Penny sighed in frustration. She still wanted to lash out at the boy who had terrified her so, but it wasn't going to accomplish anything. "No reason not to, I guess," she agreed reluctantly. "Just make sure you heal it from the inside out."

"He knows that," Flame said. "Here, Roi, is this the salve you wanted?" She opened a small jar and held it out to him. "Peacemint and aloe, from the smell."

***

"It's not that he wasn't wrong about the warnoff," Flame told Penny after they had stopped for the night. "But he knew he was wrong. Didn't you see his face, when you mentioned the warnoff and he realized what he'd done? And he gets himself wrapped up in guilt so easily. You would have made him feel even worse if you'd kept on, but there's nothing you could have said to make him any more careful about not doing it again."

Penny broke another egg into the folding cup, decided it was undeveloped enough to use for the custard, and tipped it into the mixing bag. "I know," she said. "I was lashing out at him because he'd frightened me so badly." She chuckled. "I'm still not sure I should have let him try to make amends by milking those bison, though."

Flame grinned at her as she folded foil around the last of the grouse, now stuffed with honey, herbs, rose hips dried on the brambles and a few nuts from a squirrel's forgotten winter horde. "He knew what he was doing," she said. "And with fresh milk along with the eggs and honey, we can have dessert. How's the pit coming, Roi?" she added as the sound of his footsteps approached them.

"Almost ready," he replied. "Timi's adding a few last branches to the fire, but the sandstone in the bottom is good and hot. You can start

151

cooking in a few minutes. This cleans up our food, doesn't it, Penny? How much farther to the supply cache?"

"Only a few hours' ride," the guide replied. "I didn't want to try the ford at night, though, and I don't think we could have reached it before sunset."

"It's nice here," Roi agreed. "Uh, Penny? Do you mind if I do some sketching while it's still light? There's a good spot over by the rocks. I'll keep my warnoff on."

"You'd better," Penny told him. "Sure, go ahead. You've done your share for today. There'll be moonlight enough to walk back by, when it gets too dark for you to work."

Roi

They had camped by an unexpected outcrop of red sandstone, the first solid rock they had seen for days. There was a spring-fed pool northeast of the main outcrop, which was several times their height and a good deal wider, and the water was surrounded by trees wherever the soil was deep enough. Their camp was close to the pool, just at the south edge of the wooded area. The pit oven, dug in the open away from tree roots, had been shallower than they had intended, bottomed out in solid rock.

Roi was sitting on one of the smaller rocks, near the outlet stream where he and Timi had bathed after digging the pit and starting the cooking fire. The main outcrop was red gold where the setting sun flowed over it, and shaded from wine color to almost black in the shadows above the pool. The cloudless sky was harder to depict, pale blue overhead shading to lemon and pink to the west and a darker blue in the east. The moon, not quite half full, was high behind his back and so far not affecting the colors on the outcrop. He'd come back after dinner and see how it looked in moonlight, he decided. Right now, he wanted to capture the bison and mammoths.

Most of the bison herd had already watered and left. Two young males were engaged in a pushing contest between Roi and the pool, their sleek red summer coats and black manes and beards glowing in the red light of sunset. No, not just their manes were black, he decided. Backs, chests, bellies and tails were black, too. The overall effect was of a black animal with a large chestnut patch on each side. The half-dozen cows finishing their drinks were a lighter shade of red, with umber markings where the males were black, and the calves were a startling reddish fawn. When one moved out of the shadow of the big rock, its coat glowed like liquid gold.

Roi thought about the brief trip he and Xazhar had taken to Earth a few months ago. The Falaron bison shared ancestry with the bison he had seen flowing like water over the wide North American plains, barely seen as yet by European explorers. But something had happened with the end of the glaciers on Earth that had wiped out the horses and mammoths and changed the bison into a smaller, shorter-legged, shorter-horned animal with a cape, chaps and bonnet of long, dense hair quite different from the relatively smooth-coated, wide-horned animals before him.

And the mammoths were gone forever from their home planet. Roi was glad they had survived here on Falaron. Two were at the west end of the outcrop, rubbing against the sandstone. Like the bison and horses, they shed much of their dense winter undercoat with the coming of spring, but unlike the smaller animals, they were not built for rolling. Roi had seen mammoth hair caught in trees several times, but this was the first time he had caught shedding mammoths grooming themselves. As he watched, the animals moved a few steps away from the cliff and began plucking at each other's coats with their trunks to remove the loosened hair. Their winter coats were a rusty black, but the summer coat looked as if it would be more of a dark brown.

The red sun was deflating against the horizon to Roi's left, flattening as it dropped behind the edge of the world. The last glint of sunlight highlighted a dust-colored cat near the top of the outcrop. Roi flinched, reminded of his own stupidity. He had been thinking of mentioning his poor precognition to Kyrie or even his father. The incident with the puma was far and away the worst example yet. But he couldn't bear the thought of confessing his carelessness with the warnoff. With his precognition not working properly, his father might even refuse to let him finish the trip if he knew what had happened.

Roi looked back at his sketch, then picked up an ocher stick and added the puma. It was getting too dark to fill in the color, but he had it in his mind. He laid a protective sheet over the drawing, and began to pack up his color sticks. The sky to the east had taken on a soft, grayed violet color, and the last of the bison cows was herding her calf away from the pond. To the right of the water a campfire slowly brightened into visibility in the darkening landscape. Roi sat on the sun-warmed rock, his arms around his knees, and watched the first stars appear at the corners of his eyes.

Roi? We're about ready for supper, Flame's mind-voice came into his head. He nodded agreement mentally, picked up his drawings and materials and headed back toward the camp, watching his moon-shadow slowly appear as the sky darkened.

***

With plenty of dead wood available, the travelers had built a campfire for light as well as the cooking fire in the pit. They sat around the flames to devour the roasted birds and rabbits, and to savor the crude but tasty custard after most of their hunger was assuaged. Their fire and the tents were just inside the edge of the wooded area, and firelight on the branches overhead gave an illusion of movement in the trees. Roi was reminded of the puma's attack, and kept checking his warnoff.

Amber started the singing, and they all joined in. For a while they stuck to songs they all knew, and then Timi sang them a Clan song he had learned from Filomako, and Penny taught them a couple of traditional Falaron songs. One was a song of unrequited love, and Roi was reminded of the ballad he'd been singing that afternoon. "Hey, Penny," he said when the song was done, "tell me if this song would make sense in your culture."

In Scarlet Town, where I was born
There was a fair maid dwellin'.
Made every lad cry, "Welladay!"
Her name was Barb'ra Ellen.

Roi was the only one of the five who knew the words, but the others quickly caught the tune. Flame had brought her lapsinger on this leg of the trip, and by the second verse she was brushing out chords on the strings. Then her clear soprano rose in a wordless descant above Roi's baritone, and one by one the others joined in, humming harmonies.

"The story's a bit like several songs of ours," Penny said after the last verse. "Boy dies of unrequited love and girl dies of remorse because she didn't love him back while she could. The rose and the briar's not in our version—I liked that—and I've never heard a version where the boy asks his friends to be good to the girl. More often he asks them not to let her forget him, and sometimes I think the girl winds up killing herself to get away from their accusations. In *Malorie* the lover comes back as a ghost and haunts her 'til she dies.

154

"And it's silly. Why should a girl be expected to fall in love with any nitwit who fancies he's in love with her? We've other songs enough where the girl does give in, and the boy abandons her. And that's the girl's fault, too, from the songs."

Roi chuckled. "Don't get mad at me," he said. "It makes no sense at all to me, and not much in terms of Central society. But the culture it came from has the other kind of songs, too. The boy gets the girl pregnant, and then blames her. Or he just gets tired of her and walks out, and it's always the girl who's blamed."

Penny nodded. "It's not that things really work like the songs," she said. "Except if a girl gets pregnant. That's a worse disgrace than *anything* a boy can do."

Roi nodded, absently humming the first lines of *Careless Love,* and turned away toward the pond. His own mother might still have been alive and free if he had not been conceived, and he had never quite come to terms with that fact, or felt able to talk freely about it. Would it have made any difference, he wondered, if his father had been able to find her? He remembered her enough to know she had loved him. If only they could find her, to let her know how much that love had meant to him, to let her share in the family he had found.

The moon, a late waxing crescent, was only a little southwest of overhead, bright enough to compete with the coals of the dying campfire and dim the stars in its vicinity. It touched the top and the south side of the big outcrop with silver, and when a breath of wind ruffled the pond, crescents danced in the ripples. He heard footsteps, and Penny came up beside him and stopped. "We've been here almost two moon cycles, haven't we," he said after a minute or two.

"Thirty-six days," she agreed. "A moon cycle's twenty. We don't have to rush, by the way. We lost time on both storms, and the Company bigwigs said after the first one to take all the extra time you wanted to, to make up for the time we spent snowbound." The breeze strengthened, curling around their bodies with an unexpected chill, and Roi felt Penny shiver beside him. Automatically he slid an arm about her shoulder, sharing his body warmth.

"So how do you handle the conflict?" he asked, curious. He had meant the question to be general, but Penny apparently didn't hear it that way.

"Oh, I'll get married some day," she said. "I'd like to stay with the Company, but guiding's work for young people. I'll meet someone someday whose children I want to have, and if I'm lucky, he'll feel the same way about me. I'll take a few years off while my children are too young for school, and then go back to the Company on a desk job. I'd like to be a trekmaster some day."

"You'd be a good one, I think. But—ah—some of the Falaron men I talked to on the ship seemed to think wives had no business working away from home. That likely to be a problem?"

"It could be, with the kind of man in your song." She didn't go on, and Roi wondered if he had touched something in her past that bothered her.

They had been walking as they spoke, around to the south side of the outcrop. The pool was black from here, reflecting the dark woods behind it, while the rippling grass and the huge rock itself were a ghostly silver in the moonlight. "Let's walk all the way around," Roi suggested.

"It'll be pretty dark in the woods," Penny pointed out.

"I can use my perception to find safe footing," Roi replied. "And I've got my warnoff on."

"I'm glad the lesson sank in," Penny said. "Don't feel quite so badly about it, Roi. I've had older and more experienced clients make worse mistakes. I just wasn't expecting that kind of carelessness from somebody as generally sensible as you are, and then seeing that puma on top of you ...." She shuddered.

They walked on in silence, the grass rustling around their legs. Roi was storing images in his mind, watching how the light on the outcrop changed as they moved. An owl winged silently between them and the shadowed rock, its feathers frosted by the light of the huge moon. They paused briefly at the edge of the woods while Roi felt out a path, far enough north of the rock that moonlight fell through the gaps in the leaves. They walked along side by side, pausing when breaks in the trees allowed them to see the black bulk of the rock with its glowing top. When they rounded the east end of the rock, the moon made a silver path on the pool.

They followed the edge of the pool back to the camp. The campfire showed only an occasional gleam of red among the ashes. "We left the fire burning for you," Flame's voice came out of the darkness, faintly reproachful.

"I'll take care of it," Roi called back. "Good night, Penny." He brushed his lips against the corner of her forehead. They'd already dumped the water they'd washed the dishes in, so he picked up an empty pail, filled it repeatedly at the pond, and poured several buckets of water over the ashes of the campfire before undressing and sliding into the double sleeping bag with Flame.

Chapter 12

Roi woke with a start to the sound of shouting and a great banging of metal. Something smallish and heavy was treading on his leg through the sleeping bag, a good many other things were making unpleasant noises all over the camp, and there was a rank smell in the air.

He opened his eyes to find himself nose to nose with a head the size of a small pony's, with an elongated, dirt-covered nose, small eyes set wide apart and high in a deep skull, and dauntingly sharp tusks. The whole was covered with bristly hair, banded in yellow and black. When it backed off a step to get a better look at him, Roi saw that the head blended, without much benefit of neck, into an unfinished-looking body, its considerable bulk supported on four unexpectedly slender legs ending in cloven hooves. The back was about the height of a table top—not all that large from the viewpoint of a standing man, but more than impressive when viewed from ground level.

"Penny?" he called uncertainly, rolling his eyes to look around the camp with as little movement as possible. There were at least a dozen of the things rooting around the camp in the gray predawn light, including a smallish one with its head stuck in the honey pail, two others quarreling over the remains of the custard, and a litter of five or six happily nursing from an adult stretched out in the ashes of last night's campfire. Timi stuck his head out of the next sleeping bag over, took one appalled look, and ducked his head back into the bag.

"Up here," Penny's voice came from above, and he rolled over on his back to see her shivering on a tree branch well over his head, barefoot and wearing only the thin night shift she insisted on keeping on even in her sleeping bag. "Roi, could you tell them to go away? They're not interested in eating us, and all the warnoffs are doing is telling them they don't have to be afraid of us." She gave another halfhearted bang on the branch with the water bucket she was holding. The things didn't even bother to look at her.

"What are they?" Roi asked as he eased himself out of the sleeping bag he shared with Flame, careful not to startle the animal nearest him.

"Flatheads," she replied. "Flat-headed peccaries. *Platygonus compressus*, if you want a formal name. They're not actually predators, though they'll eat carrion if they're hungry enough. And they can be very dangerous if they think you're threatening the piglets. That's why I'm up here. They'll eat just about anything, including everything we saved for breakfast. I didn't realize we were getting into peccary country, or I'd have hung everything from trees before we went to bed last night."

Roi opened his mind to the peccaries, and began gently broadcasting that this was an undesirable place. Too many places for predators to hide, no food (and there probably wasn't by now, he thought to himself), bad water .... One of the boars scratching his back on the trunk of Penny's tree wandered over and whuffled at the nursing sow. She grunted back at him and heaved herself to her feet. Striped piglets squealed in protest as their breakfasts were jerked from their mouths, while others managed to hang from their dam's nipples for a few steps before falling away and adding their voices to the cacophony. The sow turned and called them, then she and the boar trotted into the underbrush, the protesting piglets and the rest of the little herd following.

Soon the only animal left was the hapless adolescent with its head stuck in the honey pail, who was galloping blindly around the camp colliding with one tree after another. Roi tried reaching for its mind, but the creature was in such a state of panic he couldn't make contact.

"Timi," he called, and a black head slid cautiously out of Timi's sleeping bag.

"Did you see ...." Timi started to say, then broke off and dived back into the sleeping bag as the unfortunate peccary in the honey pail headed straight for his head. When the animal was past, Timi reappeared. "I guess you did," he said weakly. "Weren't there more of them?"

"Yes, but I sent them away," Roi replied. "Give me a hand at catching this one, will you? It's so scared I can't reach its mind." He had been pulling on his clothes as he spoke, and Timi hastily copied him, no more inclined than Roi to try catching the thing without clothing for protection.

"It's got a mind? What are we supposed to hold on to? It doesn't seem to have a neck, or a waist either."

"Just lie on top of it, or maybe grab the rear legs. I don't think it's full-grown. How about it, Penny?"

The guide was descending the tree, doing her best to keep her shift down around her legs in the process. Roi politely kept his eyes on the remaining peccary, and Timi's attentions were divided between the animal and the boots he was pulling on.

"Probably a yearling sow," Penny replied as she headed for her clothes. "A full-grown one couldn't have gotten its head far enough into the bucket to get caught like that. Be careful. It won't have the tusks a boar would, but it can still give you a nasty rip."

"At least it can't use its tusks through the bucket," Roi said. "All right, Timi, it's coming back this way. You aim for the rear, and I'll try for the pail." His mind touched Timi's with just enough contact to synchronize their movements. *Ready—now!*

They dived in from opposite sides of the mad, blind creature, shoulders brushing as Timi's weight collapsed the animal's hindquarters and Roi landed atop the shoulders. The peccary's frantic squeals, amplified and directed by the bucket, reverberated in Roi's ears, and its odor was rank in his nostrils. Its coat was as rough and bristly as it looked, harsh against his hands and arms.

It wasn't totally blinded, Roi saw. The handle of the bucket was caught behind the sow's ears, and the eyes were set so high in the skull that he could see them, rolling wildly, from where he lay. But it could not see ahead of itself. Roi opened his mind and used his physical contact with the animal to force his own awareness into the animal mind, controlling its struggles as he had quieted the three horses during the storm. "Hang on to the rear legs until I tell you to let go," he told Timi, and began struggling to get the handle of the bucket back over the flathead's ears.

It wasn't an easy job, and he found himself wondering how the animal had managed to get itself trapped to start with. He finally had to twist the bucket sideways, shoving the young sow's nose hard into the corner of the pail. Even then, the folds of skin behind the skull had swollen around the handle, and he had to use his Healing ability to get the swelling down before he could even begin to work the handle over the small ears. Flame and Amber were up by then, and Flame finally found a bottle of soap the animals had overlooked. They used it to lubricate the skin behind the ears enough that they could get the bucket off.

"Let's get her pointed the same way the others went," he told Timi. The girls retreated warily to climbable trees while the two boys used their mass to wrestle the peccary around. They released her simultaneously, jumping back toward the trees, but the freed animal was interested only in getting away from this frightening place and rejoining the herd. She took off after her companions at an unexpectedly fast gallop, her ears pinned back and her short tail almost vertical.

"Did they leave anything?" Amber asked. The sky had lightened to blue overhead while they were dealing with the peccaries, and the top of the outcrop was warming rapidly to gold. The devastation in the camp was clear in the growing daylight.

Penny picked up a slightly chewed saddle, checking the saddletree and girth before swinging it over a low branch at the edge of the camp. "Nothing edible, certainly. They even ate what was left of the horses' grain, and I think I saw one chewing on a skin cream bottle. Check the tack over; we may have to do some mending before we ride on."

Half an hour's work confirmed the peccaries' thoroughness. Penny had put aside one of the roasted birds and the remains of the custard in a stasis container, planning to stew the meat with some of the horses' grain that she had left soaking overnight for breakfast. The animals had demolished the stasis container and eaten its contents along with all of the remaining grain, the rest of Kyrie's candy, the package of emergency bars Penny had been hoarding, and every drop of the honey. Every cooking and eating utensil that had been in contact with food had been pulled out and scattered about the camp, including the horses' nosebags, which had been chewed to uselessness. "It's a good thing the bridles and saddles are made of synthetics," Penny said when their inventory was complete. "They'd have eaten leather." As it was, they'd have to mend two of the bridles and rig a substitute for Token's saddle blanket and the lining of her saddle. The odor of the horses' sweat had apparently fooled a couple of the animals into thinking the tack was edible.

"How much farther did you say it was to the cache?" Roi asked as he loaded the sleeping bags onto one of the packhorses.

"Two or three hours," Penny replied, frowning at Raindrop's bridle. It had been chewed completely through at the crown. "Roi, the only thing I have to fix this with is rope, and the only way I can see to use Token's saddle without rubbing her back raw is to use one of the sleeping bags for a saddle blanket."

"Can you contact the Company from the cache, like you could from the cabins? Get the replacement parts we need for the tack repair?"

"Sure. The cache is a cabin, really. Or they could send somebody out to make the repairs while we do some hiking, for that matter, or even just fly replacement tack out. But we need the tack to get there. I'm not going to let us get split up again."

"I wasn't suggesting that," Roi replied. "But isn't a little mind touch justified? Then I could ride Raindrop without a bridle, and I'd just as soon ride bareback, anyway. Flame can use my saddle on Token, and we can load her saddle onto one of the packhorses. And the reins from my bridle can go on Dusty's. It'd be a lot faster than trying to make temporary fixes, and I'm hungry."

"Can you?" Penny asked. "I mean, I know you need a lot of energy to do your esper stuff. Can you manage a couple of hours of mind touch without anything to eat?

Roi chuckled in reply. "Mind touch with a cooperative mind—and Raindrop's gotten used to it—takes less energy than hauling on the reins. It's not like Healing, or telekinesis, or levitation. There's no real work involved. Besides, with Raindrop it's only a backup. She handles fine with weight shifts." He finished rolling up Flame's sleeping bag and his own, and began loading them. "I'm ready for the cookware, Amber," he added.

"All right, we'll do it that way," Penny said as she unfastened the reins from Raindrop's bridle, and then picked up Dusty's. "Go ahead and load Token's saddle."

***

They didn't usually get moving this early, Roi thought half an hour later, but then they didn't normally leave without breakfast, either. The sun was low and blindingly bright in their faces, not yet high enough to burn off the chill of the night. He was wearing a jacket—bright red, of course—over his tunic, and the warmth of Raindrop's body between his legs was comforting.

The grulla cantered easily beneath him, her gait as comfortable as an old chair. She might not have quite as smooth a jog as Dusty, Roi

162

thought, but her walk and canter were as good as those of any horse he had ever ridden. Beside him, Token's trot was forcing Flame's weight into her stirrups, and Penny on Freckles was openly standing in hers. Dusty's stride was too short for him to trot comfortably at the speed they were traveling, and Roi could hear Timi's slight grunt at each stride of the buckskin's canter. Little Splash was cantering, too, but Amber was in tune with her mount and rode soundlessly.

They splashed across a shallow creek without breaking gait. There was no sign of recent flooding, and Roi thought they must be outside the region affected by the thunderstorms of a few days earlier. Then the sun dropped back behind the steepening slope before them, and Penny raised her arm in warning before reining Freckles to a walk. Roi rocked his weight back on his seat bones, and Raindrop shortened her next two strides and then dropped into a smooth walk herself.

Roi stroked the mouse-colored shoulder affectionately. His own horse, Flight, had been bred and trained for cross-country obstacle work, and Roi was beginning to show him in obstacle competitions, back on Central. There were other riding competitions he would have liked to try, too, including games where sprint speed, handiness and instant response were critical. Quite aside from his unhandy size, Flight tended to become unmanageable when allowed to run flat out. Raindrop, once she had decided she could trust her rider, was responsive at any speed, whether Roi was controlling her by physical aids or by mind touch. She'd be a wonderful games horse, Roi thought wistfully.

A chilly breeze lifted his hair from his forehead, and he shivered. The sun must have been warming him more than he realized. He touched his calves to Raindrop's sides, eager to get over the rise and back into sunlight, and the horse moved into a willing jog. He came up level with Penny and dropped back to a walk just as they came over the brow of the rise to find the sun.

A wide valley stretched across their path, filled with a patchwork of fog, trees, tall grass, ponds, and a broad river. Those water surfaces not hidden by patches of fog reflected the sun like mirrors. Penny glanced sideways at Roi, and then looked back ahead, eyes squinted against the glare. "The cache is on the far side of this valley, up out of the flood plain," she said finally, "but I can't spot it from here. The ford's hidden by the trees. It shouldn't be more than hock deep on the horses." She started down the slope, keeping Freckles at a walk, and Raindrop held her place at the bay leopard's side.

Birdcalls began to dominate over the sounds of the horses' legs swishing through the grass. Roi could see birds swimming on the nearest of the ponds, and other, longer-legged birds stalking through the grassy area beside it. The trail turned left as they reached the base of the slope, skirting the flat meadow. Cranes, Roi thought. Cranes and herons. Wading birds. He looked down to see that the path was moist underfoot. Water gleamed at the base of the tall grass to his right, and the smell of rotting vegetation arose from the ground disturbed by their horses' hooves.

They dropped back into single file, with Penny and her map in the lead. After days of seeing trees only in low spots where their roots could reach water, it seemed strange that these woods were on relatively high ground. When Roi mentioned as much to Penny, she nodded. "It's waterlogged here," she agreed. "We're safe anywhere the trees are growing. But some of the low places are soft enough a horse could be trapped in them. Roi, would you mind feeling ahead and warning me if you spot anything dangerous? I've got the map from a year ago, but if there's been even minor flooding since then things could have changed."

"Sure," Roi replied. The narrow trail reached a little wood and turned east into it. The sun was higher now, but the leaves filtered its glare. The path led them through tendrils of mist, especially when it lay between the wooded area and a pond where numerous water birds, including newly hatched balls of down following their parents, were feeding. Roi stopped Raindrop briefly to watch a swimming wood duck calling her brood from the nest. The younglings were clustered in a hollow high in a dead tree at the water's edge, easily twice Roi's height above the water. The ducklings looked barely old enough for their down to have fluffed out, but there was no food in the tree, and if they were to eat, they must jump to the water. In ones and twos they did just that, teetering and shoving each other at the opening of the nest until they either got up the courage to jump or were pushed off balance by the other nestlings. Then they plummeted downward to strike the water, bob up like corks and join their mother, swimming and bobbing for insects as if they had never done anything else.

The trail led back to higher ground, winding into a grove of tall elms. Woven grass bags were hanging from the upper limbs of several, and Roi tipped his head back to watch the orange and black birds that flew back and forth with offerings of insects. "Orioles," Penny said. "And the red ones are tanagers, and the little gray and yellow ones darting around in the underbrush catching bugs are warblers. There are thrushes and gnatcatchers, too, and that one climbing down the tree is a nuthatch."

"This ought to be called the Bird River," Roi commented as they moved on through the taller woods and back toward an open meadow. "Watch out, Penny, that's bog ahead." He frowned and closed his eyes, concentrating on the feel of the ground around them. "Go left about a hundred paces; it feels solider there."

Penny nodded and reined Freckles left. "The river's got its own name," she said. "Want to guess what?"

"A particular kind of bird?" Amber suggested.

"How about Marsh River?" Flame asked.

Penny shook her head. "Peccary River," she told them, and they all groaned. "I guess the peccaries are spreading. This used to be the western boundary of their range."

"Turn right here," Roi said, and they turned to cross a grassy area. The horses' hooves squelched as they moved along, but the ground stayed solid.

"You mean there are more of them?" Timi asked, looking around nervously.

"They'll be almost as common as deer, the other side of the river," Penny replied. "They're basically browsers, like deer, but they can eat a lot of other things deer don't. They'll use that long nose to dig up roots and tubers and underground mushrooms, and they have positive orgies when the berries are ripe. Especially when the fruit's starting to ferment. Not to mention seeds, and nuts, and insects and the odd bit of carrion. We'll have to hang food in trees from now on."

Roi frowned, remembering his trip to the Virginia Colony with Xazhar. "Sounds almost like black bears," he said, "though they're opportunistic predators."

"Black bears?" Penny replied, her voice puzzled. "You mean black grizzlies, or short-faces?"

"Neither," Roi replied. "It's a separate species, smaller and less carnivorous than either of those. They're fairly common on Earth, and they eat about like you describe the peccaries. Including being a major camp pest."

Penny shook her head. "Never heard of them. Whatever their ancestors were on Earth must have died out here. Maybe they couldn't compete with the peccaries."

"Swing a little to the left here," Roi said as they approached taller grass and reeds. A flock of red-winged blackbirds exploded into the air as they approached, and then settled back to their nests in the reeds. Mosquitoes and gnats rose in clouds beneath their horses' feet, and tree swallows, gnatcatchers and warblers were quick to exploit the feast. Roi slapped a mosquito probing at his neck, and hastily checked his warnoff. "Penny," he called, "my warnoff's not stopping the mosquitoes."

"Turn the intensity up," she called back. "Once they're actually on your skin, it takes a stronger signal to keep them from feeding. They don't have much brain to influence. You sure this route is safe, Roi?"

The horses were splashing through water, now, but there was firm ground a finger depth below the mud, continuing to a wooded rise not too far ahead. "It's safe," he assured her. "Is the ford a couple of hundred paces to the left of the line we're on? If it is, we can ride right down those woods ahead and straight across. Firm ground all the way, even if there's some water on top."

The edge of the wood, when they reached it, was so dense that Penny turned Freckles left and led them along the narrow fringe of damp ground next to the trees. With the trees and the slope to the east, they were riding in deep shade again, and the moist air felt clammy against Roi's face. "Penny," he called, "we're almost level with the ford. We need to get through the woods."

"There's a little break back here," Flame called, and they all gathered around her. Little, Roi decided, was a generous description.

"We could lie down on the horses' necks and put our feet up on their rumps and make it, maybe," he said dubiously. "Or lead them. Think the pack horses can get through, Penny?"

Penny had dismounted and forced her way through the break. "It's more open as you go deeper in," she said as she stepped back out of the woods, "though we'll still have to watch our heads and knees. Flame, you lead, and stay in mind touch with Roi. Head as straight uphill as you can 'til you get to the top of the ridge. I'll go next, then Timi and Amber. Amber and I can each lead a packhorse, and Roi, I want you in the rear where you can drive the packhorses if you need to."

Roi and Flame looked at each other, minds touching as their eyes met. Then Flame turned Token and tapped her heels firmly against the mare's sides. Once her mount was moving, Flame ducked her head down alongside the red-spotted neck and kicked her feet out of the stirrups. Roi, seeing through Flame's eyes as well as his own, saw the dense underbrush thin out as the shade of the trees increased. *Follow the deer trail uphill,* he told her.

Penny went next, unaware that Roi was urging on the packhorse she led, then Timi, followed by Amber with the other packhorse. Finally Roi dropped his head to Raindrop's neck, tucked his feet back onto the mare's rump, and rode after them into the woods.

Once he had broken through the dense vegetation competing for the light at the forest edge, he was able to drop his legs back to the horse's sides, though there were still plenty of branches to duck. He could see Amber and the packhorse she led, and occasional glimpses of Timi ahead of them. The packhorse following Penny was almost hidden behind the tree trunks, and he rarely caught a glimpse of Penny or Flame. Oaks and pines had joined the cottonwoods, elms and willows they had seen previously, and Roi glimpsed a scarlet bird with black wings—tanager, Penny had called it—in an oak tree.

The ground under Raindrop's hooves grew drier as the trail wound up the ridge. He could see the crest through Flame's eyes: a gravelly, rounded ridge with the glare of water visible through the trees. *Wait and regroup on the top, where the trees aren't so thick,* he sent, and felt her assent.

Game trails converged toward the ford, and by the time they were halfway down the far side of the ridge, they were on a trail broad enough that they no longer needed to watch their knees so closely. A bird sang in the treetops above them, its song seeming to blend all of the other bird songs they had heard that morning. "Mockingbird," Penny identified it. She tipped her head back, scanning the treetops. "There, see it? The biggish bird with the white breast and gray back, sitting in the top of the white oak."

They continued down the trail, which leveled out at last on a broad gravel bar sloping smoothly below the surface of the river. Penny stopped and frowned, studying the fast-moving water. Turbulence just to their right suggested deep water downstream of the ford.

"Problem?" Roi asked her, feeling through the water ahead for firm ground. There was a patch of hard shale, almost slate, beneath the current here, nearly level beneath the slope of the running water. Upstream, it emerged gradually from the sediments deposited by the river. Just below the ford, the river was nibbling at the edge of the outcrop, producing a sharp dropoff at the downstream side of the ford. It would have been safe enough if the water level had been a little lower.

"The water's high," Penny echoed his thoughts. "If we had any food left, I'd delay crossing, but .... How are you feeling, Roi?"

"Hungry," he replied without hesitation. "Feeling out the boggy spots, and now the ford, ran my blood sugar down. Not dangerously, but I do need food, and I don't have the energy to contact Kyrie and ask for more candy. The water will be belly-deep on the larger horses, but I don't think they'll have a real problem. It'll be halfway up Splash's sides, though, and that current's pretty strong."

"Could we put one of the bigger horses upstream of him? Dusty, maybe?" Flame asked. "That's what the mammoths did, when they were crossing the flooded channel of the Surprise. They stayed upstream of the baby."

"That should help," Roi agreed. "And watch the water. See how it starts swirling just to the right of the ford, and there's almost a bump in the surface? There's an underwater drop-off there. It deepens to the left, too, but that's gradual. Keep the horses as far to the left as you can without getting in water so deep they're swept off their feet. Keep at least a horse's length to the left of the swirling." He hesitated, reaching for the warning at the back of his head. "And Amber, tie your saddle rope into Splash's neck rope, and give the coil to Timi. That way if Splash does lose his footing, you won't be swept downstream."

They started across with Roi in the lead, followed by Timi and Amber, then Flame and Penny bringing up the rear with the packhorses. Roi was a little nervous about guiding Raindrop through the ford with no bridle. Feeling out the bogs and the ford had depleted him more than he had admitted, and while he could communicate with the horse without much effort, he wasn't sure he had the strength left to force his will on the animal. Luckily, Raindrop responded willingly to his leg cues, staying well away from the dangerous downstream edge of the ford.

Three-quarters of the way across, the swirling cut an arc through the path he had taken so far, and he had to take Raindrop even farther to the left, into water that foamed against his boots. The river had cut a bite out of the shale, he thought as he guided Raindrop back to shallower water on the far side of the gap.

Amber cried out behind him, and he turned to see Splash spinning in the turbulent water below the ford, Amber clinging to his neck. Timi was pulling on Amber's saddle rope, but Dusty, hardly an arm's length from the turbulence, was balking at moving upstream into deeper water, and the gap was the worst possible place for Splash to make it back onto firm footing.

Roi reached out to the struggling horse telekinetically, adding mental force to the pull of the rope. "Toss the free end of the rope to me, Timi," he shouted, "and then get Dusty over here. Don't let him cut the corner; there's a deep hole just to your right. Bring him over here where it's shallower." He caught the rope coil Timi threw him, passing the rope under his seat and around Raindrop's lower chest even as he urged the mare forward to a slightly shallower part of the ford. "All right," he added. "Let go of the rope and get on over here. Amber, just hang on to Splash. I'm going to let you drift downstream and over my way where the ford's shallower, and then pull you in and try to help Splash climb back onto the shelf. Timi, I'll need your help. I don't have much purchase, working without a saddle."

He didn't have much energy left, either. He was able to keep Splash upright when Timi released his hold on the rope and rode over to join him, but he lacked the strength to keep the horse from drifting farther downstream. The best he could do was turn Raindrop so she faced downstream and back the horse into the current. The rope was biting into his right thigh, and he sensed Raindrop's discomfort with the pressure on her chest.

Timi grabbed the rope between Roi and Amber, and kicked Dusty away from the drop-off. The ford was broad and shallow enough here that the buckskin was able to pull Splash almost to the drop-off before he balked at the deepening water. Roi's vision was starting to close in, but he somehow managed to grab the rope a couple of horse-lengths from Timi and pull, at the same time giving Splash a telekinetic boost back onto the firm rock. He felt all four of Splash's hooves strike ground, and then the world went completely black around him.

Timi

Timi had seen Roi start swaying on Raindrop's back just as Splash started to heave himself out of the swirling water. He had already started pushing Dusty forward to help Roi pull, but by the time he reached the R'il'noid's side, the rope, with Roi's hand still locked around it, was already slack and Roi was sliding off Raindrop. Timi managed to grab a handful of Roi's jacket, and then Amber was on Raindrop's other side, pulling at Roi's hand, and Timi managed to reach down and catch his friend under the arm. Between them, they got the unconscious boy back on Raindrop, his body slumped forward limply against the agitated horse's neck.

"What happened?" Penny called out from behind them.

"He pushed it too far without food," Timi called back. "Passed out from low blood sugar, I think. We've got him balanced as long as his horse is still, but I think we'd better get a lead rope on Raindrop and have somebody ride on either side to steady him."

"I'll get on his right side, Amber," Flame said anxiously. "Token's stronger than Splash."

"Can you keep Dusty far enough to the left for the rest of the ford, Timi?" Penny asked him.

Timi hesitated, painfully aware that Dusty's refusal to move upstream into deeper water was at least partly responsible for Splash's losing his footing. "I think so," he said, "but I'm not absolutely sure. Maybe we'd better play it safe and have you on his left side."

"Well, stay there for a minute while I rig a rope halter on Raindrop," Penny said, "and then you can lead the horse and I'll ride on her left. Amber, Splash has all he can handle just keeping himself upright in this current, but we're almost through the ford. You push on ahead. There's a clear trail from the end of the ford up the bank to the cache, and the cache isn't locked. Get on in and bring us back something Roi can swallow without choking."

Raindrop's ears were flicking nervously and her eyes were ringed with white, but she was making no attempt to throw her rider. Penny used the neck rope as a base to rig a halter with her saddle rope, and handed the remaining coil to Timi. Then she reined Freckles around behind Dusty and up between Dusty and Raindrop, reaching out to put a steadying hand on Roi's side. "Keep it to a slow walk, Timi," she said. "We're almost out of the worst of the current."

Amber turned Splash and rode on across the remainder of the ford, keeping well away from the line of turbulence that marked the dropoff. The current slowed rapidly as the ford became shallower, and within a few minutes Timi saw her urge Splash to a trot through the water, now no more than fetlock deep, and then to a canter as she reached dry ground. The brush on the far bank hid her almost at once.

Timi kept a steady walk, turning in his saddle every few strides to verify that Penny and Flame were still holding Roi in place, with the creanced packhorses following. It seemed a long time before they reached shallow water, and even longer before Roi moaned and tried unsuccessfully to lift his head from Raindrop's mane. By then Timi was guiding Dusty out of the water and looking in dismay at the narrow trail through the brush that grew on the bank.

"I don't think we can take three horses abreast up that," he said as they all crowded onto the toe of the slope. "Damn those peccaries! If we just had an emergency bar, or a piece of that honeycomb ...." One of the packhorses shoved against his leg, and Dusty laid back his ears in warning, then suddenly pricked them, alert to something hidden in the brush above them.

"That's Amber, I think," Penny said in relief as the other horses alerted to the sounds. "It had better be Amber. If it's more peccaries, I may start screaming."

Roi

Roi knew Amber was approaching because he could feel her concern, and he could hear the others talking. But it was hard to make sense of what they were saying. And he didn't seem to be able to control his body or even open his eyes, though he could feel the harshness of Raindrop's mane against his cheek.

Hands held his head and forced his mouth open, and there was a sudden sickening sweetness in his mouth. He swallowed as reflexively as he had been breathing. Honey, he thought. I must have overdone it and gone into esper shock.

He could feel the sugar spreading through his famished body, and continued to swallow eagerly as more honey was squeezed into his mouth. The refined honey tasted bland after the wild honeycomb, but his body didn't care. Finally he raised his head and then pushed himself erect on Raindrop's back.

"Amber," Penny was saying, "You and Timi take the pack horses and get them on up to the cache. If Roi's better in a few minutes we'll ride on up with him, but if we're not at the cache within half an hour, you'd better come back."

"I'm better already," Roi said shakily. "My body and my ability to use my esper talents just sort of shut down to protect my brain when I go too far, that's all." He would have been in serious trouble if he'd slid off Raindrop into the current, but he didn't feel like pointing that out. "I could use some breakfast, though. Let's head for the food."

"When he starts wanting to eat everything in sight, he's all right," Flame commented. "Come on, Roi." She guided Token into the path up the bank. Roi followed, and Penny brought up the rear.

Their path on this side of the river led up to a lightly wooded, well-drained terrace rather than the boggy lowlands of the west bank. The cache—really a log cabin much like the ones they had stayed at earlier—was set in a grove of oaks a few hundred paces back from the bluff overlooking the river. Timi and Amber were unloading the packhorses just inside a generous fenced pasture. When they forded the stream running through the pasture, Roi could feel heat rising from the water—a welcome contrast to the chill of the Peccary River. "Warm spring?" he asked hopefully, and Penny nodded.

"There's a hot pool at the spring," she said, waving her arm toward the rise behind the cabin. "Let's get some breakfast into you, and then you can soak for a while."

"I'm fine, now," Roi assured her. "No sense worrying my folks." He knew he could influence what Penny told the Company, but he also knew what Marna would have to say about any such unethical use of his talents. It wasn't worth it, though that certainly didn't stop him from hoping Penny would mention neither the puma attack nor the problem at the ford. Maybe, he hoped, she'd have too much to do arranging for the tack to be replaced to remember her problems with him.

Penny

They had a late breakfast of flatcakes saturated with melted bison butter, maple syrup and hot spiced apple puree, with fresh domestic peccary chops on the side. Penny had commed the Company while Amber and Timi fixed breakfast, and she was smiling as she speared a couple of flatcakes and sat down. "How big a hurry are you in?" she asked.

"Are you asking if we'd like to stay here for a while?" Roi asked.

"Well, yes, sort of," Penny replied. "To be honest, several of the Company carryalls are down for repairs, and the rest are being used nonstop. Lots of places they have no choice but to land in daylight, and the schedule is tight as long as the sun's up. There's a beacon here, so they can bring the replacement tack in after dark, and they'd prefer to do it that way. But it would mean overnighting here."

Roi grinned. "Anybody object to a bed?" he asked.

"And a hot spring to soak in today and tomorrow morning," Flame said happily.

"And a stove instead of a campfire," Timi added. "Amber?"

"A door to keep the peccaries out," the youngest girl replied. "Don't misunderstand us, Penny, I think we've all enjoyed sleeping outdoors, even in the storms when we have to put up the tents. But a night's break sounds lovely." She paused and thought for a moment. "Is there any way we could reset the warnoffs so they actually repel wild animals, at least at night?"

Penny nodded. "I'll ask for a perimeter repellor when I confirm the night delivery on the tack," she said as she pushed her chair back from the table and stood up. "Let me get back to the Company, and then we'll head for the hot spring."

The four wanted to go exploring after their soak, but Penny put her foot down as far as Roi was concerned. "You're taking it easy the rest of the day," she told him firmly. "The others can take a lunch and go hiking if they want, but you stay right here and sketch."

Roi looked briefly defiant, then thoughtful. "Two conditions," he said.

"Such as?"

"First, if I get hungry again, you let me contact Kyrie and teleport in more food."

"Agreed. I was wrong this morning. I was thinking about a missed meal or two as just a minor discomfort. I'm afraid I forgot that it's a real health issue for you."

Roi grinned. "Only if I'm using my esper talents," he said, "and I wasn't thinking I'd have to, until I was so worn down I couldn't have contacted Kyrie anyway. Second, Penny, please don't tell my parents about the stupid things I've done the last couple of days. It'll just worry them." His bronze face was flushed with embarrassment.

Penny wasn't so old that she had forgotten how painful it had been to admit peccadilloes to her parents. Besides, Roi's collapse this morning had been as much her fault as his. She fixed her most severe look on Roi. "Promise you'll be more careful from now on?"

"Definitely," he said with a fervor that convinced her he meant it.

Central: Zhaim

Zhaim stared gloomily at the contents of his wardrobe. Those of his garments that appealed to him at the moment were not those that gave the impression he wanted to make at the Council meeting. He must be serious, competent, and above all, accepting of his current position—no longer Lai's heir, but still the ranking R'il'noid member of the group. At least that would be his position until the bastard reached maturity. If Zhaim could manage it, the brat never would.

He ground his teeth in frustration. He wanted to blame Derik for his present plight. Whoever would have thought that Derik, notorious for his daredevil stunts, would have pounded into his students' heads that they should remove anything that might hang up on the gliders before flying?

He'd had everything planned out so carefully. He'd control the black slave's body to reverse the compensation on the brat's glider, at the same time installing a self-destructing screamer circuit that would be triggered if the bastard attempted to use its esper talents to escape. He would also control the black slave during the flight as double insurance, making sure that the slave died also. Lai would probably find that the slave had handled the control circuit, and with no living mind to probe, he would assume that the slave was responsible for the crash.

The day of the planned flight he had reached for the black slave's mind and found—nothing.

Had there been a Council meeting that day, he would have been far too shaken to attend it. As it was, it was close to a day before his increasingly desperate attempts to contact the slave were successful and he found that, in accordance with Derik's training, it had removed the amulet and packed it up with the tri-dee recording equipment before the flight. Even the slave chains had weak links, which had shocked Zhaim to the core. The control circuit drew its slight power from skin contact, so with it packed away, he had been unable even to locate the group. The best he could do when he eventually made contact was suggest to the superstitious and infuriatingly loyal mind that not wearing the "good luck" talisman had somehow contributed to the problem with the scarlet glider.

That, of course, was a temporary solution only. Sooner or later Lai would examine the glider, find traces of the slave's involvement in the accident, and read its mind, by force if need be. He would not find the amulet—as long as that was powered, Zhaim could exchange it for an innocent copy. But Zhaim had no illusions about his father's ability to draw conclusions from limited evidence. The slave had to die before his father could read its mind. And it had to die—preferably with the bastard—in a way that would leave no evidence pointing to Zhaim.

The thing that had saved him so far was the distraction value of the situations designed to attract both Lai and Marna off-planet. That, and the bastard's own late-waking independence. He didn't know why the brat was refusing to pass information on to their father, but that refusal was providing him with a breathing space.

He walked along the line of costumes, rejecting one as too frivolous and another as too informal. Perhaps this, with a deep sapphire body stocking under a knee-length tunic of metallic silver?

He would not take a chance on physical sabotage again. The two deaths must look natural—and since the party was in a stable continental interior, that meant manipulating the weather. There simply were no geological instabilities he could manipulate to produce an earthquake or a volcanic eruption, and it had taken almost three fivedays to find an atmospheric one he could exploit to produce a flash flood. And that one had been foiled by the libido of a horse and the bastard's choice of the one camping place in the area where his tornado, however well steered, had been unable to reach the ground.

Luckily the Kablukolelli situation had blown up into such a mess that Lai could not spare the energy he would need to teleport to Falaron and check out Roi's glider himself. Now if Marna had been on planet at the time of the thunderstorms .... Zhaim shuddered. That had been the main reason he had delayed as long as he had.

He would wear the sapphire and silver, he decided. Its rich conservatism suited the image he wanted to project. Most of the meeting would focus on Kablukolelli, as the brat's progress was only occasionally touched on at the meetings, but he still might learn something.

***

"We could use Roi's help on this one," Lunia sighed in frustration. "I don't suppose you could pull him back for a day or two?"

Most of the other Inner Council members looked hopeful, but Lai shook his head. "In the first place, there's no reason to think he's got any special expertise on Kablukolelli. In the second place, this is the first real vacation he's ever had. He's already blown up at me once for interfering, over that glider incident. I don't like his refusing to contact me or let me contact him, but if I try to force the issue he's perfectly capable of heading off on his own without even a Company tracer. At least the Company is monitoring tracers on all of them. They're behind schedule by a few days—held up by a flash flood at one of the fords, the Company representative thought—but within a few days' travel of that lake they're going to sail across."

Derik grinned and stretched. "They were fine on the seventh," he said. "Roi cadged some more candy and a fresh satellite map off Kyrie then. Kyrie said they planned to try a possible ford about half a day's ride upstream on a small river that turned into a big one after the storm, and from what you said, that's probably just what they did. He's not totally isolated, Lai. Give him a chance to be a normal kid for once in his life. He'll be stuck with enough Council business when he's grown up."

So they were not aware that the party had lost one of their packhorses, or that Roi had gone into esper shock during one of the fords. He himself had learned that less than an hour ago, and the others might still learn it from the Company. But so far, the slave-bred bastard had evidently not been passing his problems on, or the others would know about the puma attack, at least. Certainly there were no hints that the others even suspected that Zhaim was in any way responsible for some of the party's problems. The fact that the brat had gotten itself into some major problems no doubt helped.

"I keep forgetting how young he is," Kaia said ruefully. "Eighteen may be the edge of adulthood for a Human, but for a R'il'noid—well, Derry's right. Mature as he is, he needs time to be a child. We've all been asking way too much of him." She leaned back into her interface, briefly reviewing the increasingly frustrating situation in the Kablukolelli cluster. "But I have to admit I'm plain out of ideas."

Lai grimaced. "We'll try once more to get them to back off, then," he said, "and let them know I'll be out there myself if they don't cooperate. They've passed the point where I can justify a little mind-bending, and they know it. So we'll hope I don't really have to go, but if they don't respond within a few days, I don't see any other choice."

Zhaim could hardly believe what he was hearing. Marna and Lai both off planet and well out of unboosted range? He thrust his thoughts down, refusing to let himself think of the implications until he stood again looking over his own mountain stronghold.

From what Derik had said, Roi had been concealing his problems. Zhaim would have to find a chance to slip off to Falaron. There were places he had to be on Central today and tomorrow, but the next day, perhaps .... He might arrange to have his agents purchase some of the huge dogs used in the hunting preserves, and the crates to keep them in. It was the crates he was really after, though he might find a use for the dogs, too. There were a few other things he would need to buy, very discreetly indeed. And he'd have to do some thinking about those tracers.

He took a deep breath from the oxygen tank he carried. Living on the roof of the highest mountain range on Central had its costs. His home was pressurized, but when he wanted to step out onto the open balcony, to look across the immense distance of which he was lord with not even a force screen to come between, he had to carry extra oxygen. Just now, his exhilaration made it worth the trouble.

Of course he dared not count, yet, on his father's leaving Central. If he saw a safe opening to get rid of the bastard and its slave, he would take it. He was beginning to hope he wouldn't find an opening before Lai left. It would be so much more fun to take care of the brat that had usurped his birthright face to face.

Chapter 13

5/16/38

Eversummer: Marna

The planet's name, Marna thought, must have been picked out by a publicity agent. Everspring would have been more accurate, or Everfall, or perhaps Constancy. Maybe even Boredom.

The planet, with its rotational axis almost perpendicular to its orbital plane, had no seasons. The poles were bitterly cold, glaciated wastelands where the sun forever rolled around the horizon. The equatorial belt was an unchanging steam bath, the permanent home of daily tropical thunderstorms, varied by hurricanes along its poleward borders. The desert belts, inevitable result of the conflict between the planet's rotation and its unequal heating by its sun, were broad and sharply defined, with no transition zones where the rains came seasonally. The temperate zones, between desert and polar ice, were swept year round by equinoctial storms, varied only by occasional droughts. No monsoons, no seasonal blanket of snow to protect the dormant land, no regular alternation of wet and dry seasons.

All of the settled planets Marna had known or studied—long-lost R'il'n itself, Riya, Central, Falaron, Kovee, Earth—had axial tilts between fifteen and thirty degrees, and a regular progression of seasons. Those seasons might be subtle in the tropics, but they were present. And she was beginning to think they were a lot more important than she had ever realized.

"So let me be sure I have this straight," she said, her voice echoing in the isolation suit. "Of the Terran crops your ancestors imported from NewHome, only the tropicals and a handful of temperate annuals do well here, so your staples are yams, legumes, cassava, and a wide assortment of fruits and nuts in the tropics, and a few varieties of wheat, rice, legumes and vegetables in the temperate zone. Domesticated animals were poisoned by the native vegetation, and none survived the initial colonization. Native animals simply are not eaten." She looked questioningly at the acting head of the planetary government, who was looking unexpectedly green. "Are you feeling well, Acting-First Anden?"

The man jerked himself erect. "I am not ill, Lady Marna," he assured her. "It is just that the thought of eating such filth ...." He gulped and swallowed. "We honor our dead by taking their bodies into ours. We take in the clean fruits of the land that we may live. To eat such filth as the native animals—It would be to dishonor our ancestors and friends, Lady."

"Understood," Marna agreed. "And you did say that the plague has been treated from the start as one of those diseases which require that the body be cremated, given back to the air rather than taken back into the blood and flesh of the family?"

Anden sipped from the mug of beer before him, looking embarrassed. "We try, Lady," he said. "But the country people—well, when a family falls ill all at once, the bodies are burned. When there are survivors, they bring the bodies for burning, but the number of missing fingers or toes—I cannot blame them. Indeed, when my own wife and children died ...."

"A token funeral," Marna agreed gently. "Tell me, though—when this happens, are the relatives any more likely than their neighbors to fall ill?"

Anden looked thoughtful. "It is difficult to say, Lady. You understand that when a town is struck, it is not easy to keep track of those who survive. Nor of how many corpses have all their fingers, or who attends the clandestine funerals. Still, we could try to find out. It would be most heartening to the survivors if something approaching normal funerals could be held."

Marna nodded. "Ah—in your funeral rites—do you—cook the deceased?"

"Oh, yes," one of the others present assured her. "There's a very nasty local parasite. If the essence of the loved one can survive cremation and escape to the air, enough cooking to kill the parasite won't hurt it." The rest of the group stared at the speaker, obviously shocked by what they considered unseemly levity. The man seemed to shrink under their accusing gazes. "Well," he said defensively, "I'm sure that's how it started."

"I would like to see the figures on deaths among those who have followed some variant of the traditional rites," Marna said thoughtfully, "if you can find such information. Meanwhile—I believe several of you have lost family members?" Of the twelve planetary residents in the room, five nodded. "Off the record—perhaps you could all close your eyes, so only I know—how many of you participated in such token funerals?" Eyes closed, and five hands were laid palm up on the table.

Country folk, indeed, Marna thought. But it reinforced her growing certainty that the plague was not contagious in the normal sense. "I see," she said briskly. "Now, do you eat anything at all that is native to the planet? Seeds, fruits, leaves, water plants, insects, shellfish? Or invertebrates of Earth origin?"

This time most of the conferees looked either nauseated or outraged. The man who had assured her that they cooked their dead before eating them—Quallo, that was his name—cocked his head thoughtfully to one side. "Lady Marna," he said slowly, "all such are unclean. There have been famines when some such are eaten. Very few survive thus. The records suggest that some do indeed die as of this plague. But that whole towns should eat such unclean stuff, while there is clean food on the shelves, is beyond imagination."

"Yes," Marna agreed. "That is indeed the problem. But I believe I've found the toxin that is producing the symptoms. Essentially, the digestive process runs wild to such an extent that the stomach and intestines digest themselves.

"My guess would be that it's produced by a single-celled organism. If the organism is actually infecting people, it's dying off before the symptoms begin. I've done extensive lab work on isolates from victims who are just beginning to show symptoms, and I have found nothing capable of producing such a toxin. What I have found is a partial antidote to the toxin. I haven't had a chance to test it on Humans, but tissue culture and limited experiments on the test mice I brought suggest it may help. But it must be given early, while the symptoms are no more than a mild malaise, and until we can find out how the toxin is being spread, that's going to be difficult. In any event, I have the formula for you, and the steps I've used to synthesize it."

She had saved that encouragement for the end of the meeting deliberately, knowing it would hearten them, but knowing also it would be no help at all, even once the antidote was available, unless they could spot the outbreaks before the fever and vomiting struck. There was no possible way they could synthesize the antidote in the quantities that would be needed to give it regularly to everyone.

Could it possibly be deliberate terrorism? she wondered after she had teleported from the isolation suit to the orbiting courier ship. She had seen nothing in the local political situation to suggest unusual unrest, and was sickened herself by the very thought that any sane person—or any insane one, for that matter—could do such a thing.

And why, she wondered, had nobody attempted to develop a safe local meat source? That was exactly the kind of thing Zhaim was supposed to be expert at doing—the good he used to justify his repugnant habits. Well, she decided, once she had the immediate problem solved, Zhaim was going to be assigned to the problem of developing a safe local protein source for Eversummer. Under her suspicious eye.

The most frustrating thing was that she felt sure the answer to the illness had been in front of her face, there in the room where her isolation suit still sat. Something had been out of place—but she didn't understand Human cultures well enough yet to identify what. If I can't figure it out in a few days, she decided, I'll contact Roi and see if anything jumps out at him.

Falaron: Roi

"Father?" Roi said, surprised. What was his father doing here on Falaron? And Lai didn't look at all pleased with his son.

"We need to talk, Roi. Come on." The R'il'nian turned, and Roi followed. The grass along the path was wet with dew, and the river bottom was lost in fog under a sky just light enough that the stars were fading out. Eventually Lai turned away from the river, following a trail into a clump of trees. The ground was drier here, but the light was so faint that Roi found himself stumbling over tree roots and into brambles. What had he done wrong this time? he wondered.

The woods opened around them, into a clearing that seemed light after the gloom of the trees. Lai looked around him, then walked over to a huge fallen log and sat, gesturing at Roi to sit beside him. "Why didn't you tell me Timi sabotaged that glider?" he asked.

Roi froze. "He didn't," he managed to say. "He did help me pack the glider up, after we landed."

Lai turned and looked at Roi, a slow, thoughtful look. "I just went over the glider myself," he said. "The compensation circuit was pretty well charred, but there was enough left that I could tell Timi had handled the circuit itself, and before the charring. Roi, he tried to kill you. Why are you so determined to protect him?"

"Father, I probed him, right after the accident. He was shocked and horrified and even mad at me, because he thought I'd been stunting and lost control. He hadn't the slightest suspicion that the glider had been sabotaged, let alone the kind of knowledge he'd have had to have if he'd done it himself."

"But you were aware it was sabotaged? And you didn't say anything to me about it?" Lai was openly angry, now.

"No, I didn't. Because I was afraid you'd jump to the conclusion you just did, and blame Timi. And Timi's not guilty of anything except maybe a little stupidity. I think Zhaim may have used his body against me, but I don't believe Timi himself knew anything about it. I'm warned, now, and if Zhaim tries anything more I'll be ready."

"You're still that paranoid about Zhaim? Roi, I know he hasn't exactly been a good brother to you, but he's not stupid. Yes, he was upset when you tested as high as you did. It shook us all up. And you had reason enough to be afraid of him, as a slave. But can you honestly say that he has made a single hostile move since he knew you were Inner Council level?"

Roi looked down, wiggling unhappily. He had no doubts about Zhaim's continuing hostility, but it was based on little things—the curl of a lip when nobody else was looking, snide remarks, emotional broadcasts Zhaim didn't seem able to control, conversations about techniques of torture Roi was sure he was intended to overhear. "The way he's seducing Timi," he said finally.

Lai looked at him, his face incredulous. "You're taking his efforts to be better acquainted with one of your friends as a hostile act? Roi, if the situation weren't so serious, your attitude would be laughable. You and Zhaim are simply going to have to learn to work together. He's doing his part, and I'm getting very tired of your paranoia about him."

Roi fought down a surge of anger. "A control circuit is a friendly approach?" he asked.

"A control circuit?"

"Yes. Zhaim gave it to Timi as a good luck piece, just before we left. Told him to keep it hidden. I saw it when we were swimming. It looks like a piece of carved amber, but I'm pretty sure what it really is. And it explains the glider."

"What makes you so sure it's a control circuit? Did you probe it?"

"Well, no," Roi replied. "I was afraid of triggering another booby trap. When I tried to probe the electronics in the glider, when it first started acting up, it activated a screamer circuit. A strong one."

"And you didn't think to mention that, either." Lai was beginning to sound really angry. "Roi, you don't have a scrap of evidence that implicates Zhaim—only Timi. Well, I'm not leaving him here to take another crack at you. I'm taking him back to Central, and if he's as guilty as I think he is ...."

"No!" Roi cried out, suddenly frightened. "Father, Timi didn't do it! I may not be able to prove it was Zhaim, but I did probe Timi, and he didn't know anything about the glider! Please, Father!" He was frightened by how much his father looked like Zhaim, even to a silver shimmer in the green and gold eyes. He'd known the features were the same, of course, but he'd never before seen the kind of expression on his father's face that he was seeing now.

"Roi," Flame's voice came to him, "it's all right, Roi."

"All *right?*" he tried to gasp, and nearly panicked as his voice refused to obey him.

"Come on, love, wake up. You're safe, and nothing's wrong." A slender arm was around his shoulders, and a supple body snuggled close to his. His father's eyes were all silver, now—no, not his father's eyes, any more, but Zhaim's. Familiar lips brushed his, and he realized he was lying wrapped in Flame's arms, his whole body drenched in sweat. "It's just one of your nightmares, Roi. Nothing to worry about."

He still couldn't seem to move, but what was it Marna had told him, about the body sometimes being paralyzed while the mind went dreaming? He reached for the part of his brain that produced the effect, turned off the paralysis, and opened his eyes.

He was facing the west window, and only the brightest stars were visible in the paling sky. A dream, he told himself. Just another nightmare.

"You're not starting to have nightmares even when someone's holding you, are you?" Flame asked anxiously.

"Wasn't my usual kind," Roi assured her. "This was—different." He lifted himself on one arm to look around the room. Timi and Amber were sharing the other lower bunk, their heads turned anxiously toward Roi, and Penny was propped up on one elbow. It was too dark to see expressions, but he was picking up definite anxiety from all of them.

183

"Nothing serious," he assured them. "I don't feel like going back to sleep, though. Anybody else feel like watching the sun rise from the springs?"

Central: Lai

Rain slanted down outside the window, flicking leaves on the citrus trees that broke up the expanse of lawn outside Lai's study. Lai stood by the window, staring out at the gray afternoon.

"You don't think they're going to make the deadline, do you," Derry said from behind him.

Lai shook his head. Outside the window, a gust of wind sent a sweet lemon tumbling to the ground, and a wheeled box scurried across the lawn to pick it up with a jointed arm. "I've thought from the start I'd have to go out to Kablukolelli in person," he replied. "I'm sorry we had to set the deadline so short—I'd rather have waited until Marna was back. But the situation's blowing up too fast. It's got to be cleared up within a couple of fivedays, or it'll be too far out of control to stop. So—a ten-day ultimatum. If things haven't quieted down by the 25th, I'll 'port out there and knock a few heads together."

"What are you going to do about Roi?" Derik asked.

Lai sighed. "Tell him I'm going. If he decides he'd rather come back here while I'm gone, I'll want you and Kaia to keep an eye on him. I almost wish he were legally adult; I'd a lot rather leave him in charge than Zhaim. Since he's not, he's probably safer on Falaron than here antagonizing his brother. I don't foresee anything major coming up while I'm gone, but I'd appreciate it if you could find enough minor problems to keep Zhaim busy."

"You're not taking him with you?"

Lai shuddered at the idea. "After the problems he caused last time? This is going to be tricky enough without Zhaim's posturings and threats. 'Fraid you're stuck with him this time, Derry."

"Actually," Derik said, "I was thinking you might take Roi along."

Lai turned to face his half brother. "It's an awfully long teleport," he said thoughtfully, "even in tandem. I wouldn't mind having him along, though, and I might offer him that as an option. But after the fight we got into over the glider incident, I'm going to leave it up to him. He's waited a long time for this vacation, and I don't want to mess it up for him. I do wish I'd had time to get over to Falaron and go over that glider. No chance now, but I'd feel better if I were absolutely certain Zhaim didn't have a hand in that accident."

Derik nodded. "Sometimes I think we've done too good a job of getting Roi to accept Zhaim. I know. Zhaim hasn't made a move against him for the last year and a half, except for his attempts to seduce Timi. But I still suspect he's just biding his time."

Lai sighed as he sat down on the cushioned window ledge. "I'm not picking up any definite warnings on my leaving," he said, "so I think it'll be all right, this time. But I could wish Roi were a little more paranoid about Zhaim than he is. For all that he's been through, he's just a little too trusting."

"The Company's tracking them, right?" Derry asked. "Have them send the daily updates to me. He should be safe enough on Falaron, with Zhaim here. We can even hope the Kablukolelli factions start seeing sense, and you don't have to go."

"I wish," Lai replied dryly as he turned back to the window.

CHAPTER 14

"Roi," Penny finally asked, "what *are* you doing with that horse?"

With no obvious signal to the grulla, Roi slowed Raindrop from a canter to a trot and moved the horse over to trot shoulder to shoulder with Freckles. "Just checking her flying changes," the R'il'noid replied.

Penny thought back to the way Raindrop had moved under Roi, almost dancing. "Changing every stride?" she asked. "What for?"

"I wanted to make sure that she changes properly from the rear," Roi replied as he loosened the reins and leaned forward to scratch along the crest of Raindrop's neck. He turned his rain-wet head slightly and looked sideways to meet Penny's gaze. "Does the Company ever sell horses?"

Penny fought to keep from laughing aloud. "The Company," she assured him, "will sell anything it can legally sell, as long as you're willing to pay more than what it would cost them to replace it. But Roi, what would you do with a Falaron horse? Surely the horses you have make these look like scrubs. And it's not practical to ship a horse from here to Central, anyway."

"I *think* I could teleport her," Roi said thoughtfully. "It didn't occur to me at the time, but I got to wondering later if I couldn't have teleported Dusty across that flooded creek. I finally tried it with Raindrop yesterday. As long as I'm taking her someplace she'd like to be, she's no problem at all. Lots easier than teleporting Flame was, and that wasn't as hard as I expected. Of course ten light years is a lot more work than a few hundred paces, but I suspect Derry or Marna either one would figure it was a good training exercise for me, and give me help if I needed it.

"As far as why, I've been looking for a horse I can use in game competition. You know, pattern racing, quick turns, stop and go stuff.

My horse Flight, back on Central, is a terrific jumper and cross-country horse, but he's headstrong at speed and he's too big to stop or turn fast. Raindrop's quick and she listens to me. I'd like to try her for speed, but she's closer to what I want than anything I've found yet on Central."

"Raindrop, huh?" Penny said. The mare's usually atrocious manners had made her anything but a favorite among the guides, and Penny had been shocked to find her assigned to Roi. But if Roi liked his mount that well .... Penny turned to study the horse.

She really was a good-looking animal, Penny thought. Her well-proportioned black head and arched neck blended smoothly into well laid-back shoulders the color of polished slate. Her body was deep without excess width just behind the shoulders, giving free play to her forelegs as well as a comfortable seat to her rider, but the barrel flared out further back for abundant heart and lung room, narrowing only slightly at the short, strong loins. Her legs were well boned but clean, darkening to black below the knees and hocks and finished with neat white anklets above striped hooves. The whole horse was set off by a black-dotted white blanket starting at the withers and running back to cover most of her body to the powerful gaskins. Even in the misty rain they were riding through, her coat shone. She was small compared to the horses Penny had seen on Central, but there was nothing scrubby about Raindrop. And her manners under Roi were impeccable.

The Company, Penny thought, would be delighted to get rid of her. "I've been meaning to ask," she said. "Would you like the same mounts after we run the canyon?

Roi, Amber and Timi replied with a chorus of affirmatives. Flame looked thoughtful. "Are you sure Token won't come in season again?" she asked.

"Not while she's in foal," Roi replied.

Penny winced. "You still think she is?" she asked.

"No question at all," he replied, and grinned over at her. "Maybe I ought to buy her, too. I'm really curious about what the foal's going to be like."

"Think about it," Penny urged. "And let Raindrop take it easy. We'll be at the lake by midafternoon at the latest, and there's a nice open area along the shore where you can set up a weaving course or something. You can't really check her out in these little meadows, or in the woods. The ground's too uneven." They rode under the trees again as she spoke, dropping back into single file as they followed a game trail through the underbrush. A fiveday ago, they'd been in tallgrass prairie with scattered areas of dry woodland in the uplands, broken by gallery forest and swamp along the river bottoms. Now they rode through rolling open woodland dotted with beaver meadows and ponds.

Penny was in the lead as the trail approached the top of a long rise. The woods seemed lighter ahead, and when she looked closely, she saw burn scars on some of the trunks. As the ground dropped away again ahead of her, she came out of the trees above an old fire scar. Fireweed and brush grew stirrup-high on the downward slope. Charred tree trunks leaned drunkenly here and there, and Penny suspected that others, lying flatter, were hidden by the new growth. "Keep it down to a slow walk through here," she called back over her shoulder. "There'll be dead tree trunks all over."

"Is that the lake?" Roi called from behind her, and she looked higher. The rain had let up, and the horizon had opened out to a line of jagged hills. From the base of the hills, a sheet of pewter stretched toward them, its near shore hidden behind the next rise in the ground.

"That's it," she replied. "We made even better time than I thought. Want to stop here for lunch, or push on to the shore? Roi? You're the one most likely to need food."

"Only when I'm doing esper work," he replied, "and I haven't been this morning. And I ate a big breakfast. Want me to feel out the downed tree trunks, like I did through the snow? I've got plenty of candy with me."

Penny legged her mount to the side and waved Roi ahead in reply.

They moved down the slope more easily than she had expected. Roi led them in a circuitous path, but he never had to backtrack. The sun came out briefly as they were crossing the shallow stream at the base of the slope, and Penny tipped her head back to look at the sky. There were only a few patches of blue overhead, with shafts of sunlight streaming through them, but to the west the sky was clear. As they came over the top of the next slope, the lake opened out before them. Shafts of sunlight played over the gray waters, and by the time they reached the shoreline, the clouds were retreating to the east. "Might as well start gathering dead branches for firewood now," she called back.

Falaron: Zhaim

There was nothing like a good religious conflict to advance the technology of torture, Zhaim thought as he ran his eyes over the implements stocking the former butchering area of his Falaron hunting lodge. The polished metal and electronics he normally favored would have been out of place in this rustic setting, but the hand-rubbed wood and intricate blacksmith work fitted in perfectly. He ran a hand lovingly over the virgin bed of the rack and smiled at the braziers with their implements. They were collectors' items; pieces he had commissioned from the same artisans who had toiled for the Spanish Inquisition, on Earth. For two centuries they had languished in stasis, a part of the museum of torture implements Zhaim had been collecting for most of his life.

For historical accuracy, the stone walls should have been dank and crusted with niter, the air fouled by primitive—or more often nonexistent—plumbing, and the light a flaring torch or two. Zhaim could project that effect, if he wanted to, and he might do just that when he wasn't in the room himself. But he preferred light enough to watch his victims' faces, and to force them to watch each other's agony, and he detested the smell of sewer gas.

The stone walls were painted white, and the ceiling glowed with modern high-intensity lighting. The west wall was transparent above knee height, which corresponded to ground level on this side of the lodge, and looked out over jagged mountains to the west.

Nothing like *his* mountains, of course. The air outside the window was dense enough to breathe comfortably, and the snowdrifts remaining north of the rocks scattered through the meadow were melting rapidly under the late spring sun. He could just see two minute figures toiling on the far side of the meadow. Almost back to their starting point, he thought. Almost time to get rid of them. He meant the first blood on the rack to be that of the bastard's black slave—with the bastard forced to watch every move. The boot, perhaps, for those two, or the flaying knife .... He walked up the stairs, annoyed by the effort he had to make. He had known the place was rustic, of course, but he hadn't realized until he began his remodeling that it didn't even have a lift shaft.

The large room that made up most of the main floor had transparent walls on the east, west and south. The fourth, interior, wall was covered with a screen showing a generous slice of the continent. A single red dot glowed on the shore of a lake more than three-quarters of the way to the eastern coast. Zhaim brought up the magnification enough he could be sure that the dot was indeed right on the shore, and then requested a weather overlay.

The warm front that had been slowly overtaking the group the last time he had looked was past the red light now, approaching the eastern shore of the lake. The pursuing cold front was well back, probably at least two days away. Ideal weather for sailing across the lake, tomorrow. Warm and clear, with a steady west-southwest wind.

He reached his mind out to the cold front, searching for any instabilities he could trigger to accelerate its movement. Nothing in the front itself, but to the east of it—yes, if he increased the heating of the ground *here*, and brought a few extra ice nuclei in *there*, he thought he could trigger a squall line that would be crossing the lake by tomorrow afternoon. He was reasonably certain that Lai would in fact be leaving for the Kablukolelli cluster by the 24th—Zhaim had agents in the cluster making sure of that. Marna might, however, be back by then—either because Lai called her back or because she herself judged that one of them should be close enough that Roi could reach help if needed. He'd limit himself to untraceable accidents until both R'il'nians were well away from Central.

He picked up an interface circlet and slipped it over his head, then dropped into one of the deep slaveskin chairs scattered around the room. He closed his eyes and reached through the control circuit into the black slave's consciousness.

Falaron: Timi

"Y'know, I think Roi's right about that horse," Amber said. "People aren't going to believe her color, but she's a real athlete."

"Long as I don't have to ride her," Timi replied. He looked back down the shore to where Roi was weaving Raindrop at speed through a line of willow poles. Flame stood where the last pole should have been, and as Timi watched, Roi swung her up behind him as Raindrop spun around her, and then began weaving back down the line. "I suppose Vara would call that a collected gallop," the slave said. "Wonder what she'll have to say about her color. I'm ready to bend on the jib sail, Amber."

Amber grinned at him. "You and your nautical terminology! Why not just say you're going to fasten the front sail in place? Here you are," she added, feeding him the upper corner of the narrow, triangular sail. "Want me to go tell Penny we're ready for her to check out the rigging?"

Timi paused to inspect his work. The mast was stepped and stayed solidly in place, and the mainsail was firmly attached to the boom, kept in place by the light dock ties. He had checked out all the control circuits, and had only to finish attaching the jib before he would be ready to hoist the mainsail. "Sure," he said. "I'll be finished by the time she gets here."

Amber stepped carefully from the bow of the boat to the dock. She wore a white sleeveless tunic and shorts against the burning rays of the sun and the hot wood and synthetics of the boat, and her legs, pale from the riding breeches, were already turning pink. "Put some sunscreen on your legs," he called after her.

Penny was in shorts also, but she had evidently remembered the sunscreen Amber had forgotten. She checked Timi's work over systematically and nodded approval. "Looks fine," she told them. "Roi wants to cool Raindrop down and then try a couple more speed events to make sure she's got more than one sprint a day in her. Did you two want to take a short sail this afternoon?"

"Somebody ought to check the boat out, if we're going to cross the lake tomorrow," Timi replied. "Ah—we might drop the sail and drift a little while we're out there."

Penny looked pointedly at the double sleeping bag stowed in the bottom of the boat. "Use the anchor," she told him. "And remember the wind's offshore and don't go so far out you can't get back before sunset. You'll have a land breeze to reinforce the offshore wind soon as the sun's down." She looked again at the sleeping bag, and sighed. "Roi and Flame were talking about a moonlight ride this evening. Ah, well, the moon's almost full. I can hold down the camp."

Falaron: Zhaim

Zhaim pulled off the circlet with a small grimace of disgust. Normal human sexuality repelled him, to the extent that he had found himself pulling away from the contact with Timi every time the slave had looked at Amber or thought of their plans for the late afternoon. He picked up the report chip he had brought with him, and lost himself for a while absorbing its contents.

When he finished the chip, he turned to glance out the west window-wall, and snarled to himself. One of the workers was jogging toward the house, and there was still a gap in the perimeter fence. They had done everything else he needed them for, he thought as he walked out the door on the east side of the lodge, then around and downhill to the west side, glancing back to be sure the window into the torture chamber was opaqued from the outside. The two young Falaronians had painted the walls and modified the lighting, but Zhaim had teleported the equipment in himself after they were through with the room.

He looked around the area inside the fence with a critical eye. The lodge was well above tree line, nestled into an old, west-facing cirque floor. The new fence enclosed the level area, including a small lake and five large doghouses, spaced out midway between the lodge and the fence. The dogs whined in their cages behind him, huge brutes, bred to hunt sabertooth, longhorn bison and mammoth, and trained to hold or kill on command. Not, the trainer had told him, that any sane hunter would send the valuable dogs in to kill a mammoth, except as a diversion to allow a hunter time to escape.

"Well, what is it?" he snapped as the man slowed to a walk in front of him. "Can't you even do a simple job like installing a fence on your own?"

"We're ready for the gate, sir," the young man said breathlessly. He was just past twenty, one of the surplus population forced to leave the planet and one who had been unable to find work elsewhere. Forced to sign up with a colonizing company, he and his friend had been willing enough to delay their departures to work for one of the company owners. So far as either knew, their names had been switched to a later ship, one departing for a more clement world than their original destination. In fact, Zhaim had seen to it that their names had dropped completely out of the company files.

"No gate," Zhaim said. "A gate's a weak point, and I'll be flying in and out. Just close the fence, and mind you both finish up inside."

He watched as the man jogged wearily back toward the almost completed fence. It was twice his own height: thick, close-linked wire hung from heavy, deep-set posts and topped with a pair of charged conductors. It was a type advertised as being able to stop a mammoth. Zhaim was more concerned that it would hold the dogs, and slow down any escapees long enough that the dogs could catch them. He glanced back again toward the cages, and a slow, ugly grin spread across his face.

It took the two half an hour to finish the last panel of the fence, load the remaining fencing and tools onto the big floater, and start back toward the lodge. Zhaim stood and watched, attention divided between the workers and the dogs. Once the floater had passed the circle of doghouses, he began letting the dogs out of their cages, giving each a "stay close" command as he released it. When all five were out and had finished greeting each other, he took two steps toward his workers and swung his arm toward them as he gave the pack the command to hunt and kill.

His erstwhile workers didn't believe what was happening, at first. They stood their ground, shouting and waving at him. Even the dogs seemed unwilling to accept men as prey, and he had to repeat the "kill" command twice more, reinforcing the command with mind-send the second time, before the animals finally closed in and pulled the men down. The taller of the two, the dark one, went down with his throat spurting blood. The shorter, with the blue eyes and silver-blond hair, went down screaming and continued to shriek as he writhed on the ground. The dogs backed off and lay down, licking the blood from their paws and lips.

Zhaim frowned as he walked toward the animals, but then remembered what the trainer had said. The dogs were taught to stop their attack when the prey was helpless, leaving their kill as little damaged as possible for trophy or meat. As huntsman, he was expected to gut the kill and feed the innards to the dogs.

He wrinkled his nose in distaste as he pulled out his force blade, then cheered up as he realized that the one who reminded him a little of his detested half brother was still alive and conscious, watching him with incredulous eyes. Deliberately he set the force blade at the base of the dead man's sternum, and drew it down through cloth and flesh to expose the steaming intestines. The dogs whined eagerly as he kicked a couple of loops toward them and urged them to eat.

The blonde's eyes were beginning to glaze with shock, and his screams had died away to unbelieving whimpers. Zhaim stepped across him, bending to slap an ampoule of counterShock against his victim's neck. He waited for the medication to take effect enough to prevent the man from fainting, watching to be sure that the dogs, unfed for over a day, were beginning to eat their way into the dead man's body. Then he bent over again, this time setting the force blade against the survivor's hip and drawing it in a crescent across the lower belly, careful to slit only the clothing on this first pass.

"No," the man cried out, "Oh, God, no! What did we ever do to you?"

"Nothing," Zhaim purred as he drew the blade across again, this time slicing skin. "You worked well, and you can thank that for an easy death."

The next stroke of the blade cut into the abdominal muscles, and the nearest dog, unable to find room at the first body, lifted its head and whined eagerly at the smell of fresh blood. The blue eyes watched in horror as Zhaim made a fourth pass with the blade, this time cutting a handwidth slit into the peritoneum and pulling out a loop of intestine. Zhaim stretched it far enough to offer it to the dog, than stood and watched, amused by the delicacy with which the animal fed.

The counterShock kept the blond from the mercy of fainting, and Zhaim watched for a good quarter hour while the big black dog pulled the screaming man's guts out through the slit. Then a second dog widened the opening, and within minutes the man was dead, half his lungs eaten. Zhaim was giggling, a high-pitched sound he hated but seemed unable to stop.

An icy breeze from the cirque wall beyond the lodge brought him back to himself, and he looked up to see that the sun had set and the world around him was purpling into evening. He looked again at the dogs, and decided to let them devour as much as they would of their prey.

His only moment of regret came when he got back to the lodge and realized he would have to move the cages down into the old abattoir himself.

Falaron: Roi

Roi shivered violently, and felt Flame's arms tighten around him. "You all right?" she said softly, and he turned to look at her.

The moonlight was so bright tonight he could see the red in her hair, and distinguish a patch of peeling skin on her nose. The sand on which they had laid out their sleeping bag, tawny in the daylight, was tarnished silver in the moonlight, and the lake beyond, ruffled by the offshore wind, reflected a tiny moon from each wavelet. He turned his attention back to Flame's face, a handspun away from his own, and forced a smile. "I'm fine," he told her. "Just one of those convulsive shivers."

Her eyebrows drew together "Sure it wasn't one of your hunches?" she asked.

"I don't think so," he replied as he reached out a fingertip to touch the twin vertical lines between her eyebrows. "More—oh, as if something unpleasant had happened."

"Like maybe a sabertooth killing that cute baby mammoth we saw this morning?" Flame asked.

"Oh, no," Roi replied. "If I started reacting every time a predator killed its normal prey, I'd be shaking all the time on this planet. That's unpleasant, especially if you like the prey animal, but there's no malice involved, just hunger. This—it wasn't just unpleasant; I picked the wrong word there. It was malicious. And it might have had something to do with us, but I can't trace it out."

Flame's hand had come up to pull at a loose strand of hair as he spoke, and now she pulled it into her mouth and began chewing on it. Roi reached out to capture the strand and remove it from her mouth, and Flame looked briefly sheepish. "Roi," she said, "Have you told anybody except us about your precognition not working properly?"

"No," he replied, looking away. The puma attack rose in his mind, and his dream of the night on the Peccary River. "Marna and Derry have both said erratic talents are a normal part of adolescence. I can't go crying to Father with every normal change that happens to me."

"I'm not talking about complaining that you're losing your talent. I'm talking about letting him know that you're not foreseeing the specific dangers of this trek. Because he's probably assuming you do, and he may want to set up extra safeguards if you're not."

"I can handle it," Roi assured her, and ran an exploratory hand down over the curve of her buttock as he leaned forward to kiss her. He knew one sure way of getting Flame's mind off anything else, and he had no qualms about using it. Because he couldn't face saying anything to his father, at least not until he could prove that Zhaim, not Timi, was behind the glider sabotage.

Chapter 15

The wind tugged at Roi's hair and rippled the grass in the fenced pasture. Raindrop's short mane was standing almost erect as the breeze tried to blow it to the wrong side of her neck, and her sparse tail whipped to one side like a badly tattered banner. Roi held his hand flat so the mare could lip up the last of the syrup-soaked flatcake.

"Roi," Penny's voice floated up to him, fighting the wind. "Roi! Hurry up! We want to cast off before the land breeze dies down."

Roi squinted into the low morning sun toward the lakeshore, confirming that Penny was looking straight at him, her feet planted wide and her hands on her hips. He reached out with his left hand to give the horse one last scratch behind the ears, then turned and jogged down the gentle slope to the dock. After a month in boots, his feet seemed weightless in the light deck shoes he now wore.

The others were already in the boat waiting for him. Their gear, aside from what they would need during their day on the lake, had been left in two piles in the cabin—one pile to be transported by the Company to the cabin on the other side of the lake, the other to be reclaimed at the end of the journey. Roi paused at the dock to sweep his right hand through the water to rinse away the syrup, then untied the mooring rope and took a single loop around the bollard.

Timi

Timi looked up at Roi's arrival. He was the best sailor of the four, and he resented the fact that Roi would be helmsman for this day trip. At least his owner had listened to Timi's warning from yesterday afternoon and pulled wind slacks and a jacket over his light shorts and safety tunic. Both scarlet, of course. Timi was getting heartily tired of the color-coding.

Timi had already released the dock ties holding the sail to the boom, and he glanced at Roi as he reached for the control panel. "Hoist sail?" he asked.

The R'il'noid cocked one eyebrow and grinned. "You're the captain for this leg, Timi," he said, and Timi goggled in surprise.

"You really mean that?" he asked.

"Of course I mean it. You're the best sailor, so you're the logical helmsman and that puts you in charge. Did I overstep in loosening the painter, sir?"

Timi shook himself together and glanced at the telltales fastened halfway up the shrouds. The wind was blowing almost directly over the bow, pushing the little sloop away from the dock. "Snub her in a bit tighter and grab the port shroud," he said, using the joystick to swing the boom out to a right angle. Roi saw what he was doing and manipulated painter and shroud to realign the boom with the offshore wind, so Timi could hoist first the mainsail and then the jib with only a slight increase in the pressure of the wind on the sail.

"Cast off and get aboard," Timi said as the sails locked into place, and watched as the scarlet-clad figure jumped lightly to the deck just behind the shroud, flipping loose the painter as he came. As soon as Roi was aboard, Timi manipulated the joysticks to bring the boom in, coordinating rudder and sail angle until they were running before the wind, sailing north-northeast with the southwest wind over their left shoulders.

"Do we have any good landmarks from here," he asked Penny, "or do I just steer a compass heading?"

"See the two hills that look like mirror images, steep where they face each other but fairly gentle on the outer slopes?" Penny replied. "Steer for the peak on the right-hand one."

"Should have taken off on the starboard tack," Timi muttered. "Get ready to jibe." The other four ducked as he manipulated the controls, bringing the boom across the deck in a controlled jibe as he steered the boat to the right until they were running east.

The southwest breeze remained steady as they ran, only lightening a little as they lost the influence of the land breeze. Jackets were shed as the sun rose higher in the sky, and by noon Timi was tacking rather than running almost straight downwind simply to give them a cool breeze across the deck. By midafternoon everyone except Timi was asleep, their stomachs filled with cheese rolls and lukewarm herb tea.

Some day, Timi thought, it would be more than a small sailboat that he captained. Someday it would be a starship, perhaps exploring for new opportunities for the Clan. He'd have to start lower, of course—but with Academy training as well as what he could learn from his Clan relatives, there was no limit to how high he, an ex-slave, could climb. A passenger ship, a freighter—not a slave ship, though. He wanted nothing to do with that! And Amber beside him, as medical officer .... He yawned, stretched, shook himself and wished he could go for a swim. He was back on the right tack, headed almost directly toward the peak Penny had indicated, and the telltales were barely fluttering on the shrouds as the boat moved with the wind. Roi sighed and shifted position, and Timi smiled a little. At the moment, he felt nothing but affection for his old friend. Of course, he thought with amusement, Roi might not have been so willing to put him in command of the ship if it had been controlled directly by sheet and rudder, instead of electronics, but then Timi himself wasn't all that enthusiastic about trying to catch the wind by using brute force and a few pulleys.

He checked the sail and looked up, almost hypnotized by the intense blue of the sky. Ahead of him, Amber rolled over and opened her eyes, then struggled to her feet, yawning. Roi, disturbed by her movement, opened his own eyes, looking sleepily over Timi's shoulder. Abruptly he was fully alert and scrambling to his own feet.

"Amber, get down," he said sharply, just as Timi saw the first luffing of the sail.

Amber looked at Roi in sleepy puzzlement. "What for?" she asked.

"We're going to jibe," Timi said, trying frantically to swing the boat into the wind and knowing it was too late. A gust from the left side and the wind of their own motion had already caught the far side of the sail, and the boom was beginning to accelerate back toward the center of the boat.

Roi wasn't risking the time for Amber to finish waking up. He had his arm around her, pulling her back from the edge of the boat and shoving her down into the cockpit, almost as soon as the sail began to flutter. But he was still on his own feet when the boom swung violently across the deck. Even as Timi threw his weight sharply to the left, trying to keep the boat from capsizing with the abrupt shift of weight, the boom struck Roi and carried him overboard.

"Penny," Timi yelled as the trim circuits cut in and the boat began to right itself. "Take the helm! I'm going after Roi!" He had marked the eddy where Roi had struck the water, and was over the side and stroking toward it as soon as Penny had the joystick.

Roi would be all right, he told himself. The safety pockets in his tunic would inflate as soon as the underwater pressure triggered them, and Timi was fairly certain that the boom had caught Roi in the shoulder, not the head. He'd be shaken, maybe even have broken bones, but he shouldn't have been knocked out.

If you knocked him out, something in the back of his mind whispered, *there's a good chance he'd drown.*

That's crazy, his saner self replied. Roi's my friend.

He's your owner. How can he possibly be your friend?

He was almost back to the eddy now, and with a surge of relief—or was it hatred?—he saw Roi's head break water. The R'il'noid was pawing feebly at the water, seemingly unable to use his right arm, and he was choking and coughing.

All you have to do is hit him like this, the voice whispered, and to his horror Timi felt his hands moving, not to assist Roi until the boat could get back to them, but to kill.

Roi

Roi's first sight on waking had been the line of thunderstorms over Timi's shoulder. Startled, he pulled himself up to glance at the water off the port side, and saw the change in color where a different wind approached the boat. We'll jibe when that hits, he thought, and saw Amber on her feet. "Amber, get down," he called out, and saw that she was too sleepy to react quickly. He grabbed at her, swinging her around him and down into the bottom of the boat. The boom was already swinging, too fast for him to get out of the way completely. If he ducked, it would get him in the head. Almost without thinking he jumped away and upward, going with the boom as it carried him over the side and into the water.

He went deep, and his first startled gasp brought water into his throat. Luckily, he'd made teleporting oxygen from the air directly into his lungs a reflex. He wouldn't drown, no matter what his throat and upper airways felt like. His right arm was numb, though, where the boom had struck, and the floatation pockets in his tunic didn't seem to be inflating as they should. More sabotage? he wondered as he struggled weakly toward the surface.

His head broke into the air, and he quit trying to suppress his coughing reflex. Timi was close by, he saw with relief, and the sailboat, with Penny at the helm, was coming about in preparation for picking them up. Then Timi's hand was chopping down toward the angle of neck and shoulder, and he ducked back underwater to break the force of the blow, coming up an arm length away from his friend.

Friend? Timi's eyes were wild, and there was an odd, jerky quality to his movements, as if two minds fought for control of the same body. Which was probably, Roi thought, exactly what was happening. He increased the wildness of his own flailing, and when Timi moved toward him again, he managed to catch his good hand in the weakened leather thong around Timi's neck. The thong broke, freeing the amber pendant, and abruptly Timi was himself again, looking totally bewildered.

Well, Roi thought, that took care of any lingering doubts about the pendant. Too bad the thing was lost in the lake; he'd have preferred to keep it as evidence against Zhaim. The numbness in his right arm was fading, replaced by growing pain, and he was grateful when Timi reached out to support him.

"You all right?" Timi asked as his arm came around Roi's shoulders.

Roi winced at the pressure on his upper arm, then closed his eyes and reached into his body to assess how badly he was hurt. "Cracked right ulna," he said after a moment. "I'll need some help getting back into the boat." The boat, he saw, had come about and was headed back toward them—yes, he decided as he got a glimpse of their marker hill, the wind shift had been more than a gust. There was a fresh northwest breeze rising, and the water was beginning to roughen. Thunder rumbled faintly to the northwest.

The rest of the afternoon was interesting—meaning, as Timi said, that it would make a good story when—and if—they survived, but at the time it was concentrated misery. Roi spent the first half hour back on the boat Healing his broken arm and firmly telling his inner ears that he was not seasick. Timi had spent the same time tacking downwind, this time for maximum speed rather than a cooling breeze. They all scrambled back into jackets, and by the time Roi recovered enough to pay attention to his surroundings, the squall line had swallowed the sun and thunder was rumbling behind them almost continuously.

"How much farther is it?" he asked.

"Not far, at this speed," Penny replied. "But the storm's catching up with us, and we may have to drop sail pretty soon."

"Can we anchor and ride it out?" Roi asked.

Timi shook his head. "It's too deep here," he replied. "Best we could do is rig a sea anchor, and this close to a lee shore I'd rather take a chance on beaching her under some kind of control." Thunder crashed, far too close, and Timi glanced anxiously at the tip of the mast. Roi could feel the charge building up on the boat, and began bleeding it off. The faint glow Timi had been watching vanished, and the helmsman sighed in relief. "Keep doing that, would you?" he asked. "It helps if I don't have to worry about lightning."

"Right," Roi agreed, pulling himself up to sit on the windward deck. He could see surf pounding on the shore ahead of the boat, and when he twisted to look farther left, toward their landmark hill, he saw the dock, rising and falling on the choppy waves. They were sailing with the sail wide to the right and the wind from the left and behind, and as Roi studied the shore, Timi hauled in sail and reset his course somewhat to the left, aiming for the base of the dock. "Deep water inshore?"

Timi nodded. "Penny says we're safe a boat length from shore, and the dock's four or five times that long. I'm going to try to come about just downwind of the dock, and drop the sails. Are you recovered enough to jump the mooring lines over to the dock? We'll be tying up on the right side."

"Long as you can kill enough speed," Roi replied. The sailboat was cutting through the water at a rate he had rarely seen, and didn't really want to see. "Penny, do we have some more emergency bars? Just in case I have to levitate?" She looked a little green, he thought as she handed him the bar. In fact, all three girls looked a little green. "Want me to try to do something about that seasickness?" he asked, and Flame shook her head.

"You concentrate on getting us moored," she said.

Roi nodded and pulled the mooring lines from their stowage under the foredeck as he chewed and swallowed. The painter was still attached to the bow, the coil tied loosely to the mast. He lay on his belly and wiggled forward on the foredeck until he could attach a second line. It wasn't raining yet, though a gray curtain was moving steadily toward them, but waves were breaking over the left side of the boat and Timi had Flame and Amber bailing. The foredeck heaved under him as he worked, water sweeping completely across the textured synthetic, and he was glad to get back to the cockpit with the second line. The rear mooring lines were easier to attach. He coiled one and clipped it to the transom, and carried the other forward outside the right shroud.

They were getting close to the shore now, and Timi was spilling wind, trying to lose speed before the tight turn he had to make. Reflected waves from the coast were producing a chop that felt as if it was shaking the boat apart, and Roi felt the first drops of rain stinging his face. The girls and Timi were all on the left side, leaning out as far as they could to counter the effect of the wind on the increasingly close-hauled sail. Roi released the jib sheets to let the jib sail flap free and crouched on the right foredeck, bracing himself against the shroud and fighting to keep his eyes open against a sudden downpour of rain. Then the rudder went hard over and the boat heeled sharply as they turned into and past the wind. The dock slid by, almost too close and moving far too fast, and Roi jumped for it.

He landed running, and nearly fell anyway. He snubbed the stern rope around a bollard, adding his weight to the push of the wind as the boat came about, and saw the mainsail drop. The boat strained briefly at the snubbing rope, and he tossed a loop of the bow line around another bollard. Then Penny and Amber were on the dock with the extra lines, and together the three of them cross-tied the boat, springing it to ride out the storm. Flame was fastening the dock ties around the mainsail and jib, both already soaked, and Timi sat in the stern, wide-eyed and shaking, rainwater dragging his soaked curls down his forehead and dripping off his nose and chin.

***

"There wasn't a sign of a squall line on the satellite images until just before noon," Penny told the others as she scrubbed at her hair with a towel. "That's three major weather systems that have caught us by surprise on this trek."

"And I didn't even pick up a warning on this one," Roi said through the red sweater he was pulling over his own damp hair. "Any chance you could get that weather receiver back? The way we're going, we'll get a flash flood while we're rafting the canyon." He poked his head through the neck opening and pulled the sweater down to find Amber, hair turbaned in a towel, offering him a mug of hot peacemint tea. Timi, wrapped in a blanket and still shivering, was sitting on the bench by the window with another mug cupped in both hands.

Penny gave Roi a shaky grin. "They aren't giving me much choice about it," she said. "They're bringing one out as soon as the squall line's past. Roi, why didn't you teleport to safety?"

Roi took a sip of the hot tea, savoring the sweetness of honey in the mint and citrus taste of the herb. He walked over to the window of the cabin and looked out toward the dock. Rain was still falling in sheets and the boat was rocking at her moorings, but the lake to the west was almost too bright to look at, and there was a strip of yellow along the western horizon. "I had a teleport set up," he said slowly, "but there's no way I could have taken the rest of you with me. As long as there was a chance I could help you by staying with you, that's what I had to do. If it were a choice between all of us being killed and all except me being killed, I'd have saved myself." I think, he added mentally.

"Squall line will be past in no more than an hour, I'd say," he added. "Looks like we ought to have a nice evening."

"I'm the one who should have spotted it coming," Timi said miserably. "If I'd just taken a look behind me now and then ...."

"You might," Roi said as he seated himself next to Timi, "have seen it coming maybe an hour before that first gust hit. I suspect we were more than halfway across the lake before the first cloud poked itself over the horizon. Certainly there was nothing showing when I dropped off to sleep; I was feeling a very little bit uneasy, and I checked. I should have felt beyond the horizon, but I didn't. So suppose you'd seen the first little wisp of cloud. Could you have done anything but run for this shore? And would you have gotten here any sooner?"

Timi looked at him with an expression of surprise. "Maybe five minutes from sailing faster for that hour, and another fifteen if that jibe hadn't knocked you overboard. And if I'd noticed the clouds I'd have been watching for the wind shift, and done a controlled jibe before it hit."

"So I wouldn't have gotten a dunking, and we'd have gotten here before the wind slacked off. It did, you know, when that downpour started. I'm not sure we'd have made that docking if it hadn't. You did a great job, Timi, and we all learned something."

"Aren't you leaving out a broken arm?"

"Cracked, and I Healed it." He thought about telling Timi the true nature of the pendant—he considered getting rid of that worth a broken arm—but he didn't want to upset Timi by telling him what he'd done—and to all appearances completely forgotten—under Zhaim's control. "Whose turn is it to fix supper?"

"Yours," Timi said promptly, and Roi groaned.

"It's not that I mind doing the cooking," he muttered as he checked out the supplies, "it's just that I have to eat it. How about stasis-packed beans and cheese? I can't mess that up too badly."

Flame winced. "I wouldn't count on it. And I am not going to eat beans when there are fresh steaks in stasis. Let's trade. I'll take supper tonight, and you do breakfast in the morning. Pretoasted grain flakes and milk, for preference."

Roi glanced over at Penny, who nodded approval. "You mean everybody else hates my cooking as much as I do?" he asked plaintively.

Penny chuckled. "Let's just put your cooking in the same category as Timi's bandaging a horse's leg," she said. "He can do it, but the poor horse doesn't appreciate it. And there are so many other things you're good at, like bringing in wood." She glanced pointedly at the almost empty rack."

Roi looked out the window. The rain had died down to scattered drops, and wet sunlight lay on the ground and sparkled off the dripping trees. "Half an hour more," he said. "Let the trees dry out a bit first."

Zhaim

Zhaim yanked the circlet from his head and flung it across the room, following it with a volley of curses. Damn that black maggot! All the time he'd spent cultivating the little nonentity, and it had actually fought his commands. And then to lose the control circuit just as he was on the verge of overcoming its resistance and feeling the accursed bastard die under its hands! For several minutes he prowled the room, pausing now and then to hurl loose articles against the transparent walls.

He stomped down the stairs to the torture chamber, but the empty cages mocked his need to hurt someone, anyone. He could only fondle the pincers and branding iron, rack and wheel with loving hands, and think about the bastard and its slaves stretched open and inviting to his caresses. If he had succeeded now, he tried to convince himself, he would have lost the chance of that future pleasure.

He wasn't happy as he climbed back to the main floor, but he had calmed down enough to remember that the detested crew still had to deal with the squall line. Even without the direct link to the slave, he had ways of finding out what was going on there.

The red dot on the wall map was gone, no longer in contact with a sentient victim. Zhaim brought up the satellite weather overlay with a thought, and smiled wolfishly. The squall line had developed even better than he had dared hope, and the cloud shield now covered most of the lake. He activated his tap on the Company satellite communications link, setting up the particular coding used for the bastard's Challenge journey, ordered food and drink from the autokitchen, and sat back to listen for the inevitable search operation.

Daytime on this part of Falaron was night at his home on Central, and since he had always declined to switch his activities there to Enclave time, no one questioned his inaccessibility while he supposedly slept. He had gone short of sleep off and on for most of Roi's trip, and it caught up with him now. It was doubly shocking, then, when the communications tap came alive, not with a search, but with the voice of the trek guide.

"Penny Ansdor, checking in from Surprise Lake East camp. What kind of a bloody incompetent weather forecast was that you gave me this morning?"

"Penny! Everybody's all right? You made the cabin?"

"Yes, everybody's all right, no thanks to the information you gave me this morning! Roi went overboard when the first gust hit and we jibed, but we picked him up with no trouble and then ran for shore. Lucky for us Timi's a super helmsman and actually got the boat in to the dock. Have you any idea what that's like with a strong onshore wind? I didn't think we'd make it 'til we did. Tell the planners we need an alternate harbor on the east side of the lake that's sheltered from west and northwest winds, even if they have to blast one out. Now, what happened with that weather forecast?"

Zhaim, listening, snarled in frustration. Not only had he not succeeded in forcing the slave to kill its master, it seemed no one had even noticed. Except to make it a hero for defeating his storm.

"There was less than ten percent chance of a squall line developing when you left the west shore, Penny," the voice from the speaker continued. "The first indications didn't show on the satellite until after noon, and then it exploded. The supervisors are meeting right now about it, and—whoops, they've been listening, and just requested an active line."

"Ansdor," a new, authoritative voice cut in, "given the kind of weather events you've had, we've decided to issue you a weather receiver for the rest of the trek. In fact, we're making it standard for the Surprise River route for the immediate future. We'll have one out to you as soon as the squall line has passed over. Do you have any other recommendations for changes?"

Zhaim tensed and listened closely. He had made plans that should convince the Company the group was alive and well long after they were in his hands, but the wrong kind of change in procedures, a daily voice check, for instance .... "Emergency coms in the sailboats," the guide's voice replied. "If that boom had caught Roi in the head instead of the upper arm, I'd have needed a medical team right then, and they'd have had to come in knowing what to expect. Matter of fact, I'd feel better having an emergency com along right through with this group. It's not them. They're great. But Surprise River's a new route, and Challenge or not, we've had a few too many problems."

"You've got it," the authoritative voice said. "Anything else?"

"Not right now," Penny said. "I'll be thinking about it for the next hour or two."

"Good trekking, then."

"Good trekking," the guide's voice replied, and the line went dead.

Zhaim leaned back with a sigh of relief. An emergency com would give him no more problems than the emergency caller the guide already carried. He would have to make sure the guide was unconscious before she could get out a call, and he had already planned that for the whole party. He caught himself in a yawn, and decided it was time to teleport back to Central and get a few hours of sleep before his official day started.

Penny

"Much better than beans," Roi pronounced as he finished his last bite of steak and pushed his chair back. "I'll do the dishes at least, Flame. We have enough wood, Penny?"

Penny glanced toward the heaped wood rack and the fire burning merrily in the open fireplace. "Plenty," she assured him, and fought back a grin. She knew she wasn't supposed to know Roi's status as a future Inner Council member, but it still amused her to watch him hauling wood and washing her dishes. It made up a little for her terror at seeing him go overboard earlier in the day.

"What's the plan for tomorrow?" Timi asked. He still looked a little upset about something, Penny thought.

"Hiking," she replied promptly. This cabin had the necessary connections for a holographic map projection, and she hooked her portable map up to the projector as she spoke. "The trail goes from here to the Front Falls, then under the falls. That's not a long walk from here, no more than half an hour, and if we start early enough we can watch the sun rise through the falls. Really a beautiful sight."

Roi had finished washing the eating utensils, and left the cookware soaking as he joined the others at the projection. "Will the cold front be through by then?" he asked.

"Good question," Penny admitted. "The Company meteorologist thinks the squall line took a lot of the energy out of the cold front, and speeded it up as well. The front itself is due through tonight, now. There may be some fog over the lake in the morning, and I'm just not sure about the falls. Do you want to get an early start in case it is clear at the falls by sunrise?"

"I'd like to try, as long as we can see the trail," Roi said thoughtfully. "We could cut the extra steak up and wrap it in bread for breakfast, and eat at the falls."

"I'll take care of that," Flame said. "Where after the falls?"

"We're actually on the south shore of the Surprise here," Penny said. "The trail down into the gorge is on the north side, and we go under the falls to get there. Then it's on down into the gorge. It's a steep hiking trail, not mountain climbing, with lots of switchbacks. The east slope and the gorge are dryer than it's been the last few days; we'll have to pack drinking water with us. If we hit the falls at sunrise, we should make the raft camp by late afternoon. It's not far downstream; if it's light and clear enough we should see it before we go under the falls. We'll be covering more vertical distance than horizontal. But I guarantee your legs will be feeling it by the time we get there."

Roi leaned over the map, tracing their route with one fingertip. "Mine are sore just looking at the trail," he said. "Penny, do I have to keep wearing bright red? I feel so conspicuous dressed this way."

Penny looked at him in surprise. "No, we don't have to keep up the color coding if you don't like it," she said. "I'd thought we'd start the trail wearing the wind pants and jackets we used today, but I can ask for them to drop neutral-colored stuff at the raft base. It's not as if I need color to recognize you any more."

"Good," Roi said with a yawn as he returned to washing dishes. "I'm for an early bed tonight."

Chapter 16

Falaron: Roi
5/23/38

Roi?

Just a minute, Roi thought back, and shook his head as spray splashed across his face. Water boiled ahead, and he dug in the sweeps just enough to avoid a particularly nasty-looking fang of rock. "Penny," he said aloud, "could we skip the rest of the lesson? Marna's trying to contact me."

"When we're level with that leaning tree on the right bank," she replied, and Roi grimly dodged three and a half more rocks. The half he missed sent the raft spinning, but got them into the relatively calm water by the tree. Penny slid onto the seat beside him and took the sweeps, straightening the raft with a couple of well-timed strokes. "Very good for a first lesson," she smiled at him. "I'll go ahead and get us on that bar for lunch."

Roi flopped into the bottom of the raft and closed his eyes. *Ready now, Marna,* he sent, and felt her amusement.

Having a good time? she asked.

Overall, yes, he replied. *But Penny had me reading the river without using esper.* He opened his eyes and raised himself on his elbows to look back at the short stretch of rapids he'd just run. Somehow it looked a lot tamer from this point of view.

What's wrong with your legs? Marna asked.

In reply he visualized their hike down from the canyon rim the day before. It had started out better than they had dared hope. The air had smelled newly made as they walked down the trail to the waterfall in the growing pre-dawn light, and the sky had been as clean as the air. The near-cave behind the falls had been cold and damp, but they had all agreed that the way the rising sun turned the waterfall to a curtain of jewels had been worth the chill.

As the sun rose higher and they worked their way down into the canyon, though, they had begun to wish they could have brought the chill and the moisture with them. The sun, reflected back from the golden rock of the canyon, baked the water from their bodies, and legs hardened to riding tired rapidly of walking steadily downhill. They all carried canteens, but Penny had emphasized from the start that there were no places along the trail to refill them.

Flame and Amber both had developed blisters, but refused to complain until Roi saw how badly they were limping and made them take off their hiking shoes. By that time, he had to Heal not just blisters, but open, bleeding sores on both girls' feet. The candy he'd swallowed to give him energy for that job had made him even thirstier, and his canteen was almost empty. By the time they'd reached their campsite, Penny was the only one not limping. They hadn't complained about the camp chores, but they had certainly wanted to.

You'll have to draw the falls for me, Marna said, and Roi had the feeling she was trying hard not to laugh at him. *No, I'm not laughing. But you're the one who wanted a wilderness adventure. Now, I need your help.*

My help? What for?

The epidemic here is being caused by a toxin. I've identified it, but I still don't know how it's being spread. I think there's a clue somewhere in what I've learned from the planetary authorities, but I can't quite find it. You understand Human society better than I do. I want to feed you everything I know and see if you can spot something out of place.

I'll try, Roi thought dubiously, *but I really doubt I can help.*

You can't hurt. Roi felt her take a deep breath, and then her memories of Eversummer slid into his mind. Meeting after meeting, for the most part, with planetary authorities, medical specialists, and survivors from areas where a large fraction of the population had died. Something about those survivors .... *Marna, he thought, do all the survivors have beer bellies like that?*

He felt her surprise. *Come to think of it, I don't think I've seen a survivor drink anything but beer—or something stronger—or one of the local herbal teas. I remember thinking at one point they must metabolize alcohol better than most Humans—but since then I've found they can get quite drunk.* She didn't give him the full context of that.

Roi was following up a different line of thought. *If they drink that much beer, they wouldn't be drinking much water,* he worked the thought out slowly. *Marna, how do they treat their water? And what would it take to inactivate the toxin?*

Alcohol denatures it, she replied, *and so does boiling. As to treatment, I believe they rely primarily on microfiltration. But Roi, there have been three outbreaks since I arrived. I've tested the water supplies on all of them, and I've found no trace of any problem. It's good, pure water.*

Roi frowned in concentration, barely noticing when the tough-skinned foam raft touched the sand bar and the others jumped out to secure it. *What's the incubation period?* he asked.

Four days, more or less, based on when the sporadic cases left the general outbreak areas, Marna replied. *What does that—Oh! How could I be so stupid! It needn't still be in the water system when we're testing!* Roi felt her mind racing, working out ways of finding out what had been in a water system before an outbreak. *Roi, I think you've found a starting point. Thank you, love. I'll see you in a few fivedays.*

Once you've got the epidemic licked there might be a couple more crops they can grow, too, Roi added. *Maize and potatoes. They're experimenting with both at the Virginia Colony. I think they come from high elevations in the tropics, but I don't think Central has either.*

I'll check on them, Marna assured him as she broke contact.

Roi sighed and stood up, joining the rest of the group on the sandbar. Maybe his ability to catch what was significant, an ability closely allied to conditional precognition, wasn't as bad as he thought. But why couldn't he do any better at forecasting the weather, then?

It didn't occur to him that his failures had a common factor broader than the weather—his own safety.

***

Penny led them up a tiny side canyon to a hidden spring for lunch. Plant life had been rare in the main canyon mainly, Roi thought, because there were so few horizontal surfaces for it to grow on. The little canyon with its trickle of water seemed as barren as the rest of the gorge at first, but as they came around the third corner they were met first by a honeyed floral smell, and then by a miniature jungle. Water burst from the cliff twice their height overhead, arching out and down into a clear pool no

211

wider than the height of the falls. Ferns and flowers carpeted the narrow bench surrounding the pool and grew in every cranny touched by the spray from the waterfall. Roi, bringing up the rear with the sketching materials Penny had suggested he might want, stopped short as he saw the spring. He was barely aware of Flame taking his hand and leading him to a rock big enough for both of them to sit on, and later holding a meat roll for him to bite off pieces as he sketched the hummingbirds that seemed to appear out of the air once the visitors had settled down to eat.

They drank and filled their canteens at the waterfall. Penny assured them the water was safe, and that there was a spring at the night's camping place as well. "This beautiful?" Roi asked.

"No," Penny admitted, "but there's a good deal more room for camping."

Roi finally allowed himself to be dragged away with one finished drawing and half a dozen pages of sketches, and they returned to the river for the afternoon.

They were all eager to learn, and Penny let them take turns at the sweeps through the shorter and easier rapids, reserving the difficult stretches for herself. There were quiet reaches, too, where they could drift with only an occasional touch of the sweeps, and where Roi leaned back in the raft with a small sketch pad and recorded what he saw—gauze-winged insects dancing over the shallows, a bobcat lapping daintily at a trickle from another side canyon, an eagle plummeting down and rising with a fish flopping in its talons, and above it all the warm golden walls of the canyon, cutting off all but a narrow strip of sky.

They carried a small stasis chest with food supplies in the raft, and toasted stick biscuits and cubes of meat over the coals of their campfire for supper. They had built the campfire back up and were sitting around it singing when Roi felt his father's mind touch his.

Father? he thought on the surface. Behind his inner shields, he worried. Had his father heard something about his fall overboard from the sailboat?

Sorry to bother you, his father said, *but you need to know what's going on. Remember the problems we've been having with the Kablukolelli cluster?*

Roi had to stop and think for a moment. Kablukolelli was a cluster of stars, four of which had inhabited planets, within a few light years of each other. For some reason he had never fully understood, the cluster had proven a magnet for extremist groups. Each of the four inhabited systems had been settled and entered the Confederation separately, so Lai had the right to force arbitration of their differences—which were considerable. *At least you can do something,* he thought. *Not like Goodnews, where it's all internal affairs. What's the problem this time?*

Funeral customs, his father replied wearily.

Like the people on Eversummer eating their dead? Roi asked. *Marna said they're very reverent about it; they just figure that something's going to eat the body, and the most honorable stomachs are those of the family. Cremation's next best, but they do not like it.* He remembered what Marna had told him of the token funerals for the epidemic victims.

Right, Lai said. *The Kailonites do that, too. The J'koan consider that the only reverent way to treat the bodies of the dead is to give them back to the soil of the planet, the Folaanni go for cremation and the Lirrilo feed the flesh to a local water animal, tan the skins, and mount the skins and skeletons to keep in their homes. They all treat the bodies with reverence, and mourn for their departed friends and relatives. But the residents of each planet look at the other three planets and think sacrilege, abomination, and disrespect for the dead. Traders and embassies have been attacked, and it'll turn into a holy war if it isn't stopped. So I'm going to have to go out there physically and force a little sense into their heads. Want to go along?*

Roi considered. He didn't think he'd be much use, with his precognition acting up the way it was. And in spite of his occasional griping he was thoroughly enjoying Falaron. *When are you going?* he asked.

Tomorrow, Lai replied. *You'd have to come back to Central now if you want to go.*

If he went, he could quit worrying about Zhaim. No, that wasn't quite true. If he went he himself would be safe, but his friends would not. And if his father ever suspected that he had come along simply because he was afraid of Zhaim .... No, he wouldn't give in to his paranoia that easily, he decided. Timi no longer wore the control circuit, and with that change he should be safe enough. He didn't really want to go, and if his father had really wanted him to come along he would have told Roi, not invited him. *I'd rather not,* he thought back. *I don't know anything about the situation, and I really do want to finish the Challenge. Besides, it's in the opposite direction from Eversummer, and Marna had me brainstorming with her earlier today. If I went I'd be too far away for that, even with her being boosted.*

All right, Roi. Be careful, will you? And Derik will stay open to you for any problems you need help with. Zhaim's going to be in charge, this time.

I hope you're not going to be gone too long, Roi thought. *Could you bring me back some tri-dees?*

Of course I will. Take good care of yourself, Roi. And enjoy your vacation. You've earned one. His mind slipped away after a last mental hug.

Roi had stopped singing while he conversed with his father, and when he came back to himself the others were looking at him with questioning eyes. "Father called," he explained. "He's got to go out to Kablukolelli for some arbitration." Flame nodded and began brushing out another tune on her lapsinger, this one a Clan song Timi had learned from Filomako and taught to the rest of the group.

Roi leaned back against a rock, feeling how it held the day's heat. He was singing with the others—he should have split off a little of his attention to keep on doing that while he conversed with his father, he thought—but he was thinking, as well. Had he really done the right thing, in choosing to stay here? He had a lot to learn from watching his father in action. But then he had a lot to learn from Marna's medical detective work, too. He sighed and wiggled his back against the rock, trying to scratch an itchy spot.

The firelight washed orange highlights across Timi's cheekbones, and woke reddish glints in Amber's hair. Penny's, too, and he thought briefly how alike in appearance the two girls were, especially since they had started copying each others' hair styles. The fact that they'd dropped the color-coding helped, too.

He turned his head slightly to look at Flame, and saw her eyes slide sideways to meet his in open invitation. *Later,* he thought at her, and tipped his head back to look up at the strip of sky between the canyon walls. His pupils had contracted in the firelight, and he opened them deliberately, seeing the darkness overhead shift to a midnight blue, studded with points of light, in a narrow streak between the blackness of the canyon walls.

His friends' voices and the chords of the lapsinger died into silence as the last song ended. A coyote howled, far away—somewhere on the rim above the canyon, Roi thought. "No moon for him to sing to, tonight," Flame said softly, a little regretfully.

"It'll rise in a couple of hours," Penny said, "but it'll be after midnight before we see it here." She looked up, gauging the steepness of the south canyon wall behind their campsite. "No, I take that back. We won't see it here; it'll stay behind the cliff. But it'll be shining on the north cliffs, across the river."

"I'll watch it from my sleeping bag," Roi said, yawning. "Douse the fire, Penny?"

The guide glanced around the gravel shelf where they were camped. "No need," she said, "there's nothing here to catch fire. Just let it burn out.

"You mean *our* sleeping bag, don't you?" Flame said as they walked away from the fire together. Roi just grinned at her.

"Shall I wake you up when the moon reaches the cliffs?" he asked.

Eversummer: Marna

Marna wiggled in the increasingly confining—and, she suspected, unnecessary—isolation suit as she looked across the table at Acting-first Anden. "I know you filter your water and test it periodically," she said patiently. "But I've gone over all the tests you use with your techs, and none of them would pick up the dissolved toxin. As of right now, there is no cheap, simple test for the toxin, though your people are working on one.

"But I spent the night going over my notes from interviews with hundreds of people who lived in epidemic areas and were not affected. I offered most of them something to drink while I spoke with them. Not one asked for plain water. Most took beer; those who did not asked for various herbal infusions made with boiling water. Boiling denatures the toxin, and beer isn't mixed with local water. Those I've talked to who were from areas the plague hasn't struck most often asked for water or watered fruit juice."

"But you can't be sure it's the water," Anden said fretfully.

"No. I can't prove the toxin is somehow spreading in the water supply, and I cannot even verify that all of the survivors habitually drank water only if it was first boiled or had been stored. But at this point, it's the strongest lead I have. Boiling all drinking water is a minor nuisance, compared to the effect of the toxin. All I am asking is that you publicize that boiling drinking water may cut down on the spread of the plague."

"They won't do it, M'lady Marna," the acting-first pleaded. "They expect that water from the distribution system is safe to drink. That's been basic for generations."

Marna sighed. "I very much fear some will not," she said. "But others will. I would much rather find proof in some other way, with no more deaths. But if some people in the next area struck—and there will be a next area, I have no doubt about that—are boiling their drinking water and survive, while those drinking your pure water untreated do not—then we will know. But you must publicize the need to boil water, or we will take much longer testing random samples until we find a sample with the toxin and discover that four days after we took the sample the people drinking that water were struck by the plague. Because it is totally against the odds that we will find the next area to be contaminated early enough to warn people not to drink the local water."

"At one time," the acting-first said, "people did not trust the water distribution system. They got their drinking water from contaminated wells, or from ponds and streams. If we start saying the water distribution system is unsafe, they'll get their water from sources we *know* are unsafe."

"Emphasize that *all* water is suspect unless it is boiled," Marna replied. Roi had given her the basic idea late the previous evening, and she had then worked through the night without sleep. Her eyes were burning, and she had to use Healer control to keep from yawning. And she was having less and less sympathy with this stiff-necked bureaucrat. "You were the sole survivor of your family," she said, regretting the cruelty even as she spoke. "What did each person in your family drink three to five days before the plague struck?"

The administrator dropped his face into his hands, hiding his features for a long moment, and when he lifted his head his eyes were wet. "I don't remember," he said, "but usually I drink beer or tea. The only water would have been to brush my teeth—and I usually don't swallow that. The baby got a high-calcium protein drink—but it was made up with water right from the pipes. The older children mostly watered fruit juice or plain water. My wife drank some tea, but she often shared the children's fruit juice." He shook his head, and Marna thought that for the first time he believed she might be right.

"Am I right in assuming that most of those drinking beer and drinks made with boiling water, and rarely or never drinking raw water, were adult men?" she asked. "That the pattern in your family was not uncommon? Because it would explain why most of those not affected were adult men and infants drinking sterilized formulas."

"Yes," he said numbly. "Yes, it would, wouldn't it? I'll make the announcement, Lady Marna. But I think the best we can hope for is that enough people boil their water that the next outbreak demonstrates whether it really helps."

Central: Lai

Derik stood gazing out the window of Lai's study. "So he didn't want to come?" he asked his half brother.

"No," Lai replied. "It should be all right. He was in contact with Marna earlier today; that's one of the reasons he didn't want to come. Eversummer to Kablukolelli is just too far." He walked over to join Derik at the window. "I can't CP any problem from leaving him on Falaron. It's just—oh, I don't know. I just can't trust Zhaim. Not since that incident when we were coming back from Riya."

Derik sighed. "And you're a lot better at using conditional precognition than I am," he said. "I'm just being paranoid for Roi, I guess. I wish he were a little more wary of Zhaim."

"He was, when we rescued him," Lai replied. "But they have to be able to work together. And Zhaim does seem to be accepting Roi."

They stood together for several minutes, watching the winter sun slide toward the ocean. Lai's azure and white tineral, Spring, crammed herself onto his shoulder, and he reached up with his other hand to scratch the soft feathers between her front limbs. "You're getting a little big for that perch," he told the animal, and Derry chuckled in spite of himself. Lai, unlike his son Roi, had never been interested in animal pets until he had met Marna and the tinerals on Riya. Spring and several of her relatives had bonded almost at once to the strange R'il'nian, and while the others spent most of their time in Roi's aviary, Spring refused to be separated from Lai.

"Going to take her with you?" Derik asked Lai.

"No, it's too long a teleport," the R'il'nian replied. "Davy's taking care of Roi's while he's gone, and she can stay with them in the aviary."

"I'll drop in now and then," Derik said, and looked back out at the sun, now flattening itself against the horizon. "About time for Zhaim's final briefing, isn't it?"

Lai nodded. "Might as well get on down to the interface room." He still had not felt it wise to reset the shields that kept Zhaim away from most of the Enclave outside the interface room.

Zhaim

Zhaim managed to keep his expression, his outer mind, and even his emotions held tightly to business during Lai's briefing. At a deep level, he was still blocking any conditional precognition relating to Roi's safety, but that had become a reflex, so deep in his mind that no casual probe would touch it. All his father—or Derik—saw was a talented R'il'noid eager to show what he could do when left in charge.

And that cover was genuine. He had every intention of seeing that things went smoothly with the rest of the Confederation while his father was away. His father would be upset and angry at Roi's death when the trek party failed to return. Zhaim intended to do such a perfect job of running the Confederation that his father would never think to connect him with the unfortunate accident that would occur as a result of dead power packs in the warnoffs. The Company would take the blame for that.

That wasn't what would really happen, of course, as he let himself think once the briefing was over and he had returned home. Zhaim smiled at the blizzard raging outside his aerie. He would have at least ten days, perhaps twice that, before the horses wandered close enough to Safeport that they might be seen, and during that time the challenge party would be his guests, inhabitants of the newly redecorated abattoir.

Everything was ready on Falaron, he thought gleefully, hugging himself. He wouldn't return to the wilderness planet until the day after Lai was safely away to the Kablukolelli cluster. Late morning here, and he'd be sure to get plenty of rest tonight. Evening at the Enclave—Lai would have finished his supper, be busy with his final, personal arrangements. Near midnight for the travelers, sleeping in the canyon after their first day on the river.

It had been an annoyance to lose the control circuit the black slave had worn, but not a serious setback. Zhaim had obtained the equipment yesterday that let him pick up the Company tracers the travelers all carried. He'd seen the maps, and knew exactly where they would be climbing out of the gorge, day after tomorrow. Tomorrow night, for him.

Snow drove at the broad window wall, the violence of the wind perceptible even inside the building. Nothing was visible beyond that swirling gray atmosphere. Like his block on any precognitive awareness of his half-brother's danger, Zhaim thought. Today and tomorrow to wait, and do his duty as Lai's deputy. Thirty-six hours.

He wouldn't touch the bastard, at first, not beyond what was needed to immobilize the brat. Not until he had extracted the last nuance of suffering from the slaves the idiot boy was foolish enough to care for, with the boy forced to watch every moment of their suffering. He'd still rather have used all of them as raw material for his art, but that was too dangerous. He smiled and licked his lips in anticipation, watching the violence of the storm with greedy eyes.

Falaron: Flame

"Flame?" Roi whispered.

"It's still dark out," she replied, thick-tongued with sleep. "You want?" She shifted her hips toward him and he lifted his hand to her face, stroking a stray tendril of hair back from her forehead.

"Maybe after," he chuckled. "Look across the river."

She rolled away from him, toward the river, and gasped in delight. The waning moon was hidden from where they lay, but it shone full on the cliffs across the river, and even lit the water's edge. "Like they're made of silver," she said softly "with a river of carved glass. Oh, Roi, it's beautiful. Thank you for sharing it with me."

"Look lower," he said softly, "near the mouth of that wide side canyon just upstream from us. The grassy bar we noticed earlier."

Flame shifted her attention, caught movement, and blinked a time or two to bring the moving creatures into focus. "Wild horses," she breathed, "but they're so dainty. And they're not striped like the ones we've seen so far. Silver, with dark points. Oh, look at the baby!" She felt her expression shifting into a fatuous smile, but she didn't mind. Roi wouldn't care.

"I suspect gold, in the sunlight," Roi replied softly. "And they're so tiny! I noticed the vegetation on that bar, and I'd swear it's no more than ankle deep. But it's halfway to their knees."

Flame sighed happily and wiggled back against Roi's chest. "Wouldn't it be fun to have one for a pet?" she said, and felt his laughter vibrate through her body. "Well, it would," she said as she turned back to face him and pulled his face down to hers.

Later, when they were both almost asleep, she thought how wonderfully peaceful the canyon was.

Chapter 17

Roi lay back in the raft and blinked up at the sky—brilliantly blue today, with one or two puffy fair-weather clouds for decoration. The sun was just past the meridian, and the north wall of the canyon, rusty here rather than gold, was sunlit right down to the water's edge. As the raft swung toward the left, the sun itself peeked over the south wall, bathing the rafters in its brilliance and heat.

The walls of the gorge seemed lower than they had the day before, Roi thought, and looked back at the sky. It wasn't always this clear. Storm, the glider sabotage, flood, another storm with Zhaim trying to use Timi against him .... He remembered the dream by the Peccary River, with his father's accusation of his being paranoid about Zhaim. But was he really? Blizzard, thunderstorm-induced flash flooding, the squall line across the lake—but surely Zhaim wouldn't have been so stupid as to try to use weather control repeatedly to kill him. Once, maybe, and it might even explain his own difficulty in foreseeing the weather problems. But three times?

"Penny," he asked drowsily as the motion of the raft smoothed out and he judged she would have time to talk, "is the weather here always so extreme?"

Penny chuckled. "We don't usually have three violent storms on one trek," she replied. "At least not that violent."

"But is it usually this nice between storms?" Roi persisted.

Penny screwed her face up, thinking. "Well, we did have that light rain, the morning before we got to the lake," she said, "and several foggy mornings. But you're right. I'd say the total amount of bad weather on this trip has been about normal, but it's almost all been in those three big storms. Hang on, there's more rapids coming." The raft heaved under them, and Roi pulled himself into a sitting position.

Definitely not the beginner rapids Penny was letting the travelers scull through, he decided. The flexible, foam-filled rafts were designed to take punishment, but even with Penny at the sculls they were glancing off enough rocks to test their craft. He hung on and kept his mouth shut until they were back in deep water, and saw that the others were doing the same.

"That's the last big one," Penny said cheerfully. "Ready for lunch and a couple of hours of hiking?"

"Hiking?" Timi asked.

"Right," Penny replied. "After lunch. There's a combination of long bars and shelves on the right bank. We'll pull in at the top end for lunch, and then practice climbing to the downstream end. We can get a better look from there at the route we'll be climbing tomorrow than we can from right under it, where we'll camp tonight. It'll be a good place to discuss climbing strategy." She had been guiding the raft to the south bank as she spoke.

Roi lay back again. He still was not ready to mention his suspicions of Zhaim to his father. But if Marna contacted him again, he decided, he would certainly say something to her. Too bad he couldn't initiate such contact, but quite aside from knowing he was by far the weaker telepath of the two of them, even Marna couldn't reach this far without boosting. And he had no power source that would let him reach her. Or his father in the Kablukolelli cluster, for that matter. The contact he had managed from the glider to Central had shocked both of them, and he didn't think he could repeat it, even if his father were still on Central. He found himself wondering if he had made the right decision not to go with his father.

Penny

They weren't really practicing climbing that afternoon, just moving horizontally along the canyon wall. Eventually their traverse took them around an outthrust spur that had hidden the gorge downstream. Penny heard one exclamation after another as her clients rounded the obstruction and got their first good look at what lay to the east. Finally it was her turn to crab her way around the final barrier and see the river open up before her.

The canyon walls dropped rapidly downstream, but the travelers were cut off from an easy climb by rapids and a waterfall Penny had no intention of attempting. Upstream of the rapids, across the river downstream, was a tributary canyon exposing layers of rock slanting back from the river and upstream. Thick bands of dark rust, fawn, and lighter red were easy to pick out and stood in bold cliffs, separated by thinner, softer bands of greenish-black and gray-white. Roi, who had insisted on packing along his sketching supplies, was already sitting on a piece of driftwood and laying broad streaks of ochre and sienna on his sketch pad with the long edges of the sticks.

"Anybody see the trail?" Penny asked them, waving her arm toward the canyon.

Timi frowned and squinted at the brightly illuminated north wall. "Up the canyon?" he asked uncertainly. "Or does it end in a waterfall?"

"It does," Penny replied. "That's where the trail starts, though."

"The wall looks stepped," Amber put in. "See how that black layer between the dark red and buff cliffs is sort of cut in, with the dark red stone sticking out a little below it? And the buff is the same way where the white layer is eroded below the light red cliff. Like two sloping ledges, rising up toward the Surprise and downstream. The lower one looks like we could climb the canyon to reach the lower end, and then follow it back out and up to get more then halfway to the top ...." She paused, trying to see the rest of the route. "It looks like the buff cliff leans out, though."

"You had us practicing horizontal traverses today," Flame said slowly. "If we got as high as we could on the first ledge, maybe just a little around the corner, there, then we could use the anchors in the buff rock to work our way back left and into the canyon again, until we hit the second shelf. And that looks like it goes just about all the way to the top."

"Like this?" Roi said, delicately touching in a zigzag line on his drawing. Into the pictured canyon, diagonally up the boundary between dark rust and ochre, another diagonal back to the left across the lighter, yellower area until it reached the upper area of sienna, then along the bottom of the lighter red area to the top of the cliff.

"Basically right," Penny said as he began sketching five tiny figures crawling across the cliff. "A little more angle up on the traverse between ledges. We'll put Amber in the lead," she added, "and I want her climbing as light as possible, since she'll have to carry the anchors. I'll carry her pack as well as mine. You go last, Roi, and pick up the anchors, and I'll take the middle."

Amber

That was the way they arranged themselves as they began the hike up the side canyon the following morning, though Timi insisted on carrying Amber's pack. Amber led the way up the narrow trail into the canyon, her climbing belt heavy with its freight of clanking force anchors. The air was cool, shadowed by the canyon walls and resinous with the junipers and pines that bordered the trail. To her left, a stream chuckled over boulders as it hurried to the Surprise behind them. Now and then a gust of damp air touched her face, and the sound of the stream seemed to grow louder. The waterfall, she decided, and fastened her jacket tighter.

"We've climbed almost to the lighter rock," Timi said behind her. He was carrying her lunch and water bottle and even her tracer, as well as his own, and had her pack folded into his. None of them were carrying much beyond lunch and water. They had left most of their gear at last night's campsite for the Company to pick up. Riding clothes—neutral in color this time, like the climbing clothes they wore—would already have been delivered to the corral where the horses awaited them, and Flame's lapsinger and most of Roi's drawing materials would be transported to another cabin, where they would stay tonight. Not that Roi wasn't carrying a small sketch block and a handful of color sticks in his chest pack. Probably, Amber thought, he would stop and make a sketch or two on the way up the canyon wall!

The little canyon opened out as they approached a side stream coming in from the west, and Amber stopped short as she saw the inhabitants of a pocket meadow across the main stream. *Roi,* she thought, pushing the image toward him, *are these the little horses you and Flame saw? They're gorgeous!*

She felt his mind respond in a delighted affirmative, and then he was slipping past the others, moving from the rear of the line to her side. The tiny animals, their backs hardly visible above the thigh-deep vegetation, threw up their heads and turned to face the intruders, and for a moment Amber was sure they would whirl and bolt. Then they relaxed and a couple went back to grazing. The tallest of the herd, with a stallion's heavy crest and a mane and tail almost as long as those of a domesticated horse, remained on alert, head high and ears almost touching at the tips.

Roi must have told them not to be afraid, Amber thought, and felt his agreement as he turned to wave the other three into the edge of the grassy area. He had already pulled his sketchpad and a handful of color sticks out of his chest pack. After half an hour of steady uphill hiking, with a grueling climb ahead, Amber was willing to sit on a boulder and watch the animals for a few minutes, and let Roi make his drawings.

"You were right," Flame said softly as she came into the clearing. "Golds and rusts and tans, not silvers." Roi didn't even seem to hear her, but Amber took a closer look at the herd. The stallion was gold, all right, or perhaps a gold and copper alloy, with his flowing mane and tail jet black. As he walked toward them, one curious step at a time out of the tall grass and onto the gravel bar on the far side of the stream, she could see that his legs were black, too.

"Like a miniature of Butterscotch," Timi said, handing Amber her water bottle.

"Wouldn't it be fun to have a couple in the aviary?" Amber replied after a long pull at the bottle.

Timi shook his head. "The tinerals would have a ball pulling their manes and tails," he replied. "They could keep the grass grazed down at the north end, though." Amber nodded slowly, looking beyond the stallion to his harem.

One of the mares was a lighter shade of the stallion's color, but with an upright brush of a mane edged by almost white hair. The others were darker, ranging from fawn to a soft red that mimicked the color of the upper canyon walls, two with brush manes and the red with a softer, longer fall of hair. With their heads down, it was hard to tell them from fallen rocks.

Roi caught his breath, a happy, excited sound, and Amber turned her attention back to the stallion. No, she decided, not the stallion. A foal, too short to be seen in the taller grass, had followed the golden horse onto the bare gravel bar. He was duller in shade than the adults, with a bare hint of a mane and a silly little scut of a tail that he seemed unable to keep still. The stallion turned his head and snorted, and the foal stuck his neck out, chewing air in submission but far too curious to leave.

"Are they ever available, Penny?" Roi asked.

"Surprise River miniatures?" she replied. "Only if the wardens decide in the fall that there are more of them than the pockets of grazing in the canyon will support over the winter. Can you tell how many are in this band?"

Roi closed his eyes briefly, his hand still over his sketchpad. "Nine mares and five stallions in this side canyon," he replied. "One of the mares is a yearling and three others are two-year-olds, but four of the other five are nursing foals. The bachelor stallions are spread out all over." He opened his eyes and looked toward Penny. "Is that more than can winter over? How common is the longer mane?"

"I've never seen it before," Penny replied. "Matter of fact, they may take out the stallion and the red mare to try and keep the herd typical. On the other hand, they might decide to see if a long-maned race develops." She grinned over at him. "Tell them you want to try to establish a long-maned captive herd on Central. This is a big group for the available feed, and I bet you could get an older mare in foal to that stallion, at least."

He'll do it, too, Amber thought, and felt a brief pang that when she followed Timi to space, she wouldn't be staying on Central to watch the herd develop. She craned her neck to see that Roi had covered several sheets of his sketchpad with quick, bare sketches of features and attitudes.

"Back to the trail," she announced firmly as she stood up and started around the edge of the clearing.

The sound of falling water grew louder as they worked their way upstream, and within another quarter hour the waterfall was visible, falling from the top of the tan cliff to the darker red rock at its base. The diagonal ledge that would be their road out of the canyon angled up directly from the base of the waterfall. Amber stopped as she reached the ledge, and turned back to Timi. "I want a drink before we start," she said, "and I think we'd all better get our masks out now. About half the climb up the ledge will be over water, and there may not be another good place to stop and get things out of our packs."

Timi nodded. "I'll keep your water bottle on my belt with mine," he told her as he handed her the bottle and the baglike breathing mask.

"Don't hesitate to use anchors if you feel unsteady, and Roi, you remember to pick up any that she puts in," Penny said. "Flame, you and I can take some of his stuff at the top of the ledge, so he won't be carrying too much weight. Everybody ready? All right, Amber, lead out."

The ledge was wide enough at the base that they could walk it—carefully—with their hands free. They climbed rapidly above the scrubby vegetation, actually making better time down the canyon than they had coming uphill in spite of the steeper path. Amber paused for another short drink when they reached a point above the meadow where the miniature horses still grazed, then pushed on until they came out of the side canyon and began to swing eastward, following the rock face until the sun abruptly came around the cliff into their faces and they had to pause to put on goggles.

The ledge here was nerve-wrackingly narrow, and Amber began putting in anchors as a bulge of rock ahead of her again hid the sun. Beneath her, the rock face dropped sheer into a swirl of deep water. She squinted downstream as she worked her way around the final bulge and back into the sun, and decided that the pool behind and beneath her was no place for a dive—there was no place to get out of the river before the rapids. Mentally she reviewed Penny's instructions in case of a slip—get the breathing mask on and fastened while you're falling. Then try to hug the near bank, where the rocks were fewer and the waterfall was a double drop into deep pools, and go with the river, feet first and relaxed. If she slipped, she decided, she'd scream and hope Roi could catch her telekinetically. The rapids looked far worse from above than they had yesterday from upstream and across the river.

She reached a wide point on the ledge, followed it far enough that they'd all have room to stand, and stopped. The sun was shining almost directly on the rock face, and the ledge was beginning to slope downward as the cliff turned into the next side canyon. "Time to start climbing?" she asked, and Penny nodded.

Amber had studied the tan rock as they had worked their way back out of the side canyon, and observed that while the rock in reach was generally smooth, it developed fissures and cracks higher up the cliff. She moved along the shelf, searching for possible holds. Finally she found what looked like a possible handhold, set her first anchor at chest height, and snapped in one of the arm-length lines from her safety belt. She slid her fingers into the tiny crevice and twisted, then explored upward with one foot. The soft rubber toe of her climbing shoe found and clung to an irregularity, and she reached up for another handhold, raising her other foot from the ledge only when both hands and a foot were securely anchored. When her belt came level with the anchor she had planted, she clung with one hand and both feet while she placed the next one.

Slowly the cliff slid downward before her sweating face, and hand- and footholds became easier to locate. She began angling left, the sun shifting from her back to her right shoulder as she worked her way around the curve of the cliff. She heard the others climbing below her, and after a few moments she looked to her right. Timi grinned at her, black curls plastered to his forehead, and beyond him she saw Penny and Flame. Roi was below Flame, clipping an anchor he had just removed to his belt.

"Don't look down," Penny cautioned.

"Not likely," Amber replied, as she set in her next anchor.

The sun came briefly and blindingly into her eyes as she worked her way into the shaded stretch above the pool, and then the rock was sheltering her from its glare. Roi's mind touched hers. *Hold up a second, Amber. Timi's got a snap jammed.* Amber glanced idly to her left, where the dark shadow of the buttress that shaded her gave way to brilliant heat-shimmer on the pale rock beyond.

Okay, Amber. You ca .... The thought cut off like a knife. She started to turn her head to the right, to call out and ask what had happened, when some change, barely glimpsed from the corner of her eye, pulled her attention to the cliff on her left. The heat-shimmer had vanished, and the shadow of an airvan was starkly black on the cream of the rock. As she watched, a second shadow separated itself from the buttress shadow: the shadow of a human body, head and limbs tumbled awry, moving toward and into the van. From the way the hair fell and the suggestion of a chest pack, she thought the limp body was Roi's.

Amber was not aware of any kind of decision. She could have argued that the sudden cutoff of Roi's mind-touch, together with the distort that must have hidden the airvan, leaving only the suggestion of heat-shimmer, meant a kidnapping, and that the kidnapper would not willingly leave witnesses behind. At the time she knew only that she was pulling the breathing mask over her head with one hand. She looked down, very quickly, to be sure she was indeed over the pool, and then she released both anchors and let go, pushing away from the rock face just enough to clear the thread of shelf below.

Zhaim

Zhaim could hardly believe the way his luck was holding. He hadn't quite anticipated having to TK loose the snaps on the safety lines, but that was a minor problem. Very minor, with the bastard's limp body at his feet. Hastily he reached for the loaded hypodermic and emptied it into the flaccid arm. At least twice the normal dosage of raw hiControl.

And the raw drug wouldn't wear off, the way the refined stuff did. The brat wouldn't be able to use any of its esper abilities until it was given the antidote. Which it wouldn't be—Zhaim had no intention of taking any risks he could avoid.

He turned back to the cliff where the three slaves hung slack from their safety lines, still unconscious from the stun field he had centered on Roi. Methodically he TK'd them loose from the cliff, this time releasing and collecting the safety anchors as he went. Not until all four youngsters were safely bound in the airvan did he realize that the guide was missing.

Zhaim gritted his teeth in vexation. She would have been in the lead, he decided, around the bulge of rock. He swung the airvan back to the left, examining the rock wall. A couple of anchors were visible beyond the one the blackskin had been clipped to, but no sign of another climber, or of any place a climber could have escaped to—except down. He looked down, and then studied the rapids beyond the pool. No chance she'd survived, he decided, but he needed all five finders. They weren't very accurate, but if the guide's body with the emergency caller and one of the finders were swept downstream, the Company would certainly notice. He kicked at the black's body in frustration, knocking the slave over onto its back and revealing the finders clipped to its belt.

Finders? Hastily Zhaim knelt by the slave's side, finding it carried an extra water bottle as well as two finders. And the blond slave had the emergency com, while the redhead carried Roi's finder as well as its own. Zhaim relaxed with a sigh of relief. They'd used the slaves as burden beasts during the climb, of course, so he had all of the finders.

He looked again at the rapids below the pool. The guide's body was unlikely to be found, he decided. He might have to find another body of the right age and physical type for his final stage setting, but it was unlikely enough of the guide herself would get through the rapids to be identified.

He set the airvan back into motion, following the angle his captives had been taking up the cliff at a crawl, then back along the second ledge. If anyone at the company happened to be monitoring the finders, they would see five finders zigzagging up the canyon wall, as expected. He did not anticipate any visual check—the carryall to pick up the raft and the supplies to be moved to the next pickup point wasn't due until well after noon, after the party would have saddled up and left for the next cabin—but he did take the precaution of reactivating the distort circuit to make the airvan less conspicuous. He chafed at the slow speed, but as long as he carried the finders, he had to keep the van moving at a foot pace. Anyway, he wanted at least one of his captives conscious by the time they reached the corral and tack shed. He had no interest in catching and saddling horses himself.

Timi

Timi's head pounded like the inside of a badly maintained starship propulsion plant, and the rest of him didn't feel much better. His arms and feet were bound together and to each other in a manner that arched his back the wrong way, and he was lying on a hard, swaying, vibrating surface. He couldn't remember how he had gotten here. They'd been climbing out of the Surprise River canyon; he remembered that much, and then nothing. Had he fallen and been carried through the rapids, perhaps gone out of control from a head injury? But even if they'd had to restrain him they wouldn't have tied him like this.

He managed to force his eyes open, and saw Roi's face, slack and drooling, a handspan from his own. Roi was bound, too, as were the two girls beyond. Kidnapped? Timi thought dazedly. Was he feeling the aftermath of a stunner bolt?

He rolled his eyes, trying to see as much of his surroundings as he could without actually moving his head. A cramped, low-ceilinged, metal box, lighted from panels—no, translucent windows, he could see the light changing as he felt a turning sensation. An airvan, that was it. They had been tied and shoved into the rear section of an airvan.

The swaying intensified briefly, and Timi fought to keep his stomach in place. Then the motion ended with a slight jolt, and a moment later the vibration stopped. He sensed movement behind him, followed by a sharp jab in the small of his back, just where the muscles were already cramping from the unaccustomed stress. "Get up," a familiar voice said.

"M'Lord Zhaim?" Timi gulped with an irrational surge of relief. Zhaim was his friend, after all—but why was he tied? "I can't, M'Lord. Not tied like this."

The response was another kick, this time to his shoulder, rolling him onto his face, and the thrust of an unfamiliar mind into his.

Timi was used to Roi's mind-touch, and he had endured mental probing from earlier owners. This—this mental rape—was far worse than anything he could remember. Zhaim was making no attempt at all to control the emotional overtones of his probe, and what Timi felt was so totally alien to anything he had thought of Zhaim that his outraged stomach could no longer contain itself. He lay heaving, struggling not to drown in his own vomit, and tried not to hear Zhaim's high laughter echoing in the cramped airvan.

"You're even softer than I thought," came the harshly scornful voice as his bonds fell away and his body climbed to its feet. Timi tried to reach up and wipe his hand across his mouth, only to find his body no longer responded in the slightest to his will. Zhaim giggled again. "Yes," he said, "I left you conscious this time. I couldn't risk that when you sabotaged Roi's glider, or drugged the food. Go catch the horses and get them ready to ride."

Timi fought the barrier between his mind and the body that walked to the airvan's cargo door, waited for the door to open, and stepped out, falling to its knees when an ankle turned on the uneven ground. Zhaim snarled behind him, and Timi felt the slimy intruder in his brain twist on itself, seemingly spawning a part of itself in his consciousness. "There," Zhaim purred. "You can't go against my will, but I'll let you handle the details. I've got other things to do than control every reflex of your body." He turned away, and Timi looked quickly around.

The airvan had set down on a gravel area near the corral and tack shed they had been climbing toward. Five familiar horses were milling around the corral. What did Zhaim want with them, he wondered as he opened the tack shed and brought out a scarlet saddle and a blue one, laying them over the top rail of the corral. Dusty came to him, nickering hopefully, while Raindrop stood on the far side of the corral, snorting uneasily.

Whatever Zhaim was up to, he decided, he wanted no part of it. He didn't think he could escape himself, not with that slimy bit of Zhaim's mind mocking deep inside his, but perhaps if he were careless, if he let the horses escape .... He knocked against the gate latch as he brought out the next two saddles, letting the gate swing open. The thing in his mind kicked, exploding his diminishing headache back to full strength, and his body caught the swinging gate and closed it, his clumsy hand catching in the latch. He felt the middle finger of his left hand all but crushed, and realized there was no escape from doing exactly what Zhaim wanted. For right now, at least, he was better off cooperating and keeping his body as uninjured as possible for any chance of escape when Zhaim wasn't actually present.

The first four horses weren't difficult. They practically walked over him, stepping painfully on his poorly protected feet, to get to the grain bucket. Dusty needed a more or less perfunctory knee in the belly while Timi was tightening the girth, and he couldn't seem to get Token's girth buckled into the right hole. Usually, he remembered, her girth had to be retightened after a few minutes actually on the trail. Still, he had all of the horses except Raindrop tacked up and tied to the rail by the time Zhaim approached from the airvan, his hands gloved and a box in his arms.

"Which one's the guide's horse?" Zhaim asked abruptly, and Timi felt the thing in his mind shift, ready to punish any lack of cooperation.

"The bay leopard on the end by the tack shed, M'Lord," he replied, shaking the grain bucket enticingly toward Raindrop. Horse care was one chore Roi had never even suggested swapping away, and Timi couldn't remember even touching Raindrop since that first day, let alone catching her.

Raindrop clearly did not consider that Timi was any substitute for Roi. She stood just out of reach, ready to swing her heels toward Timi if the boy approached, and fixed her eyes on the grain bucket. Maybe if he put the bucket down, Timi thought, he could step in and grab Raindrop's neck rope while the mare was eating. Carefully he tipped the bucket toward the horse to let the animal see that there really was grain there, then set the bucket down at his feet and stepped back.

The horse took a cautious step forward, eyes fixed on the boy, and lowered her head into the bucket. Timi stepped up, reaching for the neck rope, and found himself stumbling backward as the grulla jerked her head up and half reared, striking the bucket with one forefoot. Grain sprayed over half the corral. The thing in his head lashed out again, and only the fact that he staggered into the fence kept him upright.

"Incompetent idiot," Zhaim hissed. "Can't you do anything without supervision?" He turned his attention to Raindrop, who was circling the corral, clearly intent on jumping the fence. The horse stopped short, shaking and wild-eyed. Mind control, Timi thought at the back of his mind. And she doesn't like it any better than I do. His body walked up to the trembling horse, clipped the lead rope he'd been carrying to the neck rope, and led the bewildered and suddenly docile animal back to the fence.

A little control came back, then, but by now he knew better than to try to fight Zhaim's will. Docile as Raindrop, he reached for the grulla's saddle and swung it over the spotted back. Zhaim seemed quite unconcerned that Timi hadn't brushed the animal before saddling.

The R'il'noid approached, ignoring Timi totally, and began attaching something to Roi's saddle. Roi's finder, Timi saw. He began to understand. Aside from tonight's cabin, where they would pick up the packhorses and the rest of their gear, they would have been camping again for the rest of the trip. The horses would be sent on, carrying the finders, and to the Company monitoring the finders, it would look as if the travelers had picked up their mounts and moved on.

Zhaim was certainly able enough to send the horses drifting toward Safeport, and to anyone checking the finder locations, it would simply look as if the travelers were taking their time and enjoying themselves on the final leg of the trip. Something would happen, Timi suspected, before the horses reached the town, but until then no one would even come looking for them.

"Ah, yes," Zhaim purred, "the cabin. I'm glad you reminded me to swing by the cabin this evening. It wouldn't do to leave what you're expected to pick up there." He turned his head, studying Timi, and the thing in the boy's mind sat up and whimpered with eagerness.

"Get the others' clothing, and get out of your own," Zhaim ordered. "Leave it where they'll expect it, here in the tack shed, and take the riding clothes for all five of you back to the airvan and toss them in. Wait for me outside the van."

That was when it hit Timi that there had been only three other bodies in the back of the airvan. Zhaim wanted to hurt Roi. And he knew the best way to do that was through the three slaves Roi loved. He didn't need Penny, so he must have killed her, as casually as he would have swatted a fly. How had he ever thought Zhaim's friendship could be worth a fraction of Roi's? How had he ever been such an idiot as to let Zhaim use him as a tool against Roi?

He had already found the cabinet that held their riding clothes and boots, and it took only a moment to carry the fresh clothing back to the van. He couldn't bear to look closely at the three bound bodies, nude now, and moaning a little. Their clothing and climbing equipment was piled just inside the cargo door, and he picked it up and carried it back to the shed, sick with misery. Zhaim had been adjusting the creance anchor on Freckles' saddle when Timi had left, and by the time he returned, the

R'il'noid was holding the horse's head between his hands, his scowling face intent on the animal's left eye.

Timi shoved their climbing stuff into the cabinet and began stripping off his own gear, watching Zhaim out of the corner of his eye. The thing in his mind kicked just as he added his own clothing and shoes to the pile, and his body walked over to open the corral gate as Zhaim released the horse's head. Token knocked Splash sideways as the horses surged through, and Timi's mind cried out in pain as Splash's hoof came down on his bare foot. Zhaim laughed and shoved him back toward the van, where Timi's body held hands behind it to be rebound, then lay on the floor and arched itself for his hands and his bruised, gravel-cut feet to be tied together. Only when the van lifted and turned under him did the controlling presence fade from his consciousness.

Chapter 18

Someone was cursing nearby.

Penny didn't think it was her; the voice was too deep for hers and half the words were totally unfamiliar. Besides, the cursing didn't stop when she moaned. Neither did the pain in her head, nor the cramps in her limbs. She tried to shift her position, and realized that she was lying folded up on an open grillwork of some sort, and her hands were fastened down to it.

She managed to get her eyes open, and shut them again almost at once as fresh pain lanced through her skull. On her second try she was ready for the pain, and managed to focus on the grid at her side. A cage?

She levered herself up on her elbows, wincing as the bars of the floor cut into them, and tried to get a better look at her prison. This time she recognized it for what it was, a traveling cage for one of the huge hounds used in the hunting preserves. It wasn't big enough for her to stand, or sit up, or even lie down without doubling up her legs, and she wanted very badly to stretch her cramped limbs. And when she looked down, she saw loops of cable on both of her wrists, with a short additional length connecting them beneath one of the floor bars.

She looked out beyond the bars of the cage, where red light lay like blood over a room filled with strange furniture. To her right was a window, and beyond it the sun lay like a deflating red balloon, pricked by the mountains it was sinking behind. She looked hastily back into the room, wanting to see what was there while the light held.

Another cage stood on a table across the room. Within it, a white-haired body lay on its side, shuddering so violently that the whole cage shook slightly. Not the source of the cursing, though, she thought.

That sound was coming from her left. She swung her gaze past the staircase climbing along the inner wall to two more cages set next to hers. Flame was crammed into the closest, her face turned anxiously across the room. Beyond her, Timi was curled into a ball, muttering to himself and now and then erupting with more curses.

Penny turned her head back across the room. "Roi?" she said. "Roi? What happened? How did we get here?"

Roi managed to roll over and lift his head enough to look at her, and she saw that the shudders that wracked him were close to convulsions, and his teeth were chattering so loudly that she could hear them across the room.

"D-don't know for sure," he replied with some difficulty. "I-it feels like Zhaim, somehow. I think somebody gave me one hell of an overdose of hiControl. I can't pick up anything. B-but I should have felt danger, before, if he was after us. Only I didn't."

Timi lifted his head. "It was Zhaim all right," he said. "I was on the edge of the stun field—came out of it a little before he landed by the corral. He—he just took me over. Made me get the horses ready and sent them off with the finders and warnoffs. He—oh, Roi, he said I'd sabotaged your glider. And, I, I tried to kill you out on the lake, and I thought it was a nightmare afterward ...." He buried his face in his bound hands.

"He used your body, yes," Roi sighed. "That amber pendant he gave you—it was a control circuit. I knew as soon as I was able to feel out the glider that you were the only one who'd touched it. But I probed you right after it happened, and you didn't know anything about it, and you were fighting with him to control your body out in the lake. It wasn't you, Timi. You trusted him too much, but I don't believe you ever willingly cooperated with him against me. Making mistakes is part of growing up. And yours were nothing like as bad as mine in thinking I was being too paranoid about Zhaim. If—if I'd just said something to Dad about not feeling danger ...."

Timi swallowed visibly and looked back at Roi. "I'm pretty sure he's recording what we do," he warned. "I don't know where he is now, but he went up those stairs."

Roi glanced out the window to where violet peaks thrust into the red sky. "Sunset took about as long as usual, so we're probably at the same latitude, close enough." He turned, looking squarely into Penny's eyes.

"Amber," he said, with an oddly deliberate emphasis on the name, "you're the expert on Falaron. Any idea where we are?"

He must not have gotten a good look at her before the sun set, Penny thought. But before she could straighten him out on who she was, Flame jumped in. "You spent enough time studying the maps, Amber." Again the emphasis on the missing girl's name.

Beyond Flame, Timi turned to look at her closely, and caught his breath. He looked back at Roi for a long moment before speaking. "I think Zhaim killed our guide," he said. "Either that or she died in the rapids. I doubt he'll tell us which. So Amber, if you don't remember where there's mountains at this latitude, we don't know where we are. I do know we were in the air for an hour or two, and I think we were headed west. The left window was brighter, anyway."

It wasn't all that dark yet, and there was a growing light source within the room. Even if Roi hadn't recognized her, the others would have, and besides, Amber had paid probably the least attention to the maps of any of them. So for some reason, Penny thought, they want me to pretend to be Amber. She wasn't sure why, since it seemed likely from what Timi had said that Amber was dead. But then if Zhaim thought he had killed the guide, it wasn't safe to be Penny in his hands. Maybe that was the idea.

"Probably we're somewhere in the Spine Range," she said. "I don't know of another range this jagged at this latitude, and Timi's flight time and direction would be right. We started out with the sleds on the east slope of the Spine, and the really rugged stuff like the cirque outside is about a time zone west of there. Say halfway between our starting point and Wilderness City."

"And Falaron's day length is close enough to Central's that the relative time zones won't have slipped much since the blizzard," Roi said. "If you're right about where we are, sunset here is close to sunrise at Zhaim's place, and since he lives about six hours west of the Enclave, he'll be on an early schedule while Dad's gone. I'd guess he's very visibly back on Central, and likely too busy to get back to Falaron until it's morning here. Father told me he set things up for daily council meetings while he was gone, and with us here Zhaim won't dare attract attention by not being there except when everybody'd think he was asleep."

Penny wanted to ask why this had happened, why Zhaim would have kidnapped them. But the others seemed to understand the situation, so probably Amber would have, as well. She'd better try to think like Amber, she thought. Pretend she was in love with Roi and Timi both, to start with. She remembered the shared bed in the blizzard, the night they had shared a sleeping bag for warmth after the thunderstorm, the evening they'd walked around the outcrop in the moonlight. As far as Roi was concerned, she realized with a kind of shock, she didn't need to pretend.

"He wants to get rid of a rival," Flame said unexpectedly. "Roi, he knows. Shouldn't Timi and Amber?"

"If we get out of this alive," Roi said wistfully, "I don't think there's any way we'll be able to keep it a secret. Flame found out by accident, but you two might as well know too. I outrank Zhaim on Çeren index. He wants me dead—as agonizingly as possible—because he can't stand the idea of being second to another R'il'noid. Especially one who was born a slave."

For a few minutes Penny just huddled in her cage, trying to take in the implications of that statement. Pools of light within the room had replaced the sunset, and for the first time she really saw the spotlighted equipment with its attached chains and cuffs and straps, and the way Roi's cage was placed where he would have a clear view of that equipment. After what seemed a long spell of silence, she heard her own voice. "And he can hurt you worst by hurting us," she said.

Roi nodded wordlessly. "I'm sorry," he finally whispered. "If there were anything, anything at all I could do, I would. But without a miracle, he is going to kill you all before my face, and then kill me. Probably before we're due back in Safeport. And no matter what he tries to make you believe, there is nothing at all I could do to change that. Except get away from him or kill him." Another of the convulsive shudders struck him. When it was over he said, without raising his head again, "We'd better get some sleep while we can."

Roi

None of them would really sleep right away, of course. Roi knew that. But he needed a chance to think the situation over.

HiControl had been a new drug to Marna, and she and Roi had investigated it together. Roi knew his convulsions just about had to be the result of an overdose of raw drug, and knew also that the reaction, though not the paralysis of his esper abilities, would wear off within a day. He hoped Zhaim was not fully aware of two other peculiarities of the stuff. While hiControl virtually wiped out most esper talents, it had no effect on deliberate shielding, in spite of its tendency to weaken natural shields. And it did not affect empathy.

The last was almost more a curse than a blessing—he would feel everything done to his friends as if he himself were being tortured. But it gave him a shred of hope, as well. His empathic ties with his slave friends were strong enough that he didn't think Amber could have died without his knowing she was gone as soon as he had recovered from the stunner attack. And as long as she was alive and free, she just might be able to get word of their plight to someone he trusted. Now he closed his eyes and relaxed as completely as the drug reaction would let him, pushing himself into the same light trance he would have used to contact someone not too far away.

Amber. It was harder than he had thought to reach only for feelings, to leave words and thoughts behind. Sunset faded to full dark, and still there was no response. The stars wheeled slowly down the sky. He was cold, and aching in every muscle and far too many bones, including his head .... No. Not his head, Amber's. His head merely ached from the aftereffect of the stun field. Hers had discrete knots of pain, including what felt like the whole left side of her jaw, and water rippled icily over her outstretched legs. She wasn't dead, not yet, but if he couldn't urge her to her feet and find something to build a fire, she'd be dead of hypothermia by morning.

Amber

Cold. *So* cold. One of the others must have rolled up in all the covers, or she'd rolled away from them, somehow. Amber reached out, seeking the warmth of other bodies, and found only sand and rounded pebbles. Driven by an urgency she did not understand, she managed to roll onto her side and open her eyes to the night.

Starlight blazed overhead, waking faint echoes in the river washing over her feet and legs. No moon to help her see, and no faint lingering of daylight, either. "Roi?" she called out anxiously. "Timi? Flame? Penny?" Only the soft rush of the river water answered her.

The need to be doing something drove her to hands and knees, and she dragged herself slowly away from the water. She gained a body length, and then another before she collided painfully with something sharp-edged, further scraping her sore jaw and narrowly missing an eye. Her hips collapsed sideways until she was half sitting, held up only by braced arms. After a moment she managed to rock back enough to raise one arm and examine the barrier.

Driftwood, she thought hazily. That should mean something. Her hand slid back down toward the gravel, brushing her heavy climbing belt on the way, her fingers catching on one of the pouches fastened there. Penny's face came into memory. "You're going to be short of belt loops, carrying all the anchors," Penny had said, "so let Timi carry your tracer. But keep the stuff in the emergency pouch with you. It doesn't weigh that much."

Emergency pouch. Fire-making supplies, fishhooks, reflective air blanket. Fire-making supplies. Driftwood. She could build a fire. Only to do that, she would have to move, and she was so *very* tired. So much easier just to lie down and rest.

The sense of urgency intensified, and she groaned and fumbled in the pouch. Emergency blanket. She worked it out of the pouch and struggled to unfold it, finally giving up and draping the wet and still half-folded blanket around her shoulders. Fire-sparker. She dug deeper, and found a handful of the waxy fuzzballs that would ignite even when sopping wet and burn long enough to start even green wood burning. And the driftwood, while a bit damp on the river side, didn't feel soggy.

Amber ran her hand carefully over the gravel, finding a considerable accumulation of smaller bits of wood and dry twigs in a ragged line parallel to the shore. She scraped them together in a small pile and put a fuzzball in the middle, then got out the sparker and began trying to light it. The sparks dazzled her eyes at first, and it took several tries before she could get a few to fall on the fuzzball. The soft outer layer went up in a flash that eliminated the remainder of her night vision. Then the wax caught, and in a few minutes she had enough of a fire to see the larger mass of driftwood.

It wasn't a single dead tree, she saw with relief, but a row of branches a little higher up the shore than the light stuff she'd scraped together. She reached for the piece she had bumped into, and dragged it close enough so that she could put it carefully on top of her little fire, where the flames could lick at the few dry curls of bark. Once it caught, she dragged half a dozen more branches back on hands and knees. Finally her sense of urgency eased, and she shook out the air blanket, wrapped it around herself, and lay down as close as she dared to the fire.

She ached all over, she found once she was no longer moving. For a while she kept reliving the day—the sudden cutoff of Roi's mental voice, the shock as she struck the cold river water, and her frantic efforts to protect her head as she was carried helplessly through the rapids. She could not remember dragging herself out of the river onto this bar, and she must have lain here for hours. Her hand rose to touch her aching jaw, and she realized with a start that she was still wearing the breathing mask that had kept her from drowning as she was carried downstream. She didn't need it to sleep in, she thought, and pulled it off of her face. She was half hypnotized by the dancing flames, and very tired. Gradually her eyes became harder and harder to keep open.

***

The sun woke her from a nightmare. She had been somewhere else entirely, cramped into a cage. In front of her, the gray light of dawn had illuminated an appalling array of objects, and beyond the chains and straps she saw three other cages, cages that held her friends. She felt a fear that was close to panic, and with it a desperate need for help. There were no words with the vision, just a growing sense of terror as someone walked down a staircase at one end of the room, and turned Zhaim's face toward her. Then, in the manner of dreams, she had been back in Safeport, talking with Lord Derik.

Amber's whole body ached with the bruising from the rapids, and she shuddered in pain as she pulled herself to a sitting position and turned to face the river. The dream could be just that, of course, a dream. But she had the feeling that the dream had come repeatedly during the night. She had a distinct memory of that nightmare room with pools of light over the torture implements, rather than the one-sided light of dawn, and with no sign of Zhaim. Could the nightmare be truth, somehow sent her by Roi?

If it was, she had to get word of what had happened back to Lai. Even if the dream was only a dream. She thought back to the moment Roi's mind-voice had cut off in the middle of a word. Something had happened to cause that, and she didn't think that something was friendly. So far as she knew, she alone was alive and free, and she had to try to contact someone she could trust. Derik, perhaps, as the tail end of her dream had suggested. He was planning to pick them all up in Safeport, Roi had said. Or maybe the adjudicator who'd sent them the food. Amber hadn't met the woman herself, but she knew that both Roi and Timi liked and trusted her.

She considered trying to call out for help mentally, and discarded the idea at once. If it had been Zhaim who'd kidnapped the others, his mind would be open for any hint of a survivor. Maybe a com call to the Company, if she wasn't too far downstream to find the cabin where they should have spent last night. How far downstream had she been carried, anyway?

She pulled herself to her feet and limped to the river's edge. Water rushed by her, deepening rapidly away from the bar. The bank shelved gently behind her, but across the river a low cliff arose sheer from the water. To her left, upstream, white water just showed around a bend. Rapids were even closer downstream. She must have just made it to the bar, she thought with a shudder. But if she remembered rightly, the rapids ended near where the trail to Safeport came back to the river. If she could find the trail, she could backtrack and use the com in the cabin.

Her clothing had dried fairly well except where she had lain on it overnight, and on that side it rubbed wetly against sore skin. The sun was warm enough that she would be more comfortable without it, she decided, and it would dry faster draped over the driftwood on the bar. She was wearing a shirt with sleeves that could be rolled up and fastened, soft, close-fitting breeches, and climbing shoes with tough but flexible soles. Her climbing belt—more of a climbing harness, really, for it had straps around her legs and shoulders—provided back support as well as being well studded with loops, snaps and pockets. The leather had been tanned to resist water, but just now it felt slimy under her hands. She pulled off everything but her shoes and laid it out near the ashes of her fire.

She glanced back at the water, and suddenly realized the significance of the direction it was flowing. She was on the south bank, and the cabin was on the other side of the river.

A raft? She discarded the idea almost at once. Even a powered boat might not have made it across the river before being swept into the rapids, and she could see no way to get from a boat to the top of the opposite bank even if she could have made it across. And could she even build a raft? No, unless there was a lot better crossing point downstream, the com was out of reach.

She turned slowly, surveying her surroundings. The gravel was bare beneath her feet, and continued bare up to the line of debris she had found by touch the night before. Driftwood was scattered farther back than she had thought from that line. The lower pieces were only a little above the debris line, resting on bare gravel. Farther away from the water, grass grew through and around the driftwood and there were even a few living saplings. Farther yet, the meadow was being invaded by open forest. There were traces of several old fires on the bar, and when she walked up into the grass, she found a well-marked horse trail angling away from the river.

She walked back to the water's edge, picking up her climbing belt on the way, and began methodically considering her resources. The belt's loops and snaps held mostly climbing anchors, but she also had her warnoff—though she wasn't sure whether it was still working after her tumble through the rapids—and a twisted coil of thin, tough rope, no thicker than string. The reflective blanket, which could be inflated for extra insulation or worn as a rain poncho if needed, still lay by the ashes of her fire with the breathing mask. She'd have to be sure she repacked both, though she might as well discard the climbing anchors.

She must have put the sparker and the remaining dozen or so fuzzballs back into the emergency kit last night, because they were the first things she found there. Next came the fishhooks and line. She dumped the fire-making supplies back into the kit and walked upslope to search the saplings for one of the little gray-green caterpillars Penny had said made good fishing bait. Then she walked down to the lower end of the bar. An eddy formed a relatively quiet pool there, and she tied the free end of the line to the roots of a dead tree and tossed the baited hook into the pool. There was no sense leaving the bar until she had decided what to do, so she might as well try to get herself some food.

There was a flat rock next to the pool, and she eased her body into a sitting position by it. She didn't feel quite as sore since she had begun moving. She looked her bare body over as well as she could, and decided that while she was well covered with purpling bruises and angry scrapes, her bones and joints were intact.

This time, she laid the contents of both belt pouches out on the rock. The emergency kit yielded a force blade, two of the emergency food bars, a very small first aid kit and a folded packet of what looked like waterproof synthetic. She pounced on the aid kit and pulled out the tube of wound salve, dabbing it carefully on her scrapes. She should have done that last night, she thought, but she could hope it would still provide some protection.

The pouch built into the belt had three more of the emergency bars and a compass. She piled the food bars with the other two, and licked her chapped lips nervously. Five days of food, if she rationed herself to one bar a day. She had the fishhooks and line, and the twine and some of the larger pebbles would make a bola, so she might be able to supplement the emergency supplies. As if on cue, her fishline moved against the current, and she grabbed it and jerked to set the hook. It wasn't a big fish, but it would make a welcome breakfast. Or lunch. She squinted at the sun. It was directly behind her when she faced the main river channel, but it didn't seem high enough in the sky to be noon, yet.

Building a small fire on the rock, and then cleaning her catch and spitting it on a green stick to hold over the fire, took little thought. Amber fretted as she worked, wishing she had paid more attention to Penny's map as they had discussed the next phase of their journey.

She had to talk to someone she trusted, and she had to do it as soon as she could. That meant a com—though on reflection she was worried about the possibility that Zhaim could intercept a com call—or talking face to face with Derik or the adjudicator. Derik would be planning to meet them in Safeport, two or three fivedays from now. The adjudicator was based in Wilderness City, far to the west, but Roi had said she was handling the planetary circuit, and that they might see her in Safeport. She should head for Safeport, Amber decided. All the more so if her dream—especially the final scene—had been a message from Roi.

Amber's stomach was protesting with increasing urgency as the smell of the fish grew steadily more appetizing, and it took all her self-control to wait until her meal had cooled enough that it wouldn't burn her fingers. She couldn't afford burned fingers right now, she told herself firmly. She was in poor enough shape to get to Safeport as it was.

And she wasn't sure how to get there. She could try to follow the river, of course. Safeport was built where the Surprise emptied into an ocean, and there were bridges in the town. She didn't have to worry about which bank she was following once she reached her goal. She wished she could remember more of what Penny had told them about this part of the route. Amber thought the guide had said something about their taking the long way round with the horses, even though they would be following the river. The river itself curved away from the direct route, or something. If that were true, she might be better off striking away from the river and heading directly for the coast. It was east, wasn't it? And she had a compass .... The compass said the river was flowing more north than east, which meant that the horse trail she'd noticed earlier was heading almost due east. But if she left the river, she would have to carry water, and her water bottle had been on Timi's belt. She looked thoughtfully at the supplies still laid out on the other end of the rock. The synthetic packet looked waterproof. Maybe she could rig some kind of water carrier from that.

Maybe she wouldn't have to. The synthetic unfolded into a sealable bag, complete with loops on two corners that would fasten to the snaps on her climbing belt. And the lines printed on it, once she got it right side up, were a map of the lower Surprise. She couldn't mistake the lake on the far left, or the place where the river flowed into the sea, on the far right. Sure enough, the river made a big loop to the north just east of the gorge, taking it far out of the direct line to Safeport. The land within the loop and to the south was marked as a reserve for guided hunting, closed during the summer months except for aerial photography. The dotted lines must be trails, she thought, and began trying to work out her own position.

Rapids, waterfalls, canoe portages and fords were clearly marked, and she decided quickly that she must be at the break between the last long stretch of rapids, the one that began in the gorge below the waterfall and continued past the point where the walls fell away, and a shorter stretch that continued to just above the marked canoe shed on the north bank.

She just might be able to hike to below the rapids, build a raft of some sort, get across the river and pick up a canoe from those stored at the cabin. She wasn't at all sure she could single-handedly get the canoe around the numerous small waterfalls shown on the map, and if she stuck with a raft she certainly couldn't portage that. She wasn't even sure she could build a raft, or control it if she did. And she discovered she was no longer even thinking seriously about attempting a com call, especially from the cabin where they had planned to sleep last night. She had to assume that whoever had kidnapped the others knew where they were heading.

She'd have to stay on this side of the river, she decided as she turned back to the map. And that meant a choice of following the south bank of the Surprise or taking the horse trail to the east. The trail held a surprisingly direct line toward Safeport. Individual segments deviated a little, but the changes in direction were almost all at river crossings. Probably controlled by where the rivers were fordable, she thought. And all of those rivers flowed into the Surprise eventually. Still, drinking water could be a problem on the horse trail.

If she followed the south bank, she would have to find ways across the tributaries. She looked for indications of fords nearer the Surprise than the trail crossings, and found them on only two of the side streams. That could be an even greater problem than water, she decided, since she had the water bag. Anyway, there must be enough water on the trail for horses.

She forced herself to eat the last cooling scraps of the fish, and looked ruefully down at her shoes. They were designed to grip rocks, not for long hours of walking. And she would have to walk and even jog a little from sunrise to sunset for the next fiveday or two if she were to reach Safeport before Zhaim killed his captives.

The belt was almost dry, if stiff, so her clothes ought to be ready to put back on. She retrieved clothing, emergency blanket and breathing mask, filled the water bag from the fishing pool, and began preparing for a long walk.

Chapter 19

Falaron: Amber
5/28/38

One more rise, Amber decided. If there was no sign of water over the next ridge, she would at least pause to check that her aching feet weren't starting to blister. She might even have to consider making a dry camp. There were still faint red dapples of sunlight on the forest floor around her, but it was already dark enough under the dense canopy that it was getting hard to see her footing.

She didn't have to look at the map on the almost empty water sack. There was a ford ahead of her, about the same distance from the one where she'd camped last night as that had been from the first night's spring. If she were lucky, there would be a proper river in the next swale, not just a low spot in the woods, and she'd have time to put out a fish line before dark. She licked dry lips. Yesterday, she'd brought down a squirrel with her improvised bola. No such luck today. She was rationing herself to one of the emergency sticks a day, eating half a stick as she started on the trail as soon as it was light enough to see, and the other half at midafternoon. That way she wasn't too hungry to sleep, even if she couldn't find anything else to eat. But the remaining food bars would not get her to Safeport. If she couldn't catch a fish tonight, she'd have to try eating the caterpillars she used as bait.

She leaned into the slope, wearily continuing to place one foot in front of the other, her eyes on the trail ahead of her. The horse trail was easy enough to follow, but it hadn't been used much lately. Probably not since last fall, she thought. So much for finding a Company representative and asking for help.

She adjusted her balance automatically as the slope changed beneath her feet, and only afterward lifted her head as her weary mind picked up the fact that she was going downhill. It was hard to see much through the trees, but when she stopped and listened for a moment, she thought she could hear the gurgle of running water. She licked her lips again and picked up the pace a little. She wasn't sure which she wanted more: a drink of water that hadn't been sitting in the water bag all day, or a chance to soak her feet.

It seemed a very long time before the path leveled out underfoot, and even longer until she began to see light through the tree trunks. By then it was dark enough under the trees that she was beginning to stumble over tree roots and fallen branches, though she could still see sunlight on the bits of the opposite slope visible through the trees.

Mosquitoes buzzed around her, though only a few actually landed and bit. Was the warnoff still working? This morning she'd stumbled into a clearing where mastodons were browsing, and the animals had simply turned their heads and looked at her, and then gone back to stripping leaves with their trunks and stuffing their harvest into their mouths. For some reason—possibly the way their heads set onto their stumpy bodies—they reminded her almost as much of giant peccaries as they did of the mammoths.

Fish ate mosquitoes and other insects, she thought as she came out of the trees and saw the liquid silver of the river ahead of her. This would be a good time of the day for fish to catch insects, so it seemed likely that the fish would be awake and looking for food. She began checking the bushes for grubs and caterpillars to use as bait.

The brush opened out into a grassy meadow, and the trail curved sharply to the left, following the edge of the forest. The ford must be downstream, she thought tiredly, but the meadow would be a good camping place. And there was a spot off to the right where the little river had cut into the meadow at some point in its past, leaving a quiet pool that looked like a good place to fish. She turned and headed across the meadow, looking for a possible campsite.

The ground rose toward the water between the ford and the pool, and looked drier. Good as the damp ground felt to her feet, she wanted a dry place to sleep. Not too near the edge, though, she thought as she neared the river. It looked as though a piece of the bank had collapsed recently.

She came to the edge and looked down, and was startled by a high squeal just below her. The bank had indeed caved in recently, so recently that a chunk of mud and sod still lay at water level below the scar. On the precarious islet a peccary piglet huddled, eyes wild with fright as it looked up at her.

Amber's first reaction was pity for the stranded baby, but she choked the emotion down ruthlessly. She had to get help for the others; to do that she needed food, and the piglet was more than she had dared to hope for. She crouched on the edge of the bank, wondering if she could make a noose in her rope and get it around the piglet's neck to lift it away from the water. As she watched, the river took another bite from the pile of dissolving mud. She would have to hurry if she wanted to salvage this unexpected bounty.

She felt the sow's charge before she heard it, and turned barely in time to see the enraged animal. Its head was level with her own where she crouched, and she could see the fury in the tiny eyes and the saliva dripping from the tusks. She tried to jump sideways, out of the direct line to the trapped piglet, but the beast was too close. A blow to her thigh sent her flying off the bank, and the river closed over her head.

She managed somehow to hold her breath until her head broke water. The far bank was in front of her, and she didn't even bother to look behind her before swimming toward it. She could hear the piglet squealing, and the grunts of the sow, and when she dared to look back, she saw the sow herding the terrified youngling up the bank at the ford. The ford. She dropped her feet and found firm ground beneath her, the water no more than thigh deep. Guess I'll camp on the east bank after all, she thought, and began struggling toward the far side of the river. She wasn't sure why the warnoff hadn't worked. Maybe the sow had started her charge outside the range of the device, or the danger to the piglet had overridden the "harmless" message. Or maybe it had been damaged in the rapids, and the mosquitoes just weren't hungry.

Her leg began to ache abominably as she fought to keep her balance against the current, and she looked down to see that her breeches were torn and blood was streaking the water around her. Nausea gripped her throat, and her hands were shaking when she looked at them. I'm going into shock, she thought, feeling oddly detached from her body.

Roi's remembered voice came into her mind. First thing you do if you're hurt is slap an ampoule of counterShock against your skin—anywhere. Then if you're bleeding put pressure on the wound. She didn't think she was losing that much blood, but she remembered seeing a few ampoules of counterShock in the aid kit. She stopped on a shallow spot halfway across the river, and fished the aid kit out of her emergency pouch. Got to be careful, she thought. If I drop the aid kit now, I've had it. And the others with me. She managed to extract an ampoule and slip it into her breeches pocket, and then returned the kit to the emergency pouch. Then she worked the ampoule back out of the pocket, careful not to look at her mangled thigh, and pressed the active end against her left arm. The ampoule clung briefly, and then dropped away into the swirling, knee-deep water. Amber stood with her eyes half closed for a few minutes, feeling the nausea subside.

The pain continued to intensify, and she forced herself to look down at her thigh. Her breeches were torn in two places, and blood was seeping into the wet fabric around both of the holes. She forced herself to be calm. The blood was seeping, not spurting, and some bleeding would help cleanse the wounds. She had the feeling that the peccary's tusks had been anything but clean, and even with the wound dressing she carried, infection was a real possibility. Let them bleed for now, she thought through the growing pain, and concentrate on getting to the far bank and building a fire. Once she was settled for the night, she could take a dose of Suppress for the pain.

The last red light of the sun faded from the top of the slope ahead of her as she struggled on across the ford. This side of the river was shallower than the west side, varying from knee deep to just above her wounds. The water wasn't icy, but it was cold enough to numb her legs a little. Without that help, she wasn't sure she could have made it to the far bank.

She emerged from the ford onto a gravel bar strewn with driftwood, and lost no time in building a driftwood fire. Much as she wanted to strip off her soaked clothing and stay right there, she knew she needed food almost as much as she needed warmth. It took a while to find the caterpillars she was after, and by the time she baited a fishhook and tied the line to a driftwood snag next to the fire, the first stars were coming out.

She had cut half a dozen willow wands and an armload of alder branches as she gathered her bait, and pulled off strips of the willow bark even before she got out of her wet clothing. The long strips she put aside for binding the fish to the sticks for roasting—if only it wasn't too late in the evening for a fish to bite! The shorter ones she chewed, remembering that Penny had said willow bark would dull pain. The guide hadn't mentioned how horrible the stuff would taste.

She was halfway out of her breeches when the fish line jerked, and she almost fell over as she yanked it to set the hook. The pain as her waistband cut into the bruised flesh of her thigh left her shaking so hard she could barely stand. She closed her eyes and gritted her teeth. I am not going to faint, she told herself. Fainting is a shock symptom, and the counterShock I took has had plenty of time to take effect.

Carefully she teased her breeches the rest of the way off, and then hauled the fish in by brute force. It was a big one—big enough to give her dinner and breakfast both, if she could figure out a way of keeping it overnight—and she was grateful for the strength of the line from the emergency kit. The fire hadn't burned down as far as she would have preferred, but she needed food too badly to be choosy. While the fish cooked, she sat down by the fire and forced herself to examine and treat her leg.

The wounds were half punctures and half tears, as if the sow's tusks had been driven into the outside of her right thigh and then pulled halfway out before ripping sideways. She had been able to use the leg, so she didn't suppose any major muscles had been severed, and the bleeding seemed to have stopped. She pulled the wound salve out of the aid kit, and looked longingly at the Suppress tubes. It would be so much easier to treat her injuries if the leg didn't hurt so much. No, she decided, she'd have to wait until she had finished eating. She had to keep going, and if she burned herself because the Suppress kept her from feeling the heat of the fire, she'd really have a problem.

She flaked meat from the better-done side of the fish until she felt she'd be sick if she ate any more, then added lengths of green alder to the fire and hung the remains of the fish in the smoke. Maybe that way she could preserve it at least until tomorrow morning.

In the meantime, she had borne the pain for as long as she could. She dug out the Suppress and squeezed one of the tubes into her mouth. The minty coolness seemed to spread directly from her mouth through her body, and she sighed in relief as the pain vanished. Somehow she kept awake long enough to add a second layer of wound salve, this time working it as deeply into the punctures as she could, before she curled into the reflective blanket, upwind of the fire. Her last coherent thought was that she would have to cut a walking stick in the morning.

Rat

It was the most desirable object the rat had ever seen or smelled. The animal's whiskers quivered with excitement as it yearned over the perfect ring with its metal wand, hanging high above its head. Once again the rat advanced to the base of the rough wall, placing a tentative forepaw against the rough stone. After a dozen tries, however, each ending with a tumble back to the stone floor when it reached a slick area just below its goal, the rat was becoming discouraged. Could there be another such Object? One within reach?

Reluctantly the creature moved to its left along the base of the wall, now and then glancing back and up toward the Object. A low wall stopped its progress, but only for a moment. It half climbed, half jumped to the platform beyond the wall. Then a second wall, this one high and smooth, forcing the rodent away from the wall where the Object hung and up more of the low walls and platforms. It balked finally, turning back to stare at its goal.

A miracle! Out of nowhere a road had appeared, leading along the wall and around the corner to just above the Object. The rat hurled itself onto the narrow path, running back to the spot where the precious ring hung just below its feet. It lowered its head to take the divine Object into its mouth. Now it scrambled a little farther along the path and down, leaping to a grating and climbing through. One final act of devotion remained. The rat shifted the Object with paws and mouth, gripping the flat metal strip where the ring pierced it, and thrust the strip into a waiting slot.

Joy.

Ecstasy.

A veritable explosion of pleasure.

Roi

Roi pulled his hands away from the cage bottom and gently removed the magnetic key from the quivering rodent's jaws. Zhaim had dragged them all from their cages often enough that he knew the same key controlled all of their shackles and cage locks, and once the rat had unlocked his shackles, it took him only a minute or so to maneuver the key to where he could open his cage.

"I thought you said you were drugged so you couldn't use your talents," Timi said from across the room.

Roi wiggled out of the cage and pulled himself upright. He stretched once, and then hurried across the room to free Timi. "I can't; that was something different," he told the other boy. Just how much he could manage with empathy alone was his secret until he was sure Zhaim could not read that information from his friends. "Get the girls loose, I'm going to see if we can get upstairs." If they were lucky, he thought, the same magnetic key would operate whatever barrier might be at the top of the stairs. If they were really lucky, there would be a com he could use to get out a call to Kyrie.

"Can we get out?" Timi called as he released Penny's wrists. Flame was already on her feet, stretching systematically.

"It's a mag lock, anyway," Roi called back. "Toss the key up, will you, and I'll see if it works. And see if you can find our clothes."

"They're in the cabinet under the stairs," Timi replied. "Let me get it open—there. Catch!" The key came spinning up to Roi.

If Roi hadn't seen Zhaim fumbling with the lock a time or two, he might have given up. But when the lock did not respond to full insertion of the key, he tried inserting it only part way. He felt the lock give on the fourth try, and the barrier above his head disappeared. Some kind of force field, he thought. "Come on up, Timi," he called. "We need to find a com, and you know electronics best."

Timi handed Roi his clothes as he passed him. He was carrying the branding iron Zhaim had forced his body to use on Penny, no doubt hoping to jam a door open, but the barrier, whatever it had been, had vanished completely. "Bring anything you think we might possibly need and come on up," Roi called down to the girls. Carrying his clothing, he walked on into the lodge's main room, dimly lit by the sunset sky out the windows to his left.

He was facing a wall covered with a dead screen above a waist-high shelf loaded with controls. Timi already had the cover off one end of the shelf, checking the connections behind the controls. Directly ahead, along the east wall of the building, was an archway into another room. Roi walked through the arch, noting that another stairway ascended inside the partition wall, and found a food service and preparation area. His mouth was too dry to let him swallow, but—yes, there was running water, and disposable cups.

The crates had been equipped with food and water cups, but the latter had held only stinking, green-scummed water that smelled as if it had come from a sewage lagoon. By the time Zhaim had dropped gnawed bones with a few shreds of half-rotten, mold-furred raw meat into the food dishes, they had all been so thirsty that they couldn't have eaten even without Roi's warning that the bones were human.

This, however, looked like Zhaim's own food-preparation area. Roi filled a cup and took a cautious sip, then checked the stasis chest against the partition wall. Food enough for one good meal for all of them, he judged, and plenty of water. Better let Penny and Flame prepare it, he thought as he filled another cup and took it out to Timi.

"Find a com yet?" he asked as he handed Timi the cup. "Don't drink that too fast, Timi. There's plenty more. Decent food, too, if you girls don't mind fixing it after you get some water."

Penny and Flame fairly dived for the kitchen, and the sound of running water came within seconds. Timi finished his water with a sigh of relief, and checked the last section of the shelf. "So far," he said worriedly, "I haven't found any sign that anything hooks into a transmitter. Lots of stuff for incoming signals, but this setup looks like it was designed not to let anything out. I did find the recorder for his spyeyes on our prison, and erased the last couple of hours."

Roi chewed his lip nervously. "Good on the recorder, but the rest's not good," he said after a moment. "We've got some time—there's a full council meeting today, and it's likely to run longer than usual with Father gone. That's what Derry said right after Father left, anyway, and Zhaim's not going to be able to get away from it without causing a lot of suspicion. But if we can't get a message out, well, I don't think we can get far enough on foot in the dark to evade him when he gets back." He took Timi's empty cup from his hand and walked back into the kitchen, this time taking a careful look out the north window. Cirque wall, doghouse, pacing dog, and there, right under the window, an airvan. Thoughtfully he refilled Timi's cup and his own, and took them both back out to the main room.

"I can turn up the lights if you want," Timi offered. "Can't do much more here without light."

"Good idea," Roi replied. "I'll check upstairs. Maybe the com's there."

The top of the stairs ended in a door, but it, too, responded to the magnetic key. Roi pushed the door open and found himself facing a west window, with a sleeping room and outdoor deck to his left and a bathing and sanitary area to his right. "Bathroom up here," he called down the stairs, figuring that a bath would be between water and food in priority, and began checking over the two upper rooms for anything that could possibly be a com.

The storage spaces were unlocked or yielded immediately to the mag key, and there was nothing anywhere that could possibly be a com. He did find and keep a duplicate of the screamer circuit that had almost killed him on the glider, and what looked like a flyer key from a belt pocket. By the time he finished checking the sleeping room, the girls had scrubbed themselves clean, and Roi cleaned his own stinking body before he went back down the stairs.

Timi was on his back with his head in an access hatch below the shelf when Roi got back to the main floor. The wall screen displayed a map of the continent, and Penny, dressed and with her wet hair rebraided, was studying it as she ate. "Food's in the kitchen," she told him. "The blue lights on the map are our finders. I don't think the Company's going to suspect anything."

"Nothing upstairs, I take it?" Timi asked as he slid out from under the shelf and sat up. "Roi, he's a good enough esper he wouldn't need an outgoing com. If there isn't one here, what are we going to do?"

"There's an airvan parked out there," Roi replied. "There ought to be at least a short-range com in that. Might even be worth trying to fly it out. I think I found the key. But for right now, get yourself cleaned up and eat. We're probably going to have to get away from here to get a message out. Even if the van's got a com, it's likely to be line of sight and we won't be able to reach anyone while it's on the ground."

Timi climbed to his feet, his face doubtful. "I'm pretty sure the third panel of the shelf copies the airvan status," he said, "and if I'm right, its power packs are about exhausted. We're here," he put his finger on a small white light near the crest of the Spine Range, "and the nearest place I'm sure anyone could hear us is over here, in Wilderness City." He touched a green light on the west coast, farther from their present location than the distance they had covered from their drop-off point in the mountains to where Zhaim had kidnapped them near the lower end of the gorge. "Penny says it's all hunting reserve. There might be some wardens there, but she doesn't know where most of them are, or whether they could pick up anything from an aircraft com. And if that's the same airvan he kidnapped us with, I got a quick look at the controls. Looked like a really cheap com setup."

"Clean up, get dressed, and eat," Roi told his friend. "Then we'll see if we can get into the airvan and check it over. If it'll fly, we'll take it as far as we can toward Wilderness City—out of the mountains at least, I hope—and start walking. Think about what you might be able to do to keep Zhaim from using the status panel to find out where it goes down. If we can stay out of his hands for a while, there'll be searchers out looking for us.

"Penny, see what you can find in the way of water carriers and trail food. Look for weather sheets, too—there's plenty of blankets upstairs, but there's no way to keep them dry if it rains." He'd already found the markers and waterproof sheets he wanted.

"Roi?" Timi called back down the stairs. "I got a feeling while he was in my mind that he was planning to make it look like wild animals got us and the horses both. He could still do that, to stop searchers."

"Won't work without our bodies," Roi called back. "At least not without mine, they'll check for my genetic signature. If we can stay free until they find the horses, there'll be searchers. Does mean we'd better clean up those cages, and good. We don't want to leave anything of ourselves behind."

Timi

The front door, they discovered, opened without a key from inside and could be opened with the mag key from outside. Timi fiddled with one of the controls to bring up the outside lights, and joined Roi at the door. They still hadn't found weather sheets, and Penny and Flame were trying to work out the best way to carry the gear they planned to take—a blanket and a water bottle apiece, plastic bags of the limited amount of trail food they had found, and the contents of the aid kits in the basement and bathroom.

The two boys were halfway down the front steps, shivering a little in the night air, when Timi froze, suddenly aware of the paired sparks of light surrounding them. "Stand still," Roi said quietly. He studied the dogs as the animals paced toward them, heads down and crouching a little. "Sit," he said abruptly, and Timi almost sat down on a step himself. The dogs' heads came up, and they sat almost eagerly. "Hunting mode," Roi muttered under his breath, "and not happy about it. Go back up the steps, Timi. See if you and Flame can find anything to feed them. They're starving, and they've been used to hunt humans before."

"I spotted half a sack of dog food in one of the cabinets while I was searching the kitchen for a com," Timi said as he slipped back through the door. He turned to Flame. "Be ready to open the door for him fast," he told the girl. "If those brutes go for him, he won't have time to use the mag key." He ran into the kitchen, trying to remember where he had seen the dog food and the stack of large bowls.

Sack and bowls were in the third cabinet he tried, and he scooped them up and headed back out the door. Roi was among the dogs, running his hands over their bodies and lifting the skin of their backs. When they started to jump to their feet, he gave them a sharp "Down," and the animals flattened themselves obediently. Then he turned and started back up the steps to Timi.

"They're awfully thin," he said as he poured food into all five bowls, "but their skins don't feel like they're dehydrated. Must be water out here somewhere. Leave the sack just inside the door; we'll want it in the airvan later. You take two of the bowls and I'll take three. I'm pretty sure that feeding them will reinforce the idea that we're huntsmen, not prey. And they should be all right, once they're not so hungry."

Roi

Neither of the two slaves liked the idea of taking the dogs along, and even Penny looked doubtful at first. Penny could, however, see how useful the dogs would be in the wilderness. Timi's examination of the airvan had confirmed the low level of the power packs, and the doors into the bottom floor of the building beside the van had turned out to be the only ones they had encountered that were palm-locked, rather than responding to either of the magnetic keys they'd found.

"And I'll bet," Roi said as he boosted the last of the dogs into the airvan's storage compartment, "that's where the power packs and anything we could use for weapons are stored. At least the weather sheets and rope were in the airvan. Penny, you sit up with Timi and navigate—I know, but you do know more than any of the rest of us. Magnetic due west—that's the closest route out of the mountains. If you see a light, even a campfire, set down as close as you can. A com's still our best chance.

"Flame and I'll ride back with the dogs and see what we can do about making up packs, now that we've got the weather sheets and rope. Stay fairly low, and get that message we agreed on out every fifteen minutes until the get-down-or-crash signal goes on. Then give us a warning and try to set down where we can hide the van. It's going to take Zhaim a little while to get after us—especially after what we did to his electronic boards—and the longer we make him look for the van, the better chance we've got."

"I wish we had a little moonlight," Timi said a few moments later. "At least the stars are out."

"You think we should have waited another fiveday until after new moon?" Roi said dryly. "I think we were damn lucky to get off this easy so far."

"Easy?" Penny gasped from the front seat. "After what he did to us the last couple of days?"

Roi moved a little farther into the open hatch between the cargo compartment and the pilot's cabin. "For us, easy," he insisted. "We're all able to walk, even run, and use our hands. Flame and I were born slaves, Penny. Rape is something we learned to live with, no matter how much we hated it. It's harder on Timi, and it would have been devastating to you. But it doesn't slow us down any. I'm more worried about your burns."

"He wasn't even all that rough with us," Timi said, puzzled. "I didn't enjoy it, certainly, but it was nothing like as bad as being raped mentally, like when he took me over back at the corral. Or—or when he made my body torture the girls ...." He choked off, unable to go further.

"One of my owners," Flame said, "once used me to teach his son about sex. He was a fairly nice youngster, and very confused—and I'd swear he knew more about what he was doing than Zhaim did. I actually wound up trying to get Zhaim to respond properly, and I thought I did, at one point—and that's when he threw me back into the cage."

Roi gave a choked snort of laughter. "I think you've hit it, Flame," he said. "He was hating every minute of what he did, a lot worse than any of us were. You got a normal response out of him, broke his physical and mental control enough that he was liking something he has always detested—and it scared him silly. What I don't understand is why he did it. Usually he's more into breaking bones and removing skin."

"Power," Timi said. "It can be a dominance thing, and I bet he thought he could make us crawl. You especially, Roi. Well, he picked the wrong victims. We won't get off as easy if he catches us again." He keyed the mike and repeated their distress message, then turned up the receiver. All they could hear was a faint hiss of static.

"How's the power holding out?" Flame asked.

"We've got maybe five or ten minutes more," Timi replied. "Roi, you've got the best night vision. How 'bout getting up here and trying to pick out a landing spot?

Roi glanced back at the dogs. Two were on their sides, sleeping, and the other three were lying down with their heads resting on their paws. "Stay," he reminded them firmly. He couldn't read the dogs' minds, but animals had more emotions than thoughts. These dogs had been used to hunt and kill human beings, but they had fought the hunt and he believed they would be safe as long as they were fed.

He slid into Penny's seat as the guide moved aft to join Flame, wishing he still had conscious control of pupil size. The terrain below them was gently rolling and forested, dark under the stars. Off to the right there were faint glints of light—water, he thought. A river. He thought back to the map at Zhaim's. If this was the river he thought it was, they could probably bury the van in it. If they could find a landing place on a bluff overlooking deep water.

He found what he wanted just as the computer voice spoke: \Five minutes power remaining. Land or crash.\ "Over there," he told Timi, pointing. "There, heading's right. Now nose down—there. Hold your glide slope."

"What are we landing on?" Timi said uneasily. "I can't see a thing on the ground."

"Grassy bluff above a deep river," Roi replied. "I'll trigger the landing lights at the last minute. No sense wasting power we'll need to get down .... There!" The landing lights brought up a grassy area barely large enough for a steep, slow landing, with an undercut cliff dropping to the river on the right, and dense forest on the left. Timi killed forward speed and let the van settle to the ground. They touched down with a firm thump that somehow seemed to echo in Roi's head.

"Grab everything we'll need, get out the left side, and run for the trees, fast," he ordered abruptly. There was a faint tearing sound, barely audible, as he followed Timi out of the drivers' compartment door. Flame and Penny had thrown the packs and most of the dog food toward the forest before jumping out, and he scooped up his pack and the remaining dog food and called the dogs as he ran. The ground shuddered under their feet, and Roi looked back to see the pale tan dog jump a widening crack, black in the glare of the landing lights, on the forest side of the van. Then the earth shuddered again, and the ground on the far side of the crack dropped away, carrying the airvan with it.

They paused just inside the forest, the dogs crowding against their legs, and listened as the dislodged chunk of earth and its load roared downward, ending in a tremendous splash that sent spray flying well over the height of the bluff. Cold noses thrust against Roi's hands in the darkness, and he counted dogs by touch as he broadcast reassurance. Two faintly lighter patches in the darkness must be Flame's and Penny's faces, he thought, and he could see the lightest dog's head, but Timi and the other dogs were invisible. "Everybody here?" he asked, and they responded with a quick roll call of names.

"How'd you know what was going to happen?" Penny gulped.

Roi frowned into the darkness. "Not esper," he said. "When we touched down .... It just felt wrong. Like it—echoed, maybe."

"I think I know what you mean," Timi said. "There's always a little vibration after a hard landing like that, but there was a slower vibration, too, kind of beating with the fast one from the van. The loosened ground, maybe. Only I didn't take it as a warning, and you did. Well, I think we did a pretty good job of hiding the airvan, even if it wasn't quite how we meant to do it. What next?"

"This has got to be the Wilderness River, if we were headed due west," Penny said. "We can follow it down to Wilderness City. Or there's at least one year-round camp, where the Mastodon flows into the Wilderness. There'd be a com there."

Roi shook his head. "That's exactly what Zhaim will expect us to do," he replied. "It's worth trying for the camp, but I think we'll have a better chance if we cut straight south here, and try to put as much distance as we can between us and the river. Maybe we can pick up the Mastodon River later on, and come in to the camp from that direction." He found his crude pack by touch and shrugged into the rope straps, then picked up the remains of the dog food. "Let's make tracks."

"We are, you know," Penny said, and he heard the rustle as she swung her own pack onto her back. "If he finds the wreckage, and our footprints leading directly away from the river ...."

"He won't," Roi replied. "It would take an expert to find our tracks under the dogs' tracks, and he's not an expert. And he doesn't dare get help to track us, unless he plans to kill that help—and he'd have a hard time covering the death of an expert tracker."

"Esper tracking?" Timi asked uneasily.

"I could, if it weren't for the drugging," Roi agreed, "but I don't think he can. That kind of reading takes control, not power, and he's never been good at control. If he gets this far, he'll see dog tracks all over the top of the bluff, and then going into the forest. With luck, he'll figure the dogs panicked and jumped out—or that we landed to put them out—and that we were still in the van when the bluff collapsed. And if he finds the van, he'll find the doors wide open, and realize our bodies might have been washed out. If he doesn't find it, he might even think that we took off again after we let the dogs out. Assuming he finds the bluff at all."

Roi had sent the dogs back to quarter the remains of the grassy area as he spoke, keeping enough of an empathic contact that he could see a little through the animals' eyes. The smallest of the pack had crept to the new bluff edge and looked down. There was no sign of the van, or even of the collapsed section of bluff.

They were barely inside the edge of the forest, and Roi studied the constellations visible to the north. Penny came up beside him. "About an hour to midnight, I'd say," she said. "It's going to be too dark to see the tree trunks until the moon rises, and not much better then—it's only a crescent now. Shouldn't we get some sleep now, while we can't see?"

"Not here," Roi replied. "Zhaim's no tracker, but he'd have a hard time missing someplace we'd actually stopped and slept. The dogs have better night vision than we do; I'll tie a white towel to the tan one and put her in the lead. The other four will follow us and cover our trail. I've got the emergency light from the van, but the power pack's only about half strength, and using it for quick flashes won't help our night vision. Everybody got all their stuff?"

He whistled for the dogs and tied the white towel he had been using to pad the rope straps to the tan bitch's collar, arranging it like a cape over her back. He nudged at her emotions—something interesting to the south, but hesitation at leaving the humans to themselves. She started deeper into the forest, pausing to look back frequently at the group stumbling after her. "Attagirl, Sandy," Roi told her softly.

Eversummer: Marna

"Milady?"

Marna sighed and took a sip from the water reservoir in the isolation suit. Anden himself, so it wouldn't be something routine. Rioting at the order to boil drinking water? An outbreak in one of the megacities? "All right," she said tiredly. "What's the disaster this time?"

Anden shifted from foot to foot. "It may not be important, Milady," he said. "You know how scientists are. Something doesn't go as they expect, and the world is coming to an end. But she seems to think it's important that she hasn't boiled the water for her cultures, and you did say anything out of the way ...."

"And what happened to the cultures she didn't boil the water for?" Marna asked.

"They're sick or dying or something. What does she expect if she won't take precautions?"

Was it possible? It was something Marna should have tried herself, but it just hadn't occurred to her. "Anden, think carefully. Did this scientist use the word 'bioassay' at all?"

Anden frowned in concentration. "She used some kind of biological jargon. That might have been one of the words."

"I think I'd better talk to her."

An hour later, Marna finished examining the last of Dr. Thuruvan's dying cultures and turned to face the anxious scientist. "Ten different bacterial organisms," she said. "You've been subculturing daily, adding filtered but unboiled tap water to each new subculture. Two days ago, one of the cultures started dying off within hours of the tap water addition, and most of the other cultures from that period or later have begun to die off since. And my tests on the stasis-stored water samples from those periods confirm that the toxin showed up at exactly the right time to explain your results. That's brilliant work, Dr. Thuruvan. And the most sensitive culture's not pathogenic, so it could be used for field assays. The equipment for the test I've been using masses three times what I do. How long would it take to develop a portable assay kit?"

The young researcher flushed with pleasure. "I've got a couple of prototypes now," she said shyly, "if you'd like to take one with you. That particular bacterium is tricky to culture—that's why I didn't say anything until some of the tougher species started dying. I did notify the local water authority when the second culture went, but I don't think they paid any attention to me."

"They did to me," Marna replied grimly. "And at two days after exposure, those who drank unboiled water can be treated. How long before we can start running daily tests on every water supply on the planet?"

Dr. Thuruvan shook her head unhappily. "I've already started subculturing on sterile media," she replied, "but it's not an easy organism to produce in mass quantities, and I don't have the funding for assistants or even large numbers of stasis containers for the kits. Even with help, the best I could do would be maybe twenty kits a day."

"We start with the water supplies serving the largest numbers, then," Marna replied. "Start listing what you'll need, in terms of human resources, laboratory facilities, and supplies. I'll see that you get it. I just wish we had a screening method that would tell us where to concentrate the testing. But believe me, this is going to save thousands of lives."

Now if we can just figure out where the toxin's coming from, she thought privately, maybe we can really stop this plague.

Chapter 20

Roi
5/29/38

By a couple of hours after midnight, Roi was the only one of the group who had not fallen at least three times. Little as he liked the idea of stopping so close to the river, he finally had to admit that the danger of broken bones from a fall was even more serious. When the dogs found a clump of ancient rhododendrons surrounding a hollow where the original plant had died out, he called a halt and all nine of them, dogs and people, wormed their way into the center of the clump.

"We'll have to go on as soon as the moon rises enough to give us any light at all," he warned them. "But for right now, it's just too dark to move safely, and we do need some sleep. Penny, do your burns need dressing again? I know you'd rather have Flame do it, but I'm the one with the medical training, even if I can't Heal right now."

"They'll be all right until daylight," the guide replied. "I'm more worried about not having any warnoffs."

"That," he told her, "is one of the reasons I insisted on bringing the dogs along." He reached out for the canine emotions. Three were relaxed and protective, but he sensed growing hunger in the other two. "What kind of animals could two of them bring down easily, Penny? They're going to have to hunt most of their own food, and probably ours as well."

"Deer or small stuff like rabbits," she replied. "All five together could probably take down an elk or even a moose. Maybe a young flathead, if they caught one alone, but peccaries usually travel in groups, and they're a lot more dangerous than they look. This looks like good deer country, as much as I can see of it."

Roi reached out to the emotions of the two hungry dogs, trying to give them the idea of deer. He wasn't sure he had succeeded, but the two got to their feet and slipped out into the night. Flame and Timi were asleep already, exhaustion overpowering fear. Penny had snuggled up to Flame, and he lay down beside her, urging the remaining three dogs in close to surround the group with their warmth.

***

Roi was awakened by a cold nose against his cheek, sticky and smelling unmistakably of blood. He opened his eyes to see faint reflections on the glossy leaves over his head though the sky was still night-dark, studded with stars. He struggled to his feet and took a step or two in the direction the dog was urging him, and fell over a body.

For a moment he almost panicked. Without mind-touch, he couldn't be sure at first that all of the others were safe and alive. Then he forced himself to calm down, and realized that his emotional bond would have told him if anything had happened to his friends. He felt the thing he had fallen over, and found a short hair coat.

"Roi?" Penny said sleepily. "What happened? It's after moonrise, isn't it?"

"The dogs brought us a deer," he said softly. "Intact except for the throat, as far as I can tell."

"Well trained," Penny said approvingly. "They're waiting for the huntsman to gut it for them. There's a force blade in the emergency kit I took from the airvan. I'll get it out for you."

"What do I do with it?" Roi asked, and heard Penny chuckle out of the darkness.

"Open up the belly with a cut down the middle and—oh, never mind. I'll do it. I want to get the tenderloin for us, and I don't want it hacked up. Can you get the dogs to stand back and wait? Back off, you."

The dogs took a step backward at her command, then several more steps as Roi added emotional reinforcement. Penny worked on the deer's back for a moment, then came around and made a single long cut. Roi wrinkled his nose as the stench of the entrails reached him and Penny stood up. "Let's get upwind," she suggested. "At least they brought it in on the downwind side of the hollow. This is not a good place for a fire, Roi."

"I want us to get moving, anyway," he replied. "There's moonlight enough to see, sort of, and if we drag the deer to where we were sleeping,

264

and let the dogs eat their fill and then follow us, I don't think Zhaim will spot it as a campsite even if he finds it."

The moon was a huge crescent, lying on its back in the eastern sky. Enough light penetrated the forest canopy that they didn't run into trees as often as they had before, but it was still hard going without the fawn bitch to guide them. "You're sure they'll follow us?" Timi asked anxiously.

"Yes," Roi replied shortly, trying to use his empathic sense to muffle Timi's curiosity. He did not want Zhaim to know just how much communication he could manage through his empathy, and while Zhaim could not breach his own shields, it would be child's play for the older R'il'noid to read anything the others knew if they were recaptured.

"They're quite well trained," Penny said, "and Roi's doing a good job of handling them. Roi, if—uh—if we're captured again, am I still Amber?"

"You'll probably live longer that way," he replied. Amber was still alive; he knew that much. He wished she had been dreaming when he had tried to contact her earlier; that seemed to be the only time he could exchange anything but vague emotions. As it was, he knew only that something had gone wrong. She was really their best hope; he did not want to let Zhaim know she was alive. Let Penny and the others continue to think that they were simply trying to protect the guide. And pray that Zhaim would continue to keep out of Penny's mind.

"I'm not sure I want to live longer if he catches us again," Penny said uneasily.

Roi sighed and ducked a tree limb. "At this point," he said, "he'd keep you anyway if he realized we cared enough about you to pretend you're Amber. Better keep up the masquerade if we can." And hope we don't need to, he added to himself.

"Is it just my imagination," Timi said, "or is it getting lighter?"

Roi paused to look up. The sky was dark blue instead of black, and only two or three stars were visible. When they climbed to the next ridge and looked east, the eastern sky showed pale above a jagged horizon.

"Are we going to stop and sleep?" Flame yawned.

"Not yet," Roi replied. "Maybe for a few hours around noon. But we won't be able to travel tonight. It's almost new moon. I'd rather push on as far as we can while there's light, and then hole up some place while it's dark and sleep then."

"How about cooking the venison?" Penny inquired.

"If we can find an old campsite and reuse it, maybe," Roi replied, "though I don't like to risk the smoke. Anyway, we do not set up a regular campsite with a fire and sleep there. Might as well shout 'We're here.' We can eat it raw if we have to."

Timi grimaced, but made no other comment.

The dogs caught up with them just as the sun was rising clear of the mountains. "The dogs are going to need rest, too," Penny pointed out. "They'd normally sleep after gorging themselves like that."

"You think I don't know that?" Roi snapped back at her. "Sorry, Penny, I'm short of sleep, too. But we've got to get as far from that airvan as we possibly can before Zhaim gets hold of transportation and starts looking for us. Because he's going to be desperate to find us."

"He hates you that much?"

"Killing—or even trying to kill—someone of higher Çeren rank, or even lower if it's close enough, is about the only thing a R'il'noid can be executed for," Roi replied. "If any of us get away and manage to tell my father what happened, he's *dead*. You bet he's going to put everything he's got into finding us!"

They found an old campsite around midmorning, a fire pit on a gravel bar a little below a small waterfall. There was a plume of spray rising from the falls, and Penny judged it would camouflage the smoke of a small fire. They chose the driest wood they could find while the dogs flopped down, exhausted, and slept. Penny had packed the tenderloin in one of the food storage bags they had taken from Zhaim's, and she cut the venison into quick-cooking cubes while the fire burned down to coals. They roasted the meat on green sticks, and after they had eaten Roi gave the sticks to the dogs to chew. Then he sat on a tree trunk well above the bar and worked with a marker and waterproof film while the others napped.

The dogs were playing tug of war with a dead tree trunk when he finished. Again he reached for their emotions, and the animals dropped the trunk diagonally across the stream, diverting the water across the bar and washing out all traces of their passage. The others were awakened by the splash, and looked suspiciously at Roi. Then the dogs, quite on their own, scrambled up the bank to join them and proceeded to shake themselves dry, and Roi could feel the suspicions vanishing. He took advantage of the uproar to wrap the one of the notes he'd written around the collar of the fawn-colored bitch.

They paused for an hour's nap under a berry thicket shortly after noon. The fawn-colored bitch wandered off while they slept, and didn't return. Roi acted as surprised as the rest.

"Roi," Penny said, shortly after they resumed their journey, "Why?"

"Unh?" the R'il'noid replied, barely catching himself after stumbling over a branch. "Why what?"

"Why is trying to kill another R'il'noid the only thing that seems to be illegal for Zhaim to do?"

"Slave law," Timi snarled angrily. "We're not even counted as animals."

"Not this time, Timi," Roi said. "That's Central law. Anyway, it wouldn't apply to Penny." He shook his head violently, trying to wake up. Zhaim hadn't given them an easy day before the night of their escape, and he decided lack of sleep was catching up with him. He checked the compass and the sun, and decided it must be about halfway through the afternoon. They needed to keep going for at least a few more hours.

"But why?" Penny repeated.

"Know your Confederation history?" Roi asked.

"A little. But I'd never heard anything about—well—R'il'noids being able to just get away with anything they want to do."

Roi yawned again and blinked several times to clear his vision. The ground was level but spongy, deep with years of rotting vegetation, and he was going to fall flat on his face in a moment if he didn't start watching where he put his feet. "Goes back to the big epidemic, I think," he said. "You know 'bout the Maungs, don't you? The R'il'nai can run them off, and spot and cure parasitized humans. They agreed to do that if the Humans'd agree to let them arbitrate interplanetary disputes. Said they weren't going to bother saving a species from an outsider when they were killing each other off. Well, that takes quite a lot of R'il'nai and R'il'noids, and after the epidemic there weren't 'nough left." He paused, looking for the best place to ford the brook trickling across their path.

"So they were too important to kill?" Penny asked dubiously.

"The R'il'nai were OK," Roi replied. "They never wanted to tell anybody what to do, they just sorta got stuck with it. But there weren't enough of them left alive after the epidemic, so they started the crossbreeding project to get more R'il'noids. Father says most of those weren't too bad, an' they couldn't afford to lose any, so they were protected. But there's some—specially in the last millennium or so—like Zhaim. They want

267

power, and hurting people makes them feel powerful." He shook his head in bewilderment. He did not want power, and could not imagine ever wanting it. But wanting to hurt—he wanted to hurt Zhaim, at any rate. Or was that being like Zhaim? He thrust the thought behind him.

"Anyway," he finished, "The Confederation's really pretty much run by the R'il'noids, now that Father and Marna are the only R'il'nai left, and they're not about to give up their protected status. Maybe I can do something about it, when I'm older, but not alone."

The big brindle male trotted alongside him for a few paces, and he checked to be sure that his second message was firmly attached to its collar. Time for you to go, he thought, and again used an empathic link to aim the dog toward the west and a warden, or Kyrie if the dog didn't reach a warden first. The others didn't even notice it was missing until they curled up under an overhanging rock half an hour after sunset.

"They were never bred for endurance like the sled dogs," Penny said. "I think they're just getting too tired to keep up." She yawned. "I'm getting too tired to keep up, for that matter."

Roi nodded in the darkness and went on fastening the third message by touch to the collar of one of the remaining dogs. He had never been happy with the idea of having to try to hold the Confederation together if anything happened to Lai and Marna, but he had liked the idea of Zhaim in that position even less. After the last few days, he was fairly sure that if Zhaim succeeded in killing him undetected, Lai and Marna would not survive him by more than a year or two. Zhaim was mad for power, and he wanted that power *now*. And if he had found a way of blocking precognitive warnings—and Roi could see no other explanation for why neither he nor his father had recognized the danger Zhaim represented .... Roi didn't seriously think they could escape Zhaim for long. Not after the explosions of rage he had picked up several times during the later afternoon. But if even one of the messages he had tied to the dogs' collars got through to Kyrie, his father would at least be warned. He had enough empathic contact with the first two dogs to know that they were still heading toward the ranger station. He felt Snowflake too, for that matter, and was trying to use her to tell Kyrie that something was wrong. He wished he could be surer that he felt Smoky.

Central and Falaron: Zhaim

The joint Council meeting had lasted until almost three in the morning, Enclave time, and Zhaim was visualizing some of the more stubborn members writhing in his newly redecorated abattoir by the time the meeting finally adjourned. He was too keyed up and short of sleep to make a direct teleport to Falaron, so he flung himself onto his bed for a brief nap. By the time he teleported himself directly into the room where he expected to find his prisoners, it was the middle of the local afternoon.

He couldn't believe his eyes, at first. The cages were locked, the cable manacles in place, even the mag key hanging in its usual place, tantalizingly visible from all four cages. And the cages were empty.

He reached for his victims mentally, searching the torture chamber and then the rooms upstairs, and then grabbed the key from its hook and ran up. He needed the key to unlock the force barrier, and once he was in the main room he found nothing obviously out of place. The afternoon light poured over the polished floor and the control wall, and the cirque floor beyond the window was bare and empty, the last of the snowdrifts melted.

The kitchen, too, seemed untouched—until he opened the stasis cabinet and found it empty. He turned and ran up the stairs to the top floor, finding his bed bare of its rare vicuna and shagga-down coverings, and water on the floor of the bathroom. Those—those *animals* had dared to make themselves free of his bathing facilities!

The dogs would have stopped them, he assured himself. He went out onto the overhanging deck and circled the building, fully expecting to see the dogs crouched by the bodies, awaiting his return. Not what he would have preferred, but it would make the cover scenario all the more realistic. He had worried a little that some trace of the true causes of death would remain. The dogs, however, were not in sight. They must be in one of the low spots of the cirque, or perhaps even have the prisoners cornered on a rock the dogs were unable to climb.

He plunged out the front door and began checking the floor of the cirque, concentrating on the low spots that were especially numerous to the south. The sun was almost to the western horizon before he thought to search for the dogs with mind-touch. Nothing.

He ran eyes and mind over the fence, searching for any sign of a break, and again found nothing. Impossible! Prisoners and dogs had to be inside the fence, then. Perhaps the dogs had killed each other fighting over the remains, or the captives had managed to wound the dogs fatally before they were killed? He needed to get high, to see the whole cirque from above. He walked back to the house, checking two more ravines on the way.

He walked around the lodge, scowling as he saw that the airvan was not in its usual spot. Strange—he didn't remember moving it into the garage area. He hadn't used it for several days, of course—he might have forgotten. He palmed the door lock, and stepped into the garage.

The airvan wasn't there.

His stomach clenched. He had made a point of having no outside com lines; he had even disabled the outgoing link on the airvan com. But it had never occurred to him that his captives could steal the airvan. The keys were kept in the palm-locked garage—the only place he had bothered to re-key when he had purchased the lodge. Only—he'd left them in a belt pocket, when he'd brought his captives here and unloaded them. And the belt had been up in the bedroom.

He walked back into the lodge, forcing himself to be calm, and continued down into the torture chamber. The sun had set; he had less than an hour before he was due at another Inner Council meeting. Nothing serious to address, but he could not risk suspicion by failing to be there. He closed his eyes and felt for the impressions left by the room's occupants, trying to determine how long they had been gone.

Almost a day, he thought. Even if they had been flying an evasive course, they could have reached either Wilderness City or Safeport within a few hours. In which case the word would have been back to Central long before yesterday's combined Council meeting was over. Maybe they had become lost, or crashed.

He climbed the stairs again and went to the third control panel, keying for the location and status of the airvan. Out of power. That made sense. He hadn't actually checked the power level when he'd last parked the van, but he remembered thinking he'd need to put in fresh power packs before he tried to go anywhere. As to where—he looked unbelievingly at the map. North? In the heart of some of the most rugged country on the planet?

He considered what he knew about his half-brother's psychology. The brat had hidden for most of its life, after all. With the only two adults who outranked Zhaim several hundred light years away, the bastard might not realize just how much help it could get. Hiding in the wilderness until Lai or Marna returned might just be the natural thing for it to do. Stupid, but natural.

The readout was accurate enough and the airvan close enough he could use its coordinates as a teleport goal. Smiling mirthlessly, Zhaim memorized the coordinates, went back to the garage for one of the multilevel beamers he kept there, and set it to heavy stun. He had time enough to 'port out to the van and immobilize its occupants and still make the Council meeting. Too bad if they froze to death before he was able to pick them up; that was far too easy a way to die. He reached for the coordinates and pulled himself through, ready to shoot as soon as he saw his victims.

He had allowed a few finger widths for ground clearance, but he wasn't expecting to drop into an untidy nest of good-sized tree limbs. Something squawked behind him, and he whirled to face a creature half as tall as he was, with a vulture's head and beak and an awkward, pinfeather-covered body. A giant condor chick? he thought dazedly as he looked around for the airvan. A blur caught the corner of his eye, and he spun to see the outraged parent coming straight for him.

Wherever the escapees were, they weren't here, and there was no sense wasting energy on a confrontation with a giant condor. He teleported himself back to the main room of the lodge, and glared at the readout. The coordinates were not what he remembered. Furthermore, the sun had dropped below the horizon. Angrily he stabbed at the light button, and jumped as every light in the room exploded. The fire-prevention system *was* working properly, and treated him to a blizzard of carbon dioxide snow.

He had neither time nor energy to waste, he realized. He had to appear at the Inner Council meeting in less than half an hour, and he had to appear looking normal—or at least as normal as could be expected after the late night they had all shared. And there were things he needed from Central. Snarling, he reached for his private quarters on the administration planet, and pushed himself through.

He managed to keep the Inner Council meeting short, and was back on Falaron with two crates of electronic gear by shortly after midnight, local time. He was beginning to feel punchy from the time zone juggling—it had been early afternoon at the enclave and early morning at his eyrie on Central—and he gulped a stimulant to keep himself going.

Zhaim was no electronics tech, and at this point, he didn't dare bring one in to find out what was wrong with his control panel. He could, however, use his object-reading ability to determine who had been handling the board recently. He walked over and probed the control shelf—then yelped and put his hands to his head as every alarm in the lodge, along with a screamer circuit, went off simultaneously. He had to run down to the garage and throw the master switch manually to cut off all power to the lodge before the physical and mental cacophony stopped.

The alarms had included odorous sprays, intended to incapacitate an intruder as well as making later identification easy, and Zhaim sat on the front stairs of the lodge in darkness and simmered while the interior of the building was airing out. He knew where the screamer circuit had come from. It was a spare from his attempt on Roi's glider, and needed only a power hookup to behave as it had. Further, it had a self-destruct. He needed only to wait. And once he had waited, he managed to pick up traces of the black slave's presence all over the board. Until now, that one had been merely a means of hurting Roi and insuring his own safety. Now, it had become a target in its own right. He sat and brooded on the steps, planning what he would do once the young devil was in his hands. After he had taken over its mind and forced it to repair the damage it had done, that was.

He thought back to when the airvan had last been at full power, and how much he had used it since, and concluded that the fugitives could at best have made it halfway to Wilderness City. Probably not as far as that ranger station on the Wilderness River. Very well. His first priority must be to make sure they did not reach any of the places between here and Wilderness City where they might be able to get help. That was what the sniffers were for, and he had best get started setting them.

Too bad the brat had thought to scrub out the cages, he thought sourly. The sniffers worked best on samples from an individual. But they could be set to be species-specific, too, and his own blood and skin cells would sensitize them sufficiently to pick up his half brother. As soon as it was daylight here, he would teleport to the office he kept in Safeport. Then to a used flyer dealer who would have no awkward inquiries and whose disappearance, later, would raise no questions. He'd teleport whatever craft he could get out here, load in the sensitized sniffers, and put rings of the gadgets around each of the four com stations between the lodge and Wilderness City. The sniffer base station would operate off airvan power;

he could do without other amenities until he had his hands back on the fugitives.

His lips stretched in a savage grin as he picked up the portable light, took a few deep breaths, and held his breath while he ran into the lodge to get one of the boxes of sniffers. Methodically he began setting the species sensitivity to himself. Rings around possible communications points, he decided, and several concentric arcs around Wilderness City itself. With luck, he'd have the brats back in his hands before sundown. He refused even to think of what could happen to him if he didn't get them back.

Roi

5/30/38

Morning came with a drizzle that soon intensified to a steady, soaking downpour. Roi had not a trace of a hunch as to whether they should hole up for the day or keep going, but logic dictated that they keep traveling, even though they had no rain gear other than the weather sheets. They managed to rig the waterproof sheets to cover their heads as well as their bedding, but between the wet undergrowth and the fact that the two remaining dogs kept returning to the party to shake themselves, they were soon soaked.

"Oh, stop it," Penny exclaimed in frustration as both dogs shook themselves dry at her sides.

Roi, just as wet, sighed and sneezed, wondering what was the matter with his nose and throat. "We don't really need them for trail cover any more," he said, "though they can still hunt for us, and I suspect they're providing some defense against predators. What are the predators here, by the way?"

Penny's brow creased. "Wolves, of course, and sabertooth cats—they mostly go after young mammoths or mastodons, but they wouldn't turn up their noses at us. Dire wolves and short-faced bears. Pumas are fairly common, and jaguars wander this way now and then. Lots of smaller carnivores, as well, but I figured you'd want to know the ones that normally hunt prey our size or larger."

Roi grimaced. He had already fastened messages to the collars of the remaining dogs, and he wanted to get them on their way before Zhaim caught up with their party. One of the dogs stopped and cocked its head, listening, and when Roi concentrated, he thought he heard the whine

273

of a flyer overhead. He shivered and swallowed, painfully aware of the scratchiness of his throat.

By noon they swerved back to the west. The big black dog refused to make the turn with them, sitting and staring until they were almost out of sight, and then picking himself up and continuing southward.

The sky continued to darken and lower until it lay below the tops of the trees, and there were times when the rain came down so heavily that whoever was at the end of the little line could hardly see the leader. Any pretense that the weather sheets could keep them dry had long since been abandoned. They plodded on, beaten down by the rain when they crossed a clearing and washed by dripping branches in the trees, too wet, chilled and generally miserable to do anything but keep plodding onward.

The remaining dog found a cave of sorts, under the roots of a half-fallen tree, and made it clear that she intended neither to share her shelter nor to continue on with them. "Well," Penny said wryly, "I guess we start watching for predators ourselves." She lifted her shoulders a little, shifting the drag of the wet blanket tied behind her, and flinched as the soaked cloth of her shirt pulled across her breasts.

"Burns bothering you?" Roi asked, stepping in front of her to examine her face. Her cheeks and forehead were patterned with raw brands, and he knew more burns spiraled around each of her breasts. There was burn cream in the aid kits they had brought with them, and he had applied a generous coating before they had started out this morning. He hadn't liked the looks of her right cheek or left breast then, and he liked the cheek even less now. If she weren't so chilled, he thought anxiously, she'd be running a fever.

"Don't worry about me," she replied.

"We may have to risk a fire tonight," he fretted out loud as he turned back into the game trail they had been following. "Otherwise we'll all be sick by morning."

"If we can find anything dry enough to burn and a place sheltered enough that the rain doesn't drown any fire we could get started," Flame said dispiritedly. "Hadn't we better start looking for shelter now, Roi? My feet are so cold I can't even feel them."

"Look, sure," Roi replied tiredly. He tried to think of what kind of shelter they could possibly find in this wilderness. They'd need to find something soon; it was getting dark already under the trees. He took a deep breath and started coughing. He needed a fire, too.

The woods lightened ahead of them, and the mist lifted as they entered a clearing. Roi glanced around quickly, looking for something they could use as shelter. Nothing but grass and sodden wildflowers. He checked the compass and headed straight across, hoping the Mastodon River wasn't too far away.

He heard a thunderclap behind him when he was halfway across the clearing and spun to face it, fearful he knew what it was. Zhaim stood before him, a triumphant leer on his handsome face and a beamer swinging toward the party.

Zhaim could not have been expecting anything but cowed obedience or flight. When Roi launched himself at his half-brother, the older R'il'noid stood frozen for long enough that Roi's hand was firm on the beamer as they fell together. All that Zhaim had done to him and to the people he loved most came flooding into his mind, and his whole being exploded into an inferno of rage. He fought for control of the beamer, slamming the stock repeatedly into Zhaim's shoulder when he couldn't get it into his brother's face, using teeth and knees relentlessly. He was ready to kill his brother as that brother would have killed his friends, slowly, savoring every bit of pain he could wring from his helpless victim.

Then he felt Timi's dismayed shock, and his left arm was grabbed and twisted behind his back. When he rolled with the pull, the shift in his weight allowed Zhaim to pull away and struggle back to his feet, shaking with fury.

Roi could hear the sob in Timi's breath. Timi's body, yes, but it was Zhaim's will that twisted his arm so high that his shoulder joint screamed protest, and jammed Timi's arm across Roi's throat. The heavier boy's body pulled him to his feet, and he managed to glance around as he was jerked up. The girls were sprawled bonelessly where they had fallen, their wet clothing plastered to their bodies by the rain. Then Timi swung him around to face Zhaim, and it took all his self-control to keep his head up and his eyes steady on his brother's.

Zhaim's face was contorted with rage, and the beamer was shaking visibly in his hand. He started to raise the weapon, then looked down at it for a moment. "No," he said finally, tucking the weapon into his tunic. "No, you're not getting off that easily."

Timi's grip on Roi tightened as Zhaim stalked forward, his arm swinging back as he came. Roi tried to duck away from the blow, but Timi's hold swung him into it instead. His head snapped to the side, and then before he could recover another blow slammed into his stomach, followed by a kick to his groin.

The world narrowed to a maelstrom of fists, knees and feet. He felt ribs give, and then a tearing pain as Timi's body twisted his shoulder out of its socket in an effort to keep him on his feet. He hoped with all his heart, as the darkness closed in around him, that at least one of the dogs would get its message to Kyrie.

Falaron: Xazhar

"That's right," Xazhar said for the twentieth—or was it thirtieth?—time in the last month. "Each team of seven tries to maneuver the ball into the metal basket at the opposing team's end of the arena. The center zone, directly in front of us, is off limits to both teams, so there's no body contact. But there's nothing in the rules to stop a player from trying to hit an opponent with the plasmoid. In fact, it's really the only way to keep the opposing team from blocking the goal with their bodies."

He didn't have to think about what he was saying any more. He had four to six new guests to shepherd each day, and while some knew the game, it seemed that every day he had at least one who didn't even know what the players were trying to do. Today there were three in that category.

"But isn't that dangerous?" Camy asked. She was a low-grade R'il'noid, with dark hair worn loose and enormous violet and silver eyes. If her father hadn't been along, Xazhar would have suggested they spend some time together after the game.

"So far in the tournament," Xazhar replied, "there've been three players killed, and half a dozen more are still hospitalized. I haven't kept track of minor injuries. But it's the players' choice whether to wear protective gear. I've taken quite a few direct hits in protective gear, and it's a jolt—like a stock fence—but not really dangerous. The injuries were all to players not wearing full protective gear."

"Of course," Camy's father said dryly, "the advice of their coaches and getting their contracts renewed might influence that choice."

"I never meant to imply their decisions weren't influenced by outside pressure, sir," Xazhar replied as he turned back to the arena. "Ah, here they come for the second set."

They were into the serious games now, and for the first time Xazhar really noticed the difference between the amounts of protective gear worn by the players of the two teams. The gold team's members were almost as heavily armored as school players, while many of the blue players wore only helmets. Different planetary customs, Xazhar wondered, or different pressures from the coaches of the two teams?

The plasmoid was released into the neutral zone across the middle of the arena, and the blue team, far faster without the protective gear, grabbed control almost at once. The golds, massed in front of their goal, seemed as if they would be able to prevent the blues from scoring, but one of the blue players, moving far to the side of the arena, managed to angle the ball so that it ricocheted behind the guarding golds, scoring the first goal of the game. Howls of rage from the gold supporters were met with raucous cheering from the blue fans, and the gold team went into a quick huddle as a new plasmoid was being readied.

This time, the golds managed to get control of the ball. Their tactics were clearly aimed at getting the blues away from their goal, and at first Xazhar grinned with approval. Then the golds ignored a clear chance at a goal, electing instead to keep slamming the ball at the blue who had just scored, and he began to wonder whether they were trying to win the game or take out the opposite team's best player—possibly permanently.

He keyed for the lineups, confirming that the player who was clearly the focus of the gold attack was Rupal Sessar, the blue team captain and one of the brightest young stars in plasmaball. So far, the man had managed to dodge the ball successfully, though Xazhar thought he was beginning to realize that the golds were trying to hit him, rather than the goal. He watched as Rupal managed to spin close by two of the other blue players as he dodged, and then moved directly between the gold players and the goal, apparently giving them a perfect opportunity, but in fact setting them up for two of his teammates to gain control of the ball.

They weren't quite fast enough.

The ball touched Rupal's upper chest even as his teammates took control, and the star player convulsed in midair.

Camy gasped in horror as the play continued, four of the blue players driving the ball toward the gold goal even as the other two grabbed their captain's body and dived toward the nearest exit port. "Won't they stop to get a doctor in?" she exclaimed in horror.

Xazhar shook his head. "Not until the end of the set," he replied. "If his teammates can get him out the exit port, there'll be a medical team there, but—oh, no!" The gold team had managed to recover the ball from the disorganized blues, and sent it spinning toward the two pushing their captain through the exit port. Xazhar jumped to his feet, shouting in outrage. It wasn't actually a written rule at the professional level, but trying to interfere with a rescue attempt was at the very least a major breach of game etiquette.

The sound of the other fans was muted in their VIP box, but even so the furious shouts were hard to ignore. In the arena, Rupal's teammates thrust their captain through the emergency exit and hurled themselves away, but they didn't have time to seal and insulate the exit properly before the plasmoid struck.

Sparks blasted outward, and the arena lights suddenly flickered and went dead. The shouts of the fans became screams of terror. Xazhar reached out mentally, feeling for rapid motion and trying to stop it telekinetically.

Eleven fast-falling bodies in the arena, and far too many more overhead. The players first, Xazhar thought; the overhead spectators who'd failed to web in were sliding down the curve of the arena rather than falling free. He worked to slow the falling bodies, bringing them down to the curved bottom of the ellipsoid at a speed that left them bruised but not seriously injured. Then the few spectators whose falls hadn't been stopped by the next tier of seats. Maybe Roi had known what he was talking about when he'd claimed that Xazhar actually felt emotions, but so weakly he sought them out. Certainly the rising panic in the arena was pounding at Xazhar's head.

An arena security officer's mind brushed Xazhar's: *Oh, God, don't let them panic; if they start trying to get out they'll be crushed to death ....*

Xazhar took a deep breath, pulled himself together, and shouted, mentally and physically together, **SIT DOWN.** The shouting and screaming vanished in a single *whump* of human bodies colliding with seats.

He swallowed a time or two. His father had that ability to command obedience in an emergency; he hadn't realized that he himself had any such talent. But what next? Light, he decided. Anything to break the blind blackness around him!

If you have a personal light, get it out and turn it on, he broadcast, not quite as commandingly as his first attempt. *Stay in your seats until a security officer tells you to leave.* He felt around for some mind that understood what had happened, and found a nearly panicked engineer. He almost groaned aloud at what he read from the man's mind. The plasmoid had knocked out most of the building's electrical system, leaving only the emergency med-techs working on the injured player with power. *Security,* he added on a tighter beam, *get some portable lights in here and start evacuating people.*

Personal lights were beginning to flicker into life all around the arena now, and the panic was receding. A light flashed on two seats to his right, held by Camy's father. "Last pocket I looked in, of course," he said, and looked thoughtfully at Xazhar. "Was that your mind telling us what to do?"

Xazhar nodded weakly. "And trying to slow down the players," he said.

"Better have something to eat," the man said, pushing over a tray of small pastries he'd been nibbling. "You look like you wore yourself out."

"That I did," Xazhar said, surprised. Was this what Roi kept doing to himself? If it was, Xazhar decided, maybe Roi wasn't as much of a wimp as he'd thought. Camy reached over to hug him, and her father looked thoughtful.

"We're leaving the planet in a few days," he commented, "but I'm assigned to Central for the next few years. And we'd be pleased to continue the acquaintance."

The man's shields weren't all that good, Xazhar thought. He'd picked up the man's curiosity of what the genetics board would make of Camy and Xazhar. Zhaim's son fought back a grin. "I wouldn't mind that at all," he replied.

Chapter 21

Zhaim scowled as he dabbed antiseptic on his hands. Not only had he cut his knuckles on the brat's teeth, the young devil had managed to bite him several times during the beating. He hissed as the antiseptic foamed in the crescentic wounds on the heel of his right hand. His shoulder ached, too, but at least he'd managed to keep the brat away from his face. As it was, he would have to keep his hand and shoulder hidden until they healed. Certainly he couldn't ask Nik Tarlian to treat him. The man was a competent physician, but he was also a sentimental fool. He was very likely to spread the word that one of Zhaim's slaves had managed to defy him, or even pick up the fact that Roi had been involved, and later on, when the bodies were discovered, that might draw attention Zhaim could not afford.

He glanced at the monitor screen that showed the old abattoir. As far as he could tell, the bastard hadn't moved since Zhaim had used the black's body to thrust it into the cage. He scowled uneasily, reluctant to admit he had lost his temper and perhaps overdone the beating. He certainly had not intended to leave the brat so badly concussed that it couldn't watch what Zhaim planned to do to its slaves. Especially the black. Zhaim's scowl became a snarl.

It had seemed simple. He would take over the black's mind and force it to repair the damage it had done to the control panel. The problem was, Zhaim didn't know that much about electronics. He could control the slave's body, but he didn't know what to do with it. When he had relaxed his control over the body enough that he could read its knowledge, the creature had attacked him. When he tried to control both at once, it had fed him false information mixed with the true.

He had finally concentrated on the heating and lighting systems, both simple enough that even he could understand them. The rest could wait. By then he had less than half an hour before the Council meeting was scheduled to start, barely long enough to walk the black down the stairs and stretch its body on the rack, then run back upstairs to treat his hands. He reached for the synthetic skin spray and applied it to both hands, then pulled on a pair of thin black leather gloves. He would wear his black leather tunic and breeches today, he thought. The crested shoulders would hide his own swollen joint, and the sleeve cut, intended to emphasize that the wearer need never exert himself physically, would explain any stiffness in his use of the arm. Fashion demanded that he wear gloves with the outfit.

Derik and Kaia were already in the interface room when Zhaim arrived. Derik was in a full interface with the computer, and when Zhaim raised an elegant eyebrow Kaia grinned sardonically. "Long distance call," she said.

Derik opened his eyes at the sound of her voice. "Kyrie wants me to come a few days early with Elyra and try her new cook and a few new restaurants she's discovered," he explained. His eyes fell on Zhaim's gloves. "Slip up and get your hands instead of your victim?" There was raw hatred in the tone.

Zhaim managed a supercilious sniff. "Your ignorance of fashion is appalling," he said. He had never thought Derik would be that quick. If the older R'il'noid probed the injuries at all, he'd probably pick up the connection to Roi. He needed to get Derik away before he attempted such a probe. "Routine today," he added as the other Council members filtered in. "Derik, I have to be here every day, but there's no reason that everyone has to. If you and Elyra would like to take Kyrie up on her invitation, why don't you go ahead and take a few days off? Kaia can get hold of you if anything serious comes up."

Derik's eyes widened in surprise; then he smiled in genuine pleasure. "That's more than thoughtful of you, Zhaim. I'll tell Kyrie, and 'path Elyra to start packing." He slid back into full interface, pulling power to ease the long-distance link to Kyrie.

Falaron: Derik

"He actually urged you to come early?" Kyrie asked in surprise. "Here, try this one."

Derik nibbled thoughtfully at the tiny pastry. "Excellent. Would your cook be willing to share the recipe, do you think? Yes, he did. Not like Zhaim at all." He frowned. "Kyrie, when's the last time you heard directly from Roi?"

"A little more than a fiveday ago," the adjudicator replied. "He asked me to see if he could get breeding stock of some miniature horses that are native to the Surprise River Canyon. Something about a mutation to long manes. I think they were climbing to the canyon rim at the time. Now that I think about it, I'm a little surprised that he hasn't gotten back to me for the answer."

"More pets?" Elyra asked.

"More pets," Kyrie confirmed, "and I think he'll be able to get them." She fought visibly to hold back a yawn. "That dog he's got is trouble enough. She was delightful at first, but the last fiveday she's been absolutely impossible. Jumping up on me, howling, and even refusing to eat."

"That'd be the lame sled dog?" Derik asked. When Kyrie nodded he continued: "I don't like that. Especially since Cory commed me this morning to say he was at his wits' end about Roi's dog, Smoky. He's acting the same way."

"You think something's wrong with Roi?" Elyra asked.

"The Company's monitoring their progress," Kyrie assured her. "They're traveling slowly but steadily. Probably another couple of fivedays, at least, before they get to Safeport."

Derik frowned out the west window of the room. Stars dusted the night sky, their patterns only a little different from those visible from Central. Kyrie followed his gaze. "At least it's cleared off now," she said. "The rain was just letting up at sunset."

"Getting close to midnight here?" Derik asked, and heard a little gasp from Elyra.

"Oh, Kyrie, I forgot how different the times would be. We're keeping you up. I'm so sorry. We want to switch to your time, so if you could just show us where we're to sleep, we'll let you get to bed."

Kyrie smiled at her. "Oh, you haven't kept me up yet, Lyra," she assured Elyra as she stood up. "But you would have soon. Come on, and I'll show you your rooms. The Company office in Safeport won't be open until five or six in the morning, here."

"Well before we'll likely be up," Derik said. "Actually, I was planning to go over there tomorrow, anyway, and pick up the stuff Roi's been dropping off. Got a flyer I can borrow? One with lots of cargo space, and preferably jump capability? I don't know the area well enough for a teleport."

Kyrie looked puzzled. "What have they been dropping off?" she asked.

"Clothes and Roi's finished drawings, mostly," Derik replied. "It's the drawings I want to see. He's really good, Kyrie."

"Show them to me, too?" their hostess asked.

"Of course," he replied.

Falaron: Amber
6/1/38

Amber woke reluctantly, shivering in the dawn air. Her injured leg was throbbing even more than it had for the last couple of days, and when she pulled her tattered breeches down to check, the wounds showed an angry red. She groaned and pulled out the remains of the wound salve. She wasn't sure how much good it would do, now that infection had clearly set in, but she had to try.

The sun was golden on the eastern horizon, and there wasn't a cloud in the sky. A hot day to come, she thought resentfully. She had dreamed about rain last night, a cold, soaking rain that mocked her feverish warmth. Rain, and stumbling through a forest unlike the one around her, and—yes, Zhaim's face coming out of the mist, and being beaten .... Another of the nightmares about the others, she thought, the first since she had been injured. Another dream to tell Derik. If she ever made it to Safeport. If he were there.

She was thirsty, and drank freely from the creek by her camp before filling the water bag, but she had to force down the remains of last night's fish. And she had finished the last emergency bar yesterday. She looked at the map on the water bag. Less than halfway there, and there was no way she could move faster than she had the first few days, not with her leg swelling and throbbing as it was.

For the first time, she allowed herself to realize how poor the chances were of her reaching Safeport at all, let alone while Roi and the others were still alive. If they were alive now. It would be so much easier just to stay here, and be found or die as chance decreed.

No. She might not have much of a chance, but if she gave up, the others would have no chance at all. She picked up the stick she had cut for support, and began limping down the horse trail to the east and Safeport.

Eversummer: Marna

The noon sun glared off the surface of the little pond, and the bushes shook in the steady wind. Marna paused to polarize the faceplate of the isolation suit. With the wind, she thought, the oven heat of the sun might even be enjoyable. In the isolation suit, it was sheer misery. She looked enviously at her guide, a local teenager wearing only shorts and sandals.

"We be here, Mum," the boy said. "You want more water?"

Marna nodded. "More water," she agreed. Taking samples from the marshy pond in the clumsy isolation suit might have been possible, she thought, but it certainly would not have been easy, and teleporting samples directly from the pond would have deprived the boy of feeling he was doing something useful. She watched as the boy dipped a bucket into the scummy water. He was about Roi's age, and his sun-bleached tow hair and sun-browned skin had even reminded her of Roi—for the first few minutes of their time together.

She maneuvered her suit next to a rock outcrop, and set up her portable testing laboratory. She had located the source of the toxin two days ago, in the form of a photosynthesizing single-celled organism widespread in surface waters and forming a large part of the base of the aquatic food chain. As far as she could tell, the thing she'd dubbed a pseudodiatom stored the toxin in its body, protected by a silica shell. Locally evolved animals, whether they ate the pseudos or simply drank the water containing them, sequestered the toxin and passed it up the food chain, thus becoming toxic to human beings and animals from off planet. It should be possible, she thought, to breed food animals that would break down and excrete the toxin, or better yet, use it as an energy source as they broke it down. So far, the pseudos had been in every sample of surface water she had examined. Definitely, she decided, she was going to hand this problem to Zhaim and insist that he do something about it.

She reached into the bucket with her mind, and teleported a sample of its contents into the sample cell of her microviewer. Odd—usually she could feel the activity of the organisms in a water sample. This time .... She looked at the screen of the viewer, frowning in puzzlement. Instead of dozens of the pseudos, jetting randomly through the water sample, she saw only three of the delicate crystal shells. Two of the three were almost quiescent. Normally they took in water from openings on one side of the shell and jetted it out the other, producing constant motion. Different—and she was looking for difference .... From the corner of her eye she saw the local boy scoop water from the pond into his drinking cup. "Don't drink that, Kardullo," she said sharply.

He looked at her, slack-jawed. "It be safe, Mum. I use the cup."

The cup. The cup had a microfilter built into the drinking nipple, the same kind of filter used to treat drinking water on large and small scales all across the planet. To the boy's simple mind, the cup was magic that made the water safe to drink, just as the filters made his village's water supply, piped from this pond, safe to drink. But there should have been dozens of the pseudos on her screen. Where was the toxin that would have been locked in their shells?

"This water is different," she told him carefully. "The cup may not make it safe. Can you wait for half an hour, while I run another test?"

She watched him puzzle that out as she deactivated the stasis field on the bioassay culture container long enough to teleport a few thousand bacteria into the water sample in her microviewer.

Usually, the first cell division after transfer to water contaminated with the toxin would appear normal in the microviewer. With this particular bacterium, the effects of the toxin would start showing up about the time the cells were ready to divide a second time. Instead of dividing, the cell walls would disintegrate.

On her screen, one of the few bacteria visible seemed to explode as its cell walls fell apart. Startled, she set the microcomputer controlling the system to searching out other cells. Within ten minutes she knew that the culture was dying, and dying faster than she had ever seen before. She had to confirm this with the lab test, she thought, but she had no real doubts now that the toxin normally locked away inside the silica shells of the pseudos had somehow been released to the water.

"Kardullo," she said, "this water is very bad. I have to go back to my laboratory and make some more tests. You must go back to your village and tell them that nobody is to drink the water unless they boil it first. The cups and the pipes won't work any more."

The boy looked at her blankly. "They not believe Kardullo," he said unhappily. "Never believe Kardullo."

No, she thought wryly, they wouldn't. Kardullo was the slow one, the one who had to be told everything over and over again. He knew the

285

countryside and its dangers, and she suspected he'd do better than many of his brighter neighbors if he were dropped alone into the wilderness. But he didn't seem to think in words.

"I will give you a note to give them," she told him. "You tell them not to drink the water, and that there will be people here soon, doctors, from the city. You must all do as they tell you, or the whole village may die." Especially since the general opinion in the village was that boiling water was a waste of time and fuel, she thought.

"A note?" He brightened and scribbled with one finger on his other hand. "They believe note."

He watched as she hastily wrote her message, and took it with a respect that confirmed her suspicion that he could not read or write. Like the cup, the note was magic to him. "Go, now," she told him. "I can get back by myself." He nodded and took off toward the village at a run that was equally remarkable for its inefficiency and its speed. Marna smiled briefly at his flailing arms and legs, and gathered herself for the teleport back to her borrowed laboratory at the planetary capital.

An hour later she stood, still in the isolation suit, before a mass of Eversummer's public health authorities. "The bioassay is working," she said, "but it may be several fivedays before it's widely enough available to be useful. There's no question now that the toxin is produced by the pseudos, and so far I haven't found it free in water where the pseudos are healthy. I'm going to recommend that we set up a fast assay just looking for the pseudos in the unfiltered water sources. That's something anyone with a microviewer can do with half an hour's training. Concentrate the few bioassay kits Dr. Thuruvan has put together in the areas where the pseudos are missing, rare, or abnormally sluggish. If I'm right, something's killing them, and they're releasing the toxin into the water when they die."

Quallo tipped his head to the side, his expression eager. "You mean that the filtered water is probably safe if the toxic organism is still present in the source areas?" he inquired. "What a fascinating idea. Would water from aquifers be safe, then?"

Marna sighed and started to run a hand through her hair, stopping herself as she remembered the isolation suit. "I don't know," she admitted. "But it would certainly be worthwhile to look at well water and see if the pseudos or the toxin are present. Meanwhile, the combination of the two tests may give us enough warning that we can block the next large outbreak."

"No wonder Roi wanted to get breeding stock," Elyra exclaimed. "They're exquisite!" She picked the drawing up, holding it in the late-afternoon sunlight.

"The drawing's certainly exquisite," Kyrie said in response. "Look at the way he's rendered the different textures. Rocks, vegetation, cliff walls, the bodies of the horses, and the water. And with nothing but a carbon stick. Derry, is there anything that child can't do?"

"Stand up for himself," Derik replied promptly. "And that hurts, because I'm one of the people responsible." He took the drawing from Elyra, checking the date in the corner. "Morning of the twenty-fourth, probably from memory since it's obviously moonlight. These all have brush manes, though. Wonder if there are any showing the long manes?" He began turning through the drawings. "Any idea if he'd seen them shortly before he contacted you, Kyrie?"

"He was sketching them, I think," she replied, "so there should be another one further down in the pile."

"So far, they're in chronological order," Derik commented absently. "No, it's not here. Matter of fact, there's nothing here later than a quick sketch of their campsite in the canyon, dated on the twenty-fifth. That's odd. Surely they stopped and dropped stuff off after the climb out of the canyon. They were planning to pick up horses on the cliff top, and they'd hardly have carried their riding gear up with them, or bothered to pack the climbing gear along on the horses. And I can't believe Roi wouldn't have made a few sketches on the way up, as well as the one you thought you felt him doing." He sat and stared at the last drawing, scowling uneasily.

"Dinner's ready, M'lady," a voice said politely. Derik looked up at the young woman at the door to the dining room, put down the drawing, and stood.

"If it's anything like the snacks you prepared for us last night," he said, "we can return to this later."

***

Dinner, excellent though it was, did not make Derik any less uneasy. He returned to the drawings as soon as the meal was over, putting them in careful chronological order and studying each sheet as if he expected to find some hidden message. "I don't like this," he muttered to himself.

"That," Kyrie replied, "is rather obvious. But there could be a simple explanation. The Company might be behind in recovering the things they left to be picked up. Were their climbing clothes in the stuff you brought back?"

"I haven't looked," Derik replied.

"So the Company might not have understood that you wanted all of the drawings, or might not even have picked them all up yet. The ones you're looking for could still be in Safeport or in one of the cabins."

"Probably," Derik admitted. "I'll get out there again as soon as they're open in the morning. But I don't feel right about this. I can't actually get any precognitive feeling about Roi's safety, but I don't like this." He riffled through the drawings again, pausing at one with a malignant puma perched on a gigantic red rock. "I may be out of here before you wake up tomorrow, Kyrie."

A soft chime sounded, and the door monitor lit up with the image of a middle-aged man in a game warden officer's attire. "Response on the miniature horses?" Derik said softly, and Kyrie shrugged, watching as the visitor held up his identification, and then telling him to come in. A few minutes later the man entered the room, bowing politely to Kyrie and her guests.

"My apologies for such a late visit, M'lady Adjudicator," he said, "but this had your personal code on it, and we thought you might still be up and would want to see it. And truth to tell," he flashed her a sheepish grin, "we're all eaten up with curiosity." He held out a folded and wrinkled note to Kyrie.

"That's Roi's writing," Elyra said abruptly, as Kyrie began to unfold the note. "But why on earth would he write? And why send it through the game wardens?" She turned to their visitor. "How did this get to you?"

"One of the field wardens picked up a stray hunting hound this morning," the man said. "One of the big ones used for the really large animals. This was tied around its collar."

The note had been folded and placed in a waterproof bag, and it took Kyrie a moment to spread it out. Derik was watching her face as she saw its contents, and saw her frown. "Derik," she said, "wasn't Roi called Snowy as a slave?" She handed across the note.

Roi had handled this, and fairly recently. And he had been nearly desperate at the time. Derik knew that the instant the note touched his hands. He forced himself to read the brief message: *Big brother kidnapped us. Warn Father. Snowy.* Derik crumpled the note in his hand, all his vague suspicions crystallized into painful certainty. "Big brother" had to be Zhaim. And if Zhaim even suspected that Derik suspected him .... He forced himself to look at the messenger.

"It's a joke, perpetrated by a friend of Kyrie's who's on a hunt," he said, nudging at the man's immediate memories to erase the shock he must have seen on their faces. "I'm sorry you've had the trouble, but we are most grateful for your promptness."

"Thought it must be something like that," the man replied as he bowed himself out the door, "but it could have been important."

"So it could," Kyrie managed to say. "You did well to bring it immediately. If there are any more, I want to see them at once, please. And—if you could bring the dog by ...."

"What is it?" Elyra asked after the man had left. Derik thrust the crumpled note into her hands and flopped into a contour chair, throwing his head back and reaching with all his strength for Roi's mind. Nothing. The boy was either dead or behind tight shields.

Elyra's chocolate face could not turn pale like Kyrie's fair one, but the blood left it just as surely. "What can we do?" she asked. "If he's in Zhaim's hands—Zhaim will kill him and get rid of any evidence he ever had his hands on Roi the instant he thinks anyone suspects him."

"We get hold of Lai," Derik replied. "I'll need a boost and monitoring for that. There's no one able to monitor here on Falaron, and the Council's in session right now, so I don't dare pull any of them out. And Zhaim might pick it up if I went through the Big'Un. Kyrie, have you got a power source here I could use?"

"The villa and the Hall of Adjudication are powered by a small fusion reactor," Kyrie replied. "If you can tap that ...."

Derik closed his eyes and traced power back from the lights to the generator, and through that to the reactor. "Good enough," he replied after a moment. "At least Lai's within pretty easy boosting range. I still want a monitor—Nik, I think. We'll want him once we locate Roi, anyway. I'll jump him over from Central. This chair will do, Kyrie. Can you rig something to hold a glucose drip?"

Kablukolelli: Lai

A dozen stubborn, self-righteous faces stared back at Lai. About half an hour longer, he thought disgustedly, and I'm going to start using more than words. If they can't tell the difference between symbol and reality, it's about time somebody showed them.

He shifted slightly in his seat, forcing himself to analyze what the Folaanni representative was saying. It sounded appallingly like one of the warring sects from the Goodnews system, he thought. Which was odd, because that particular sect was about as far from Folaanni beliefs as you could get. Could someone who knew the Goodnews system have been deliberately fomenting this problem?

Lai, Derik's voice ghosted into his mind. *Lai! We've got an emergency here.*

What? he thought back.

Roi. We think Zhaim's kidnapped him. I can't reach him at all, even enough to tell if he's alive.

Lai sat up abruptly, and the Folaanni representative broke off in confusion. The R'il'nian looked around the room, forcing eye contact on everyone in it. "That statement," he said, "and a number of others I have heard lately, seem to me inconsistent with your several beliefs. I am going to give you some time to think over the question of which arguments you have given me are questionable by your own beliefs, and the source of those arguments. If there are further problems before I return, so help me, I will see that when you die, your bodies are dumped in space, between the stars." *Guide me in, Derry. Kablukolelli can take care of itself.*

The diplomats looked at the suddenly empty chair and then at each other, shocked. "That's obscene," the chief J'koan representative said finally. It was the first statement in months that they could agree on.

Falaron, Xazhar
6/2/38

It wasn't fair, Xazhar thought. It would be at least two more days before the arena electrical system could be repaired and the tournament resumed. Camy and her father had left early this morning. It was the wrong season for hunting, so he couldn't hunt. Strictly speaking, he wasn't even supposed to have a flier out here without a governor that would keep it high enough not to disturb the animals, but that requirement was easy enough to evade. At least it was possible to rent a flier in Safeport. In Wilderness City, no fliers were available.

There was plenty of public transportation available, of course, from crowded transport shuttles to the luxury chauffeured flier he had splurged on when he had taken Camy out to dinner last night. And after dinner .... He smiled lazily at the memory.

He was still feeling proud of the official commendations he'd received for his reaction to the accident at the plasmaball arena, but he could have done without the recess in the tournament while the arena was being repaired. With no games in progress and Camy gone, the planet had little to interest him. He wished he knew where his father's hunting lodge was, but Zhaim had never seen fit to tell his son its exact location.

He'd swing farther north on the return trip, he decided. Maybe he'd spot Roi's party. They were supposed to be somewhere in this area by now, but on the other side of the Surprise. Of course fliers, aside from Company craft, weren't supposed to be north of the river at all, but he wouldn't let that stop him. Xazhar rarely let anything stop him from doing something he really wanted to do.

He glanced at the tri-dee monitor hooked to the downward pickup, and put the flier into a circling pattern to watch a herd of mastodons splashing in a river below him. No calves, so it must be a bachelor herd. Nice tusks on the biggest one. He tried to visualize a trophy head on the wall of the student apartment he would have next year, and grimaced. He'd need a considerably larger apartment. Roi, he thought resentfully, would have no such problem. It wasn't fair, at all.

He remembered last night again, considering the possibility of a longer-term arrangement with Camy, maybe even a child, though the idea of being father to a child appealed to him far more than living with one. Not that he'd have to. More than likely he'd be tired of Camy by then, especially if she turned off once she was pregnant, as so many R'il'noid women did. He didn't really have to worry about any child's welfare, in any case. He and Camy were both genetics board primes, and the board would make sure that any child of theirs had a secure, loving home. He could still brag of his child, as Roi bragged about Wif.

He pulled the flier out of its mindless circling and flew on, following the river downstream to where it joined the Surprise and then turning northwest to follow the big river upstream. The leaders of the first salmon run of the season were struggling upriver below him, and a grizzly was standing on a submerged bar. Spray flew as it snatched at the water foaming around its legs, finally bringing up a flopping silver fish. Xazhar watched it briefly, and then returned to his musing. Roi didn't have it all his own way, either, he supposed. Wif had been an accident, and Roi would never be allowed to have another child.

There was supposed to be a season on sabertooths before long, and a sabertooth head would fit into an apartment. In some ways, he thought, it would be an even more exciting trophy. Mastodons were, after all, fairly common. Predators were always less numerous than their prey, as well as being more dangerous. A spear-killed sabertooth, now—He visualized such a hunt, and quickly decided that he preferred modern weaponry. He sent the flier on, hoping to spot one of the big cats. He wouldn't land, of course, or even fly low enough to disturb the animals. He just wanted to see his prospective prey in the wild.

The river valley was heavily forested, and if he wanted to see a sabertooth he'd have to find more open country. He checked his map, and found an area to the south marked as prairie. He turned the flier that way, darkening the upper part of the canopy to shade his eyes from the sun. It had felt good, getting the spectators out of the damaged arena. He wondered why his father had never mentioned the satisfaction of using his talents to help people.

A herd of longhorn bison appeared below, their attention fixed on something farther west. Xazhar flew over them and followed their gaze, and to his delight saw a tawny cat crouched in the grass. Its back was turned to the bison, and it was clearly stalking something well away from them. Intrigued, Xazhar lifted higher, trying to follow the cat's stalk.

Dammit, there was a human being down there. That would mess up the sabertooth's kill for sure—and it was a sabertooth; the head had turned briefly at an angle that let him see the fangs. He looked around, trying to locate the big cat's target, and suddenly realized that the human was the prey. He aimed the pickup at the distant figure and keyed for magnification, and saw a girl, limping along with the aid of a crude staff. Even younger than he was, he thought, and she looked familiar, somehow.

Something to do with Roi—hell, it was one of Roi's slaves. What was she doing here?

Well, she could be a useful pawn. He sent the flyer down, quickly, landing as close to the startled girl as he dared and swinging the far door open. "Get in," he ordered her.

She took a half step toward him, and then froze "Xazhar K'Zhaim," he reminded her. "Hurry up—hey! Come back here, you idiot!" The girl had turned and was trying to run—directly toward the stalking cat. Swearing, he lifted the flier, racing low toward the sabertooth and wishing he had a weapon—even a stunner. The rapid approach of something the size of a mastodon and a good deal faster was enough, however. The cat left, bolting for cover.

Xazhar set down again, this time between the slave and his last glimpse of the predator, and when the girl tried to turn away again he jumped out and ran after her. She fell almost at once, and struck wildly at his eyes when he grabbed her arm. He hit her, hard, striking an old bruise on her jaw, and she wilted. He dragged her back to the flier, swearing at her unconscious form.

Now what, he thought disgustedly. He had tried to rescue her, thinking Roi would be pleased, and instead she had made him beat her up. More than likely, she would manage to convince Roi that he'd attacked her without reason. What was she doing out here, anyway? She was supposed to be with the others on the far side of the Surprise River.

Xazhar wished he knew how to find his father and ask his advice. *Better tie the slut up somehow before I take off again,* he thought. *Don't want to deal with her jumping me while I'm trying to fly. Father's lodge is out in the Spine Range somewhere, I think. I could head out that way and have a look for it. He'd probably have a closed com to home there. Getting close to noon, though, and the Spine Range is a long way off. I'd better go back to Safeport and have something to eat and repower first. Maybe rent something with more range.*

Derik

Derik walked along the sidewalk back to Kyrie's parked flier, feeling as if he'd slammed into a wall at high speed. Yes, the Company had picked up everything left at the drop points. There had been no more drawings, either at the corral above the canyon or at the cabin downstream from the gorge, but the travelers had left their climbing gear and clothing at the corral, and picked up the packhorses and food at the cabin. At least, they had left most of their gear at the corral. The youngest girl had apparently decided to keep her climbing clothing on. Unwise, but not uncommon. There were no more scheduled drop points before Safeport. They had showed him their tracking system, and given him detailed maps of the party's progress as revealed by the finders. Yes, they were moving a little slowly, but their guide had been expressly advised to take as much time as her clients wanted, to make up for the early delays. Here was the rest of the stuff the party had dropped off, M'Lord, but it was just dirty clothes they'd planned to clean before returning. Would he like to take them now? It was rather a large box. Was there anything else they could help with, M'Lord?

Derik had made himself remember that Zhaim might very well have a contact within the Company, and forced a smile. No, they had been quite helpful, and he had merely been eager to see Roi's sketches of the miniature horses that had caught his fancy. Well, he'd just have to wait until they got back. Another two or three fivedays, they thought? That would give him plenty of time to enjoy the planet's finest restaurants. There was an outstanding one here in Safeport? Oh, dear, too bad Kyrie already had her cook preparing a special lunch for himself and Elyra. If he'd known earlier, he'd have let the cook off and brought Elyra along.

This part of the town was devoted to tourists, and was deliberately rustic. The streets were paved with something that looked like raw dirt, and horses stood tied to hitching posts at the edge of the wooden boardwalk. Parking areas were discreetly hidden away. Derik walked along the boardwalk, a large box cradled in his arms, counting alleyways. The fifth one on the left should lead to Kyrie's flier. He hoped the box would fit through the alley.

An oncoming pedestrian dodged around the box, glancing sideways as he went past and then stopping. "M'Lord Derik? Please, Derik, wait up a minute. I need to talk to you."

The voice was familiar—Zhaim's son, Xazhar. Keeping tabs on Derik for his father? He had to act normal, Derik thought. How could Zhaim use his son like this? Derik would have had a hard time contemplating anything like Zhaim had pulled in kidnapping Roi, but he could not even imagine involving Coryn in such a crime.

"Hello, Xazhar," he said. "Sorry I didn't see you; this box is a little hard to see through. Mind if I keep walking? I'd like to get it into the flier."

"Can I help?" Xazhar asked unexpectedly. "Derik, I have to talk to you. I don't know exactly where father's place is, even if he were on planet, and I don't think I can really talk to him about this, anyway. I mean, I'm pretty sure what he'd say, but that's not what I want to do—oh, I'm making a mess of this. Please, could you come by my flier and let me show you? It's important. Maybe really important. I think something's gone wrong with Roi's group, maybe."

"Oh?" Derik said carefully, letting Xazhar take the box. "Company says they're just taking their time. How far to your flier?"

"Right here," Xazhar replied, turning down the same alley that led to Derik's craft. He led the way to a small, two-seat runabout. "I had to knock her out and tie her, Lord Derik. I wasn't going to hurt her, but she must have thought I was. She *hit* me." He sounded outraged, and when Derik looked closer, he saw that Xazhar's left eye was well along the way to a classic shiner.

"Who hit you?" he asked, amused in spite of himself, and then gasped as Xazhar put down the box and opened the door.

Amber

"So then I got to thinking, and it didn't make sense she'd run away from Roi at all, let alone in the middle of the wilderness," a voice said, "and I knew damn well that if father got his hands on her he'd find a way to use her against Roi. And then I saw you—it's all right, isn't it, Lord Derik? I mean, you'll help me convince Roi I was just trying to help her, won't you?"

Derik? Amber fought to open her eyes. She was in the cargo space of a flier, lying on a heap of dirty clothes, and the back of the head in the driver's seat looked very much like her old owner's. Then he said "Jump coming up," and there was that disorienting change in the light, and she found herself sobbing with relief.

"Amber?" came the familiar voice. "Awake? Good girl. We'll be down at Kyrie's in a few minutes. Can you tell us what happened? No, wait. I'm not the only one that needs to know. How about why you tried to black Xazhar's eye?"

"More than tried," Xazhar muttered, but he didn't sound as upset as she would have thought.

"I thought he was working with his father," she gulped. "Oh, Derik, it's been awful. Something or someone took the others right off the canyon wall—Roi's thoughts just stopped, in the middle of mind-talking me. And I've been having nightmares that Zhaim has them. The last one—I think it was night before last, but I've kind of lost track of time—they were in a forest, wetter than here and different plants, and Zhaim found them there and started beating Roi."

"He wouldn't do that," Xazhar said, but his voice sounded as if he were trying desperately to convince himself, rather than convince Amber or Derik. "I mean it'd be a crazy thing to do. Wouldn't it?"

"It would," Derik agreed, "but I'm not sure Zhaim is sane where Roi is concerned. Anyway, we've got independent reason to think Zhaim kidnapped Roi, and at about the time they were climbing out of the gorge. I only pray Roi's still alive."

"They were up in the mountains, at first," Amber said. "The place he had them in had a clear wall, looking west, and it was above tree line. Still some snow, at first, but later on it melted. Kind of a flat area, with a low rim to the west and I think mountains on the other sides."

Xazhar's shoulders were shaking, his face buried in his hands. "I don't know exactly where it is," he gulped, "but father has some kind of a hunting lodge in the Spine Range. I've seen tri-dees of the setting, and her description fits. It's in an empty cirque."

"You're willing to work with us, then?" Derik asked.

Xazhar hesitated for a moment. "Grandfather said once I could be my father's son or his grandson, but not both," he said shakily. "I was mad at him, and I said I'd rather be my father's son. I love my father, but I think now I made the wrong choice. Do you think Grandfather would let me change my mind?"

Derik hesitated an instant, and then Amber saw him smile just a little. "I think he'd be glad to have you back, Xazhar," he said.

Chapter 22

"Well, the infection's not antibiotic resistant," Nik said. "You're lucky, Amber. Hold still, and I'll inject this right into the wounds. You'll be fine in a couple of days."

Lai turned toward them. "We've done what we can with Amber's memories," he said abruptly. "Something's blocked Roi mentally, or he'd have yelled for help to Kyrie long since. He's got that much sense, even if he's shut me out. I think he somehow managed to maintain an empathic link with Amber, but it only seems to open enough to pass information while she's asleep and dreaming. I'm pretty sure the link is still there, and if I'm right on that, Roi must still be alive. Amber, if Nik can put you into REM sleep, would you mind if I stayed in your mind while he does it? It's a thin chance, but I might be able to get through to Roi by way of your dreams, and pick up enough information to teleport myself to him."

"Would a possible map location help?" Xazhar said.

"You think you've got one?" Derik asked.

"Maybe," Xazhar replied. He turned one of the notes and a large-scale map so both faced the others. "Look here, at the notes the dogs were carrying. This scribble you've been ignoring is the same on all of them. Could it be a map? This looks kind of like the coastline, and if that's the Wilderness River and this is the Mastodon, then the thing here that looks a little like a building in an open loop would be about here on the map. And there's a cirque at that location that matches the tri-dees I remember, and what Amber described as the view out of the window. The satellite map even shows a building."

Lai leaned over Xazhar's shoulder, studying map and drawing. "I think you may be right," he said, and closed his eyes in brief concentration. "And there's a shielded area there. I'm still going to need that empathic link with Roi to 'port in. Flying or 'porting to a location outside the building is a last resort, and only when we know Zhaim's not there."

"After sunset," Derik said, glancing out the window. The sun was high in the southern sky, just past noon. "Council meeting doesn't start 'til then. Amber?"

The girl nodded in agreement. "If you really think it'll help," she said.

"Three-way link, to start," Nik said. "I'll put her into REM sleep once you're in full empathic link, and then back out."

Lai picked up a beamer and adjusted it to a wide stun setting. "I'll need a couple of slap pads of hiControl," he said, "and Derik, you'd better link up and come along. Bring an aid kit, but be ready to drop it if I need help with Zhaim." He sat down beside the lounge where Amber lay, and reached out to take the girl's hand. Derik, behind him, placed his free hand on Lai's shoulder, and Nik, sitting on the far side of the lounge, took Amber's other hand.

Lai slid into Amber's mind and emotions as gently as he could, but he still felt her flinch at the contact. *Sorry,* he thought, *I just can't match Roi's soft touch.*

I don't think anybody can, except Marna, Amber replied. He felt her settle against his mind, adjusting herself to the sensation and trying hard to control her fear for Roi. *I'm ready when you are, Nik.*

The empathic pathway was there, all right. The girl's mind slid into sleep, and he felt the connection open wider. Carefully he pushed his own mind into the link, trying to reach his son.

Roi

Someone was pounding on Roi's head with a hammer, and the rest of him felt as if he'd been shipped all the way around the Confederation in an ore carrier. The freight compartment of a nearly full ore carrier, with the cargo loose in free fall. He hurt all over, and on top of that, he felt everything the other three were suffering. Especially Timi, who felt as if he were being pulled apart hairbreadth by hairbreadth. He remembered the rack, and decided sickly that that was probably exactly what was happening.

His headache intensified. *I've got a concussion,* he thought. *And some broken ribs, too, from the feel of it, and I can't breathe properly ....* He felt as if he had to open his eyes. There was something odd about the feeling, as if it had originated outside his own mind. The emotion felt as if it belonged to someone else, like his father. He hoped his father would get one of the notes he'd sent off with the dogs.

Four notes. Why was he seeing four notes, laid out on a polished wood table? And why did he have such an overwhelming urge to open his eyes and attract Zhaim's attention for a moment?

Roi thought about that for a minute or two, trying to ignore the pounding in his head. Open his eyes. Could he open his eyes? They felt awfully swollen. He remembered the beating, and decided they probably were swollen. Could he open them? It finally occurred to him that the logical way to find out was to try.

He couldn't open them very far, and what he could see in his narrow slit of vision was blurred. Timi was stretched on the rack, and Roi's heart twisted in his chest at the way his friend's body had been literally pulled apart. Only his skin seemed to be holding him together. He wondered if Amber was still alive. He couldn't send her this image, he thought. Not the way she felt about Timi. But yes, Amber was there, asleep, and—surely he couldn't be feeling his father's emotions! The urge to get Zhaim's attention intensified. Could Amber have reached his father somehow?

But why would his father want him to attract Zhaim's attention? Once Zhaim knew he was conscious, what little was left of his own life would become something he would struggle to escape. Had his father decided to end the friction between his sons by destroying Roi?

Shock, denial and an unexpectedly clear image of a flicker in the shadows behind Zhaim—a flicker that solidified into his father's form. He looked again into the room, rehearsing every detail he himself would need for a teleport, and this time realized that Zhaim was standing so close to a wall that there was no place his father could teleport to without alerting Zhaim.

If he was going to be able to help Timi, he told himself, he had to get the antidote to the hiControl he'd been dosed with, and to get that, he had to help his father get here. So he had to get Zhaim's attention, and hold it for the moment Lai would need for the teleport. He wished he could be certain it was his father's mind he was feeling, and not his own wishful thinking. It would be his own death and those of his friends if he were wrong.

Attracting Zhaim's attention shouldn't be too hard, he told himself. He'd spent most of his life avoiding attention, and that made him somewhat of an expert on getting attention, too. He moaned and shifted his position slightly, and began cursing, softly enough that Zhaim would have to pay attention to hear what he was saying. He had an excellent repertoire of invective, the legacy of a long string of owners, mostly words and phrases he had never dared say aloud. Zhaim actually took a step toward him and froze, his mouth wide open in shock, and Roi picked up horrified astonishment from Penny, surprise and relief from Flame and pain-fogged agreement from Timi.

There was a sudden shift of light in the shadowed corner between the stairs and Timi's empty cage, and Zhaim spun around. Roi felt his shock, panic and sheer fury as he saw their father's face, set and angry over the muzzle of the beamer, and then a sudden blankness as Roi's own eyes saw Zhaim crumple. His father moved out of the shadows, slapping his hand against Zhaim's upper arm even as the R'il'noid fell and then bending over the limp figure. Another figure ran toward Roi's cage, fumbling with the lock.

He felt like saying "Hello, Derry," or something equally inane, but his cursing had triggered a coughing fit, and the coughs felt as if they were tearing his lungs apart. He heard Derik swearing as his uncle struggled with the cage lock, and then Flame's voice, saying something about the locks being changed to a thumbprint key.

"Roi!" Derik's voice pulled him back to attention. "Can you judge your own condition well enough to know if Suppress is safe? Drop your shields and mind-talk if you can't stop coughing. I'll hear you. Zhaim's out cold and your dad gave him a double dose of hiControl on top of that. He'll be over as soon as he's tied Zhaim up."

Forgot you could hear me even if I can't push, he subvocalized. *Think I've got a concussion and some cracked ribs. And he did something to my throat. Get the others treated, will you? Specially Timi. And I need the hiControl countered, fast.* He closed his swollen eyes and concentrated on trying not to cough.

"You'll have to override Zhaim's thumb-locks, Lai," Roi heard Derik's voice, and then, a moment later, he tasted Suppress in Timi's mouth, and the slow, spreading relief from pain. Then Flame and Penny, so at last it was only his own aching body he felt, and his father's arms lifting him from the cage.

"HiControl counter," he managed to whisper between coughs. "Need to Heal."

"We'll get it," Lai promised. "It'll take about a day to take effect, though."

No, he thought desperately, Timi can't make it that long. I can't do a full Healing assessment, but I could see that much.

"Roi, you're not risking your life for Timi," Lai said.

But you don't understand ....

Derik

Derik had not dropped his link to Roi, and he heard both sides of the argument, even as he was assessing the condition of the two girls. "I think," he said abruptly, "that I'd better get Nik. Anybody know where the esper shield control is? Lai may be able to slide right through a shield, but I can't, especially with Nik along."

"Control panel upstairs," Lai replied promptly. "I dug that much out of Zhaim's mind. Along with exactly what he did to Roi's party." There was real venom in the last words.

"Derik," Timi managed to whisper, "better take my mind along. The controls are kinda screwed up. He made me fix lights 'n heat, but I fought 'm on the rest." There was a kind of exhausted pride mixed with shame in the last sentence.

Derik hesitated. "I know you hate mind-touch, Timi."

"Yeah, but you need t' know, an' you can't take my body," Timi whispered weakly. No, Derik thought as he looked at Timi. Barring a miracle, you're going to die when we slack the tension on that rack. And if a few minutes of contact helps you feel you're worth something, even if it hurts you .... "I'll be as gentle as I can," he said aloud.

He placed his hand lightly on Timi's forehead, and eased into contact with the boy's mind as softly as he could. Timi flinched but somehow managed to keep his crude shields relaxed, giving Derik a clear picture of the control panels upstairs and exactly what Timi, with help and advice from Roi, had done to them. "No wonder Kaia said Zhaim was looking harassed at the last couple of Council meetings," Derik said as he pulled the mag key off its hook and walked up the stairs.

Nik

"Heel and thumb tendons cut on all four," Nik repeated back to Derik as he packed the large aid kit. "Roi's got a concussion, broken ribs, a dislocated shoulder, and he's bruised and scraped pretty well all over. Timi's been almost pulled apart. Flame's been raped and burned, and the Company guide's badly burned and had her hands torn up. Anything else?" He added another cocoon to the pile on the table and glanced at Derik. "Sure you can teleport all this and me too?"

"If you think you'll need it," Derik replied. "You've pretty well got the serious injuries. I dosed all three Humans with Suppress—didn't dare use it on Roi, in case the concussion's serious. Roi and Lai are fighting about how long it's going to take to counter the hiControl. Roi wants to be able to Heal his friends."

"And Lai's trying to overprotect him again?" Nik asked. "Well, I'll have to see how bad the concussion is." He glanced over at Elyra. "And you and Xazhar are going to clean out the carryall and get it out there to bring the Humans back here."

"And Kyrie canceled the rest of her circuit adjudications for the day as soon as I called her. Nik, you tell us what to do, but let Kyrie and me take care of those girls. They won't want a man touching them right now. Especially the Falaron girl."

Nik made a last, quick check of his supplies. "I'm ready when you are, Derry," he said. He felt Derik's mind enfold his, and followed the older R'il'noid's guidance through the teleport.

Lai was sitting on the floor, leaning against a stone wall with Roi's body cradled against his chest. They were still arguing, though at the moment it was all mental. Roi was coughing too hard to speak. Nik took a quick look at the two girls, still locked in their cages, and at Timi stretched on the rack. The girls would have been in pain without the Suppress but were probably not in serious danger, he thought. He didn't think anyone but Roi—or Marna, but she was out of reach—could keep Timi alive for more than a few more hours. He slipped around the end of the rack and knelt by Roi.

"All right, Roi," he said calmly, "Let's see just what's wrong with you. Open up and let me monitor. Lai, get out of here for a minute and open the girls' cages. I don't want to try to monitor him in the middle of an argument."

Lai glared at Nik for a moment, and then obeyed, allowing Nik to take over the job of supporting Roi upright. Better check out that concussion first, Nik thought. If it was as bad as the pain he felt in the boy's head suggested, they might have to pull Marna in, and from what she had said about the intensity of the Eversummer plague or toxin or whatever it was, that could cost tens if not hundreds of thousands of lives. He slid his perception into the boy's brain, searching for areas of pressure, dead cells, blood clots or any other symptom of concussion. After a moment he chuckled.

"Thought you were a better diagnostician than that, Roi," he said finally. "You had a mild concussion, but it's pretty well healed. What you've got is a nasty head and throat cold. Probably the first one you've ever had, since normally you enhance your immune system without even thinking about it. That's physical—esper—so the hiControl would affect it. The shoulder and the broken ribs are real and serious, though. One rib is broken in two places, and the loose piece is threatening to puncture a lung every time you cough." He sighed. "Derry forgot to mention the coughing, and I didn't bring anything for cold symptoms. Let me TK that loose rib piece back where it belongs, anyway, and I'll get some strapping around your chest and the shoulder back where it belongs."

"HiControl antidote?" Roi pleaded. "Then I could tack-heal the ribs and maybe even do something about the cold." After Roi had done what he could for Timi, Nik thought. Maybe he could get Roi to tack-heal his own ribs to demonstrate that he was ready to work on Timi.

"Two possibilities," Nik told Roi once he had the boy's ribs lined up and was starting to wrap bandaging around the bruised chest. "Standard treatment's what your dad was saying. Refined antidote, together with a drug to keep you sound asleep while it's working. That way you don't feel everybody within reach screaming into your mind. The antidote erodes shielding and increases sensitivity during the early part of the reaction. That's what you've had before, though it hasn't taken as long because you've always had measured doses of the refined drug, not an overdose of the raw stuff. The alternative, given the dose your dad says Zhaim gave you, is likely to be very rough, but it is faster—takes a couple of hours."

"That's not an option, Nik," Lai's voice cut in.

The physician turned his face toward his half brother. "It's a legitimate medical option, and there is virtually no chance of it causing permanent damage," he said. "He's not that seriously injured, Lai, no matter how bad he looks. If there were a chance of further injury, if he really had a major concussion, I wouldn't even suggest it. There are decisions you can legitimately make for him, but this is not one of them. Now shut up and let me tell him exactly what's involved." He turned back to Roi.

"If we use the fast option," he said, "we'll have to continue holding off on the Suppress. You'll probably have some mild convulsions or violent shuddering, and we may have to use a muscle relaxant to make sure that doesn't further damage those ribs, even with the strapping. Your shields against picking up thoughts in your vicinity will go down, and you'll be hearing everyone in range at once. We'll help as much as we can, but it will be a miserable two hours."

Roi started to speak, but another coughing spell intervened. *The fast way,* he thought without hesitation. *Only thing that really bothers me is my shields going down. I don't think there are many people outside this building that are close enough I'd pick up an undirected thought, but is there anything you can do to make sure I don't pick up Zhaim? And can I have a drink of water first?*

"That we can handle," his father replied as he dropped to the floor and took Roi back into his arms. "Roi, are you sure about this? You do realize there may be nothing even you can do for Timi, don't you?"

I've got to try, Roi replied. Derik came over with a cup of water and held it to the boy's lips, and it was obvious to Nik that Roi was forcing himself to sip rather than gulp it down.

"Let's get started, then," Nik said.

Roi

The effects started slowly. Roi began to shiver much as he had with the initial overdose, and his awareness of the other individuals in the building increased. Zhaim seemed fogged out, somehow; he felt his half-brother's presence, but not his thoughts. *He's still out from the stunner,* his father said. *I'll increase the block between you later on, if he wakes up.*

"The antidote restores sensitivity first, then power, then control," Nik said. "I know you'll be picking up things from your friends, but don't try to send them anything. If you try after your power builds back but before you've got normal control, you could really hurt them."

Roi managed a shaky nod. He could feel the three Humans in the room, all right. Penny was shocked almost beyond coherent thought, huddling far back in the corner of the open cage. Flame was aware of what was happening, allowing Derik to help her out of the cage, but wondering deep down if she would ever be able to enjoy lovemaking again. *It doesn't matter, Flame,* he wanted to tell her. *It's not your body or your skill in bed that I love, it's you.* Timi was worst, though, dying and knowing it, which was bad enough, but thinking he deserved death for what Zhaim had done with his body, which was intolerable.

"Timi," Roi managed to get out between coughs, "if you die on me I'm going to kill you."

"Nik," Derik called from across the room, "I'd like to get these girls in cocoons, but Flame says she wants a good bath first, and the guide won't let me touch her."

Do you need to watch me every minute, Nik? Roi asked. *If you don't, I'd really rather you did what you could for the others. Timi needs water, and Zhaim has a very comfortable soaking tub on the top floor. And a bed.* He felt Nik's agreement and his father's protest, and Nik got to his feet.

"I've got some stuff for a soak," the physician said, "and we might as well get Roi into a bed while the reaction's running its course. And get the girls into cocoons before we move them any more." He cocked his head, listening. "Is that the carryall landing? Derry, let me get a glucose drip and a little extra oxygen for Timi, and then I'll give the girls a quick check while you meet Kyrie and Lyra. Get the blue squeeze bottle from my kit for them. Tell Lyra to fill a hot soak bath for them and put about a third of the bottle's contents in the water, and send Kyrie down here to help get the guide into a cocoon. Timi, we don't dare move you until Roi's ready to help out, but I'm going to wrap a cocoon around you as far as I can, and I'll stay down here with you once we get everybody settled."

His voice faded as Lai carried Roi up the stairs, but not his mind. If anything, Roi's awareness of the thoughts, the emotions and the physical sensations of everyone in the building grew stronger as his father tucked him into Zhaim's bed. Kyrie and Elyra, now, and a third mind, one that held an image of Amber .... *Is Amber all right?* he thought at his father.

"Yes. We couldn't have gotten to you without her help. And the notes on the dogs' collars—that's what really pushed Derry into realizing you needed help, and contacting me. How'd you ever manage that, Roi? Once Zhaim had you .... Roi, you'll be far better than he would, as my heir, but he's a lot stronger than you'll ever be."

I know that now. He hoped Lai wasn't reading more than the surface of his mind, because he was feeling profoundly embarrassed about his earlier refusal to let his father know about his suspicions. *But there were some things he didn't know or was just careless about, and I was able to use those. Like the flyer key. And that hiControl he had me on—it doesn't affect empathy, and I don't think he knew or even cared about that.* He visualized the rat, and the way he had managed to use his empathic contact with the dogs—not only the hunting hounds, but Snowflake as well. *I tried to get through to Smoky, too, but I'm not sure I managed that.*

He felt his father reach out to Derik, and then Derik's mind touched his, very carefully. *From what Coryn said, you got through to Smoky all right, but Cory couldn't get the message. Just thought the dog was acting crazy. Should have told him to read the dog's mind, or read the sled dog's myself.* The emotional overtones that came with the words were of overpowering guilt.

You *don't have anything to feel guilty about, Derry. Father, you're sure Amber's all right? How'd she get to you?*

"Xazhar found her, and then helped us figure out where Zhaim's hunting lodge was. He might want to see you." There was a question in his voice, and Roi nodded, then wished he hadn't. Thanks to the Suppress he wasn't feeling the others' pain any more, but his own head protested the movement. Worse, the nod started his coughing again.

Lai adjusted the pillows behind his head. "Thank all the gods of all the planets that you did think to use that empathy of yours. We'd never have gotten to you in time otherwise. Zhaim might even have gotten away with killing you. But you'd better rest for now."

Had he picked up a trace of "You'll have enough to worry about later" in his father's contact? He hoped not.

Xazhar

"I can't believe father would have bought a three-level building and not put in a lift shaft," Xazhar puffed as he climbed the second flight of stairs. The cocoon-wrapped girl he was carrying didn't weigh as much as he did, but she was still heavy to carry up two floors. Why hadn't they brought a cocoon with a levitation circuit?

"In here, Xazhar, to your right," a female voice called. Lady Elyra, he thought. "Just leave her to us; she's still in shock."

"Right," Lord Derik said behind him. "Nik gave them another dose of counterShock before we brought them up—Zhaim's been keeping them on it, but Flame said their last dose was early morning. And it doesn't do much for psychological shock."

"Very early," Flame agreed huskily. "He will be all right, won't he, Lady Elyra? Roi, I mean?"

"Take her into Zhaim's bedroom for a moment so she can see for herself, Derik," Elyra said as she guided Xazhar to deposit his cocooned burden on one of the benches outside the soaking tub. "We'll take it from here, Xazhar. The poor child's a Falaron native, and they have very strong nudity taboos with the opposite sex. Go stick your head into the bedroom and say hello to Roi, if you like. Derik, get Flame on in here and yourself out. I want to get these girls soaking in decent privacy."

"You need to tell me where I can get some drugs Nik wants for Roi, Kyrie," Derik said. "Teleport coordinates."

Xazhar took a deep breath and stepped into his father's bedroom. It was a big room, with balconies on three sides. The setting sun shone in the windows to his right, with the crescent moon following it about halfway down the sky. Roi was propped up in a huge bed in the middle of the floor, with Lai in a chair next to the bed, washing the dried blood from his son's face.

"Come on in, Xazhar," Lai said, and Roi turned his head toward the door. Roi's whole face was misshapen and mottled with purple amid the natural bronze, his eyes swollen almost shut and his lips split in several places. Xazhar wasn't sure whether it was worse knowing that his father had done this, or remembering that he himself had beaten Roi almost as badly in the past.

To his surprise, Roi managed a ghost of a smile. "Father tells me you rescued Amber, Xazhar," he said. "Thanks." He started to say something more, and went off into a coughing fit. His father lifted him a bit and adjusted the pillows, his face worried.

"Derik's going to get something Nik wants for Roi," Xazhar said uncertainly, and Lai nodded.

"Cold medicine," he said.

Xazhar shuffled his feet. "I'm sorry," he said miserably. "I knew father didn't like you, but I never thought he'd do anything like that. I thought your slave had just run away. I even thought about asking father what to do with her, but then I figured he'd find a way to use her against you, and besides, I didn't know how to get in touch with him, and then I ran into Derik .... I never for a moment dreamed he'd kidnapped you, though, or that the girl was trying to get help. She actually attacked me. Well, I guess that makes sense, if she thought I was working with father. I never thought he'd beat you up like that, once he knew you were R'il'noid."

"It wasn't a very scientific beating," Roi said, more carefully this time. "He plain lost his temper when I jumped him instead of coming back to his cages like a good little slave when he caught up with us. I think quite a bit of it must have been after I was unconscious. I sure don't remember getting hit in some of the places I hurt." He started coughing again.

Somehow that made Xazhar feel even worse about some of the beatings he himself had inflicted on Roi, without even the excuse of a lost temper. "Maybe he just meant to scare you?" he said uncertainly, when the coughing had abated.

"Not likely, if it's Zhaim you're talking about," Derik said from behind him. "Here, Roi. Nik says a dose cup full every two hours. I pulled rank on the drug seller to get it fast."

Roi swallowed the thick syrup obediently, carefully licking a stray drop from a split at the corner of his mouth. "Stings," he said. "Tastes kind of good, though."

"Roi, what did happen?" Lai asked. "No, you stay too, Xazhar. I think you had better know exactly what your father did, so you'll understand why we've got him tied up and loaded with hiControl."

He didn't understand that, Xazhar thought, a little resentfully. His father had certainly gone beyond allowable limits in kidnapping Roi and putting him in a cage, and at the very least he owed Roi major compensation for the injuries to his slaves and the humiliation and pain Roi himself had suffered. But why were they treating Zhaim like a rabid animal?

Roi took a couple of deep, cautious breaths, and managed a slight grin when they didn't trigger a cough. "I suspect the snowstorm was when it started," he began.

By the time he finished, Xazhar could no longer believe that Roi's injuries were simply the result of a temper tantrum on his father's part. Not given the earlier attempts on Roi, and what Zhaim had told the four of his plans to cover their deaths.

Lai had other concerns. "You mean you knew at the time that Zhaim had sabotaged your glider, you knew that he had a control circuit on Timi, and you never even mentioned it?" the R'il'nian said, his voice climbing.

"I knew Timi wasn't behind it, and I didn't want to get him into trouble," Roi shot back.

"So instead he's lying downstairs thinking he deserves to die for what Zhaim did using his body," Lai said. "Roi, couldn't you even trust me enough to think I just might believe you? Or if not me, Marna? I was worried about you. And Zhaim seems to have found a way of blocking off conditional precognition on specific subjects, like your safety, or I'd never have left you here with neither Marna nor me to protect you. As it was, you were so touchy about the glider incident that I didn't dare push you to come along with me as much as I wanted to."

"And I figured you were just giving me an out because I was so paranoid about Zhaim, and didn't really want to be saddled with me," Roi said ruefully.

"I still don't understand why it's so serious," Xazhar said uncertainly. "I mean, if father killed me, he'd have to pay a whopping fine. And he'd probably just pay it, if he really wanted me dead. I don't understand why he's so determined to get rid of Roi, and I don't understand why you've got him tied up. Unless—is Roi Inner Council level?"

Lai and Roi looked at each other, and Derik's lips twisted. "There's no possibility of keeping it secret anymore," Derik said.

Lai nodded. "Roi's Çeren index is higher than your father's, Xazhar."

Xazhar swayed and would have fallen if Derik hadn't pushed him down into a chair and made him put his head between his knees. "So he's facing possible execution," he whispered when he had recovered enough to lift his head.

"It's the only solution I can come up with," Lai replied.

Timi

It was getting harder and harder for Timi to keep breathing, even with Nik's help. His strength seemed to be flowing away into his ruined joints. He remembered Penny's explanation of tides, that first morning back in Safeport, and seeing how each successive wave seemed to come a little farther up the beach. He felt as if he were being overwhelmed by an incoming tide of nothingness, each wave a little higher and a little harder to resist than the one before.

The only thing he had left to cling to was the fact that Roi had wanted for him to live—wanted it enough to accept the pain he had to be in rather than sleep through whatever it was that they had to do .... His thoughts trailed off as another wave of darkness surged over him. Roi. Somehow he had to keep fighting for Roi. At least he had to hold on long enough to tell Roi how much he regretted ever listening to Zhaim.

"Tack-healed the bad rib all right, so I'm pretty sure I'm ready." Roi's voice?

"Go ahead and initiate contact while I'm getting the glucose drip in you," Nik's voice came through, and then, just as the next wave started to wash over Timi, Roi's mind touched his. It hurt, a little. Timi's mind was raw from Zhaim's forceful invasion. But then he felt Roi's mind shift, aware of his pain and adjusting the contact to ease Timi's discomfort. Tendrils of thought reached for his torn and stretched joints and spine, weaving a net of energy holding his body together, pulling fluids from his lungs, gently reinforcing his faltering heartbeat.

"I've got him," Roi's voice came. "You can start slacking off the tension. Keep it slow, I need to keep pulling him together and Healing in an awful lot of places at once."

Timi could feel Roi's attention jumping from one part of his abused body to another, knitting a blood vessel here, repairing a torn nerve fiber there, returning leaked fluids to their proper places.

"You're doing fine, Timi," Roi's voice came gently. "Just a few more minutes, and I'll have you stabilized and you can get some sleep. Not the muscles and tendons and ligaments; I'll have to work on them later. Only so much I can do at once. But I've got the stuff that was killing you under control, and I'll have the joints all back where they belong by the time we get you unstretched a couple of fingerwidths more. Keep it steady, Nik, that's it. There. Get the straps off and get his arms down by his sides so I can get the shoulders back in place. That's it for now, Timi. Let's kick the girls out of the soaking tub and collapse into it."

Roi's voice and mind-touch alike were exhausted. And so am I, Timi thought. *Somebody had better hold my head above water,* he pushed at Roi, *'cause I sure can't do it myself.*

Neither can I, Roi sent in reply.

Chapter 23

Daylight. Pain lanced through Penny's hands, and she stifled a moan. Daylight meant their tormentor would be there any moment, and she was terrified of catching his attention. Daylight meant seeing Roi, who had fought so hard for all of them, lying helpless and dying in the cage opposite hers.

No, that wasn't right. She had a vague memory of lying in warm water, soothed by gentle hands and a woman's voice, and—yes, what lay under her didn't feel at all like the bars of the cage. More like a bed. Cautiously she cracked one eye open.

Sunlight glowed across the floor. When she managed to roll over, she saw Flame, asleep in an adjacent bed, and beyond Flame, a wide window wall opening onto a blaze of light. As her eyes adjusted, the brilliance resolved itself into a patio with a swimming pool, and a blond girl approaching the window. "Amber?" Penny gulped as the girl slid a panel back and entered the room.

"Oh, good, you're awake," the younger girl said cheerfully. "Hurting? Lyra's in helping Nik with the boys, but she said to call her if you needed anything for the pain. Probably not Suppress; if they gave you that you'd have to stay in bed and they want you moving around to help work out the stiffness from that cage, even if you can't walk until they get those heel tendons taken care of. There was a representative from the Company by earlier, but Lai said you were staying right here until they were sure you'd be all right. They followed the finders and found the horses as soon as Lai told them what happened. Don't worry about anything; you're perfectly safe now, and between Nik and Roi you'll be fine. Oh, they're hunting up float chairs for all of you until your ankles and wrists heal."

311

"We all thought you'd been killed," Penny managed to get in as Amber paused for breath. "Yes, I would like something for pain. My hands hurt." She glanced down at the bandages hiding the remembered damage.

"I'll get Lyra," Amber replied, "and I'll tell you and Flame both all about it when she wakes up again. Nik and Roi are working on Timi, or I'd bring Nik. But I think they can spare Lyra." She slipped out onto the patio, turned left, and disappeared.

Roi was alive! For a moment that was all she was aware of.

Flame yawned and turned her head in the next bed. "I don't think Roi told us everything he knew," she said thoughtfully. "His father was saying something earlier about following Amber's mind to reach us, though I didn't see her until now. But Roi was pretty careful about not letting us know there was a chance she was alive."

"Actually," an unfamiliar voice announced, "he knew that Zhaim could dredge anything you three knew out of your minds if he wanted to, so he didn't dare let you know anything he didn't want Zhaim to know." A tiny, beautiful woman with skin, hair and eyes all the same rich shade of milk chocolate entered the room, carrying a tray with several tubes, boxes and ampoules. "I'm Elyra. Nik said you're to get a shot of this in each forearm, Penny, to numb your hands, and there's some salve for your burns. Flame, I've got a couple of pessaries for you. And Penny, Roi said you are not to worry about those hands. We can fix them so you can use them with conventional surgery, though they'll heal faster and without scarring or residual aches if you let Roi help." She sat down on the edge of Penny's bed and began administering the medications, while Amber sat on Flame's bed and began her story.

No wonder Roi had wanted her to pretend to be Amber, Penny thought. If Zhaim had even suspected that one of Roi's slaves was alive, free, and trying to get help, he would have put all of his energy into tracking her down. Instead, he had assumed the missing person was the guide, and probably thought that even if she survived, she would be blamed for the deaths of her clients. Which was pretty stupid, but she had already come to the conclusion that brilliance did not preclude occasional flashes of incredible stupidity. Look at Roi and the puma, or Zhaim's carelessness with the flyer's key.

And because of the examination of her own thoughts she had gone through in trying to think and act like Amber, she had come to realize something she might not otherwise have admitted to herself. In the terms of her own culture, she was in love with Roi. She kept thinking in spite of herself of the night they had stripped off their soaked clothing and snuggled together for warmth after the thunderstorm. And that led to the memory of his total indifference to her sex. She remembered Flame's comment, the next day. Had Roi really been indifferent, or simply trying to put her at ease? He had seemed just as concerned for her welfare as for Flame's during their brief escape.

Even if Roi loved her as much as she thought she loved him, there was no possible way he could marry her. She knew that. But was there any other way she could be with him? Her family would disown her if she went to him as a concubine. Could she accept that? Would he even want her as a concubine? And what about his obvious relationship with Flame?

"So Zhaim's son Xazhar captured me," Amber was saying, "and I thought everything was all for nothing. Then he took me to Derik instead of his father, and I just about broke down completely. I couldn't have gotten much farther. Nik was amazed I hadn't just collapsed already, the leg was so badly infected. The swelling's down this morning, though, and Roi said he'd give it a Healing session this afternoon and I could probably go swimming by tomorrow. He's concentrating on Timi right now because he's the worst hurt, but he's planning to Heal all of us. I told him to make sure he saved some energy for himself."

Heal? Penny thought. Didn't that require mental contact? She couldn't let Roi into the turmoil of her thoughts as they were now! "I'm not sure I'm ready for that," she said, and saw the real concern in all of the others' faces.

"We'll worry about that later," Elyra said firmly. "But if you want to recover full use of your hands, you're going to need esper Healing, and Roi's the only person we have right now who can do it. Think about it."

Lai
6/4/38

The Inner Council never met formally away from the Inner Council chambers on Central.

But as far as Lai could remember, as far back as records had been kept, they had never had a case of an Inner Council member trying to kill another. And while Roi was not yet a member of the Inner Council, he had that status.

313

So they were all crammed into Kyrie's largest meeting room, grumbling at the lack of interface lounges and—with the exception of Derik—horrified at the very idea of getting rid of Zhaim.

"Are you sure you aren't misinterpreting his actions?" Ramil asked.

"We don't have anyone else who can match him in bioengineering," Colo blustered as he stalked around the room, showing off his magnificent body and tossing his long, carefully curled black hair.

"What will the Human populations say?" Tethya asked, trying to look older than her age, which was even less than Zhaim's. "After all, he's pretty popular with them."

"That we police our own," Derik growled, gripping the arms of his chair. "As for misinterpretation, it's pretty hard to misinterpret what we found in that torture chamber."

"We still can't condemn him without knowing exactly what happened," Kaia said. She shook her chocolate head, so like a scaled-up copy of her niece Elyra's. "Lai, none of us can get through his shields. Could you? So we can read what's really in his mind? Roi's too, I think. Just the memories of the last few weeks."

"I won't force Roi's shields," Lai replied. "I'll ask him to open to you, and most of you have enough truth-sense that you should be able to verify the truth of what he shows you. And give him at least another day to recover, first. But Zhaim .... Yes, I'll force his shields back. But only what's related to what he's tried to do to Roi, and only for this trip. You want him now?" His son, the child he would once have defended with his life. But for Roi's sake and the sake of the Confederation, the child he must now be willing to kill.

"Might as well get it over with," Lunia said, her pale double chin jiggling. "We have to know as much as we can find out about the situation before we can start figuring out how to present our decision to the Outer Council—not to mention the rest of the R'il'noid and Human population." She sounded and looked more resigned than happy.

Lai nodded. "Derik, Kaia, would you get him and bring him up here? He's still under HiControl, so you should be able to handle him."

"Now just a minute, here," Colo snarled. "Those two are his enemies. Who knows what they'll do on the way back here."

"All right, you and Derry go get him," Kaia snapped. "And don't kill each other on the way."

Carima shook her head, a bewildered expression on her hatchet face, as Derik and Colo left the room. "What's happening to us?" she asked. "We never had this kind of rivalry when I was young."

Lai shook his head helplessly. He knew what Marna thought: that the Çeren process was to blame. But over half of those in the room owed their existence to that process. None of them agreed with what Marna—and the Genetics Board—now believed. He wasn't quite sure that he believed it himself, but it did help explain Zhaim. Those who, like Carima, were old enough to remember the desperate days before Çeren had found his solution to the problem of too few R'il'noids being born were now in the minority.

Derik—or more likely Colo—had found a robe to cover Zhaim's nakedness, but Zhaim's expression and the way he kept trying to adjust the set of the shoulders made it clear that he considered it a poor substitute for the elaborate costumes he usually wore. "Well?" he snarled coldly as he stalked into the center of the group.

Lai locked eyes with his son, sliding past the tightly held shields and forcing them open. Zhaim froze physically, his eyes widening with shock. He didn't believe I'd do it, Lai thought as he nodded at the rest of the Council members.

He'd confirmed what Zhaim had done earlier; there was no need to immerse himself in the filth of Zhaim's memories again. Besides, there was one thing in Zhaim's memories he wanted to keep shielded—how to block CP. That had better die with Zhaim. He watched the faces of the others change as they slowly read the same memories that had sickened him. In the end it was Derry and Kaia who escorted Zhaim back to his cell. Colo seemed to have lost all interest in defending Zhaim.

"Does anyone have any doubts left of his guilt?" Carima finally said.

"We still need to check Roi," Colo said. "And he's the one who has to request the death penalty. But the rest of us had better start thinking about how we're going to tell the Outer Council. And the general population."

Roi
6/5/38

"*I'm* the one who has to request the death penalty?" Roi gasped. Reliving what had happened on the trek for the whole Inner Council had been bad enough, though he'd done his best to cooperate. He'd even included his own carelessness with the warnoff, though he didn't think

Zhaim had anything to do with that. But it had never occurred to him that he would be involved in the decision of what to do about Zhaim.

"Under Confederation law, yes," his father replied.

It wasn't that he didn't want Zhaim dead. He wanted that now as much as he'd wanted it when Zhaim had recaptured the group. But killing Zhaim then would have been in hot blood, and in immediate defense of his own life and those of his friends. And it still would have stayed with him, warped him. He remembered all too clearly the first time he had killed in self-defense, and he hadn't even made any choice about that. A brain-stem reaction, Derry had told him when he'd forced Roi to revisit the incident many years after it had happened. Pure self-defense reflex, and nothing he could have done anything about.

Making such a decision consciously, in cold blood ....

"I need to think about this," he gulped.

Xazhar
6/6/38

The adjudicator's villa was built near the crest of the low ridge separating the gently rolling forests inland from the narrow coastal plain occupied by Wilderness City proper. Like most Confederation administrative posts, it was built in the form of a hollow square, with the ground floor providing adjudication rooms for disputes heard in Wilderness City, meeting rooms for official functions, and a few holding cells in the center of the square. One of those cells currently held Zhaim, while the rest of the Inner Council had spent much of the last three days in one of the larger meeting rooms. The raised central courtyard with its heated swimming pool, level with the second floor of the villa, was currently occupied by the guide and one of Roi's slaves. Not really people, of course, just Humans. Intelligent animals. But Xazhar found he did not want to face them.

He sighed and started another circuit of the second-floor balcony that surrounded the building. The ground sloped away in all directions, and he could see low, forested hills reaching eastward to the horizon. The Spine Range was somewhere beyond that horizon, but the roiling snowmelt filling the Wilderness River was the only visible sign of its existence. Xazhar followed the river with his eyes as he came around to the south balcony, turning and walking into the rapidly sinking sun to the west. The river caught the sun like a mirror where it flowed into the ocean, almost blinding him. Perversely, he slitted his eyes and leaned against the western parapet of the balcony, watching the red sun touch the ocean and begin to sink into the endless water. The sun would come up again in the morning, he thought, but for his father there was no direction left but down. He was a little surprised that Zhaim was still alive, but then he couldn't recall ever hearing about a situation like this before. And if the Council was creating a precedent, they would take their time to make sure it was right, no matter how much mental suffering the delay caused his father. The worst thing, he thought, was that he couldn't even defend his father's actions to himself.

The upper rim of the sun floated on the ocean, blinking an unexpected emerald green just before it disappeared. "Hey," Roi's voice came from behind him. "I've heard of that, but I've never seen it before."

Xazhar turned to see Roi beside him, the float chair Nik had found hovering high enough that Roi's eyes were level with his own. "The green flash?" Xazhar asked condescendingly. "Ought to be pretty common at the Enclave."

"The west wing of our building's derelict," Roi replied absently, his eyes dropping to the city below them. "I think I've really watched more sunsets on this trip than I have in the last two years. Maybe in all my life." He paused.

The float chair reminded Xazhar of Roi's first arrival at Tyndall, a smaller, badly frightened child in a smaller float chair, still with a slave's habit of avoiding conflict and even eye contact. *I don't think Father could talk me into thinking he's really a slave if I saw him for the first time now,* Xazhar thought to himself. *He's grown more than physically. Of course there's still that nonsense about thinking of slaves as people ....* Amber's face came into his mind, twisted with fear and defiance as she had struggled to escape him. The distance the injured girl had managed to cover in six and a half days still amazed him, as did her determination to carry news of Roi's plight to someone she could trust. And that emphatically had not included Zhaim's son. But it was hard not to realize that she was a lot more than a clever animal.

"Xazhar," Roi said hesitantly, without looking up from the city below, "tell me. Why should your father live?"

Xazhar glanced across at Roi, startled by the question, then looked toward the city. The first stars were beginning to come out, and the traffic-responsive pavement lighting surrounded the moving surface vehicles and the much more numerous pedestrians with pale gold halos. Why should his father live? Why was Roi even asking such a question?

"He can make people obey him," Xazhar said slowly, thinking out what he was saying. "He misuses it, but it's a valuable ability in an emergency."

"If what he tells people to do is the right thing," Roi agreed. "You've got that, too. I heard about the accident at the Arena. I'm not good at it, and probably never will be. And he's supposed to be a genius at abstract mathematics. What else?"

Xazhar sighed and leaned on the rail. His mental shout at the Arena had been the first time in his life he had done something to help people on instinct, without stopping to analyze how the situation could be turned to his own advantage. And even aside from the change it had made in the attitude of Camy's father, it had been one of the most satisfying things he had ever done. He still could not understand why his father had never mentioned that effect. Could it be that his father just didn't feel that way? His father *had* done other things to help people, though.

"You know that fruit and grain stuff we had for dessert last night?" he said.

"Whitefire rice and fruit torte," Roi agreed, licking his lips at the memory. "One of my favorites. What's that got to do with your father?"

"One of the few things you have to thank him for, then. He was one of the colony sponsors on Whitefire. They knew it would be a high-UV planet, but it turned out to be so high they couldn't grow food. Father's a bioengineer, when he can be bothered. He bioengineered just about everything that grows on Whitefire today. The flavor was serendipity. Some of his early successes tasted really super, and it turned out to be a side effect of the UV resistance. In fact, his plants turned out to need high UV levels—that's why they can only be grown on a few planets. And the flavor's so unique that every one of those planets has a thriving export trade in gourmet foods.

"He's done a lot of that—breeding and engineering plants and food animals to grow on planets where existing types don't thrive. They're not often as successful commercially as the ones he developed for Whitefire, but they feed people that'd starve otherwise. I don't think anybody else is as good at it. I think he's working on something now, for some planet where they can't keep meat animals alive. Only—if father lives, he'll wind up killing you. He's—obsessed, that's the word." More stars were out, now, and the streets of the city below were awash with soft light.

"And if he kills me," Roi said sadly, "he'll wind up having to kill Father, and Marna, and Derry, and probably Kaia .... most of the Inner Council, I suspect. He might have managed to fool them this time, especially if one of the storms had worked. Never again, though."

"No," Lai's voice came from behind them. "As long as he's alive, we'll never believe in an accident to you again. Though he still denies the puma attack, and I think he's telling the truth on that. You're not usually that careless, Roi."

Roi winced visibly. "Penny made that very clear."

"I should hope so," Lai replied. "We're eating in about a quarter hour. Want to join us?"

Roi looked down. "I'd rather eat with my friends by the pool," he said. "Nik ought to be there by now, and maybe Timi and Amber are back from their meeting with the Clan representatives. I've finished Healing both of them, and I've almost convinced Penny to let me try to Heal her." He glanced sideways at Xazhar. "If Xazhar wants to eat with us ...."

Xazhar shook his head hastily. He was getting to like Roi, in some ways, but treating human slaves as equals was too much. "Not if you're going to be Healing," he said hastily. "Bothers me to watch." He turned and headed into the villa.

Roi

"Roi, you can't keep evading the problem like this," Lai said after Xazhar had left. "We have to destroy Zhaim; he's too big a risk to the whole future of the Confederation."

"Then do it and get it over with!" Roi snapped back. "Just leave me out of it!"

"We can't," Lai replied. "He didn't actually kill you, though our group examination of his memories and yours makes it clear enough he intended to. Since you survived, you as the victim have to request the death penalty. Roi, do you want him alive and a constant threat? Not just to you, but to anyone else he feels threatened by?"

"Including you and Marna," Roi agreed. "No, I do want him dead. That's why I can't ask for his death, don't you understand that?" He was sweating, even more frightened by his father's demands than he could remember being in Zhaim's hands. It wasn't his body that was at risk this time; it was what made him himself. If only he could talk to Marna! She would understand; she'd taught him the Healers' Code. *Never make a decision for death of another in the presence of negative emotions,* she'd told him. *If you hate or even dislike a patient, if you benefit in any way from that person's death, leave the decision to another.* And he'd gone way beyond dislike, in Zhaim's case.

But was that true when more than his own safety might be at stake? How to balance the slaves who would die at Zhaim's hands if he lived against the lives rescued from famine? And what of the lives he himself could save, as a Healer? If he asked for Zhaim's death, wanting it as he did, could he ever again trust his judgment enough to Heal? Could he even keep himself from becoming another Zhaim? Wasn't there any other way to control the R'il'noid?

"Roi," his father repeated, and Roi felt the same rage that had overcome him when he had grappled with Zhaim.

"You think you're going to get rid of Zhaim that way?" he spat out. "You push me into agreeing and you'll have another Zhaim—me! You're asking me to deny the part of me that keeps me from being like that, and if I once step over that line I'm not sure I can ever get back. And I won't do that. I'll die before I turn into another Zhaim! Hells, I'd be worse than Zhaim. I've got the Healing talent to misuse!"

Lai stepped back, his face startled. "You?" he asked. "Roi, that's ridiculous. You're not at all like Zhaim!"

"You weren't in my mind when I jumped him," Roi blazed back, and thrust the memory at his father. He watched Lai's expression change as he absorbed the impact of Roi's emotions.

"Self defense. Of course you were furious at him," Lai said, but it was obvious to Roi that he was no longer nearly as sure of himself as he had been a moment before. Roi turned the float chair away, still shaking.

Lai sighed and put his hand on the back of the chair, nudging it toward the passage into the courtyard. "I wish you'd take the time to finish Healing those cut tendons," he said.

"They're tack-healed," Roi replied. "I've still got to finish Flame's, too, though I finished with Timi and Amber before they left this morning. I just wish Penny would let me work on her. And I couldn't manage more than two or three hours a day Healing even if I weren't having to spend so much time on what to do about Zhaim."

They came out of the passageway into the enclosed courtyard. The pool glowed softly, and other lights washed discreetly across the paved patio and a table with hot and cold foods laid out ready to eat. Timi and Amber were there, loading plates. Roi felt his father's hand grasp his shoulder in a gentle squeeze. "Eat, before you try to do any more Healing," Lai said. "And—Roi, would it help if you talked to Marna?"

"Yes, but I don't want to drag her away from that epidemic," Roi replied, and suddenly remembered that his father, too, had been dealing with an emergency situation. "Father, I just thought—what about Kablukolelli?"

Lai chuckled. "Guess I shocked them into reexamining their own arguments when I took off," he replied. "I'll check on them when this mess with Zhaim has been taken care of, but this morning's report says they're really talking to each other for the first time in years. There's still going to be a lot of prejudice on an individual basis, but I think the higher-ups are starting to think a little straighter. Roi, I'll contact Marna sometime before tomorrow morning—I'll have to figure what time it is there—and if the epidemic's still got her stumped, I'll at least arrange a three-way mindlink. Now get some food into yourself." He turned and left.

"It's roast baby peccary," Amber said with an oddly brittle happiness in her voice, "and I'm going to make up for the one I didn't get 'cause its mother showed up. And we finally talked Penny into letting you try to Heal her hands, so you'd better eat plenty. Flame and I will take turns feeding her tonight, and maybe you can Heal her enough that she can use her hands to feed herself by tomorrow."

Roi smiled sympathetically at Penny. "I know how it feels," he said. "Took me over a year before I could pick up a set of eating tongs." He looked around at the group as he loaded his plate.

He hadn't bothered to Heal bruises and scrapes, concentrating instead on those injuries that would have crippled or scarred. Flame's facial brands were barely visible, but the poorly pigmented skins of all three girls were patterned with hues from dull yellow-brown to still-vivid purple and green. He and Timi would probably look even worse if it weren't for their darker skins. Flame and Penny were still confined to float chairs, as was Roi himself. Penny had so far resisted his offer to Heal her, and her angry burns and bandaged hands made it difficult to believe that Flame had been in even worse physical condition a few days earlier. Roi hoped that Amber was right about the guide being ready to let him try to help her. He liked her far too well to want to see her left scarred or crippled.

At least he could manage the Healing. The problem of what to do about Zhaim was more difficult, and one on which he knew everyone's advice would go against his instincts. He hoped Marna would be in touch soon.

Eversummer: Marna

Acting First Anden fairly danced into the laboratory, relief written all over his face. Marna turned the isolation suit to face him and raised her eyebrows. "Aren't you going to ask me how many new cases?" he asked excitedly.

"Down from yesterday, obviously," she chuckled. "Under—oh, five hundred?"

"One hundred and thirty-seven!" he proclaimed, swinging his arms wide with such exuberance that Marna hastily locked telekinetic braces on every piece of equipment in his vicinity. "Only a hundred thirty-seven new cases, and over half of them early enough they're treatable!" Tears were running into the corners of his smile.

"I take it everyone's boiling their water now, especially since the early warning system is in?"

"Oh, yes, yes, the new cases were mostly people drinking water from streams with filter cups, or those who couldn't afford the energy to boil their water. We're working on a distribution system for boiled water for drinking now, but it can't be done all at once. We're testing three different methods of mass-treating the water supply to destroy the toxin, and two of them look promising, oh, very promising. My Lady, you've saved our world. If there is anything, anything at all, that we can do for you, please, please, just ask."

At the moment, Marna thought, all I want is to get out of this isolation suit. Only I promised Lai I wouldn't. Ah, well. I can go home soon, now. Aloud, she said, "But it's been a fascinating problem. I don't believe I've ever run into a situation before where a microorganism caused an epidemic because it became ill itself. And the real credit goes to my young stepson, Roi. He's the one who noticed that so many of the survivors drank beer rather than water, and pointed out that a water-borne toxin might not still be in the water by the time the symptoms appeared." A sudden thought struck her, and she added, "Your water treatments don't include that idea of adding alcohol, do they?"

Anden actually laughed, the first time, she suspected, since he had lost his family. "We did consider it, M'Lady. We could have evaporated the alcohol and recovered it. But the energetics were almost as bad as boiling the water before we distributed it, and we had to rule that out early. Just too costly. Anyway, who wants to bathe in the equivalent of stale beer?"

Marna grimaced. She'd spent the last two nights in the isolation suit, and even a bath in beer sounded good at the moment. "Well, have your techs let me know what the treatments are. I've put together a report on the causes I'll leave with you, and I think I'll be heading back home as soon as I get caught up on my sleep. There are some references in the Big'Un I want to check out."

Anden bowed and started to back out. "Of course, Milady. As I said, let us know what we can do for you."

"Wait," she said abruptly as something tickled at her mind. *Lai?*

Yes. How's the situation there? He was boosting, but she thought not from the Enclave generator.

Better than I'd dared hope. I'm getting ready to go back to the courier and sleep for a couple of days.

Any chance you could come straight back here? Derry and I can help you with the jump.

Lai, what's wrong?

Roi. Zhaim found a way to block him and us from picking up normal precognitive warnings about his safety, and then almost killed him. Steady, love, he's all right. A little the worse for the experience, but nothing he can't Heal. But I think he needs to talk to you. Calm down, I said. You'll need to find an energy source at your end.

Ten minutes, she told him, and broke the link. "Anden, I need to get back home. Now. Have you a power source I can use for a direct teleport?"

Falaron: Roi

Roi lay on his back in the heated pool, watching the stars. He couldn't really swim, yet; his ankles wouldn't take the strain of kicking. But he was too tense from his session with Penny to sleep, and floating on his back, the patio lights dimmed, was a comfortable way to watch the stars. He heard Nik shift position on the poolside lounge, and glanced briefly at the physician before looking back at the sky.

The half moon was declining into the west, almost hidden by the wall behind him and leaving the sky to the stars. He found the Dolphin easily enough, though its eye seemed a little out of place. And the Sailboat was missing the bright star that topped its mast. He felt suddenly sheepish—of course that particular star was missing. It was Falaron's sun. On the whole, though, ten light years didn't change the familiar constellations much.

Healing Penny's hands—or more accurately starting the job—had been both easier and harder than he had anticipated. Easier, because Penny had been cooperating with him so much better than he had dared hope. Harder, because she had no idea whatsoever of how to shield. He'd taught his friends that, first thing. Not that any of them could have resisted a hard probe from Zhaim, or from Roi himself, for that matter. But they knew how to keep from shoving their private thoughts into Roi's mind.

Penny's thoughts had been impossible for him to tune out as he worked, and all too many of those thoughts had been fantasies involving Roi. He considered teaching her a basic shield technique before their next Healing session, but it wouldn't change what he had picked up today. And he wasn't sure that was right for her.

"Roi?"

Marna! He whirled toward her, choking and sputtering as his instinctive move sent his head underwater.

Marna

Marna's first reaction on arriving had been to question Lai. "You are asking him to make the final decision for Zhaim's death?" she had asked, shocked, once she had understood what had happened.

"Under Confederation law, he's the only one who can," he'd replied. "And he won't. Says it would turn him into another Zhaim."

"And you haven't considered that he may know himself better than you know him? Lai, I will talk with him. But if I think there is even a chance he is right, I will not ask him to do this. What you are asking would be hard for any empath with his ability, even an adult. At his age .... I think he may be right in refusing."

***

Marna watched Roi for a minute or two before she spoke his name. Thinner than she remembered, and vulnerable in a way she did not remember seeing him before. He must have been deep in some private thought, for her first words very obviously startled him.

"It's all right, son of my heart," she said gently, once he was holding the side of the pool and breathing easily again. "Your father told me what they'd been trying to do to you, and I told him why he was wrong. We'll find some other way to protect you."

"Marna, you didn't abandon a plague planet just to help me, did you?" Roi asked. "I mean, I'm awfully glad to see you—I don't have the words to say how glad—but I don't want people dying for me."

"I'm an empath, too, Roi. I know what you're feeling, remember? No, the plague is under control, and there's nothing I could do there I can't do better on Central. Not that I wouldn't have come anyway, love."

"So was it the water?" Roi asked as he levitated himself out of the pool. The night air was chill, and he grabbed a hooded towel on the way to the float chair. "Anything to do with the beer bellies? Come on, Marna, tell me. And I bet Nik would like to know, too."

"All right, but then you tell me what happened here," she replied. "Yes, it was in the water. But I'll have to start with the Eversummer ecology." Nik joined them, eyebrows raised.

Roi listened, wide-eyed, as she told them of how she had unraveled the causes of the epidemic.

"How did the early settlers survive?" Roi asked, snuggling deeper into the towel.

"The pseudo-diatoms are fair sized," Marna replied, "large enough that a pile of their shells feels gritty, and quite big enough that the intact organisms can be filtered out of the water supply, and that's what the colonists did. And some pretty strong cultural taboos developed against eating the native plants and animals—though I'm not sure that was necessary as far as land plants are concerned. I'm pretty certain now that the imported food animals died from ingesting the pseudos in the water, not the native vegetation."

"Your pseudos wouldn't be in a land plant food chain," Roi agreed. "Probably a good idea to make sure the higher plants don't have similar toxins, though."

Marna nodded and continued. "Sometime fairly recently, probably this year or even in the last month or so, a virus began killing off the pseudo-diatoms. It spread fastest in blooms, of course, and I suspect it was carried between watersheds on the furry feet of the local bird-equivalent. And when it killed its victims, their cell walls disintegrated, and the toxin flooded into the water in soluble form."

"And the filters wouldn't catch the dissolved toxin, of course," Roi said.

Marna nodded. "And the water purification system relied entirely on filtration. The toxin would clear out of the system before any symptoms appeared, since exposure to atmospheric oxygen destroys it within days. A major bloom somewhere upstream, virtually complete mortality of the affected pseudo-diatoms within two days, and a surge of toxin moving downstream. It would be past and the water pure again by the time people started showing overt symptoms."

"So it wasn't still in the water by the time anyone tested it," Roi said. "What did you do once you figured out it might have been there earlier?"

Marna grinned at him. "You figured that out, remember? I knew what the toxin was, and that boiling would destroy it. I talked the planetary administrator into urging people to boil their drinking water. The next major city to be hit, nobody who was following instructions got sick. When word on that got around, everybody started boiling their drinking water, and by then we had a usable test for the toxin. The new case rate was under two hundred this morning—and we know the toxin hit the water supply in the capital city four days ago. Two weeks ago, they would have had close to a quarter of a million victims."

"You really do have it under control, then," Nik commented.

"Yes. I didn't isolate the virus that was affecting the pseudo-diatoms until early this morning, though, and I still need to confirm the pseudos' place in the local ecology. They'll undoubtedly evolve resistant strains, in time. Right now, though, the disease is likely to send a major shock through the native food chains. There are already reports of massive dieoffs of water dwellers, with all the signs of mass starvation."

"So my beer belly observation really helped," Roi said wonderingly. "I thought it was stupid, but you said anything that struck me, and that did." He grinned at her, lopsidedly because of a swollen lip.

"If it had taken me another two days to spot the things you noticed," she told him, "and I think that may be optimistic, probably another fifty to a hundred thousand people would have died. That's why your safety is so important, Roi. Not only because your father and I love you, but because you have the potential to help so many other people. Now, how about telling me what Zhaim did to you."

He looked at her, sadly, and in the light from the pool she saw that his cheek and jaw were scored, swollen and bruised. Evidently he'd been Healing everyone except himself. "That's the same argument they use to justify letting R'il'noids kill people if they feel like it," he told her. "Like Zhaim. From what Xazhar told me, his bioengineering talents have saved a lot of lives—probably more than the number of people he's killed. But it's not right, Marna. I don't care how many lives Zhaim's saved; it doesn't give him the right to do what he does to his slaves, never mind what he did to us."

"What did he do?" Marna repeated patiently.

She watched his face and hands as he spoke, seeing his stress even as she felt his emotional reaction to what had happened. "He didn't really do much to me physically," he told her as she reached out to monitor his physical condition. "Just lost his temper that once, and crippled me enough I couldn't make a second try at escaping. Timi's the one he almost killed, and the two girls were in pretty bad shape, too. Marna, what scares me most is that he has me thinking and feeling like he does. I want revenge. That's why I can't go along with Father and ask for his death. I'd never be able to trust my own judgment on life or death decisions again. But is there any other way I'll ever be safe from him?" He broke off to cough, and Marna repeated her monitoring, concentrating this time on throat and lungs.

"He's still got a cold," Nik's voice startled her. "He's a lot better, but not well enough yet to sit out here on a rapidly cooling evening after a swim, even a swim in a warm pool."

"Agreed," Marna said promptly. "Your room, Roi? I'm sharing with your father."

"Nik and Timi are with me," Roi replied as they moved back into the warmth of his room, "and the girls have the next room. Kyrie isn't really set up to have the whole Inner Council as guests." He looked rueful. "I'd rather have the girls with me, too, but Penny wouldn't have been comfortable with me or Timi, and I was afraid she'd have nightmares totally by herself. Marna, could you possibly take over her Healing? I think I'm going to have problems. Not technical, but she doesn't know how to shield, and she—uh—thinks she's in love with me." Under the pigmentation and the bruises, his face was red.

"And it's mutual?" Marna said, amused. "I'll consider the Healing. But you're going to have to be the one to resolve the personal situation. However much you like her, remember she's from a monogamous culture. She may not be able to share you with Flame. Sure you're not having nightmares?"

"Derik 'ported Smoky over to sleep on the bed," Roi replied, "and that helps. Snowflake took care of me the first night, but then Penny started having nightmares, so I sent Snowflake over to her. Marna, isn't there any way to keep us safe from Zhaim without killing him?"

Zhaim's your problem, Marna, a familiar voice whispered in the back of her mind. She groaned inwardly. Win had told her that, at the same time he'd urged her to accompany Lai to her new home on Central. She'd tried her best to forget that portion of his advice, telling herself repeatedly that there was nothing she could do for someone as old and as hardened in cruelty as Zhaim.

Roi had turned his chair around and was staring at her round-eyed. "Marna," he asked tentatively, "who was that?"

Who was that. As if Roi had been as aware of the comment as she was. *Well?* Win's voice prompted. *Aren't you going to introduce us?*

"You heard him?" she asked, and watched his hesitant nod. "A ghost," she told him. "My guardian angel. A persona adopted by my subconscious. I don't know, Roi. He told me I'd have you as a son, long before Lai came anywhere near Riya."

"Whose ghost?" the boy asked.

Her knees were shaking, and she sat down on the edge of Roi's bed. "Win. He was a Healer who died in the epidemic on Riya, two centuries ago. We were lovers, planning a child, when the plague came. I was on an isolation satellite; he was in the thick of the epidemic. When the life support system on the satellite broke down, long after everyone on the planet died, and I was waiting to die there, I started hearing his voice now and then. Never to my harm, but I've never been sure he wasn't my own imagination. I was so lonely by then."

"Does it matter what he is, then, if you trust him?" Roi asked. "And what did he mean? How could Zhaim be your problem?"

"All I can think of is the technique used to build an artificial conscience for a child born without empathy," she replied. "I thought of it when I first met Zhaim, but only in terms of what a pity it was that someone hadn't given him the therapy he needed when he was a baby. I know the technique in theory, but I've never actually done it, and I have no idea if it would work on a resisting adult."

I have, Win said. *It was my specialty, remember? It will work if he doesn't actually fight you, though it should probably be reinforced every quarter century or so. I'll guide you.*

Marna shuddered, appalled by the thought of actually working within Zhaim's mind. *He deserves to die,* she started to think, and then pulled herself up short as her Healer training asserted itself. Nobody deserved to die, not in that sense. Deserved the right to die, when all other hope was gone, yes. And Roi deserved protection from a brother who had shown he would kill the younger boy, and revel in doing it. If killing Zhaim was the only way to protect Roi, then the killing would be justified, but that was balancing a lesser against a greater wrong. Expediency, and to be greatly regretted, but not a deserved punishment. Especially not if there were an alternative, and if she trusted Win, there was an alternative.

If Zhaim didn't fight her. Would he, if it were a choice of submitting to her therapy or death? She looked again at Roi, who was shivering in his damp towel. "Get yourself ready for bed," she told him. "I need to think this out."

By the time Roi had levitated himself into the bed and she had tucked the covers around his bruised body, Marna had decided that Zhaim should be given a choice. He could submit to her therapy and be given an artificial conscience—and incidentally required to do the necessary bioengineering for Eversummer—or he could choose death.

"Roi," she said thoughtfully, "do you think you could act as if you were going to demand not only that Zhaim be killed, but that he be killed as he would have killed you and your friends?"

Smoky slid through the door and jumped up on the bed, nuzzling the boy's face, and Roi wrapped an arm around the dog's neck. "Scare him?" he said. "You're going to try to frighten him into letting you cure him? I'm not sure I could keep it at the pretending level, Marna."

Marna nodded, thinking. She would have to tell Lai, she decided. How many of the rest of the Council? Then she turned back to Roi. "I was going to finish Healing you tonight," she said, "but I think the more bedraggled you look tomorrow, the better. Do you mind?"

"Take care of this blasted head cold, will you?" he replied. "It's the one thing I can't really blame on Zhaim, and I haven't figured out how to handle it, and I'm never going to laugh at a Human with a cold again."

Roi

Timi and Amber walked into the room, hand in hand, a few minutes after Marna left. They looked almost frightened, Roi thought as he sat up, and wondered what news they had received from the Clan. Well, he'd give them his news first. "Company rep was here this morning after you two left," he said. "She said Zhaim's interference was way outside the parameters for a Challenge, so we can pick up the trail again at the horse corral on top of the canyon wall. They're giving us credit for the climb we hadn't quite finished, and the rest is basically trail riding and camping out. Father wasn't exactly happy, but Uncle Derry got him to agree."

Amber looked down, and Timi took a deep breath. "Not us," he said, without quite looking at Roi.

"The horses? But Timi, what's left is canoes and horses both. You don't have to ride at all if you don't want to."

Timi swallowed hard as he looked up at Roi. "It's not that, Roi," he said. "I, well, it turned out I do have relatives alive with the Clan, including an uncle I met today. He, he wants me to apprentice on his ship. And, well, slavery isn't legal on Falaron. I'm going with him, Roi, and so's Amber."

"Timi, if you want your freedom, here or Central, I'll give it to you—you don't have to grab it now just because Falaron doesn't recognize slavery. And remember what Filomako said about the advantages of rejoining the Clan with Academy training? And about Amber—do you really want to bring her into a situation where she may not be accepted or given a chance to become what she can be? You don't have to go back on the trail if you don't want to, Timi, but do think twice about taking off now. Stay with me until you've graduated, at least."

Amber lifted her head, her eyes meeting Roi's squarely. "Going with him is my choice, Roi," she said. "Don't try to use my future to influence him. Please."

Timi broke in almost before Amber had finished speaking. "I can't stay with you, Roi. Not after what I did to you."

"Zhaim, not you, Timi," Roi replied. His precognitive sense was back to normal strength, and every future he could see for Timi was bleak if the boy went back to the Clan now. But the futures he foresaw if he insisted that Timi stay with him for even a few more years were worse. "Not you," he repeated as he swung his legs over the side of the bed. "Zhaim's got incredible power, Timi. There's no way any pure Human could stand against him once he'd decided to take them over. I don't blame you for what happened on the trip. Even Father doesn't. I'm the one who's to blame, for not contacting him or Marna as soon as I realized someone was trying to kill me. Timi, there is no way you're responsible for the fact that Zhaim used your body."

"I'd blame me, every time I saw your face," Timi replied. "And I think you're wrong about Zhaim's being able to do what he did. Oh, not that I'd have been able to do anything if he'd tried to take me over, but I think you'd have picked it up if he'd done it by brute force. I let him in, little by little, and there were times I was all for him and hated you for having everything. I think he used those feelings to take me over so gradually I didn't know it was happening. God, I cooperated with him—of my own will—on keeping that 'good luck charm' of his hidden."

"And I knew you had something of the sort as soon as he used it to sabotage the glider," Roi replied, "and I was the one who chose not to tell anyone back on Central."

"To protect me," Timi replied, "and that gave Zhaim another chance at using me against you. Roi, I don't for a minute think you'd ever blame me, but I'd never feel right living with you again." He was blinking as he spoke, his eyes brimming, and as Roi watched, a tear trickled down one cheek—Timi, who'd had all of the tears beaten out of him long ago, whose eyes had stayed dry even in Zhaim's hands, crying.

Roi squeezed his own eyes shut and reached forward for the possible futures, trying to find something, anything that he could do here and now to help Timi. Nothing that would give a better future than giving Timi his freedom, now. Amber? She had never been able to accept Roi's near-immortality, and he had long ago realized that she would leave him, probably choosing to stay with Timi. But moving into a society where she would be shunned for nothing more important than the color of her skin and hair? With none of the training that might give her some value in the Clan's eyes? Roi opened his eyes and felt tears trickling down his own cheeks. "Amber," he started, but she broke in before he could say anything else.

"I told you, don't try to use me to influence Timi!"

"I'm not," Roi choked out. "I just wanted to ask you, for my sake, to get that space medicine training you were planning on, so I'll at least know you have an ability the Clan should prize. It doesn't have to be on Central, if you don't want that. If it turns out to be an expense you can't handle, let me know and I'll help. God knows you've earned that, by saving all of our lives. Both of you, really. There were times enough I'd have gone totally around the bend without Timi—without all of you—to keep me sane. Please, leave if you must, but let me know how you're doing."

"I'll do that," Amber said, blinking back tears even as a ghost of a smile touched her face. "Poor Flame, getting stuck with you all by herself. You know, Penny would stay with you, if you asked her. And Flame thinks you should."

"I know," Roi said bleakly, and forced a smile to his face. "How much longer can you two stay? And can I meet this uncle of yours, Timi? Just to make sure he really cares about you?"

For the first time since he'd entered the room, Timi managed a smile. "He'd like to meet you, too," he replied. "Day after tomorrow all right? He'll come out here if that's what you'd prefer, or we can all go down to the Clan trade depot. His ship leaves in about a week, and I've got some training to get in before we lift off. Uh—you'll tell me if you pick up anything wrong, won't you?"

"You bet," Roi assured him. "See you tomorrow, then, after we're through with Zhaim?"

Timi's face relaxed into a more natural grin. "Right," he replied, as he and Amber linked hands and turned toward the moonlit patio. Looking for a place more private than they could find in the shared rooms, Roi thought. He wished them luck, thinking that they'd need it, given the crowded state of the Adjudicator's residence.

He slid back under the covers and stopped fighting his tears. Damn Zhaim. Wasn't what Zhaim had done to them physically enough? Now he'd lost two of the few people he had treasured as friends. And he would hold Zhaim's life in his hands, tomorrow.

Could he condemn Zhaim, without making himself into someone who would also condemn Timi?

It took him a long time to get to sleep that night.

Chapter 24

Roi
6/17/38

Timi and Amber had left early, and Nik was conferring with his colleagues in town. The pool that kept drawing Roi's eyes was empty under a gray sky, as was the rest of the patio. "You understand what to do?" Marna asked.

Roi sighed. He'd spent over an hour before Marna arrived this morning using all the conditional precognition he'd learned as far into the future as he could reach, concentrating on the welfare of the Confederation. He knew what he wanted—Zhaim dead. But every combination of variables he'd run confirmed that such a choice on his part would have disastrous long-range effects. He thought he knew why. If he chose death for Zhaim, when there was another way of stopping him, the decision would make him another Zhaim.

Doing what Marna and Lai wanted—trying to scare Zhaim into accepting Marna's therapy—gave much better results, though there was something in the far future that bothered him. That didn't matter, he told himself. If he made the decision to end Zhaim's life, the Confederation—at least in any form he could live with—wouldn't last that long.

"Act like I'm eager for Zhaim's death," he replied. "Even argue a bit with you. Like I don't believe you can really do it."

"And I'm going to sound pretty doubtful, too," Lai said. "I'll check him out when you're through. Though I'll be watching pretty closely while you work, as well as holding his shields open."

Marna nodded. "Roi, I'll want you watching what I do, too. If anything ever happens to me, you're going to have to be the one to reinforce Zhaim's bonds every quarter-century. Oh, don't look so doubtful. You'll be able to do it by then, with the Council backing you."

"Just don't let it be obvious that you're acting," Lai said.

Acting? The only acting he'd be doing was when he had to agree to let Marna try to cure Zhaim. "That law's stupid," he muttered. "I don't want to be the one to decide."

"It needs changing when the victim's as young as you are," Lai agreed, "but we're stuck with it this time. Come on. Let's get to the adjudication chamber."

Roi followed his father and Marna into the same room where he'd shared his memories with the Council members. The others were still trickling in, and he halted his float chair facing the window wall, observing the storm over the city and the ocean beyond it. Only when Marna touched his arm did he turn his back to the window.

Kyrie didn't have enough interface lounges for all of the Council members, so several were in rather uncomfortable-looking straight chairs, arranged in a rough semicircle, with a single empty chair at its center. Only Marna and Lai had interface lounges, with Roi's float chair crammed between them. "He's been notified?" Derik asked.

"Yes, but he's not responding. I'll get him," Lai said, and then vanished.

Roi swallowed hard. He hadn't seen Zhaim since his rescue, and while the force field he perceived around the chair was reassuring, it wasn't reassuring enough. I don't need to worry about him, he told himself. I just need to keep myself under control. His eyes, like those of every other person in the room, were fixed on the door through which Lai would bring Zhaim.

Zhaim

There was nothing intrinsically unpleasant about the cell, aside from the fact that Zhaim couldn't get out of it. It was small—four steps one way by three the other, with a ceiling he estimated would have been around two and a half steps high, if he could walk up the wall. What he wanted was to walk through the wall. The cell was beginning to make him claustrophobic.

What were they thinking of, to treat him like this? It had been bad enough to awaken tied to a chair in his own hunting lodge, mentally deaf, blind, dumb and paralyzed. When he had tried to point out that they could not do this to him, his father had gagged him. The R'il'nian must be getting senile, he thought angrily. Time and past time that the

Confederation was taken over by someone with the strength and will to rule properly. He jumped up from his seat on the simple box bed and began again to pace the floor.

Pastel patterns swirled across the softly glowing ceiling and walls as he paced. If he lay quietly on the bed, he knew, the walls would darken to slow washes of deep blues and greens, as if he lay deep in an ocean current. He stopped short, snarling at the pastel prettiness around him. Couldn't the fools see he'd been working for the good of the Confederation in trying to eliminate that weakling bastard?

No possible weapon had been left him. The bunk was in a warm corner, but had no coverings. His body was bare, bruises still faintly visible against the bronze skin where the young devil had attacked him. His food came on a piece of bread, to be eaten with his fingers, and the washing and sanitary facilities were molded into the wall and floor. No pickups were apparent in the walls or ceiling, but he had no doubt they were present. And unable to levitate, he could not reach the ceiling to check more closely.

He had been taken from the cell—taken, not released—just once, to find himself facing the rest of the Inner Council. Not only had they questioned him verbally, they had dug into his mind about his treatment of Roi, his father forcing his shields open as if he were a common criminal. Even his half-sister Tethya had acted as if he were something unclean. He had thought she was as remorselessly logical as he was himself. It seemed not.

He wasn't sure how long ago that had been. He had always relied on his sun perception to determine time, and with that blocked, and the lighting responding only to his own activity, he had no idea how long he had been in the cell. They couldn't do this to him, to the Lord Zhaim, to the rightful heir in power to a senile father. Lai must not be followed by a weakling. He had tried to do them a favor, and they were acting as if he had committed a crime. He glared at the wall, which at the moment resembled a waterfall, stalked to the bed and threw himself on it, face down.

He never knew how long he lay there. The lighting dimmed, and he might have slept a little. Certainly a voice spoke out of the air, but he refused to acknowledge it, lying immobile on the bed. He would not allow them to treat him as some worthless slave. He refused to move even when the door opened behind him.

"We could, of course, stick you in a cocoon and float you to the meeting," Lai's voice said. "Or you can walk in under your own power. It's up to you." Something broad and soft struck his hips and the back of his thighs, and he turned to see silver gray leggings and a tunic of the same color lying across his body. Seething, he stood and pulled on the obscenely plain garments, settling them into place as well as he could. He would not bear the humiliation of facing the Council nude.

***

All Zhaim saw at first, when he stalked into the meeting room, were the eighteen faces turned toward him. Hostile faces, all of them. Marna's face closed, angry. Roi's with a smoldering hatred that somehow shocked Zhaim—he hadn't thought the bastard had the guts to hate like that. He broke his own gaze away from those accusing eyes, looking out through the window walls at the storm over the ocean, and for the first time he really believed that they might try to kill him.

Kill him. As often and as casually as he had dealt out death, he had never thought that his own life might end, much less that the other Councilors would ever consider killing him. And drugged as he was, there was nothing he could do to protect himself. Surely they wouldn't kill him without even an opportunity to defend himself. He wasn't a mere Human slave!

He was led to a chair near the center of the room, and a force field closed around him before he could realize what they were doing. He froze, staring at Roi and Marna, sitting between him and the freedom of the ocean beyond. Roi's upper lip lifted a little, and his eyes never left Zhaim's face.

"We all know the facts at this point," Lai said abruptly as he sat by Roi. "Zhaim captured Roi and his party, terrorized Roi through torturing his slaves and the tour guide, and beat Roi himself severely enough that he was still suffering from a mild concussion and broken bones two days later. He had made plans to dispose of Roi's body, and had previously tried to destroy the party or at least kill Roi four times—three times by illegal tampering with the weather and once by sabotage of Roi's hang glider. He clearly intended to recover his old place as my heir by murdering the new heir. If he had succeeded, we would not even be discussing whether he should die; he would already have been executed.

"Roi must be protected. The only question I have is whether this is even possible without Zhaim's death."

"That brat's no fit heir," Zhaim said, outraged even in his fear.

"You're no fit heir," Derik shot back at him. "Does that give me the right to murder you, and take back my old position? Not that I wanted it back. The Çeren index is flawed; we all know that. But it provides an objective measurement that was designed to avoid exactly this situation, and as far as you and Roi are concerned, it ranks you rightly. Do even you want to see this Council degenerate into rivalries and assassination?"

Derik, murder him? For an instant he almost saw the parallel, but he managed to pull away from it. He was Zhaim, not some slave-bred brat!

"He ought to feel what Timi and Flame and Penny felt," Roi said thickly, his face distorted with anger, and Zhaim saw Marna turn quickly, almost as if to correct the boy, and then deliberately stop herself. He glanced around the rest of the circle, dry-mouthed. Was everyone against him? He looked back at Marna, who seemed to be the only person in the room not willing his death.

"My Lady," he pleaded, "surely you cannot be a party to this."

"I will not sacrifice Roi for you," she told him coldly, "though I had hoped you could do something to help with the situation on Eversummer. There's a toxic microorganism, a kind of poisonous diatom, widespread in surface waters on Eversummer. I'm sure now it's what killed off the livestock imported by the original colonists, and left the settlers without local animal protein. I had hoped you might be able to engineer stock that would excrete or neutralize the poison instead of dying or storing it in their bodies like the local animals. But it's not worth the risk to Roi."

Zhaim's stomach clenched. If she ever realized what he had already done .... And why hadn't the possibility of tackling the problem at the other end occurred to him?

"Didn't you say something once about some kind of artificial conscience treatment that was used on Riya?" Lai asked. "If that would work ...."

Marna frowned. "That technique was developed for use with children, and it depended on their full cooperation. Applying it to a resisting adult would be impossible. And I wouldn't trust it long range—even if it would work, it would have to be repeated regularly."

Zhaim looked at the hostile faces around him, and saw death in every pair of eyes. "I wouldn't resist, My Lady," he pleaded. Humans might have to live with the constant knowledge that death would someday put an end to their existence, but he had always known that he would live forever. No matter what this artificial conscience meant, it was preferable to dying.

"If the rest of us held his shields open, it might be worth trying," Kaia said grudgingly. "He didn't actually succeed in killing Roi, after all. And we can always execute him if it can't be done. Lady Marna, can you be sure whether he's under proper control, if you're willing to try?"

"I'd know if it succeeded, yes," Marna replied. "Though I'd still want to recheck him every quarter century or so. I hate the thought of touching his mind, but if you really want me to try ...."

Zhaim forced himself to relax mentally as his father's mind reached into his, forcing his shields back and holding them there. Only the naked hostility in the faces surrounding him, and the knowledge that it was this or death, kept him from struggling, especially as he saw Marna turn to Roi and take the boy's hand. "Follow and watch," she said. "You need to learn this."

Zhaim closed his eyes, mind and body rigid with his effort to relax. He was aware of a feather-brush against his mind, then an unexpectedly soothing touch deep within himself. Was this what was meant by the Healer's touch? he wondered.

Roi

Roi gulped and tried to follow Marna. He'd never actually gone into Zhaim's mind before. At most, he had tried to manipulate his brother's emotions, blunting any thought that the guide might have survived, and steering his sexual assaults from Penny to Flame. Reading the memories of some of the things Zhaim had done sickened him.

He's done some decent things, he reminded himself. Like the bioengineering. Didn't Xazhar mention some project he was working on? Can I find that? Maybe help Marna see it?

Zhaim

Marna's touch moved on, probing deep into his very soul as he fought for control. This was far deeper than the Council had probed before. And then it touched his memory of how he had lured Marna herself off planet, by releasing the bioengineered virus on Eversummer.

Her rage blossomed in his mind, followed moments later by Lai's as he discovered what Zhaim had done in the Kablukolelli cluster, and Zhaim knew he was looking his own death in the face. He lay, shaking and whimpering in fear, while Marna and Lai tore every scrap of what he had done from his mind. He wasn't normally sensitive to emotions, but Marna's fury was impossible to ignore.

Then, for no reason at all a third mind, one he had hardly felt, exploded into white-hot fury—a fury that spread first to his father, and then to the Riyan woman. He was going to die.

And he didn't even know why.

Roi

Roi had been more horrified than angry at the realization of what Zhaim had done to get his father and Marna out of the way. If anything, he felt guilty himself for being the cause of an epidemic, however unwitting a cause. But he had absorbed enough of Marna's training to know that particular guilt was false. Guilt's for something you could have done something about, he reminded himself. He had more than enough genuine guilt to deal with over his own refusal to contact his father when things had started going wrong.

He was sickened by what he was reading in Zhaim's mind, and wanted only to get away. But Marna had told him to watch, and he choked down his nausea and obeyed. He saw Flick, his death hardly worth noting to Zhaim aside from annoyance that one of his better sculptures was gone. He saw how Zhaim had perverted his bioengineering to cause the plague on Eversummer.

And then he saw his mother, mere raw material for Zhaim.

He screamed aloud, and felt his father react almost as violently. He wanted to kill Zhaim. Not just by asking for the death penalty, either—he wanted to feel Zhaim die inch by inch under his own hands. For a moment that desire to go for Zhaim physically was the only thing that kept him from demanding Zhaim's death.

Roi, think.

The mind-voice was not his father's, and not Marna's, either. Certainly not Zhaim's. Not familiar enough to be Derry's or Nik's ....

You killed once. Self defense, and not consciously willed. What effect did it have on you?

Roi winced. Derry knew about that episode, as did his father, Nik and Marna. No one else, as far as he knew. He'd been an eight-year-old slave, a powerful but totally unsuspected esper with no training or blocking, and the death of the guard who had tried to kill him had been pure reflex. Yet that unwilled death still played a large part in his persistent nightmares. The rest—himself looking through Zhaim's eyes, mostly.

Not the nightmares, the voice in his mind said. *What lies behind them.*

Behind them? What had he told his father? That agreeing to Zhaim's death would be taking the first step toward becoming another Zhaim himself? He wanted Zhaim's death as he had never wanted anything before. But he did not want to make those nightmares reality!

Think, the voice had said. And thinking was leading him into some very uncomfortable conclusions. Zhaim had to be stopped. But if he himself took on the worst of Zhaim, was that actually stopping anything? And the voice itself ....

You're Win, aren't you, he thought. Was he picking up Marna's subconscious? Was there really a way of stopping Zhaim without killing him? He almost found himself wishing there were not.

She can put and keep him under controls that will stop him from doing anything like that again, but still let him contribute what he can to the Confederation. He probably will not like it.

Logically, it made sense to let Marna put Zhaim under her control. Emotionally, he wanted revenge for his mother's death.

Would she have wanted you to avenge her? Or would she have wanted that no one else should ever suffer what she did?

Roi flinched. He'd been thinking—as far as he was thinking at all—of both. But what he'd said to his father .... If it was a choice between the two ....

He didn't remember his mother very well. It had, after all, been ten years since he'd been sold away from her. But what he did remember, combined with what his father had told him ....

She'd have put protection of others above revenge, he thought.

"No," he said aloud. "I will not let him make me over in his own image." He opened his eyes to see both Marna and his father looking at him. They had wanted revenge too, he thought, but they had gotten over it before he had, and all he felt from them now was pride.

He had trouble following everything that Marna did, but he knew that she took everything that she and Lai had dredged out of the sewer of Zhaim's mind, changed it somehow, and fed it back. Changed it how? He didn't think Zhaim was capable of true guilt. And he thought she had somehow tied what Zhaim had done into his physical reactions.

Zhaim

Time crawled by. The light brightened behind Zhaim's closed eyelids, and finally he opened his eyes. The storm was passing, letting the sun appear below the cloud deck with only the automatic darkening of the window to tame its brilliance. They had let him live.

Marna and Roi gave identical deep, exhausted sighs, slumping into their chairs. "Want something to eat?" Lai asked them, and Zhaim felt the mental restraints fall away.

Marna shuddered, and Roi said "Not right after that, thank you. I think I'm going to go and be sick."

"I'm going to scrub myself clean," Marna replied. "It worked. I'll need to check him in about a month, though." She shuddered again.

Zhaim lifted his head, shaking. What he had done on Eversummer—he had Marna's perspective now, as well as his own. He'd get the bastard for that—he gasped at the pain that shot through him as his body arched in a violent convulsion. He was being flayed, burned, hurt in every way he had hurt his victims over all the long years.

He had wished more than once that he could share his victims' emotions; see his power through their eyes. But not like this! For the first time in his life he felt small, contemptible, disgusting. He looked after Marna's retreating form in horror, and she turned to face him with a grim smile.

"It's a substitute for guilt, Zhaim," she told him. "From now on, you'll experience what your victims feel, and not as something you can savor. And if you even think of hurting someone again, your body will punish you. You'll get over the initial wave of feeling, but if I were you, I'd find myself a new hobby. And you can start with clearing up the situation on Eversummer."

Roi

"So he really is suffering what his victims felt?" Roi asked as Marna pushed his float chair into his room.

Marna nodded. "That's why the emphasis was on treating children, I suspect," she said. "All the guilt he should have been accumulating for the last few centuries hit him at once, in a form he could not block out. I finished Healing Penny this morning, by the way. Take a bath and get yourself feeling clean again, and I'll get those heel tendons of yours back to where you can walk."

Somewhat to Roi's surprise, a long, hot soak did seem to clean the filth of Zhaim's mind from his own thoughts. Marna was coddling him, he thought as she reknit his heel and thumb tendons and gently Healed his scrapes and bruises, but he was in no mood to resent the coddling. In fact, he enjoyed it.

He looked out at the patio as she worked, and saw Derik and Elyra, sharing a lounge and oblivious of anyone else. The other travelers were there as well, and so was a smaller figure. Wif? "I 'ported him over, once the situation with Zhaim was cleared up," came his father's voice. "Feline didn't approve, of course. And I doubt she'll ever be able to accept the amount of mind-touch necessary for a teleport. But I thought that if Timi and Amber weren't coming back, Wif should have a chance to say goodbye to them."

Roi nodded, looking at his son, who was snuggled between Timi and Amber with an unusually serious look on his face. Neither Roi nor Feline, slaves then, had had any choice in Wif's conception. Roi, once he had gotten used to the idea of having a son, loved the little boy uncritically, happy to share him with his own father, Derik, Nik, Timi and his old physical therapist, Davy, and completely unbothered by the fact that Wif looked on him more as a big brother than a father. Feline, on the other hand, lived only for Wif and expected him to love only her. The fact that Wif adored his Grandma Marna and was perfectly happy with his "Aunts" Flame, Amber and Elyra upset her, and that in turn was not helping Roi's already stormy relationship with the mother of his son.

"Done," Marna said as her mind dropped away from his, "and I'm starved. Let's get something to eat." The others were already digging into filled plates.

Fish of some kind tonight, Roi thought as he piled his own plate high, and delicately herbed wild rice, and a medley of small vegetables lightly cooked and retaining much of their crispness. He walked over to a chair beside Timi and Amber, and Wif looked up at him, lower lip trembling.

"I don't want Uncle Timi and Aunt Amber to go," he said. "Make them stay, Daddy. Please?"

Roi sighed, put his plate on the broad arm of his chair, and held out his arms to Wif. "I don't want them to go, either," he said as the little boy snuggled into his lap. "But Timi's found his own family, and he wants to go back to them. You wouldn't want to keep him away from his family, would you?"

"But he's part of our family," Wif protested.

"He's got two families, and they're in different places," Roi said. "He had to choose between them. That doesn't mean he doesn't love you."

"Wif," Timi said, "you know I was raised on a starship, and Amber and I always planned to go back to space. That's where my family lives. I'll be going back a little sooner, that's all."

"Will you give me a ride on your starship?"

"Someday." *I'll ask my uncle about a tour,* Timi's mind whispered into Roi's.

He saw Penny watching him, and realized that most of his ambiguity about her lay not in his feelings toward her—he would welcome her into the family he was building for himself—but about hers toward him. What she had seen on the trip was incomplete, lacking both the chaos of his family structure—parts of which he suspected would shock her to the core—and his often conflicting responsibilities. Maybe if she were exposed to a little of that chaos and conflict, she would be better prepared to make her own choice.

He touched Flame's mind with his idea, and met enthusiastic approval. *Feline won't like it,* she told him gleefully. Marna's mind came in—Flame wasn't very good at directing her thoughts—and to Roi's surprise she also approved. *Leave Feline to me,* she told them both. *I think the separation will be good for her, and it certainly will be for Wif.*

"Elyra," Roi asked aloud, "has the Genetics Board taken a good look at Flame's genetics, yet?"

"Still thinking about having your father sire a child on her that you can raise as yours?" she asked. "She's fine." *Not as intelligent as most mothers of crossbreds,* her mind told his privately, *but nothing we'd have a problem with. And she's been a much better mother to Wif than Feline is.* "I'd wait a few years, though, until Wif is older and you've had a bit more education."

Penny looked shocked at the idea, but it was a thoughtful kind of shock. Good. Now the next part. "Penny," he said, "the rest of the trip's pretty easy, isn't it? Trail riding, canoeing and camping out, mostly?"

Penny looked puzzled by the change in subject, but answered readily. "That's right. And since there'll be so few of us on the final leg of the trip, the Company's approved your idea of using esper to guide the horses along the banks while we're in the canoes, and moving the canoes along when we're on the horses."

That would make things easier, Roi thought. "Do you think the Company could come up with a pony?" he asked.

There were times, he thought as Wif gave a heave in his lap that almost upset his plate, when his son was a little too quick to make inferences. "A pony?" Wif demanded. "Can I go too, Daddy? Please? I'll be good. Really, really good! I'll do everything you say. Please?"

"To start with," Roi said as he swung the little boy to the floor, "you can let me eat my supper! Penny? He really is a well-behaved child most of the time, and he's ridden enough to manage a few hours a day on a pony. Flame and I can take turns carrying him double or even in a backpack if he gets too tired, and if we alternate riding and canoeing he may not even need that. If we do take you along," he added to his son, managing to catch Wif's eye as the little boy spun excitedly around the patio, "I expect you to sit quietly and wear a float jacket when we are in a canoe."

"I will, I will," Wif assured him, jumping up and down with excitement.

Penny's expression had changed from shock through bewilderment to open amusement. "I suspect the Company would approve just about any request from you, at the moment," she told him. "I can com them from here and ask. They do guide family parties, at times, so I suspect they keep some suitable ponies. But Roi, I'm not a family guide." Her emotions were agitated, but he didn't think that was because of any reluctance to stay with them.

"You know us, though. Flame and I will take care of Wif—he's not a difficult child." No, in fact both Marna and Elyra had told Roi repeatedly that he was an uncommonly easy one.

Penny's emotions had brightened, and she jumped to her feet. "I'll com and ask them," she said, and ran back into the building.

Marna and Elyra. Marna was all the mother he had, now. He hadn't realized until he had seen his mother's death how much he had clung to the hope that someday she would be found. *She gave you a good start, Roi,* Marna's mind touched his. *And I think she'd be very proud of the man you're growing into. Especially today.*

Roi lowered his eyes. His instincts still screamed for revenge, and he was far from certain he had done the wisest thing in letting Zhaim live. But if he had chosen otherwise …. He had come near enough to the edge to feel how close he was to Zhaim. And he could not have condemned Zhaim without forever changing himself.

"They agreed," Penny's voice broke into his musing. "But we're going to make one change. You're in charge of firewood, general horse care, and dishwashing for the rest of the trip."

For once, Flame was ahead of Roi. "And we," she added with a gesture that included Penny, "will do all the cooking."